"Oh," Mary said, scrutinizing his face again. "You've come to tell me something serious." She glanced at her ladies. "Can you leave us alone for a moment?"

"Yes, Your Grace." The Marys all curtsied and exited promptly.

Mary gestured for Francis to take a seat on a chair near hers. He did.

"Is everything all right?" Mary asked. "Are you unwell?" She looked genuinely worried.

He cleared his throat. "I'm perfectly well." His heart was pounding. He had to say it now, or he'd never be able to say it at all. "Mary, we're getting married."

MY
CYNTHIA HAND
CONTRARY
BRODI ASHTON
MARY
JODI MEADOWS

HARPER TEEN
An Imprint of HarperCollinsPublishers

HarperTeen is an imprint of HarperCollins Publishers.

My Contrary Mary

Library of Congress Control Number: 2020951699
ISBN 978-0-06-293005-7

Typography by Jenna Stempel-Lobell
22 23 24 25 26   PC/LSCH   10 9 8 7 6 5 4 3 2 1

First paperback edition, 2022

For the people who feel like they have to be perfect.

And for France: we're sorry for what we're about to do to your history, but it was your turn.

The present time, together with the past, shall be judged by a great jovialist.
—Nostradamus

In my end is my beginning.
—Mary, Queen of Scots

MY CONTRARY MARY

Prologue

You may think you know the story.

All right, all right. We know. We just had to get it out of the way.

But now that we have your attention, we'd like to remind you that you actually have heard of this particular Mary. Does "Queen of Scots" ring a bell? If you're a history buff (or if you watch TV), you probably know that this Mary was married (to a prince! Aw!), but she didn't get to live happily ever after, because her beloved died young (of an ear infection! Boo!). After that, Mary bounced around from place to place (and husband to husband) simply trying to stay alive. But she posed a threat to another famous queen—Elizabeth I of England—and eventually the politics of the day caught up with Mary, and (gulp!) she lost her head.

It wasn't the happiest of endings.

But you know us—we're never satisfied until we've fixed the tragedies of history (which means changing things around a bit from what you'd read in the history books, like *cough* dates, names, and a few major details). So boy, have we got a story for you about Mary, Queen of Scots.

In those days (think 1560), the world was sharply divided between two groups of people: Eðians and Verities. The Eðians believed that inside every person was an animal—a creature you could become whenever you wished. One Eðian could become a dog, for instance, and another could transform himself into a horse (call him G). The other faction—the Verities—was not amused by these shape-shifting shenanigans. They believed that people should be people, period.

The friction between these two groups led to a lot of conflict. Like, a lot. Wars were fought. People on both sides were thrown into prison and tortured. And more than one person lost her head.

Which brings us back to our story, starring a teenage queen who hates being told what to do, a prince who has never felt particularly charming, and the daughter of a famous seer who's about to be dragged into a political game of cat and mouse.

One thing's for certain: it's not easy being queen.

 ONE

Imagine, if you will, dear reader, the Louvre in Paris, France, in the days before it became a museum: an enormous marble palace stretching along the banks of the Seine. Then imagine a garden behind that palace, a large expanse of meticulously upkept greenery, fountains, and courtyards. In the back of one such courtyard was a . . . butt. No, dear reader, not a backside-type butt, but an archery butt, which is the thingy with the bull's-eye on it that archers shoot arrows at. And roughly fifteen paces from the butt, there stood a girl.

But this girl was not just a girl. She was a queen.

Not a princess. Not a lady.

A queen.

Her name was Mary.

At the moment, Mary was concentrating on the butt.

She lifted the bow in her arms, drew it back, and aimed. One brown eye squeezed shut, while the other focused sharply on the bull's-eye. She blew out a slow breath, then loosed the arrow.

It flew fast and true, striking the butt with a solid *thwap*.

The four ladies-in-waiting standing around her all clapped enthusiastically.

"Well done, Your Majesty," exclaimed one.

"You're getting better," said another.

"You were always quite good, I thought," said a third.

The fourth one was not much of a talker, but she smiled approvingly.

The queen strode over to inspect the butt herself. It had been a very good shot, hitting nearly, but not quite, the exact center of the bull's-eye. She'd been about a thumb's width off.

"I'll try again," she said resolutely, and marched back for yet another attempt. One would have thought she intended to murder that poor defenseless butt by the way she narrowed her eyes and scowled it down.

Thwap.

This time she was a pinkie's width off.

Mary resisted the urge to stamp her foot, because queens do not stamp.

"One more time," she said tersely.

One of her ladies-in-waiting sighed. "Again? We've been out here for ages. It's time for lunch."

(Some helpful backstory: Mary had come to live in France when she was only five years old, to be the fiancée of the dauphin—aka the prince—while her mother ruled Scotland on her behalf. To this new life, Mary had brought along her four best friends—think the world's longest sleepover—every single one of whom also happened to be named Mary: Mary Fleming, Mary Seton, Mary Beaton, and Mary Livingston. The girls all had nicknames, to avoid confusion, but collectively they were known as "the Four Marys." The particular Mary who'd just complained was Mary Fleming, whom everyone called Flem, for short. Flem was the one of the four who was most ruled by the dictates of her stomach.)

Speaking of stomachs, the queen realized she *was* a bit hungry. She'd only nibbled at breakfast.

"It's getting rather hot," said another Mary, this one Mary Livingston, also known as Liv.

All of a sudden Mary noticed that she was feeling overheated. The combination of the morning's exertion and her heavy green velvet gown was causing her to sweat—oh, we mean glow, of course, since queens do not sweat.

"A shipment of lemons and oranges arrived from Spain yesterday," noted Mary Beaton—nicknamed Bea. "Perhaps there's lemonade."

Mary did love lemonade.

The fourth lady, whom everyone called Hush, said nothing but appeared a bit parched and wilted and looked hopeful at the prospect of going inside.

"One more time," Mary said.

But really she meant however many times it took until she got it perfect.

The next shot was an entire hand's width from the bull's-eye. Mary's foot did a little shuffle forward that was definitely not a stamp. She twisted her amethyst ring around on her finger—a habit she had whenever something displeased or troubled her.

"Oh, look," Bea said suddenly. "Here come your uncles."

Mary turned, and yes, strolling in her direction across the courtyard were Francis de Guise and Charles de Lorraine.

She handed the bow off to Liv as everyone all did the appropriate bowing and curtsying.

"Ah, my dear," said Uncle Charles, taking her hands and drawing her in to kiss her cheeks, his beard scratchy against her face. "How lovely you look. Did you know that the writer Jean de Beaugue recently described you as 'one of the most perfect creatures that ever was seen'?"

"Yes, you're always so exquisite," added Uncle Francis (kiss, kiss). "And only yesterday I read what Jacques de Lorges wrote about you as being 'so charming and intelligent as to give everyone who sees her incomparable joy and satisfaction.' I was so very proud."

(We, as your narrators, think this is a little much, but we get it: Mary was undeniably beautiful, with dark auburn hair that fell nearly to her waist, a fine complexion, and rich, expressive brown eyes. There was just something about Mary: a regal bearing, a grace and confidence that seemed well beyond her seventeen years. But to us, it seems like a lot of pressure.)

"Thank you," Mary said humbly, because the best queens are humble.

Uncle Charles looked at the butt. "Are you still playing at archery? I'd have thought you would have given that up by now."

Mary's chin lifted. "I quite enjoy archery, I find."

Uncle Francis went over and examined the butt. "Not quite hitting the bull's-eye, though, are you?"

"I will," Mary said steadily.

Uncle Charles smiled. "No doubt, my dear. You keep trying."

"You've got to hold the bow steady," advised Uncle Francis.

"Yes, I—"

"And stand up very straight, and have you tried closing one eye?"

"Yes, Uncle, I—"

"And you should exhale, right before you—"

"Yes, Uncle," Mary said more firmly. "I know."

Her uncles were the only people Mary knew who dared to interrupt her, but she allowed it. These two men were, in essence, her guardians. She knew they only cared for her welfare, even if they could be a bit overbearing at times. They were family.

"I'm so pleased to see you," she said warmly. "But is there a particular reason you've come to visit me?" When she'd been younger they'd done monthly inspections of her rooms, her clothing, her companions and tutors, to make sure she was being brought up properly, but that had stopped more than a year ago. She liked to think that was because now they trusted her to use her own judgment of such things.

Uncle Charles looked grave. "We've had a letter from your mother."

"She wrote to you?" Mary glanced quizzically at her lady Bea, who handled all of Mary's correspondence with her mother. She'd received no recent letters. "What did she say?"

Uncles Charles reached into his doublet and pulled out a slightly damp fold of parchment bearing a royal seal on one side, and the handwriting of Mary's mother on the other. He handed Mary the letter.

She took it and unfolded it right away, walking off a few paces while she read quickly. "She says there's trouble." Her brow furrowed. "Some malcontent named John Knox stirring up problems."

"He's a filthy Eðian," Uncle Charles muttered. Uncle Charles was a religious man, a cardinal in the Verity Church, which meant that he wore the red robes and the oblong red pointy hat, and also that, more than anything, he hated Eðians.

"He means to instigate a full-out rebellion against your mother," added Uncle Francis.

"Yes," Mary murmured, continuing to read. "He claims that she is not the rightful monarch of Scotland."

"No, he claims that *you* are not the rightful monarch of Scotland, being a woman," said Uncle Francis. "And your mother, as regent, is even more of an abomination in his eyes."

"He seeks to overthrow the power of the Verity Church in Scotland." Uncle Charles looked grim. "Starting with you."

"But—" This was just so frustrating, considering. "What's to be done about it? He won't succeed, will he? Is Mother in danger? Perhaps I should—"

Uncle Charles took her hand and patted it. "We'll take care of it, my dear. We always do."

Mary nodded. They always did.

"Yes," said Uncle Francis almost gleefully. He was a military man, a general who had led many a battle in his time, and he relished any chance to use his strategical prowess. "We can handle Scotland."

Mary was grateful for her uncles, even though she knew they could be a bit wicked in the pursuit of their goals. They were wicked, she knew, on her behalf. She probably would have lost her crown a hundred times by now if her de Guise relatives hadn't been there to intervene for her. Still, it went against her better judgment, letting others take care of what Scotland needed. Part of Mary always felt that she should go back there and take care of it herself.

Otherwise it was like she was a queen in name only.

She twisted her amethyst ring.

"Now, don't worry your pretty head about all of this dreary political nonsense," said Uncle Charles. "Why don't you come inside and read to us for a while? I simply love to hear the dulcet tones of your sweet voice."

"Thank you, Uncle," Mary said, er, sweetly. "But I'd like to stay out here and continue my practice."

Both uncles frowned.

"But it's so hot out," said Uncle Francis.

"And it's almost lunchtime," Uncle Charles said.

"That's right!" exclaimed Flem, and the other Marys murmured their agreement.

"Nevertheless," said Mary. "I will stay."

"Very well," said Uncle Francis finally. "You should join us for supper, then. We're dining with the king tonight."

Mary inwardly groaned. She'd been looking forward to a quiet evening in with her ladies, doing embroidery by the fire, perhaps some knitting or shoe design if things got crazy. The last thing she wanted was to be stuck at a stuffy dinner with her uncles and the king. Of course, Francis (her fiancé Francis, we mean) would undoubtedly be there too, which would make it all more bearable, as the two of them always came up with amusing things to do to pass the time.

"You must come," Uncle Francis said. "We insist."

All four of the Four Marys caught their breaths.

Mary smiled tightly. She never did like to be told she *must* anything.

"I'll consider it," she said softly.

After her uncles retreated into the palace, Mary picked up her bow once more. She swept her hair over one shoulder, adjusted her stance, drew, and let loose.

The arrow struck the bull's-eye hard, burying itself deep into the straw at the exact center.

Mary handed the bow to Liv.

"*Now* can we have lunch?" asked Flem in relief.

"Yes."

They moved toward the palace, the Four Marys flanking her on every side.

Mary was frowning.

"You're worried about your mother," Liv said.

"Of course." She was always worried about her mother these days. Things were heating up between the Eðians and the Verities everywhere, but especially, it seemed, in Scotland.

"Would you like to draft a letter for me to take to her?" asked Bea.

"Yes. Not tonight, though," Mary said. "I want some time to think about what I should say."

"Do we really have to go to dinner with the king?" whispered Hush.

"The food will be good," said Flem cheerfully. That was true. The king did like to eat.

"Yes, but the king and the uncles together are quite insufferable," said Mary. "They can't seem to stop congratulating themselves on being the masters of the universe."

"But they *insisted* that you attend," said Bea.

Mary's lips pursed. "They can insist as much as they like. I am not theirs to order about. I am the queen of Scotland."

Sometimes it was good to be queen.

"We could use a girls' night out," Liv said lightly.

All five Marys stopped and looked at each other.

"Oh, let's!" Flem clapped her hands.

"You mean a *boys'* night out," said Bea, tucking a strand of her black hair behind her ear and smiling slyly.

"It's been ages," said Liv.

"I like the music," murmured Hush.

Mary smiled. A night on the town sounded like just the remedy to her worries. "All right," she agreed. "Let's."

"I want to be the one to wear the false mustache!" Flem exclaimed a few hours later, as the queen and the Four Marys put the finishing touches on their disguises.

"You got to wear it last time," argued Bea.

"I don't want to wear it," said Hush softly. "It itches."

It was decided that Flem would wear it, because she really, really wanted to, and besides, she looked so funny wearing a mustache that they all couldn't help but giggle at the sight. Flem was the shortest and stoutest of the ladies, with curly chestnut-colored hair and wide brown eyes.

"Well, gentlemen," Mary said as they donned their feathered hats. "We make a fine company of men."

Liv had been right—it felt like ages since they'd played this game, in which they dressed up as boys and sneaked into the city to their favorite tavern. They always had a merry time chatting with the townsfolk, drinking ale, and dancing to the lively music, a much better time in general than they did at the palace's most lavish parties.

And even though Mary's bosom was wrapped up tight in

layers of cloth to flatten her curves, as they helped each other climb over the garden wall, she felt like she could finally breathe.

Tonight, she'd push her worries for Scotland and her mother from her mind.

And for just a few hours, she'd forget she was a queen.

TWO

Ari

Nostradamus was losing his touch. In the past hour the world's most famous seer and revelator had started to refer to his own daughter as "Galileo" instead of her given name, Aristotle—or Ari, as she liked to be called. Then he'd broken her best glass vial trying to brew a remedy for unrequited love. (Ari wouldn't have minded if that one had worked.) But when he predicted that France was soon going to be ruled by a frog, she decided she needed to get out of the palace for a while.

He isn't well, she thought glumly as she made her way down the Place de l'Opéra, avoiding the larger cracks in the cobblestone. He hadn't been well for some time. At first she'd thought it was simply a matter of failing eyesight, as he struggled more and more to read the labels on his mystical concoctions. But then he'd started to forget the names of things. Like, *What the heck is a Galileo?* she thought. (Galileo Galilei, the astronomer and physicist, had not been born yet, dear reader.) And then Nostradamus began to use a cane to walk, that is, when he did walk. And his sleeping patterns had changed, so that he was staying up half the night, frantically scribbling predictions onto random pieces of parchment and dropping off to sleep at all times of the day, sometimes in the middle of a—

Which made Ari's patterns of behavior change, as well. For instance, now she needed to "take a walk" more and more frequently, in order to "get some air."

The best air in Paris was at Le Chien Hirsute (or Shaggy Dog to non-Francophiles). Ari pushed her way inside and took a deep, cleansing breath. It smelled like ale and armpits. She claimed her regular seat by the window. After a few minutes the owner approached her with a wide smile.

"Back again?" he boomed. "This is the third time this week."

"Hello, Louis," she said. *Louis, not the king,* the owner always felt the need to clarify whenever he introduced himself, as if there was a chance he would be confused with one of the many former kings of France named Louis. (Reader, there were eleven former Kings Louis: Louis the Stammerer; Louis III through V; Louis the Fat; Louis the Young; Louis the Lion; Louis the Saint; Louis the Quarreler; Louis the Prudent, the Cunning, the Universal Spider; and Louis, the Father of the People.)

The owner of Le Chien Hirsute called himself Louis the Aleslinger. Ari thought that was a little on the nose.

"It's always an honor to serve you, Little Nostradamus," he said.

"I'm not quite so little anymore," Ari replied good-naturedly. "And please, call me Ari."

Louis patted her on the head. "Try the pottage."

"You know I love your pottage," Ari replied.

Louis chuckled and disappeared into the kitchen. A serving girl poured Ari a cup of ale. As she sat there, slowly drinking it, she became aware that people were staring and talking about her. They'd clearly heard Louis call her "Little Nostradamus." It would only be a matter of time before—

"Hello," mumbled a tall, red-faced peasant, stepping forward. "Are you Nostradamus?"

She swallowed her swig of ale. "I'm *a* Nostradamus."

He thrust his palm into her face. "Tell me my fortune."

"Um, well, you see. I don't . . ." Ari started to explain that palm-reading was not how the Nostradamuses did their prognosticating, but the man didn't give her a chance.

"Is my dog an Eðian?" he blurted out.

This drew more looks from across the tavern.

Ari lowered her voice. In general, it was unwise to talk about Eðians in public. "Have you seen your dog change into a human?"

"No, but sometimes I swear she acts just like a person."

"Sometimes a dog is just a dog," Ari said sagely. "I think someone once said that about things we see in dreams." Then she held out her hand.

He peered into her palm. "Um, I guess you have quite a long love line?"

"No. I meant, that will be three livres."

"What, you want me to pay you?" he asked incredulously.

"You asked me a question. I answered it. Three livres, please."

He scratched his head. "Well, I thought that you would just tell me my fortune, and I would tell everyone what a great prognosticator you are. It would be good exposure."

"Nostradamuses don't need more exposure. We need to be paid for our work," Ari said.

"Pay the girl for her services." Louis appeared with the dish of pottage. He set it down in front of Ari as the peasant grudgingly put three livres into her hand. "Now let's have some music!" Louis belted out before anybody else could ask for their fortunes to be told.

Three men with fiddles started up a jig in the corner. Men in their britches and women in their work dresses held hands and danced in circles around the floor while others clapped with the beat. Ari felt a flash of gratitude toward Louis.

It wasn't that she didn't want to tell people their futures. It was that Ari's ability to see the future was a little substandard.

She was the only one of Nostradamus's many sons and daughters who'd inherited any of her father's talents. But what Ari was truly good at was making potions, everything from tinctures to bind small cuts and scrapes, to complicated elixirs that could produce a more—let's say—*supernatural* effect. This had been discovered one day when Ari was a toddler, playing in the kitchen while her mother cooked dinner. Ari had pretended to cook dinner as well, adding this and that to a bowl and stirring, until suddenly a poof of smoke shot out of the bowl, and little Ari's straight brown hair instantly curled into ringlets. Her father had been so proud. He'd begun to refer to her as his "heir," which was a huge deal considering that she was a girl. He taught her everything he knew about potion-making. He said that she would take his place, when the time came, as the spiritual adviser to the queen of France, Catherine de Medici. But whenever he tried to instruct Ari on seeing the future, she inevitably failed.

"What do you see?" he'd ask her over and over, making her sit still in a quiet room and concentrate for hours.

Ari did sometimes see things, but nothing that made sense:

"I see a princess from the moon. She punishes all of the evildoers."

"I see a girl with pale hair singing in the snow. She wants to let it go, but I don't know what *it* is."

"I see a child. He sees dead people."

After that, her father stopped asking her what she saw. Ari thought this was a bit unfair. After all, her father's visions weren't always crystal clear themselves. Take today, for example. "A frog," she muttered. "A frog ruling France."

The musicians started up with a new song. Ari watched the dancers wistfully. Then her breath caught when she got a good look at the face of one of the dancing men. He was weaving his way gracefully through the twirling masses and ducking underneath raised arms.

After the end of one such move, he bowed low, his head tilting charmingly, and a long curl of blond hair escaped his hat.

Ari dropped her spoon into her bowl of pottage. That man wasn't a commoner. And he wasn't a "he."

"He" was Mary Livingston, also known as Liv.

Mary's lady-in-waiting spun around the dance floor with a smile that was its own light source. Nobody seemed to suspect that she was a woman, but Ari knew. She knew the shape of Liv's face and each line of her features. She and Liv had once shared a look (you know the kind) across the dinner hall, many months ago. And then in the corridor as they passed each other. And again in Queen Catherine's chambers as Ari arrived to deliver a tincture when she hadn't expected Queen Mary and her ladies to be there. In fact, if Ari were counting the days, she would guess it had been nearly an entire year of . . . looks.

She'd never thought anything could come of it. Ari was meant to be "the next Nostradamus," taking over for her father, and Liv would be waiting on Mary until she was matched with a suitable nobleman to be married off to. But in this moment, in this tavern, Liv caught Ari's eye, and without any hesitation, she sashayed closer to Ari and stopped right in front of her.

Ari bit her lip to keep her smile from reaching all the way to the walls. Liv bowed grandly. "May I?" she said, her hand outstretched.

Ari glanced left, then right. "Um, I'm Ari," Ari said.

"I know," Liv said with a laugh. "You're the girl who never talks to me."

"Because you're a lady," Ari said.

Liv tilted her head in that adorable way that had given her identity away just moments ago. "Why should that matter?"

Then she grabbed Ari's hand and they were spinning and dancing and laughing and the rest of the crowd parted, including *Queen Mary herself* and the other Marys, who were similarly dressed as men. Funny how Ari hadn't noticed them before. They were all watching Ari and Liv, and they were smiling and clapping. Including the queen.

"Do you do this often?" Ari said over the music as Liv guided Ari back and forth across the floor as if she'd always led and never followed.

"What? Dress like a man? Or dance?"

"Both." Ari's head was spinning. Liv's hands were as soft as she'd imagined, the kind of soft that hadn't seen a hard day's work. Liv was such a lady.

"Sometimes a lady needs a break from all the extravagant gowns," Liv said. "Do you realize how heavy they are?"

"I'm sure they're a lot heavier than what you're wearing now." Ari blushed, but Liv just smiled.

As Ari lost herself in Liv's hazel eyes, the three fiddle players began to sound like a full-blown symphony. Liv smelled of lemons and lavender. They were alone in the room. No, they were alone in the world.

"Aristotle?"

"Call me Ari," Ari said, breathlessly.

"That wasn't me," Liv said. She pointed toward the counter where Louis was waving at Ari. "Aristotle!" he shouted again.

"Just a minute," Ari said. She did *not* want to let go of Liv's hands. When would she have another opportunity to hold them?

"Your father sent a message that you are to return to the palace at once," Louis informed her.

"How does he even know where I— Oh." Ari sighed and reluctantly dropped Liv's hands.

"I'm sorry," she said. "I have to go."

"Of course," Liv said. "It's your father."

As Ari gathered her cloak, the symphony in her mind died down again to three measly fiddles, and the lights that had seemed to glow on the dance floor suddenly dimmed. She pushed out the door, but before it closed behind her, she caught one more long look from Liv.

This time it felt different. It felt like the start of something.

By the time Ari made her way from the tavern to the palace courtyard to the servants' entrance to the secret pantry to the second laboratory, which was hidden below the first laboratory, she was out of breath.

She blew through the door and was immediately shushed by Greer, the lab assistant.

"He's sleeping," Greer said.

"Why was I summoned so urgently, then?" Ari asked.

"He had another vision while you were gone," Greer whispered. "He's been having them all night. He said it was important."

Show-off, Ari thought. She gave her cloak to Greer to put away. Then she clanged some pans and loudly set mugs upon the table. But her father didn't stir, so she tiptoed to his desk, where he was slumped over with his cheek stuck to a piece of damp parchment.

"What have you seen, Papa?" she whispered. She brushed a strand of his wild white hair from his face. He looked so old, so frail, that her heart gave a squeeze.

She didn't want to lose her father. What would happen when he was gone? Or when the queen inevitably found out that Ari's visions weren't exactly extraordinary?

She'd be cast out. She'd have to find some man somewhere to marry so she could be taken care of.

Ew, she thought. She'd much rather be dancing with Liv.

"Queen Catherine sent you a message as well," Greer said. She reached into her apron and produced a small folded piece of parchment with the queen's seal on it.

Ari tore it open, read the contents, and then went about the alchemy laboratory, gathering white fir needles, spruce needles, tendrilled fritillaria bulb, and pinellia root.

Greer studied the ingredients. "The queen has a cough?" she guessed.

"One of the queen's ladies," Ari answered. "And yes, she has a cough." And by "cough," Ari meant an ailment one contracts by

20

too many close encounters with members of the king's guard. "Will you hand me that mulberry bark?"

Greer, who was younger than Ari but much taller, reached up to the top shelf, pushed aside some bound herbs, and brought down the requested bottle.

"Thank you, Greer," Ari said.

Greer had become kind of an apprentice to Ari, in a similar way that Ari was an apprentice to her father. She lacked any of the more spiritual abilities of Ari and her father, but she could throw together easier medicinal tinctures, and she was especially great at retrieving things from top shelves.

Across the room, Nostradamus came to with a startled snort.

Ari rushed to his side. "Papa? You sent for me?"

Her father looked at her with glazed eyes. She waited for recognition, which was taking longer and longer these days. "Galileo? Is that you?"

She took his hand. "It's me, Papa. Ari."

His eyes cleared. "Daughter, we must go to the queen at once."

"What is it?" Ari asked.

"Traps. Betrayal. The crown in jeopardy."

"But it's late," Ari said.

Nostradamus took her by the shoulders with surprising strength. "This is an emergency! Lives are at stake! The succession of the crown. The future of the country."

Ari knew he meant business. The succession of the crown was everything to Queen Catherine. Her son Francis was destined to be the next king. Catherine would sacrifice anything to make sure that happened.

"We must go now!" Nostradamus started to rise, but Ari put a hand on his shoulder, and he sat back down.

"Father, they are all in the middle of dinner. You will not be allowed to interrupt."

"But once she hears—"

"They won't even let you in the door. For now let's sit and write what we know, and interpret what we don't know."

Nostradamus sighed. "Very well." He struggled to stand up and then began to ever so slowly pace the floor using his cane. Ari licked her graphite and readied herself to take notes. Her father was obviously extremely agitated, but at least he sounded like he had his senses about him.

Nostradamus raised a finger. "The first and most immediate threat is . . . *the biscuits.*"

Then again, maybe not.

THREE
Francis

"Someday, son," King Henry said, waving a hand to encompass the Louvre Palace's grand banquet hall, where the royal court was dining. (Yes, at 10:00 p.m.! Your narrators have already gone to bed at this point.) "All of this will be yours. Everything the light touches."

Francis noted that the light did, in fact, touch everything. The hall shone with hundreds of candles, which burned in crystal chandeliers, golden sconces, and elaborately wrought candelabras. There were no pockets of shadow in the banquet hall—not one. Francis had a feeling that if he looked under the table, there would be candles there, too, just to prove King Henry's point.

"That's impressive," Francis said dully, but Henry wasn't actually listening to him.

"This is truly the best banquet we've had all week." Henry

gazed down the length of the long, crowded room. The feast was laid out down the center of the grand dining table, upon which lay a lace tablecloth of the finest spun silk. Bottles of wine stood like guard towers over the platters of veal, rabbit, and pies, while crystal goblets shone in the candlelight. Lords and ladies clothed in their richest velvets and silks, their faces painted with white makeup and vermillion spots on their cheeks, sat in order of importance down the table, with King Henry II (and Francis) at its head.

All of this will be yours, the king had said. *Everything the light touches.* He said it regularly. He said it when it wasn't even part of the topic of conversation, as he was proud to have a son, and even prouder that his son would one day marry a queen, and prouder still that the Valois line would last for centuries beyond his own final days.

Fortunately, his final days were a long way off. King Henry was young and healthy, which was a good thing, because every time Francis thought about becoming king, his hands got sweaty and his chest grew tight. Sometimes his eye started to twitch.

Henry loved being king. He always said that when he'd been Francis's age, he just couldn't *wait* to be king. Francis, however, had never wanted it. He'd never felt he would be good at it, but the one time he'd voiced his concerns to his father, the king had replied that ruling was in his blood. He would know how to do it when the time came.

"What do you call a serf in the royal palace?" Henry asked Duke Francis (Mary's uncle, if you recall), speaking over Francis's head to the uncles on Francis's other side. Usually, Mary was seated beside Francis, softening the effect of the king and her uncles bellowing back and forth, but she was, ahem, indisposed tonight, leaving Francis to face the three men on his own.

"Hmm." Duke Francis tapped his chin. He was a war hero and had the scar on his face to prove it; he liked to tell the story of the lance piercing him through the bars of his helmet and how he'd ridden, unassisted, to his tent, where the surgeon removed what remained of the weapon. The duke claimed he hadn't even flinched, in spite of the incredible pain. His military career had only grown more impressive from there.

King Henry, of course, *adored* him.

"I don't know, Your Grace. What *do* you call a serf in the royal palace?" the duke asked.

"A cockroach on two legs!"

Francis cringed, but the duke guffawed and slapped the table. His brother, Cardinal Charles, gave a bawdy laugh, too. "If this king business doesn't work out for you," the cardinal said, "you might have a future as a court jester."

Henry stopped laughing and leveled a hard glare at Cardinal Charles.

Color rose in the man's face as he sobered instantly. "That is, I mean—you're exceedingly funny, Your Grace, when you put your mind to telling a joke. No monarch has ever been as good-humored as you. Yet, you still maintain an air of regality. It is a delicate balance, I'm sure, but you manage it masterfully. You are a true king, truly."

Henry started to laugh. "I'm just kidding. That was hilarious! You should have seen your face."

The Cardinal of Lorraine relaxed, letting out a long breath as he laughed faintly. Duke Francis smiled nervously.

"What a king you are," said the duke. "The best king in the whole world. Good-humored, thoughtful, and not so bad with the ladies, if you know what I mean."

"I'm sure *I* don't," said the cardinal, chuckling.

"Ah, I do know what you mean." King Henry stretched his arms up over his head, then wrapped one around a woman's shoulders—shoulders belonging to a woman who was not his wife yet was seated at the head of the table with him. This was Diane de Poitiers, his official mistress. Usually she was a lot more polished, but tonight she shifted uncomfortably and tugged at her sleeves and the bodice of her gown, as though it wasn't fitting correctly.

Meanwhile, Henry's unofficial mistresses were scattered about the banquet hall like bright flowers, all their faces turned toward him, as though he were their sunshine. They were easy to spot, and the length of time it had been since the king had called for them was clear in the relative eagerness of their expressions. Francis would have felt sorry for them, if he hadn't been busy feeling sorry for his mother.

Queen Catherine de Medici, Francis's mother, sat on the far end of the table from the king and Francis. Francis wished he could talk to her without yelling down the table, even if a conversation with Catherine had its own set of pitfalls. She was, as Mary liked to say, a playful sort of evil. Catherine loved to stir up trouble wherever she could. She'd been known to tell her ladies-in-waiting that there was going to be a themed costume party and laugh at them when they showed up in silly attire to a formal event. She'd arranged several marriages between couples who were bizarrely mismatched, like the son of a wealthy pig farmer to a noblewoman who fainted at the slightest whiff of a foul odor, or an exceptionally portly girl to an extremely skinny man. She was also known to dose the tea of certain women at court with laxatives and then tell them a long story and watch them squirm but not dare to interrupt her to excuse themselves.

In short, Francis felt Mary's description of Catherine was accurate. Still, he loved his mother, even though he sometimes wondered how he'd been born of these two people, since he wasn't very much like either of them. But he'd been told never to wonder such things aloud, as he had two younger brothers, either of whom could take the throne if there was ever a doubt of his legitimacy. Legitimacy was a surprisingly big deal for kings.

With a sigh, Francis turned to his father, ready to ask about the recent boar hunt he'd gone on (it seemed safer than inquiring further about his father's extramarital conquests), but King Henry was in the middle of trailing his fingertips down Mistress Diane's neck.

Gag.

No, Francis wasn't like his father.

Not even close.

The king winked at a woman across the table, one of the dozen or so Catherines in attendance who was not Queen Catherine. She giggled and rested her fingers on the large brooch she wore, which showed off her, ah, gown's plunging neckline.

Francis noticed something else that was plunging: his will to pretend he was comfortable with any of this.

Perhaps he could excuse himself—

"Bring the next course!" cried King Henry, and servants rushed to lay out yet more food. They had already eaten a stew of spiced duck, quail, and pigeons, a fillet of duck, chickens cooked on hot embers, a fillet of beef, a quarter of veal, two hens and four rabbits, and some salad because vegetables were important once in a while.

The third course was an enormous partridge pie, fruit (so no one got scurvy), slices of roast beef, and—please make sure you're sitting—fried sheep's testicles.

Francis really wasn't hungry anymore.

More drinks were poured (wine, liqueurs, and other things meant to get the nobility ridiculously drunk), and somehow, even after consuming all that food, the king and his court still managed to eat more.

"Where is my niece tonight?" Cardinal Charles mused.

Francis gazed down the table. It was a fair question, if belated. Everyone who was anyone was in attendance—except the queen of Scotland. There was the ambassador from England (no one was speaking with him), and the ambassador from Spain (quite popular, as Francis's sister had just married their king), and lords from holdings across France. This was a typical night of revelry in the Louvre Palace, because King Henry loved revelry.

"I'm afraid Her Majesty is"—Francis tugged at his collar, thinking of the note she'd sent earlier—"not feeling like herself tonight."

(At this very moment, Mary was still partying in the pub like it was 1599.)

The duke frowned. "When we saw her this morning, she seemed quite well. I made it clear that she must join us for dinner."

Francis suppressed a smirk. Mary's uncles clearly didn't understand that insisting that Mary do something was bound to make her do the opposite.

"She's assured me that it will pass," he said.

"Ah." Cardinal Charles looked at his brother. "She was out in the sun too long today. We should check in on her later. Perhaps send a servant to bring her chicken soup."

"That won't be necessary!" Francis said, a little too fast. "That is, I mean, I've already taken the liberty of sending a meal for her. There's no need to worry. She only requires rest."

The uncles both gave reluctant nods.

"You are such a good match for her, Your Highness," Duke Francis said. "We could not imagine a better future husband for our beloved niece."

Francis flushed at the thought of becoming Mary's husband. She was clever, kind, powerful—not to mention breathtakingly beautiful. There was nothing that Francis didn't admire about Mary. Becoming her husband would be a dream come true. Or it would have been, if there was any chance that she felt the same way.

Oh, Mary loved him. Francis was certain of that. But he was equally certain that she didn't spend night after night lying awake, thinking about him. Francis, however, was intimately familiar with the complete darkness of his ceiling, as he passed hours staring at it, thinking up ways to make Mary laugh, or planning small gifts for her, or—let's be honest—imagining what it might be like to kiss her rosebud lips.

As it was, it would be a marriage of one-sided adoration. That would have to be enough.

Anyway, marrying Mary was a long ways off. They'd been betrothed since they were children, and there hadn't once been talk of setting a date.

"I'm honored that you think so," Francis told the uncles. "Queen Mary is a remarkable young woman." Remarkable. Incredible. Maybe—and Francis knew very well this was her least favorite descriptor, but he thought it anyway—perfect. He sighed admiringly, just thinking about her smile.

The third course continued. Francis pushed his food around his plate, and the courtiers grew ever more drunk. Soon, they wouldn't be able to sit up in their chairs. Even the king was red-faced and slurring his solicitous words to Mistress Diane.

If Mary had been here, they could have laughed at everyone. But Mary was not here, which meant Francis had no one to laugh with, and therefore Francis wished he weren't here, either.

She used to offer to let him join her to go dancing. Sure, they wouldn't have been able to dance together, but they'd *be* together. And without his fancy clothes and attendants, nobody in Paris would be likely to recognize him as the dauphin. But Francis had always declined. Going out with all those strangers, stuck in some loud and alcohol-stinking room had sounded utterly nightmarish. Of course, King Henry's royal banquets turned out basically the same.

He was nearly free, though. He just had to make it through dessert, and then he could escape back to his rooms and read.

Just then, the double doors at the opposite end of the banquet hall burst open, admitting a trio of guards and a . . . seagull?

The bird's wings were strapped down with someone's belt, and its talons were tied up with a bit of string. Even so, the seagull struggled, screeching as it tried to escape the guard's grasp.

The banquet hall went quiet as every eye swung toward the seagull and soldiers.

"*Now* what?" Duke Francis murmured.

King Henry rose to his feet. All eyes swung toward him now. "What is the meaning of this interruption?"

"This is no mere seagull, Your Majesty. It is an Eðian spy. Our sources at Kershaw Place say that she arrived as a bird, changed into a human, and delivered a message. She tried to escape as a seagull again, but we caught her."

"I see." The king's expression was serious now, all his

merriment from earlier vanished. He even seemed, somehow, less drunk. "What were the contents of this message?"

It could be nothing, Francis thought. *It could have been a love letter, or a recipe, or anything. They have no proof this seagull is a spy.*

But Francis didn't say those words out loud. He couldn't. France was a staunchly Verity kingdom, and to be branded a sympathizer at a time when tensions ran so high . . . Francis had no illusions about how difficult ruling France would be; it would be impossible if anyone suspected the truth.

"Here it is, Sire." One of the guards, a man with a wide, bushy mustache, pulled a folded paper from his pocket. "Shall I read it aloud?"

"No, no. It could be something inappropriate for the dinner table. Give it here." Henry snapped his fingers and the guard put the paper into the king's hand. He read it briefly with no change of expression and then handed it (over Francis's head) to Duke Francis, who read it and handed it to Cardinal Charles.

"I would also like to see it," Francis said after everyone, it seemed, knew what the paper said but him.

Henry nodded. "Give it to my son. He loves to read." Henry motioned vaguely at Francis, and the cardinal slid the paper down the table to Francis.

Slowly, Francis looked it over, and a chill worked its way up his spine. This wasn't a note. It was a pamphlet, entitled "Eðians Must Rise: Why Scotland Will Fall If Verities Are Allowed to Continue Ruling," written by a man named John Knox. The contents were even more sinister than the title.

Verities are incomplete souls. That they cannot change form
tells us the truths of their spirits—they are lacking, less than,
and unworthy of this world. Scotland should no longer suffer
under these deficient rulers. We Eðians must rise up and take
our natural place as the true leaders of our country.

We will take on the hollow Verity queen. We will chase
out the Verity regent. We will make a monarchy of our own, with
strong Eðian men who will produce strong Eðian sons.

It went on like that for a while, dragging both Verities and
women through the mud. It ended with a rather gruesome depic-
tion of a girl with her head on the chopping block, an axe racing to
meet her neck. Resting on the girl's hair was a golden crown.

Mary.

His Mary. His Mary, who was away from the palace right now,
with no protection but her ladies. His Mary, whose life had been
threatened more times than either of them could count. And here
was another threat, a pamphlet delivered to a tavern in Paris on the
exact night that Mary was out dancing in a tavern in Paris. Was it
the same one? Her note hadn't said where she was going.

Francis hurled the terrible pamphlet across the table, then
tried to hide his shaking hands under his legs.

"Well," said the king darkly. "I believe my son's reaction
says it all. The only matter left is to deduce whether this is actually an Eðian or simply an unfortunate seagull." He nodded slowly,
thoughtfully. "Have you seen it change shape?"

"Not personally, Sire, but our sources—"

"Yes, you said there were witnesses." King Henry stepped away from his seat at the head of the table and strode toward the men and their captive. The gazes of everyone in the court followed along, eager anticipation in their eyes, until finally, he stood before the struggling, squawking seagull. "Change," the king commanded. "Change back into a human."

The bird merely continued struggling.

"Change," commanded the king. He was an imposing figure, the king of France, dressed in his royal robes and wearing his crown—because a monarch should never squander an opportunity to remind his underlings that he was in charge. "You will change immediately, or my guards will wring your neck and we'll have a fourth course on this table." He gestured to the silver platters filled with various kinds of fowl.

Francis's heart skipped a beat. Surely his father wouldn't do something so terrible as that. And besides, didn't Eðians revert to their human forms once they died? Would Henry actually—

A white light flared through the room, and by the time the glare cleared, a woman stood before the king, long brown curls concealing her unclothed body.

Everyone in the hall gasped, as though they'd never seen an Eðian change shape before. Maybe they hadn't. Maybe the only Eðians they'd ever seen had been in books or pamphlets about what to do if they saw one. (The books and pamphlets all said the same thing: report to the nearest guard so the Eðian could be arrested.)

For a moment, Francis let himself hate this woman. She'd been carrying that vile pamphlet, which literally called for the death of Mary, Queen of Scots. It was because of her that those terrible words, that awful image, had entered his mind.

But then he caught himself. Just because the guards *said* the pamphlet was hers didn't mean it was true. It could have been planted with her, or they could have discovered it somewhere completely unrelated to Kershaw Place and brought it here as "evidence." It would hardly be the first time a man or woman had been accused of being a spy simply because they were an Eðian in a Verity kingdom.

So Francis could not rush to judgment. He didn't have enough information.

He bit his lip—and then stopped. No one appeared to be looking at him, but all it took was one glance.

And to protect the person he cared about more than anyone in the world—more than himself, even—he could never let anyone believe him a sympathizer.

"Well." The king's gaze roamed down the woman's body. "How interesting. You *are* an Eðian."

The woman didn't speak a word, and now that she was in her human form, she was no longer struggling or screeching. But she was trembling with terror. Even from the far side of the hall, Francis could see her shaking. His heart twisted. Surely there was something he could do.

"Tell me about the pamphlet," King Henry commanded.

She remained silent.

"Was it yours?"

She kept her gaze firmly on the ground.

"Are you part of Knox's little Scottish rebellion?"

Still nothing. Just that fearful trembling. This poor woman. Maybe she was a spy. Maybe she wasn't. But surely, no matter what she was, she didn't deserve the humiliation of standing naked before the entire court. Before the king.

"Tell me now!" roared the king.

The woman only closed her eyes. She must have understood the danger she was in, but still she refused to speak.

Francis couldn't take it anymore. Spy or no, she deserved some dignity. He started to stand, started to remove his jacket—

A chair scraped as Queen Catherine rose to her feet, sniffing derisively. "I'm appalled," she announced, slipping the pamphlet into the folds of her gown. "We're in the middle of supper. And you"—she leveled her royal glare on the guards—"intrude with such a trivial matter? No proof? No allegations beyond your assumptions and a scrap of paper that you *claim* belongs to her? No good reason to bother the king during a meal with *this*?" The queen curled her lip as she glanced toward the Eðian woman.

Francis's heart pounded. There was one thing he could always be sure of when it came to his mother, which was that he could never be sure what she was about to do. It seemed entirely possible she would have all three guards and the Eðian woman sentenced to death, right here and now, because her meal had been interrupted.

(You see why Ari had been more than a little hesitant to come rushing in with news of Nostradamus's vision.)

The queen of France swept off her silk shawl and draped it over the Eðian woman's shoulders. "Cease wasting our time, soldiers. Take her to the dungeon and find a blanket or something to cover the rest of her filthy peasant body."

Duke Francis nodded. "Yes. Get her out of our sight. I will interrogate the prisoner personally. Find out what else she knows."

Queen Catherine glared at Duke Francis as if she'd like to argue, but instead she turned to the nearest servant. "Send dessert to my rooms. I have grown bored of this company." With that, she left the banquet hall without waiting to be dismissed by the king.

Tension hung low over the hall until King Henry sighed and waved the guards away. "Go on," Henry said. "You heard my"— the word practically choked him—"wife."

The Eðian woman clung to the shawl as the guards led her from the room, and one at a time, courtiers returned to their meals, murmuring frantically about the interruption and the queen's rather rude exit.

"Do you think she is a spy?" Cardinal Charles asked his brother as they resumed eating. "She looked English to me. That Eðian-loving queen has no shame."

"Perhaps she's Scottish. The pamphlet was written by that Knox fellow, after all." Duke Francis stabbed one of the fried sheep's testicles. "I'll find out soon enough. But it doesn't really matter, does it? She's an Eðian. She should be put to death."

At least they weren't asking *Francis* about the pamphlet. For the moment, the uncles had forgotten him. All the better. He kept his gaze locked on his plate as he listened to the uncles talk about the woman, and then encourage King Henry as he began to boast about how he'd hunt down all the Eðians in France.

"They're a menace to all of France," said Cardinal Charles.

"They deserve no mercy," agreed Duke Francis.

More clearly than ever, Francis understood this truth: for all that the uncles lavished Mary with praise, saw to her every need, and maneuvered world politics to benefit her, they were not on her side.

An hour later, the furor inside the banquet hall had finally died down and Francis was, at last, returning to his chambers.

It was always exhausting, putting on his best face to be the dauphin people expected. (His best face wasn't exactly convincing. Nobody—literally nobody—was fooled.)

Perhaps, he thought, he should send guards into Paris to search for Mary. She was out there with Eðians and Verities alike, and John Knox had just called his Eðian followers to have her killed. Francis could send a few guards, only men he trusted, to search the usual pubs for Mary and her ladies and have them brought back to the palace. He could pay them off, so they'd never talk about retrieving Mary, or how all five Marys were dressed as boys.

But Mary would be furious if he did. She loved going out, and she had so few freedoms already. . . .

Francis paused at a window, peering out into the night. From here, he could see the lush palace gardens, the wrought iron gates, and the long drive that separated the Louvre from the rest of Paris. "Come on," he whispered.

She didn't usually stay out *too* late.

If anything happened to her—he couldn't say what he'd do, only that he would never recover from losing her. Never. Not even if he lived a thousand years.

His fingertips brushed across the glass, as though he could reach out and find her himself.

He must have stood there for half an hour, waiting and hoping and worrying, wondering whether he should send guards after all, when finally movement flickered over one of the garden walls. A figure dropped down into the grass. Then another. Then three more. They moved swiftly toward the palace, their cloaks billowing behind them. One moved ahead of the others, and even from this distance, Francis knew her shape. He nearly sagged in relief.

Mary, Queen of Scots, was home.

FOUR

Back in the queen's chambers, Bea helped Mary out of her men's clothes and into a lavish purple dressing gown. Hush took down her hair and brushed it until it shone. Liv built up the fire in her room. Flem fetched her a cup of tea. Then the Four Marys went off to their own chambers, still talking and laughing, energized from their night in the city. Liv, in particular, seemed alight. Mary smiled as she remembered the way Liv had danced with Ari de Nostradame, after all this time spent gazing at the seer's daughter from afar. It was nice to see her happy. Lately Liv had seemed preoccupied with some worry she didn't speak of, a constant furrow to her brow, a hint of sadness in her eyes.

Perhaps it was because Liv realized that it would soon be time for the Four Marys to be, well, married. That was the main reason their families had sent them from Scotland along with Mary all those years ago: to find prestigious, well-connected matches in the French court. That sounded good, in theory, marrying well, but what it actually meant was that each of her ladies would have to wed whoever Mary chose for them, namely a lord with loads of money and a title. Most likely a complete stranger.

In that way, Mary considered herself lucky. It felt like she'd always known that she would be Francis's wife. There had been a period a few years ago when she'd briefly considered running away to England and marrying Edward Tudor, the boy king, just so she could do something unexpected and not simply obey the adults around her, but that had been a passing fancy. Francis was all she'd ever known. She'd grown up in the chambers next to his, been taught by the same tutors, breathed the same air in the same rooms for most of the past twelve years.

She knew Francis.

She would even say she . . . well, yes, she loved him. Not the romantic kind of love, of course, the kind the poets wrote sonnets about, but then Mary had always known she wouldn't marry for love. That was impossible for a queen, and she'd always been a queen. But a sisterly kind of love . . . well, no, it wasn't exactly sisterly. Sometimes when she looked at Francis, she became aware of how pretty he was. His blue eyes could be quite startling, and she liked his halo of golden hair, and the funny little twist of his smirk. And she knew they would make a handsome couple together. Even if she was so much taller.

As for her ladies, she'd try to find a suitable husband for Liv, when the time came. A man who was gentle and sensitive, who would appreciate Liv's golden beauty *and* her strong, loyal heart. Although it was hard to say who that could be.

Unfortunately for Liv, it could not be Ari de Nostradame.

Mary twisted her ring around her finger. Her gaze fell on the ornate oak desk. She thought about the letter from her mother. Then she took out a quill and some paper.

Dear Mama, she wrote, then stopped and bit her lip. She didn't know what to say. *I'm sorry to hear that things are such a mess? Keep up the good fight on my behalf? Why did you write to the uncles about the problems with John Knox, and not to me?*

She wished she could offer her mother some news or information that could be helpful. What Mary wouldn't give for a bit of true excitement. A plot she could uncover. An enemy to foil. A way to prove herself.

(To which your narrators would say: be careful what you wish for.)

She hadn't seen her mother, Mary de Guise, in many years. (Yes, it's *another* Mary to keep track of—we're sorry.) Lately it was getting more and more difficult for Mary to remember her mother's face, the exact color of her eyes or angle of her nose. But one thing she could never forget was her mother's strength.

Mary de Guise had been twenty-one years old when her husband, James V, had up and died, leaving her with a newborn daughter who now happened to also be the queen. Not that the elder Mary had particularly mourned her husband, who'd believed that the "forsaking all others" part of their wedding vows was more of a guideline than a rule. He'd had nine official mistresses at the time of his death and a veritable army of illegitimate children. It had been all the elder Mary could do to keep herself and her daughter alive, as one power-hungry man after another tried to assassinate them both and steal away the throne. Mary's earliest memories, in fact, were of being on the run from some terrible menace, a wild flight from one castle to another, stronghold to stronghold, tucked into the pocket of her mother's dress.

The last time Mary had been in Scotland, her mother had walked her onto the deck of the ship that would bear five-year-old Mary away to France.

"I don't want to go," she sniffled, clutching her mother's sleeve. "I want to stay with you, Mama."

Her mother knelt beside her. "You will be fine." She grasped Mary by the shoulders and looked deeply into her eyes. "I am sending you on this very important mission for me. You must not forget your duty."

Mary nodded gravely. Her "duty," in the official capacity, of course, was to be raised by the French king and his family and marry, when the time came, the French king's eldest son. But the duty her mother spoke of was something else. "You are to use your little gift," her mother had explained to her the night before, by which she meant Mary's ability to sneak in and out of the tightest of spaces. "I want you to watch all of them—the king and those closest to him, and the queen as well, for heaven knows the queen is full of her own deviousness, and you must report back to me all that you discover. Every detail. Every scandal. I must know."

"I will, Mama," Mary promised, although her heart had thumped wildly at the idea. "I won't forget."

"Good," her mother said, touching the tip of Mary's nose. "You've always been my good girl." She drew Mary close and hugged her tightly. "Oh, my clever darling. I shall miss you. Remember, we are a team, you and I."

Now, back in her chambers at the Louvre, Mary went to the door and locked it. Then she walked to the back wall where there was an intricate medieval tapestry of a rearing unicorn.

She unfastened the dressing gown, let it slip from her shoulders, and stepped out from where it pooled at her feet. Her long auburn hair tumbled all around her.

She closed her eyes.

There was a bright flash of light, and when the light dissipated, it seemed that Mary had vanished. But she had not. If you direct your attention lower, dear reader—much, much lower, near the floor—you'll see her.

A mouse.

She was gone in an instant, darting through a small hole in that wall, not much larger than the circumference of a coin. If you were small enough to pass through this hole (which of course you wouldn't be, but let's pretend, for the sake of the story), you could follow a dark and dusty path along the inside of the wall, which would connect to another path along another wall, and then another path, and so on, a circuitous journey through the various rooms, passageways, and *secret* passageways of the palace, which would lead you, at long last, to another tiny hole in the wall of the royal bedchamber of the king of France, himself.

The king was asleep (or had passed out in a drunken stupor—you decide) and was sprawled on the bed, arms and legs akimbo, his head thrown back and his mouth open.

The king was also drooling. And snoring. Loudly.

Mary-the-mouse crept out of the hole and stood for a minute, watching the king drool and snore. She twitched her mouse nose in distaste. But she knew that the king often talked in his sleep, so she waited, listening. And soon the king did speak.

"You're looking fine today, my dear Catherine," he slurred. "Would you like to see what the bedroom of a king looks like?"

Ew. If Mary had been human right then she probably would have gagged. Instead, she called up a list of the women she knew named Catherine. (During this time in history, approximately 92 percent of women were named one of four names: Mary, Anne, Catherine, or Jane, which led to many cases of mistaken identity.) There were no fewer than ten women at the French court named Catherine. The king couldn't be referring to Queen Catherine (aka Catherine de Medici, his wife, the queen of France), because he'd called her "my dear." Queen Catherine and the king had given up such pleasantries ages ago—now if they addressed each other directly (which was rare) they typically went with "hey, you." Also, Mary was fairly certain that King Henry wasn't the least bit interested in Queen Catherine visiting his bedchamber.

So it wasn't the queen King Henry saw in his dreams, but that still left an abundance of Catherines. And, in what seemed a sort of miraculous defiance of probability, none of the king's current romantic entanglements (that Mary knew of, anyway) was a Catherine.

"That's a beautiful brooch you're wearing," continued the king, still fast asleep.

Mary cocked her mouse head, trying to recall the brooches she'd seen recently.

"It nicely accentuates your bosoms," added the king. If it were possible for a person to leer in his sleep, he did.

Mary gave a mouse-sized sigh.

It didn't really matter *which* Catherine. The only thing to be gleaned here was that Henry was considering the procurement of a new mistress. And that, to Mary, was old news. Henry was always procuring a new mistress.

She waited a few more minutes to see if there'd be any further relevant mumblings from the sleeping king, but there were none. At one point he'd called out "Gowns! Wine! Women! Bells!" but that was all keeping with his brand (except for the bells part—what was that about?). So Mary ventured on to the next room: that of Diane de Poitiers. But she didn't learn anything revelatory there, either, only that Diane needed to order all new dresses, as she had recently (cough) outgrown her old ones.

Perhaps she's been eating too many bonbons, thought Mary, and scurried along her hidden path toward her next destination.

On the way, she passed by the kitchen, but she didn't venture from her hole there, as the kitchen was one place in the palace where the servants were vigilant about exterminating mice. She did happen to overhear that the cook intended to feature her fluffy buttermilk biscuits on the palace menu this week, biscuits with breakfast, lunch, dinner, and dessert. With marmalade, too, as Bea had been right about them receiving a shipment of oranges and lemons from Spain. This bit of news caused a shiver of anticipation to travel from Mary's nose to her tail.

A little-known fact about Mary, Queen of Scots: she loved biscuits.

With her stomach now grumbling, she made her way to her final hidey-hole: in the chamber of the French queen. The queen's room was always an exciting place to eavesdrop, one of Mary's favorites, for the simple reason that Catherine de Medici was (as we've already established) evil.

Tonight the queen was sitting at the fire while her lady-in-waiting filed her fingernails into sharpened points.

"And then I directed the seamstress to take in all of her gowns overnight, so that when next she wore them, she was nearly bursting out!" Catherine said with a laugh. "She didn't have a bite to eat all evening, for any good it did her."

The lady-in-waiting laughed, too, a little too heartily, Mary thought.

"Oh, my, Your Majesty. Such antics you pull. What will you do tomorrow? I wonder."

"Tomorrow," said the queen with a devious smile, "she'll get taller."

Mary's whiskers quivered in a silent giggle. She did like the queen, for many reasons, but most of all because the woman was so fearless in the pursuit of what she wanted, and so unapologetic in being herself. Both were qualities that Mary wished to emulate, in the times when she was not a mouse.

The queen put a thoughtful finger to her lips. "I wonder if I could also locate some kind of itching powder that would stick to a piece of jewelry, like, just hypothetically, a brooch? I'd want it to itch, of course, but also give the wearer a terrible rash."

"I have never heard of such a thing, Your Grace," said the lady-in-waiting. "But I can ask around."

Catherine waved her hand dismissively. "Never mind. I'll ask the Nostradamus girl. She's sure to have something that will suffice."

There came a knock at the door.

"It's Nostradamus, Your Majesty," came a voice from the other side.

"Speak of the devil," said the queen. "Enter!"

The door opened, and in stepped the famed seer: a stooped, aged man sporting a stern expression and a long gray beard. He was accompanied by Ari, who must also have just returned from her own adventure into the city. She still looked a bit aglow, herself. Mary felt a flash of happiness for Liv, followed by a twinge of guilt.

Nostradamus bowed. "My queen."

They began to make small talk, but Mary hardly registered what they were saying, because she had made a new and wonderful discovery: tonight the queen's dessert tray had been set upon the floor next to the wall. Upon the tray was a plate of strawberry crepes, which was of little interest to Mary, but there was also one of the cook's aforementioned biscuits. With marmalade.

Mary gave a delighted gasp. In that moment it was like the clouds parted and a beam of light shone down from heaven, in the company of angels singing, upon the golden biscuit. The smell of flour and honey and sweet, sweet goodness crowded Mary's sensitive mouse nose. Her mouth started to water uncontrollably. She felt instantly famished, as if she were starving and one bite of this providential biscuit would save her life.

The humans were still talking as Mary-the-mouse crept slowly but purposefully across the room to the tray. She didn't like to fully enter a room where there were people (awake ones, that is), because she had a delicate body and no desire to be squashed, which was always what people wanted to do if they spotted a mouse. But she couldn't help herself. Once she reached the tray, she hid under the napkin for a moment before she ventured over to the biscuit.

She broke off a corner, held it between her tiny mouse hands, and took a bite. Her eyes closed. It was delicious.

"My queen, I have had a vision of grave importance," Nostradamus announced raspingly.

Ooh, this could be good, thought Mary. She broke off another chunk of the biscuit and stuffed it into her mouth.

"It is about deadly biscuits," the old man said.

FIVE
Ari

He led with the biscuits! Ari dragged her hand down her face.

"Deadly *biscuits*," the queen repeated. "This is why you interrupted my nightly routine?"

Nostradamus nodded solemnly.

"Biscuits like the ones served with tonight's dessert?"

They all turned toward the dessert tray on the floor, where Catherine had left one untouched biscuit. Untouched, that is, except by the mouse that was currently gnawing on it. The mouse froze, and then threw itself against a spoon in some kind of mouse-like Heimlich maneuver.

"Is that a mouse?" the queen asked slowly. "In my bedchamber?"

"Don't worry," Ari said. "I'll take care of the mouse. Father, why don't you tell the queen about the *other, possibly more important visions?*"

Ari gave her father a knowing look and then lunged toward the tray and made a shooing motion with her hand. In an instant, the mouse disappeared through a tiny crack in the wall. It seemed to be a physical impossibility. It was like a lemon disappearing through the eye of a needle.

"Thank you, Ari." A suspicious glint entered the queen's eyes as she stared at the crack through which the mouse had escaped.

This visit was not going well.

"Your Majesty," Ari said. "The biscuits are not the reason we are here tonight."

"Really?"

"Well, not the only reason," Ari amended.

"Tell me, girl," the queen said. "Have you figured out an elixir that will"—she waved her hand in the air as she thought—"make a man's testicles climb ever so slowly up and back into his body? Like two little itty-bitty sloths?" She made a mini climbing gesture with her hands.

The queen was always asking for potions such as this, and she always did it with a mischievous smile. Ari used to think she was jesting, but after so many requests, she'd begun to wonder.

"Not yet," Ari answered, "but if you have an unsightly blemish, Your Majesty—not that you would ever have such a thing—"

Nostradamus thrust his cane forward. "Your Majesty, as I was saying, there is more to my vision."

"More than biscuits?" she said, turning back toward Nostradamus.

"Indeed. My vision came in separate parts. They were not clear revelations, which I believe is due to the current position of the asterisms in conjunction to the moon—"

"Bother the moon," the queen interrupted. "Get on with the vision."

Nostradamus took a dramatic pause as he sank down on the queen's chaise lounge. He held his cane with both hands as if it were a sorcerer's staff. "There's something about Mary," he said.

"Mary?" the queen asked. "You mean Francis's future wife?"

"Yes, Your Majesty."

"Mary," the queen repeated. "Queen of Scots."

"Yes."

The queen glanced at her desk. Upon it, Ari saw a folded pamphlet. Something about the evils of Eðians.

"And you've had no visions about Francis?" The queen was always asking about Francis's future. She seemed paranoid that some terrible fate was about to befall him.

"Not lately. Francis will be perfectly fine."

The queen pursed her lips, unconvinced. "All right. What is this vision about Mary?"

Nostradamus leaned closer. "I have seen a trap, laid open and baited, and it is set for the queen. And it is deadly."

"A trap?" the queen asked.

"It might not be a physical trap," Ari explained. "It could be a metaphorical trap."

"Yes, Aristotle and I have not come to any conclusions as to the meaning of the trap," Nostradamus said.

The queen looked again at the pamphlet. "But who has laid this trap? The heathen John Knox?"

Nostradamus shook his head. "Someone allied with the court. But the face is unclear. I have also seen a betrayal."

"Against Mary?"

"By someone close to her."

"There have always been threats to Mary's life," the queen said. "But those close to her, particularly her ladies, seem loyal. And the French court reveres her."

"This is why we think the vision is urgent," Ari said.

Queen Catherine sat down next to Ari's father. "Who, wise Nostradamus? Who will betray her?"

"I do not know," Nostradamus said. "Those near her must be watched."

The queen frowned and nodded. "Can you tell me anything else?"

"I cannot," Nostradamus said. "Not at this moment."

"Thank you, my dear friend." She held out a hand.

Nostradamus gripped it tightly. "And do not forget about the biscuits. There is death in those crumbs."

Ari winced, but the queen ate it up, so to speak. She always took his advice. Ever since Nostradamus had predicted the untimely death of a cousin of Catherine's, he'd been in her employ and under her protection as a trusted adviser. He'd predicted many other events that had kept his job safe. Ari hoped this would continue to be the case.

The queen snapped her fingers. "Jane!"

Her lady-in-waiting came to attention.

"Please go to the kitchen and try a biscuit, and then return here so that we may monitor your condition."

"Your Majesty?" Jane said, her voice shaking.

"Or you can eat the one on the floor." She gestured to the biscuit the mouse had been nibbling on, as if she were doing the lady a favor by not making her go all the way to the kitchen to eat a deadly biscuit.

"But, Your Majesty?" Jane's words were a plea.

"Oh, all right," Queen Catherine said. "Go and inform the kitchen that for the next month, biscuits are to be banned."

"Yes, Your Grace."

"But if there is a biscuit revolt, I'm blaming you."

Jane gave a curtsy. Oh, to be a lady-in-waiting to Queen Catherine de Medici. It was like being in a fun house full of trick mirrors and daggers. And clowns.

"Should we ban baguettes as well?" the queen asked Nostradamus.

"No, Your Majesty. That would be madness."

Oh, to be French.

"Very well. Also, Jane . . ." She turned toward the dessert tray. "Have the servants put out some mousetraps." The queen then waved away Jane, who bowed and scurried out of the chambers.

"As for the rest of your warnings . . ." The queen paused for a moment, thoughtful. "Queen Mary is very private and very loyal, especially to her ladies. It may prove difficult to keep an eye on those close to her. But she is the future of a secure France. We need a live Mary. A dead one would do us no good. At the expense of everything else, she must marry Francis." Then she smiled a wicked smile, and Ari knew she was up to something, well, wicked. "We need to find someone who can get close, someone who can keep an eye on her. To ward off any evil intentions, of course."

Ari didn't take time to think, or to reason, or to waffle. "Your Majesty!" she blurted.

"Yes?"

"I would like to volunteer to keep an eye on Mary."

The queen pressed her lips together. "How?"

"Someday, I shall be the adviser to the king of France." Whenever she and Francis were in the same room together, there was a definite "next king of France" and "next Nostradamus" vibe, which weighed visibly on them both. "So for now, put me in as a lady-in-waiting to Queen Mary." She lowered her eyes. "If you please," she added. That was what a lady-in-waiting would say, wasn't it?

Ari offered this solution for three reasons. One: she really could watch out for a trap and a betrayal because she knew it was coming. Two: she would further solidify her usefulness to the future king and queen. And three: well, if her arm were twisted, and she had to tell you, all right, fine, she wanted to be closer to Liv.

Queen Catherine looked skeptical.

"I promise it will work," Ari said, having absolutely no idea if it would work. "I can keep an eye on her while at the same time I can listen to"—Ari pointed to the heavens—"divine things. If I see anything coming, I can warn you." Yes, she'd just pulled the "divine information" card. She just hoped she wouldn't actually be asked to see the future. . . .

Queen Catherine raised a dubious eyebrow. "Turn to the side, child."

Ari faced one direction and then the other.

The queen took in Ari's attire, her plain dress, and her well-worn shoes. Her stockings used to be white, but they had gathered a bit of dirt on her walk back from town. And her hair was a bit frizzy. She wasn't filthy, by any means. But she wasn't ladylike, either.

Queen Catherine scrutinized her with narrowed eyes and then held a finger to her lips. "Hmmmmm."

Ari nodded as if it were a question.

"You will watch Mary," the queen said.

"Yes," Ari agreed.

"Every move."

"Yes," Ari said with only a hint of hesitation.

"You will know where she is at all times and what she is doing at all times, and whom she is doing it with at all times."

Ari swallowed. "Yes."

"And you will do all of this knowing that your future in this court depends on it," the queen said.

Ari gulped. She had not intended to gamble with her future. But at this point what could she do? Queen Catherine was not someone to be trifled with.

Yet here Ari was, doing all sorts of trifling. "Yes." Those three little letters weighed as much as an elephant on Ari's shoulders.

The queen clapped her hands. "You will visit the court seamstress at once. Tell her I sent you. Tell her you need a dress befitting a lady." Her gaze focused on the mop of messy brown hair on Ari's head. "And do you not own a hairbrush?"

"It's very steamy work, making potions," Ari protested. "Oh! By the way, I have your lady's cough remedy here." She handed the queen a small vial. "And I will get a hairbrush at once."

"Now, we cannot alarm Mary, or the rest of the court, about any prophecy regarding her well-being. She is a strong-willed, contrary girl. She would not take well to any interference in her life. Besides, there are threats everywhere. Earlier tonight, a pamphlet was discovered, one derogatory to all Verities, especially Queen Mary."

"Oh no," Ari said.

The queen continued. "Everything will be fine once Mary and Francis are safely married, but who knows how long that will take. And if everything's not fine, I suppose I'll know who to blame."

Ari took a deep breath. "I swear it will be done."

SIX
Francis

"Am I not king of my own kitchen?" King Henry shouted. "Why does that woman insist on tormenting me?"

Francis sighed. All morning he'd been trying to slip away to see Mary, but the king had summoned him to the royal chambers to share lunch. And to add to Francis's torment, the king had invited Mary's uncles, too. Francis had been forced to sit there while servants set the table with trays of fine cheeses, breads, and decanters of wine. Then the king had asked about biscuits and been informed that Queen Catherine had taken biscuits off the menu for a month.

"The queen is a woman," murmured Duke Francis from his seat beside the king. "Women live to torment men."

"Indeed," agreed Cardinal Charles. "If they are not

tormenting, they are tempting. We men face challenges like no one else, I'm afraid."

Well, that doesn't make any sense at all, Francis thought. Anyway, they were just biscuits. That was to say, Francis wouldn't have minded a biscuit right now, but he'd never have shouted at the staff in order to get them.

Finally, when lunch was set and the servants had retreated to the safety of the far side of the room, the king looked at Francis and said grandly, "My son, I've had a vision."

The uncles both clapped politely. "Well done, Sire," said the duke cheerily.

"You have the most glorious visions," agreed the cardinal.

Francis stifled a groan. This again. The king was always having "visions," which were different from Nostradamus's. The kings visions usually led to parties, banquets, and other exciting ways to drain the royal treasury.

"It hasn't been a full day since your last vision," Francis said, thinking of the banquet last night. The vision before that had been only two weeks ago. There'd been a surprise festival—one to celebrate the beauty of the moon, or maybe it had been the trees? Either way, Francis was still recovering from the small talk with people feigning admiration while they fished for favors.

"Visions don't come on a schedule, son." King Henry took a long drink of wine. "Aren't you curious as to what I've seen?"

Francis knew that the king would tell him even if Francis leapt to his feet and fled the room. "Of course, Father."

A smile curved the corners of the king's mouth. "I see gowns," Henry proclaimed, motioning with his goblet. "I see feasts and merriment and beautiful ladies. I see wedding bells."

"You see wedding bells?" Francis asked.

"I hear them, too." Henry took another long pull from his goblet, then held it still as a servant rushed to refill it.

Francis frowned. His sister Elizabeth had recently been married to King Philip II of Spain, a fact that she reminded everyone of in every letter she wrote. *My husband, the king of Spain* . . . As if anyone could forget that her wedding had allied France with the most powerful kingdom in the world. She'd been married by proxy at Notre Dame, with the Duke of Alba standing in for the king, and then traveled to Guadalajara for another ceremony with the man himself. Like anyone needed two weddings. But Elizabeth had always insisted on the finest dresses, the most elaborate hairstyles, and the gaudiest jewelry. Two weddings was on brand for her, even if France would be paying for the first one for another three years.

And now there would be another wedding. Hopefully the crown wasn't paying for it, too.

Francis knew he shouldn't ask, because Henry liked to imagine himself a matchmaker, usually because he needed to politely remove a mistress from his company. Three out of his four most recent unofficial mistresses had been acquired—and then disposed of—at weddings. But if this was happening, Francis should probably know what kind of gifts he should bring. "Who's getting married?"

Henry used his teeth to tear off a bite of baguette and grinned. "You, son! You're getting married." He waved his arm to encompass all of Francis, as if every body part was getting married. "It's time for you to marry Mary."

Francis went totally still, hardly daring to breathe. "Marry Mary?" he repeated. "But . . . why now?"

"To secure the alliance, of course." Henry said it as though Francis were a complete fool. "We must unite France and Scotland for eternity."

From the corner of his eye, Francis could see the uncles nodding agreeably. Eagerly, in fact.

"We've been thinking about this for some time." Duke Francis sipped his wine. "Especially after we saw that terrible pamphlet from John Knox last night."

"Indeed." Cardinal Charles's mouth curled in distaste. "It is, unfortunately, a common problem. Those barbaric Eðians in Scotland are always threatening our dear niece."

"They are vile creatures," the king agreed.

"We take all threats against our niece seriously, of course," Duke Francis went on, "and this only invigorates our desire to see sweet Mary married and with child. Only when she is a wife and a mother will she truly be safe."

Francis frowned.

Duke Francis turned to him. "And how fortunate, my boy, that you're already such good friends."

Well, that was true.

"You are both of age," the cardinal said.

They were sixteen and seventeen.

"Plenty old enough to begin making a brood of sons who can inherit both thrones," Duke Francis finished cheerily.

Thrones. It always came back to thrones. How much of this was about Mary's safety, and how much was about securing the inheritance of more kingdoms?

"I've decided on a date." The king leaned forward, delight shining in his eyes. "The twenty-fourth."

Francis blinked. "Of this month?"

"Of this month."

"Of this year?"

"Of this year."

But . . . that was only five days away.

Francis's eye twitched. Marry Mary. Make heirs. Secure the royal line of succession.

"The twenty-fourth?" he asked, like triple-checking would change anything. He'd never before been so aware of how short a time five days was. If he'd realized he was approaching his last hours as an unmarried man . . . well, he wouldn't have made different decisions because none of his decisions were his own, but maybe he'd have appreciated the relative lack of expectations more. Because in five days, he'd be expected to produce heirs.

With Mary.

Gulp.

"The twenty-fourth," Henry confirmed. "We'll hold the

ceremony at Notre Dame. I've already got everything picked out. I adore weddings. And you're going to love it, too."

Francis didn't have anything else scheduled for the twenty-fourth, but this wedding seemed pretty last minute. "Father, I'm not sure this is the best time . . ."

"Don't be foolish, son. If you don't marry Mary soon, some other suitor is sure to make her an offer. We need to keep Scotland dependent on us, and Scotland needs France. They are overrun by Eθians! That Knox fellow is only one example of the danger they face. Which means that you'll marry Mary and seal the deal. And when you are wed, you will apply a gentle but firm pressure to bring that kingdom back to its Verity roots. Mary is a Verity. You are a Verity. Your children will be Verities. The kingdom must follow."

"I want to do what is best by France, of course." Francis squirmed with discomfort. "I'm just worried about"—he lowered his voice so the servants couldn't overhear—"the wedding night. We've been friends forever, but she's never given me an indication that she sees me as anything other than a friend." Francis tried very hard not to look at Mary's uncles.

"Bah!" Henry waved away that concern. "Mary will do her duty. She needs an heir even more than you do. She will obey. I will see to it."

Mary and *obey* could not usually be used in the same sentence. Wait— "What do you mean you'll see to it?"

"I'll be there, of course."

Francis blinked. "You'll be there?"

"Of course," Cardinal Charles said. "There's nothing unusual about a father-in-law observing the consummation of a long-awaited wedding."

Francis begged to differ.

The king nodded. "My father observed your mother and me. Unfortunately it didn't take right away, but you came along eventually."

Francis's throat went tight. "Did he, um, observe every time after?"

"Of course not. He had a kingdom to run, and believe it or not, there was a time your mother and I did not hate each other. We were quite energetic in those days, if you know what I mean."

Francis did not want to think about what Henry meant, and he certainly did not want to think about his grandfather, ahem, observing. He decided to move on to the point of the conversation. "I'm just not sure I want to—"

"Oh, you will," Henry assured him. "Mary is a beautiful girl, and you should enjoy her." He said it as though she were a new toy he was offering Francis.

In his head, Francis gagged a little. (Your narrators are gagging, too.)

"And once you've made an heir," Henry went on, "if you get tired of her, then you'll be able to take a mistress."

"Well, now." Cardinal Charles frowned. "That's not a thing to speak of in front of Mary's uncles, is it?"

The king smiled innocently at the uncles. "Not that anyone could ever tire of Mary. She's quite the prize."

Prize? Francis was really going to be sick.

"But in a normal marriage," Henry said to Francis, "sometimes the man and the woman realize they despise each other more than anything else in the world. Sometimes the woman cuts off the biscuit supply for no reason. Sometimes she's just mean. Therefore, a man with needs must find satisfaction elsewhere. Or are you worried that you won't know what to do?" Henry mused, stroking his beard as he shot Francis a challenging look. "Should I send a girl to instruct you?"

Francis blanched, then reddened, then blanched again. "No, no! I know what to do!" At least, he was reasonably sure he knew what to do, because as a sixteen-year-old boy, he thought about it approximately 432 times a day.

The king smiled slowly, menacingly. "Good. But let me know if you change your mind."

Francis would not change his mind. He had no intention of becoming his father.

"The announcement will take place this evening, followed by a feast." Henry stood and brushed the bread crumbs out of his beard. "It should go without saying that you're expected to attend."

"Of course," Francis mumbled, hating everything. "Does Mary know about this yet?"

"Oh, goodness, no. Why should she concern herself with the details?" Duke Francis shook his head, like there was nothing wrong with the idea of four men holding a meeting about a woman and her reproductive future.

"I see." It would fall to Francis to tell her, then. Otherwise, she would find out tonight in the worst possible way.

"Congratulations, Your Highness," said Duke Francis. "I'm so pleased that I'll soon be able to call you nephew."

Cardinal Charles smiled widely and shook Francis's hand.

"Son, you are dismissed to prepare for the feast." Henry waved him out the door. "If you see Catherine out there, send her in."

"Mother?" Francis tilted his head. Were they meeting because of the upcoming—gulp—wedding?

The king scoffed. "What would I want with her? No, I mean Catherine with the amazing"—he leered a little—"brooch."

Francis barely escaped the king's chambers with his dignity intact. Brooch Catherine wasn't in the hall, thank goodness. He didn't think he could stomach facing another woman Henry would soon grow bored with.

Francis would marry Mary, and no matter what kind of relationship they had, he would never do to her what Henry did to Catherine every day. Francis would give her the respect she deserved.

Starting by telling her that Henry had set a wedding date.

With a sigh, Francis trudged toward Mary's rooms.

Five. Days.

He needed to figure out how to tell her.

"Mary, I regret to inform you . . ." No, that sounded like he was delivering news about a dead relative.

"Mary, you know how we're supposed to get married?" No, too awkward.

"Mary, my father plans to watch us on our wedding night."
Gah. Worse.

He was still mulling it over when he arrived at Mary's door. The usual guards were outside, and they gave him stiff, formal nods in greeting. Which meant if he didn't want the guards to stare at him while he loitered out here, he needed to knock. But if he knocked, then he'd need to tell her about their upcoming nuptials.

Mary was his best friend. She would understand why he was so conflicted.

Francis knocked.

"Who is it?" he heard from the other side of the door.

"It's me," he said, and then realized that wasn't terribly helpful. "I mean, it's Francis."

The door swung open, revealing a Mary. Not Mary, Queen of Scots, his impending wife, but one of her ladies-in-waiting.

"Good day, Your Grace," Liv said cheerfully. "Please come in."

Inside he found Mary—his Mary—seated at her vanity, with Hush arranging her long hair into an elaborate updo of twisting braids.

"Hello, friend." Mary smiled at him through the mirror, making his heart skip.

Francis tried not to think about it, because Mary was his friend first and his future wife second, but she was really, really beautiful. Probably the most beautiful person he'd ever seen in his life. And when she smiled just for him . . .

"I'm glad you're here," Mary was saying. "There's to be a

party tonight, have you heard? I'm not sure what we're meant to be celebrating, but I've been told it's a grand affair."

"Yes," he said. "About that—"

"Do you know what you're going to wear? I've been thinking about my cream gown with gold trim, you know the one." She tilted her head to clip a pearl earring onto her earlobe.

He nodded. "That one's nice. But—"

"And you could wear your blue velvet doublet that sets off the blue of your eyes. That way we wouldn't match, but we'd complement each other nicely, don't you think?"

"Yes," he said. "I'll wear the blue doublet. But . . ." His voice trailed off. Now was the time. He had to tell her.

She stopped as she was putting on the other earring and turned to look at him, her forehead rumpling. "What's wrong?"

He took a deep breath. "Nothing's wrong, exactly."

"I know you hate these parties, and I agree, they're wasteful and extravagant, but I promise, we'll find a way to have some fun."

He smiled faintly. She always did try to make things more bearable for him at social events. Last time she'd made up a game where they had a sip of their wine every time Henry drunkenly called someone by the wrong name. By the end they'd been quite tipsy themselves.

An idea came to him. "Oh, I know! What if we silently added the phrase 'in my pants' after everything my father says?"

Mary's dark eyes twinkled with mischief. "That could keep us properly entertained for hours!"

She laughed. The Four Marys laughed with her. Francis laughed, too. It was a funny idea, but— Droppings. He'd come here for a reason.

"Oh," Mary said, scrutinizing his face again. "You've come to tell me something serious." She glanced at her ladies. "Can you leave us alone for a moment?"

"Yes, Your Grace." The Marys all curtsied and exited promptly.

Mary gestured for Francis to take a seat on a chair near hers. He did.

"Is everything all right?" Mary asked. "Are you unwell?" She looked genuinely worried.

He cleared his throat. "I'm perfectly well." His heart was pounding. He had to say it now, or he'd never be able to say it at all. "Mary, we're getting married."

SEVEN

Mary gazed at Francis blankly. "I know that." She'd known for what seemed like forever that she was destined to marry Francis. She remembered well the evening when the king had announced their engagement. She had been five years old, just arrived in France. Henry made her stand before a huge assembly of courtiers, and he gave a long, grand speech, most of which Mary hadn't understood, because she didn't yet know French. But at the end of the speech he'd said, "I present to you my daughter, the queen of Scotland."

His daughter, he'd called her. As if the wedding were already over and done.

Francis rubbed the back of his neck. "He announced our engagement years ago. But tonight he's announcing our wedding. Which is set to take place on the twenty-fourth."

She blinked a few times. "Of this month?"

He nodded.

"Of this year?"

"That's what he told me," Francis sighed.

"But that's . . . Thursday."

"Yes," he said weakly. "Thursday."

Her mouth was hanging open. She shut it. "But that's in *five days*."

Something in Francis's throat jerked as he swallowed. "Yes."

"Who gets married on a Thursday?" she cried.

"Us, apparently."

A myriad of emotions rushed her. Fear. Excitement. Nervousness. Elation. Trepidation. Resignation. And then back to fear. But Francis was watching her face carefully, his eyes full of a worried hopefulness, so she produced a smile.

"All right. Well. That's wonderful news," she said finally.

"Yes," he said. He was saying yes a lot.

She stood up and began to pace back and forth across the room. "That's very little time to prepare. I will need to have a dress made, and pick the colors, and arrange for the flowers and decide on the menu, the venue, and the seating, and hire a good traveling minstrel. . . . There's not nearly enough time." She stamped her foot indignantly, without so much as a thought about the appropriateness of a queen stamping in front of her fiancé. "How can I be expected to do all of that in five days?"

"Not to worry. I think my father has made all the arrangements," Francis said. "Not that I know any of the details, except that the wedding will be held at Notre Dame."

She knew Francis probably meant to reassure her, but she scowled and stamped her foot again. "But *I'm* supposed to make the arrangements! It's my wedding, after all!"

"Our wedding," Francis corrected her.

"Yes. Of course. Our wedding. But I'm the bride, and the bride is generally expected to play a large part in the planning of her wedding! I've basically been planning since I got here. I had it all thought out. I'd wear a white dress—I know that's not a typical color for a wedding, but I've always looked good in white, and I would wear my hair down and simple, and I'd carry a bouquet of white cowslips, and there would be doves, and a lovely pair of swans for supper, and my mother would . . ." She sank to the chair. "Oh. My mother won't be there." Even if Mary sent a letter right away, it would take weeks for her mother to make the journey from Scotland.

Her mother would not get to see her wedding.

"I'm sorry," Francis said. "I could ask my father to postpone. Would that help?"

She shook her head. "No. My mother would tell me to go ahead. If the king wants us to marry so soon, it must be for a reason. It's a good sign," she said more to herself than to Francis. "He's finally honoring his promise, after all this time. Our countries will be united. France and Scotland will be partners. Like we are partners, you and I."

Francis nodded. "Partners. Right."

"What is it?" she asked. "What aren't you telling me?"

He rubbed the back of his neck, his eyes still troubled. "The reason my father is in such a rush for us to be wed is because your life is in danger."

He told her about the pamphlet, the drawing of her being beheaded.

"So someone wants me dead. What else is new?" she said, trying to make light of it in spite of the fear that prickled her. "Does your father really suppose that my being married is going to change that?"

Francis was quiet for a minute. "I don't know. I just know that he said our marriage would protect you. And Scotland."

"All right. We all know that what the king wants, the king gets. So Thursday." She bit her lip, which she knew was a dreadful habit, but she couldn't seem to help it. "I'm not busy Thursday. It is awfully soon, but I suppose we will just have to make it work."

She met his eyes. *I would be content to look at those eyes, that nose, that shapely mouth, for the rest of my life,* she thought, which startled her.

He was leaning toward her now, his knees nearly brushing hers. "You don't have to marry me," he said softly, "if you don't want to."

She straightened. Her heart was beating strangely. She'd never been fond of surprises, least of all surprise weddings, least of all her own. But it sounded just now like Francis was questioning her commitment to him. "Of course I want to. Do *you* want to marry *me*?" she shot back.

"I suppose so," he said, like she'd just asked him if he'd like to sample a new type of French pastry, and he wasn't sure he'd like it, but at least he'd give it a try.

He was attempting to be funny, she thought. But still she glared at him. "You suppose so."

"I know so," he admitted. He pulled at the collar to his doublet. "As a matter of fact, as arranged marriages go, I'd say we're lucky. We know exactly what we're getting into. And we like each other, at least we do most days. We're friends."

"Yes." She nodded. "Yes. We're lucky."

They smiled at each other. Then Francis seemed to have a sobering thought. "But back to Thursday. When we're married . . ."

"Things will go on quite the same, I think," she said. "Henry is so young and strong. We won't be king and queen of France for a long time to come."

He nodded, then winced. There was still something, she realized, that he hadn't told her. "That's true," he said. "But *right after* we're married . . ."

She gasped and sat back in her chair, her hand flying to her mouth. "On Thursday night! Yes! We'll be expected to . . ."

"Yes," he said. "And my father wishes to . . ."

Her nose wrinkled. "You don't suppose that he will insist upon . . ."

"He intends to," Francis said grimly. "He told me so himself."

"That's barbaric! Surely we've progressed beyond such vulgarities. This is the sixteenth century, after all!" Mary's face flushed, her cheeks heating to the point where she felt feverish, like that one time she'd had smallpox. She was well aware that marrying Francis would mean bearing children to be the heirs to the thrones of both Scotland and France, and she'd imagined, in a few lonely, secret moments, what that might involve, but she'd never considered that it would all be presided over by her father-in-law.

She shook her head firmly. "No. Just . . . no. That is not acceptable, Francis. We must find some way to keep your father out of the wedding night . . . activities."

He laid his hand over hers. "I will. I'll figure out a way for us to be alone when . . ."

"When we . . ." she murmured. "You know . . ."

"I know." He squeezed her hand gently. "We don't have to, though. I mean, eventually—yes, but not right away. Like you said, my father's going to live for ages yet. And we're still . . ."

"So young," she agreed, relieved. "We have plenty of time to produce heirs."

"Yes," he said. "And because that's the only reason we would ever . . ."

"Right," she said. "I'm glad that's settled."

They sat for a moment in awkward silence, Mary lost in thought over the smaller details of the wedding she might still have time to work out, and Francis thinking about . . . whatever boys thought about when it came to their own weddings.

After a time, Francis cleared his throat and said, "So have you enjoyed any recent adventures as *la petite poucette*?" The word *poucette* literally meant "thumb," as in "thumb-sized," and it was their secret code for Mary as a mouse.

Mary had told Francis about the mouse thing when she was seven (and he was six) years old. It had been one of those rainy days when they'd had to stay indoors and their tutor had been indisposed with a terrible cold, so Francis and Mary had been playing cards all day and were wildly bored. So Mary thought she'd pass the time by telling the dauphin her deepest, darkest secret: that sometimes, when she especially wanted to hide, she could transform herself into a mouse and sneak around wherever she pleased.

"I even have whiskers," she'd confessed.

Francis's wide blue eyes had grown even wider. He glanced around to be sure they were truly alone, then leaned forward to whisper, "Does that mean you're an . . . Eðian?"

Mary nodded. "I suppose so. My mama says I'm never to tell anyone, ever." But she'd told Francis, because, even then, she'd trusted him. And he had kept her secret faithfully all these years. In fact, one of the best things about being a mouse was creeping about, gleaning all the best gossip of the kingdom, and then returning to Francis to tell him about it, the two of them giggling and speculating and taking turns acting shocked by the nefarious secrets and scandals that Mary uncovered around the palace.

She turned to him now eagerly, hands clasped together. "I learned that your father has a new conquest."

Francis cringed and squeezed his eyes shut. "As always. But I already know this one. It's Catherine. Brooch Catherine. You know, with the . . . brooch."

"Oh." Mary deflated a bit. But then she remembered a much more amusing bit of intrigue. "Did you know that Diane thinks that she's outgrown all of her gowns?"

Francis's lips pursed. "Outgrown them? How could she outgrow them?"

Mary puffed out her cheeks, and Francis laughed. "But she hasn't really outgrown them," Mary explained. "She only thinks she has."

"I see," Francis said, like he was being serious. "And why would poor Lady Diane"—he stopped to smirk, as he was never inclined to pity Diane de Poitiers—"think that she had outgrown her gowns?"

"Because your mother had the seamstress take in the seams overnight," Mary said. She lifted her eyebrows expectantly. Then they both burst out laughing.

"I saw her at dinner last night. She looked most uncomfortable," Francis said when they could speak again.

"And now you know why." She was tempted to tell him about the unfortunate incident with Nostradamus and the "deadly biscuit," but she still felt too foolish about it.

"That proves it," Francis sighed. "My mother really is evil."

Mary nodded. "Let's resolve to stay on her good side." (If only, dear reader, she'd be able to keep her own advice. But we're getting ahead of ourselves.)

"Yes, let's," Francis agreed.

There was an impatient bark from outside the door, which

signaled the return of the Four Marys. Francis rose reluctantly from his chair. "I should go. I've lots to do. I'm getting married at the end of the week, you know."

"I've heard," Mary said. "Congratulations."

He arched an eyebrow at her. "Thank you."

She reached out to touch his arm—well, his sleeve, anyway. "And I wish to thank you, Francis. I am glad it was you who told me about the wedding. And I'm glad that we're finally . . ."

"Getting married. Yes. I am, too," he said. Then he bowed to her politely, because she was still a queen and he a prince, and made his exit.

The Four Marys bustled in, this time as three young ladies and one very excited spaniel, who leapt up into Mary's lap the moment she was allowed.

"All right, all right," Mary laughed, scratching behind the dog's ear. "I'll tell you everything." She gazed around at her ladies. "I'm getting married on Thursday!"

There was then a great deal of screaming and jumping up and down. Then they all sat, and Mary relayed what details she knew.

"Men really shouldn't plan weddings," Liv said with a snort when Mary was finished. "Who gets married on a Thursday?"

"That's exactly what I said." Mary sighed. "I do hope there are doves. I always wanted doves."

"I'll see what I can do with my contacts," said Bea. "And I'm sorry your mother won't be able to attend, but I'll get a message to her right away. Write a letter, and I'll be off with it tomorrow."

Mary smiled at her friend gratefully. "Thank you."

"And what shall we do with your hair?" added Hush quietly. "I know you've always imagined it down, but perhaps I can find a way to curl it so it falls just right."

"I'm sure you will," Mary said.

"Bark!" said Flem.

(We should probably explain about the barking. The Four Marys had been chosen, dear reader, because they each possessed a rare gift that they could use to assist their mistress. Strong, brave, and nimble Liv was Mary's guardian and protector; Bea was Mary's informant and messenger to and from her mother; Hush was Mary's hairdresser and principal seamstress; and Flem, well, Flem was Mary's most enthusiastic companion, in both human and Eθian form.)

"So it's finally happened," Bea said when everyone was quiet again. "I was beginning to wonder if we'd ever see the day when you two would be wed."

"I know. We've waited so long. Strange that it would suddenly feel so rushed," Mary mused.

"But you're pleased?" Liv asked.

"Of course I am," Mary answered. "This is all I've ever wanted."

"Good," whispered Hush. "We only want to see you happy."

"I am happy," Mary said, twisting her amethyst ring.

"And once you're married," said Liv with a small frown, "I suppose it will be time for us."

"I suppose," said Mary, and gave her a sympathetic smile.

Flem gave a happy bark and wagged her tail. Flem loved the idea of being married. She already had a list of a half-dozen suitors she was interested in.

"Will you marry us off right away?" asked Bea a bit tremulously. Bea didn't have a paramour, as she was extremely independent. She liked to spend long hours alone, and had on more than one occasion announced that the idea of courtship and matrimony quite disgusted her.

"No," Mary said. "I plan to take my time with that, of course. There's no rush."

Hush gave an audible sigh of relief, and Liv and Bea also relaxed.

There was a loud knock at the door, which startled them.

Bea went to answer it. She stuck her head out briefly and spoke to the party who wished to have an audience with the young Queen of Scots. They heard her say, "One moment, please!" before she pulled her head back in and shut the door.

"It's the queen!" she gasp-whispered. "Queen Catherine, I mean!"

EIGHT
Ari

Ari stared at the door to Queen Mary's bedchamber. The muffled sound of shuffling came from inside, but Ari didn't mind waiting because at the present moment she couldn't breathe.

The corsets of servants were made of cloth, and rarely did a servant have another servant tighten the laces for her. They learned to be very bendy with their arms.

The corsets of ladies, however, had things like whalebone in them, and were pulled as tight as if a team of horses had been attached at the ends of the strings and then whipped into action while the lady held on to a bedpost for dear life.

Ari was now standing in said corset, outside the door to Queen Mary's chambers, trying to breathe.

"Do you need a bit of liquid courage?" Queen Catherine

asked, holding out a flask she'd produced from somewhere within the drapery of her royal clothes. (Ari had heard rumors that the queen ordered her seamstress to add all sorts of secret pockets to her dresses.) "It's the strong stuff made especially for me."

"No, thank you, Your Majesty," Ari said. "I'm ready." Just because she couldn't breathe didn't mean she was nervous. She would be fine.

As long as Queen Mary didn't ask her to see the future, that is.

Besides, Ari had actually spent the night before concocting a potion she called *Your Best Self*, which had little to do with liquor and more to do with licorice root, mixed with *Ganoderma* mushroom, amber, and a splash of incantation from her great grandfather's grimoire. (Since magic could be considered heresy, the grimoire was hidden in the lab under the cover of *A History of Beets: Volume Five*, which nobody in their right mind would want to read.) Not many females of non-noble birth could read, but Ari's father had taught her from the moment her gifts began to manifest.

"Now remember, my dear girl, I must be told of everything that happens to Mary," Queen Catherine reminded her. "Down to the least significant-seeming detail."

Ari nodded. "Yes, Your Majesty."

Finally, a voice called: "Please, come in."

The guard opened the door, and Queen Catherine stepped inside, followed by Ari.

It was one of the most majestic rooms Ari had ever seen, besides Queen Catherine's. Ornate tapestries hung from ceiling to floor and the moldings and decorative woodwork were covered in gold leaf. In front of the largest of the windows sat Queen Mary on a chaise lounge, surrounded by her ladies. One sat on the chair beside the queen, two sat on stools at her feet, and then there was Liv, who sat on the windowsill, with her legs crossed and one foot hanging daintily off the edge.

Suddenly, Ari's corset felt a little tighter, her flushed cheeks felt a little, well, flushier. Liv returned her gaze with a lopsided grin, and Ari wondered if maybe she should have taken some of Queen Catherine's liquid courage.

Queen Catherine cleared her throat. "My dear Mary," she said. "May I introduce Aristotle de Nostradame."

"I know of Aristotle," Mary said with a significant smile at Ari. Of course the queen wouldn't mention that she'd been merrymaking in a tavern with Ari only last night. "Isn't she meant to be the next great prognosticator?"

Inwardly Ari cringed. "Actually, my greatest strength is in potion—"

"Yes," Queen Catherine interrupted. "But for now she will be your new lady-in-waiting." The queen gestured to Ari, which was her cue to curtsy.

Ari had only learned the basics of a true lady's curtsy that morning, and it was from the seamstress, who, due to being a little top-heavy, fell over every time she demonstrated. Slowly, and very aware of the heels on her shoes, Ari set her right toe behind her left foot, bent her knees, and bowed her head.

The *Your Best Self* elixir must have been working, because she didn't fall over. But when she lifted her head, she saw every one of the Marys stifling a smile, except Liv, who didn't stifle her smile at all. Ari blushed, her hands trembling. She shoved them behind her dress.

"I thank you, Queen Catherine," said Queen Mary, "but I am not in need of any more ladies-in-waiting."

Liv lightly touched her foot to Mary's shoulder. (For us non-royals this would be akin to kicking a friend under the table, but no one would ever kick a queen.)

Mary and Liv shared a look. It was one of those looks only best friends could understand.

"I mean," Mary said slowly, "we would be lucky to have her."

"Wonderful," Queen Catherine said, clasping her hands together. "You may think of Ari as your own little fortune-teller."

Mon Dieu. They were back to the topic of seeing the future. "I also make potions," Ari blurted out.

"Do you?" Mary said.

"Yes, Your Majesty." Ari worked hard to regain her composure. *Remember,* she told herself, *you are the daughter of the great Nostradamus.*

"I will leave you all to get acquainted," Queen Catherine said. "Try not to eat each other." She swept out of the room, and they were all left to themselves to try not to eat each other.

"Well, Aristotle, these are my ladies," said Queen Mary. "They are all named Mary. But you may call this one Bea"—she pointed to the lady next to her on the chair—"this one Flem"—she pointed to one of the stool Marys—"this one Hush"—the other stool Mary—"and I believe you know Liv."

Of course Ari already knew all the Marys' names. Especially Liv's. But she said, "I am very pleased to meet you all, formally. Please call me Ari."

There was a moment of silence.

"So, you are Nostradamus's daughter," said Mary.

"Yes."

"And where do you live?"

"In chambers near the lab."

"The main lab or the secret lab?" Queen Mary asked.

Ari hesitated. "Um, the main lab."

"How come I don't see you around the palace very often?"

"I tend to blend into the background," Ari said.

"I don't agree," Liv murmured.

Ari glanced at Liv, and the glance turned into a longer glance, and then it was a downright gaze. There was just something so comforting about Liv's face. It was like a warm blanket.

Queen Mary stood and took Ari's hand and led her to a chair. "So, you get to be my very own Nostradamus. Show us your talents."

"Yes, yes," Flem said, clapping her hands. "Predict something."

Oh crap. Had her corset not been so tight, Ari's heart would have beat out of her chest. "Well, I'm really better at potions than prognostication. In fact, I brought you something, Your Majesty." Ari reached into the waistband of her dress and produced a small bottle.

Queen Mary took it and held it up to the light. "What does it do?"

"It's nothing much," Ari said humbly. "But if you sprinkle it lightly over your dress, any wrinkles will disappear. It took me five months to perfect."

Ari didn't mention that at the time, she had been trying to make wrinkles on a *face* disappear, at the request of Diane de Poitiers, who was Queen Catherine's senior by twenty years and well aware of it. Ari still hadn't quite mastered that one yet. She wasn't too worried, though, because her loyalties rested with the queen and not the king's mistress.

"That's nice." Queen Mary tossed the bottle to Flem, who caught it midair with one hand. "Now give us a vision."

"Yes, a vision," Flem said, sniffing the bottle, which Ari found a bit odd.

"Well, visions are not an exact science." Ari tugged uncomfortably at the lace around her neck. "They can be very vague, and you never know when they will come true. It may not even happen in your lifetime."

"Even so, please try," Queen Mary said.

Ari thought fast. During her training, her father would tell her that the quickest access to the far reaches of the mind was through the nose. Aromas. Odors. Pleasant or disagreeable. The first time

Ari had a vision—another one that hadn't made any sense—her mother had sent her out to gather some mint for tea.

"I need a sprig of mint." Ari hoped she was remembering it right.

"I have just the thing." Bea strode across the room in such an elegant way that it almost seemed like she was floating and not walking. She returned with a bound cluster of herbs, green leaves with purple blooms at the top. "I saw them as I was—um—traveling, and I thought they were pretty. It's mint sage."

Traveling? Ari didn't think the ladies went anywhere without Mary.

Bea handed Ari the bundle.

Ari sniffed at it. Nothing happened. Perhaps she could make the smell stronger by burning it. Ari spotted a lit candle on Queen Mary's writing desk. She gulped and walked over. She considered lighting the top, but that might turn it into a torch. So she held the green bottoms of the stems over the flame until they glowed but did not ignite.

"You might want to stay back," Ari said, even though she was only burning a bunch of herbs. It probably wouldn't work. Maybe she could make up a vision. (But readers, we ask you, have you ever tried to come up with a prophetic vision on the fly? It's difficult.)

Ari took a pillow from another chaise and placed it on the floor. She sat down, cross-legged (most unladylike), held the glowing end near her face, and waved the fumes toward her nose.

Nothing happened again.

"Is she supposed to be doing something?" Flem whispered. "I feel like she's supposed to be doing something."

Ari held the bundle closer and inhaled deeply. The aroma of mint went straight to her head. Suddenly her eyes rolled back and she felt that strange floating sensation. This was it!

She remembered her breathing, as her father had taught her. Then she belched, which her father had not taught her. The giggles of the Marys became muffled and then gave way to the sound of waves. Ari found herself hovering over a vast expanse of water. It was dark. There were screams and a far-off horn. She sank closer to the water, looking down upon two people.

Ari spoke softly. "I see a boy and a girl. They are floating in the ocean."

She heard some oohs in the distance, and then a shushing sound.

"It's very cold. The breath coming out of their mouths freezes instantly." Ari shivered. "They are not in a boat. They are on . . ." Ari squinted and saw the metal hinges of a latch. "They are on a door? The boy is slipping into the water. The girl is holding his hand. She is promising to never let go. She will hold on forever and they will be together— Oh wait, she just let go."

Ari jolted back into the present.

The Marys were staring at her, their mouths open.

"Was the girl Queen Mary?" Liv asked.

The queen glanced at Liv and then Ari.

"No," Ari said. "At least I don't think so. She had red hair."

"Mary has brown hair," Flem said.

"Technically, it's auburn," Hush argued softly. "Auburn is a shade of red."

"The hair color doesn't matter," Queen Mary said. "What happened to the boy?"

"He drowned," Ari answered. "Or froze to death. I'm not sure which came first."

The Marys collectively deflated at the news.

"I'm sorry," Ari said. "It wasn't a very pleasant vision, I know. But at least the girl survived."

"That doesn't make it better," Flem sniffed. "Somehow that makes it sadder."

Ari's shoulders slumped. "Well, remember, we don't know when this will happen. It could be tomorrow, it could be, say, four hundred thirty-seven years from now. Like I said, visions can't really be counted on." At least not any of *her* visions.

"Couldn't they both fit on one door?" Bea asked. "Seriously, look." She gestured to the giant oak door to Queen Mary's chamber. "That could fit all five of us. I mean"—she glanced at Ari—"all six of us. So, I've solved the vision. It must be a murder on the girl's part."

"It wasn't necessarily a puzzle to solve," Ari said. On one hand, she was relieved that she'd even been able to conjure a vision on demand like that. But on the other hand, Queen Mary and her ladies all seemed disappointed that it hadn't been a better one.

"I think it was," Bea said. "I think I won the vision!"

The ladies laughed.

Ari turned to Queen Mary. "Were you hoping for a specific type of vision?"

"No, no, of course not," said Mary lightly.

"We just thought, with the queen so soon getting married—" Flem blurted out.

This was a revelation to Ari. "Oh. Is Queen Mary getting married soon?" Ari glanced at all of the ladies, and then at Mary, who smiled demurely.

Liv jumped to her feet. "Queen Mary and Francis are to be wed on the twenty-fourth."

"Of this month?" Ari asked, flabbergasted.

Queen Mary sighed. "Yes."

"Of this—"

"On Thursday. At Notre Dame. But not many people know yet."

"So naturally we were hoping you might have a vision concerning her rapidly approaching state of matrimony," said Bea.

"Yes, we want a vision about the wedding!" Flem said.

"Um, I didn't know about the wedding," Ari stammered. "I've had no visions . . ."

"It's fine," said Queen Mary. "Anyway, I already know the wedding is going to be . . . perfect."

"Yes, and we're all going to dress up and attend her at the ceremony," said Flem excitedly.

"Including you now, I suppose," said Bea.

Ari's stomach did a flip. It was one thing to dress up in fine clothes and wait upon the queen in private. It was quite another thing to parade one's unrefined self in front of thousands of people at Notre Dame.

Suddenly she was feeling a bit sick. But when she thought about it, she realized this was why she'd signed up for this job. The wedding could be a good opportunity to present herself as the next Nostradamus and secure her relationship with the dauphin and Queen Mary.

"I'll need a new dress," she said.

"We'll add your order to ours," said Bea, who then began to circle around Ari, taking her measurements.

Hush immediately began to fuss with Ari's curls.

Liv touched Ari's shoulder. "If you want, I can help you with the curtsy, and other things a lady is supposed to know."

"I'd love that," Ari said too eagerly, which caused Liv to laugh.

Now imagine, dear reader, a makeover montage, in which Mary's ladies hovered around Ari, holding up samples of fabric, tucking in tufts of hair, and spritzing her with fine aromas.

It was the first time Ari had ever been the center of anything.

She knew she should excuse herself as soon as possible, to report the momentous news of the wedding to Queen Catherine. It was obvious the queen didn't know about it, and it would be best if she learned of it from Ari. It would prove that Ari was indeed useful to her as one of Queen Mary's ladies.

But just for a few moments, Ari lingered to chat with Bea and joke with Flem, to have her hair done up into elaborate braids by Hush, and to try on one of Queen Mary's jeweled necklaces. All the while, she basked in the warmth of Liv's hazel eyes.

"I'm so glad you've come to join us," Liv said merrily. "Now you have an excuse to talk to me. Regularly, I mean. Without me having to be in disguise."

It seemed miraculous, this idea that she'd be seeing Liv, and yes, talking to her, every single day.

Ari smiled at her. "Nothing would make me happier," she said.

NINE
Francis

That night, the wedding announcement went something like this:

Henry called every noble in Paris to join him in the throne room, packing people so tightly there was hardly space to breathe. Then he gave a long speech about France's alliance with Scotland and the importance of great friends. At some point in there, servants had thrown open the windows and started fanning the edges of the crowd, because the heat was unbearable. People had started to sweat, filling the room with the toxic reek of body odor and too much perfume.

By then, either someone had suggested that Henry might start wrapping it up, or he too had begun growing weak from the heat and smell and so decided to finish before everyone fainted. Either way, he finally got to the point, motioning for Francis to step forward and for Mary to approach the throne.

Nerves crowded in Francis's throat. This was it.

"For years, these two young lovebirds have been promised to each other," Henry said as he made Francis and Mary hold hands. "After much deliberation, I've decided that now is the time for our two houses—our two kingdoms—to be joined in holy matrimony."

A ripple of excitement wove through the crowd.

"The royal wedding will take place in five days' time, at Notre-Dame Cathedral. Everyone who brings a gift is invited!"

A cheer rose up, filling the hall with joyful thunder. At the front of the crowd, Mary's ladies all clapped and giggled. Flem made kissy faces in their direction.

Francis felt his face turn red. He hated the feeling of everyone watching him, but he'd do his best to make a good impression, since it reflected on Mary as well. He straightened his shoulders and met her brown eyes. She looked beautiful, wearing that cream-colored gown she liked so much, and her hair done up in a twisting braid with her crown set atop the auburn tresses.

She was taller than he was, only by three inches (although Francis hoped he might still grow to meet her height one day, or maybe even taller, because come on), and she carried herself so regally. If he had to get married, he was glad it was Mary.

She smiled.

He smiled.

She gave his hands a reassuring squeeze.

It was all part of the show, of course, but even so, when he lifted her hand to his lips and kissed her fingers, he meant it.

* * *

An hour later, all the most important nobles had been seated in the banquet hall and served confit de canard, a glass of red wine, and personalized invitations to the wedding.

From their places at the king's table, Francis and Mary sat through approximately fifty thousand toasts in their honor, and even though Francis had done his best to keep his sips small, he could feel heat crawling up his neck and face, not to mention the fogginess creeping through his thoughts. It took longer and longer to figure out how to say thank you to the various well-wishers. By the time Guillemette de Sarrebruck raised her glass to offer her praise of the happy couple, Francis was barely touching the liquid to his lips. He'd had too much a thousand toasts ago.

Henry, of course, was done for. As the meal progressed and his goblet was continually refilled, the king spoke louder and louder.

"My son is getting married!" he'd shout occasionally, setting off another round of toasts and cheering. "Francis will be making heirs by the end of the week, just you wait! A virile young man like this will keep Mary pregnant for years."

People whooped and leered in Francis's direction. Or maybe Mary's. It was hard to tell when the room tilted this way and that.

Francis looked at Mary, whose smile had become somewhat wooden. It must be difficult, Francis had always thought, being a woman in King Henry's court.

He desperately wanted to make a joke of some kind—reassure her that as far as he understood, pregnancies didn't last multiple years and she'd give birth far, far sooner than that—but it seemed extra awkward given the conversation about how one *becomes* pregnant and that Francis still needed to find a way to stop his father from observing the wedding night.

"To the happy couple!" someone in the back shouted, and all the glasses went up, Francis's and Mary's included. Francis only pretended to drink.

"To France and Scotland!" someone else called. More glasses. More fake drinking.

"To the king!" Again with the toasting.

"This is the best night of my life!" Henry slurred as a servant hurried to refill his glass. "I'm so proud. I love wine."

Francis leaned toward Mary. "In my pants," he whispered.

The tension around Mary's jaw eased as she flashed him a real smile. "I didn't think you were serious about that."

"Of course I was."

"If I'd realized, I'd have improved so many toasts already." Her smile brightened her whole face. "We'll have to make up for it."

The king's voice boomed nearby. "Hello, my dear Catherine. You're particularly lovely tonight. And"—he paused—"I see that you've wrapped yourself up like a gift."

Francis glanced at Mary, wondering if he should say it. She frantically shook her head. Then they both looked over just in time to see one of the court ladies boldly approaching the king's table, where the queen and his official mistress both sat, finishing their meals.

Henry grabbed the woman's hand and gave it a long, lingering kiss. She tittered, while Diane stood and went to speak with someone else. Queen Catherine smiled—well—wickedly, but remained in conversation with Claude, Francis's younger sister.

"Looks like they're fighting again," Mary murmured, meaning Diane and Henry.

Brooch Catherine still had that gaudy jewel resting on her chest, although the bodice of her gown went all the way up to her collarbones. It was an interesting choice, given how she'd caught Henry's attention last night.

"Yes, yes," Henry was saying, his eyes on the brooch. "All wrapped up. I hope you intend to let me unwrap you later."

"Perhaps," teased Brooch Catherine, her hand lifting to her chest to draw Henry's eye. Francis's eyes went there too—just in time to see her scratch violently through the lace, then force her hand down to her side.

"My dear!" Henry said. "Already trying to unwrap. I knew you couldn't resist me."

Francis quickly looked away.

"Oh." Mary giggled a little. "It's Catherine."

"Yes. As we've already established."

"No, I mean"—Mary stifled another giggle—"your mother. The itching powder. Look at Brooch Catherine. She can't stop scratching, and her skin is red above her bodice."

"Oh." Francis looked, and then immediately looked away again, because King Henry was still talking about unwrapping. But yes, the would-be mistress bore the marks of frantic scratching. "My mother did that?"

"Oh, yes," Mary said. "I didn't expect it to happen so quickly.

I suppose your father won't be"—Mary made a gagging sound—"unwrapping her tonight after all."

"Mother does love spoiling his plans," Francis agreed.

"We should make the rounds," Mary suggested. "Before the banquet is over."

"Talk to people?" Francis asked, pretending that he was only pretending to be appalled. "Face to face?"

"Well, yes." Mary smiled wryly. "That is how it's done."

"Why should I talk to anyone else? You're the only one I need." Blasted wine! Francis ducked his head to hide his flush. "What I mean to say is— Everyone else— You are—" Maybe now was the time to consider becoming a monk—the kind that took a vow of silence.

Mary touched his chin. "Eyes up, Francis."

He couldn't. Not when he was more than a little tipsy and his mind kept drifting to Thursday. Thursday *night*.

"Francis," Mary said again, more forcefully. "Eyes up."

It was something she'd been telling him for years, ever since they were children and the betrothal had been announced. For days, they'd been practicing a dance together for the engagement party, both of them laughing and having fun. But at the party when they were supposed to perform the dance, Francis had frozen. He'd often been the center of attention, what with being the king's eldest son, but even at four years old, he'd understood that moment was different. What had been a fun game with his new best friend was suddenly much more serious, and as the music had started, he'd stood there while Mary began her part of the dance.

The music had stopped. Then started over.

Francis hadn't moved, instead staring at his feet and trying not to cry as the music swelled and stopped again, when suddenly a soft finger tapped his chin. "Eyes up," Mary had said, and it had worked. He'd lifted his eyes and met hers, and this time, when the music began again, they both danced the carefully rehearsed steps.

The end of the dance had called for a chaste kiss, and Francis, at four, hadn't really understood what that meant. He'd just stood up on his toes—because even then, Mary was taller—and they'd shared a brief peck on the lips. It had been their first kiss, and their only kiss, and sixteen-year-old Francis still sometimes thought about that moment with fondness.

So now, at those words—"Eyes up, Francis"—he did as he always did: he met her gaze and let her steady him. She was the strong one, he often felt, the steady one, the one who knew what to do and how to do it. She was the one who reminded him that if he solved problems one step at a time, he could endure anything.

He could endure anything if she were with him.

A full-on blush warmed his face now, but hopefully she'd think it was the wine. "You're right," he said. "It's time to make the rounds. Divide and conquer?"

Mary nodded. "I'll take the givers, you take the beggars?" That was the way they'd started classifying the people of the court: people who were always trying to give something to royalty in order to create debts owed to them, and those who were always asking for the crown's help.

"Let's do it," Francis said, but before he could extract himself from the table, his mother found him.

"Francis," she said.

"Hello, Mother."

Mary, who was already making her way into the crowd, glanced over and raised an eyebrow, but Francis motioned for her to keep going. He'd be all right with his mother.

"Walk with me," Queen Catherine commanded.

Francis walked with her. "How have you been?"

"Busy," Queen Catherine replied.

"Busy what?" Francis asked, although he wasn't sure he really wanted to know.

"Busy protecting the kingdom, as always."

"How's it going? Did you read that Knox pamphlet?"

"I did." Catherine's gaze was hard. "What a disgusting man. He really should be stopped."

"That's the point of Thursday, I'm told: to protect Mary and begin ridding Scotland of the Eðian menace." Francis felt dirty just saying it, but this was a Verity kingdom and all that. Mary had to say it from time to time, too; he knew that it hurt her deeply.

"Indeed," Catherine said. "You must be excited about the wedding. Finally, after all this waiting."

"Yes, of course." Francis offered his mother his arm. "So excited."

"You don't seem all that excited," Catherine said.

Francis went rigid. Could everyone tell?

"Don't worry," Catherine said. "No one can tell any more than usual."

"Oh," said Francis. "That's good, I suppose." He needed to get better at pretending. He needed to copy everything Mary did. Well, maybe not *everything*. "Mary and I are a good match," he went on. "I'm honored to become her husband."

"But?"

"But this all seems so, I don't know, fast. I'm only sixteen. Why should I worry about heirs yet?"

Catherine looked at him askance. "Henry will live to torment me a very long time, but there is always a need for heirs. You can't have too many. Except, of course, in the cases you do. You can't have multiple heirs competing for a single throne. That leads enterprising young rulers to taking out the competition." She patted his hand. "And that is why you need to make your own heirs. It secures your position above the competition."

"What if I'm not the right man for the job?"

"Of king?"

"Of potato peeling," he said. "No, of course of king." What else was there for him?

Catherine sighed. "You don't have a choice, son. You're next in line for the throne. You must fulfill your duty, and it's best that it happen in stages. First you'll marry Mary and work on the heir situation. You'll have plenty of time to prepare yourself for becoming a good king, just like your father."

"Just like him?" Francis frowned.

"Better, I hope." Catherine squeezed his hand. "You actually seem to like Mary."

Francis bit the insides of his cheeks to keep from saying anything about that. "We are a good match," he said again. "I just wish . . ."

"Yes?" she prompted.

"None of this is my choice. Becoming king. Who I marry. I don't even get to decide when and where my own wedding will take place."

"It's too late to change the date," Catherine said, missing the point.

Francis sighed. And it was too late to allow Mary to choose her own flowers. Cowslips, she'd said.

"But if there's something else I can help you with . . ."

Francis started to say no, but then an idea occurred to him. "I do have another concern."

"About Mary?"

Francis shook his head. "Forgive me if this sounds indelicate—"

"As though I've ever cared about such things."

"But when you and Father first married, the wedding night was, um, observed. By my grandfather." If it was awkward talking to his father about these things, it was ten times worse talking to his mother.

"Ah, yes." A frown pulled at Catherine's mouth. "Yes, that was part of the happiest day of my life. How could I forget?"

Catherine de Medici was the reason Francis himself was fluent in sarcasm.

"Then you probably know what I'm going to ask," Francis

said. "Father intends to watch my wedding night, but I'd rather not put Mary through that."

Francis could have asked for the favor for himself, but he thought his mother might empathize more with Mary. Woman to woman. Francis hoped.

"Of course," Catherine said. "There's no talking him out of anything, unfortunately, so I won't even try. But I'll think of something that will keep him out of your way. Not to worry."

Relief poured through Francis. "Thank you, Mother. Knowing you're on our side brings me a great deal of comfort."

Even now, Brooch Catherine was scratching while the king offered her a bite of strawberry cake.

Queen Catherine looked away from the scene and smiled. "Anything for you, my son." She patted his shoulder and then sent him on his way. "Go on, then. Show them the future king of France."

TEN

Dear Mama, Mary wrote carefully across the parchment. *I am pleased to inform you that King Henry has seen fit to honor my betrothal at last, and Francis and I are to be wed on Thursday.* She sat back and read over that first sentence, chewing the inside of her cheek. For some reason she was having difficulty forming the words for what should have been an easy letter to write. How would her mother respond, she wondered. Would she smile and clap her hands at the idea that her only daughter was finally getting married? Would her eyes light with joy?

Mary picked up the quill again.

All I can tell you is that I account myself one of the happiest women in the world. I have spoken to the dauphin, and he, too, is greatly pleased. It was a bit of a white lie to say that Francis was "greatly pleased." If anything, he was more anxious than usual concerning their wedding, and especially the wedding night, but it seemed appropriate to reassure her mother that she and Francis both still approved of the match. *We are fortunate, indeed, that we know one another so intimately already, and get along so well.*

There was a light tapping, tapping at her chamber door, and Bea slipped noiselessly inside, wearing only her dressing gown, her black hair unbound down her back. "Do you have a letter for me yet?" her lady asked.

Mary bent over the desk and scribbled hastily: *My only sorrow, dear Mama, is that it will be impossible for you to be here with me on this most auspicious of days. But I know that you will be with me in spirit, so I can truly rejoice.*

Your devoted daughter, she signed. *Mary, Queen of Scots.*

Bea had removed her shoes and was opening the curtains, and beyond that, the window. "Are you nearly ready?" she asked impatiently. "I'd like to go before it gets too late in the day."

Mary nodded. She skimmed quickly back over the letter, checking her grammar. Normally when she wrote to her mother it was in a cipher that only Mary de Guise had the key to translate, being that she was transmitting bits of the most secret espionage. But this letter was one that Mary would be expected to write. Even if the method of delivery would be considered unusual and also illegal.

Mary added in a postscript: *I apologize for the untidy penmanship, but I am writing hastily, so that you may receive this joyous news as soon as possible. M.* She rolled the letter into a tight tube, sealed it with red wax, and joined Bea at the window.

"It's midday, and I'm still in my dressing gown," Mary lamented, noticing the height of the sun.

"No one will judge you for it," Bea replied. "We had a late night. The other Marys are all still sleeping, especially Flem. She may have drunk more than was wise and suggested to the Duke of Brie that he consider proposing to her."

"I hope he didn't, seeing as he already has a wife," Mary said. She had partaken of too much wine herself during all the excessive toasting. Her head felt achy and the light too bright for her eyes.

Bea lifted her arms over her head, stretching. "I'll return in a day or two, depending upon the weather and how long your mother takes to pen a reply. Definitely before the wedding. Until then, be well, Your Majesty."

"Be careful, Bea," Mary warned. "The guards are on high alert for Eðians." Francis had told her of the seagull Eðian who'd been caught with the terrible pamphlet from John Knox. She wondered what had become of the woman. She was probably rotting in a cell somewhere.

"I'm always careful," answered Bea.

There was a flash of light and a rustle of feathers. The dressing gown dropped to the floor as a large, glossy-black raven fluttered to the wooden perch that had been installed on Mary's window casement for just this purpose.

Mary hurriedly bound her letter to the raven's leg. "Safe travels."

"Caw," quoth the raven, and was gone in a clapping of wings.

Mary rubbed at her temples. She should send for the rest of her ladies so they could help her dress and set about preparing for the wedding, now only four days away. There were—in spite of the king's attempt to organize everything—what seemed like a thousand tasks before her.

But Mary was still thinking about her mother. She felt a dart of jealousy that Bea would get to see Mary de Guise in person, when Mary herself hadn't seen her mother in seven years—the last time the elder Mary had come to French court for a visit. What was her mother doing now? Was she safe, or had this John Knox rebellion already arrived at her door? What could Mary do about it if it had?

The thought made all the fuss over wedding preparations seem frivolous.

She went to the door. "Please summon my ladies," she told the guards.

Within a few moments there was a tentative knock, and Ari shuffled into the room.

"You sent for me, Your Majesty?" she said.

Mary frowned. The moment that Queen Catherine had announced Ari as Mary's new lady-in-waiting, Mary had suspected that she'd chosen the girl to spy upon her. It was to be expected, she supposed. Queen Catherine was meddlesome and relentlessly cunning. So Mary had resolved to tread carefully around Ari. Still, Mary found that she quite liked this strange and quirky daughter of Nostradamus. There was just something so endearingly eager about the girl. But she definitely could not be trusted.

"I sent for all my ladies," Mary said.

Ari's mouth twisted. "I'm the only one who's not hungover."

"Then we shall have to make do with what we have. Help me dress."

But Ari hadn't the least idea how to corset or cinch, let alone what parts of Mary's gowns were supposed to go where. "I'm sorry," Ari stammered. "I can try to wake another one of the Marys, if you'd prefer. But earlier Flem tried to bite me, so I ran away."

"Don't bother," Mary said, pulling on her simplest dress. "We can manage together. Do you think you could arrange my hair?"

Ari nodded. Mary sat on her chair before the fire, and Ari, with painstakingly care, slowly combed through the queen's long auburn tresses.

"How are you finding your new position as a lady-in-waiting?" Mary asked.

"There's a lot to learn," replied Ari. "But I enjoy the company."

"My ladies are indeed good company," Mary agreed. "Liv especially."

In the mirror she watched as Ari's face pinkened. "Lady Livingston has been so helpful in explaining my duties. I am grateful for her . . . kindness."

"Yes. She seems quite taken with you," Mary said.

They were quiet for a minute as Ari struggled to style Mary's hair. (She invented the messy bun right on the spot.)

Then Mary stood. "Come, let's away."

"Away to where?" asked Ari.

"I need to speak with Queen Catherine."

"Queen Catherine?" squeaked Ari. "Speak? Now?"

Oh yes, thought Mary. Ari was definitely a spy for the queen. "No time like the present," she affirmed, and swept out the door.

Ari's face became paler and paler the closer they drew to the French queen's chambers. Mary actually felt bad for her.

"Is this regarding the wedding?" Ari asked.

"No," said Mary lightly. They had reached the queen's door. "Wait out here for me," she directed Ari. "I'll be back."

Ari startled. "I had a vision this morning of someone saying that very thing!"

"Someone?" Mary asked. "Who?"

"A large and frightening man," Ari said. "Wearing a black and shiny doublet, with darkness over his eyes. He said he was a friend of Sarah Connor's."

"Who's Sarah Connor?"

Ari shrugged.

Mary shook her head and told the guards she wished to speak to the queen of France. She was immediately granted entrance.

"Mary. What an unexpected surprise," said Catherine upon seeing her. "I was afraid you were unwell, as you missed the official engagement breakfast in your honor."

Droppings.

"I'm sure it was lovely," Mary said. "I've just been so busy with plans for the wedding. You understand."

"All you have to do is show up, dear," the queen said. "But you're excited for Thursday, I assume?"

Mary smiled and nodded. "I could not be more excited."

"Good," said the queen. "All I desire in this life is Francis's happiness. And yours, of course, my dear. You know I've always thought of you as one of my own daughters."

"And you have been a good mother to me," Mary said. "In the absence of my own."

This was true. In some ways, Queen Catherine and even Diane de Poitiers had been more maternal to Mary than Mary de Guise.

"So you're happy?" the queen asked.

"Yes." Mary twisted her amethyst ring. "Deliriously happy." Another white lie.

I should *be deliriously happy*, she chided herself silently. She had more than most people could ever dream of—jewels and gowns and all kinds of finery, and she was lucky, truly lucky, she knew, to be marrying Francis. It is the best possible outcome.

But she didn't feel the kind of euphoric happiness that she supposed a girl should feel when thinking about her wedding day.

Be happy, she told herself sternly. *Or at least content. Now.*

But her heart would not abide.

"Are you all right, dear?" asked Queen Catherine. "You seem troubled."

"I'm fine." Mary checked herself immediately. "I'm ecstatic to be marrying your son," she assured Catherine. "There is much on my mind, is all."

"I understand," said the queen, so kindly it made Mary rather suspicious. "It's a lot to carry on your shoulders, the weight of two countries. And a wedding is stressful for any bride. I was a mess of nerves before my own wedding."

"You were?" Mary had a hard time imagining Catherine being anything but exquisitely composed. "And what did you do?"

"I'm a Medici. I drank some wine and pulled myself together."

Mary nodded, twisting her ring.

"That's a lovely ring," Catherine observed.

"The stone is said to have magical properties," Mary said. "To calm the mind and ease any troubles."

"Does it now?" said Catherine wryly.

Mary felt that their entire conversation had gone a bit off course. "I've actually come to speak with you about something unrelated to the wedding."

"Oh? Do tell," said Catherine.

"Francis said there was an Eðian woman taken captive at dinner a few days ago."

Catherine scowled. "Indeed. A seagull. Pitiful wretched thing."

"Do you know what became of her?"

"Your uncles took custody of her," Catherine said with a sniff. "I imagine that they interrogated her." At that she sounded wistful, like she was missing out on some fun she would have liked to have. "And then put her to death, as befitting any Eðian, of course, but most especially any Eðian who has proven a threat to you."

Mary's chest was tight from a mixture of fear and sadness for the woman. "But was she? A threat to me, I mean?"

"She was bearing a pamphlet that called for your removal from the throne, illustrated with a charming drawing of you being beheaded," Catherine said.

Mary nodded. She knew all of this. "Do you know what became of the pamphlet?"

Catherine looked confused. "Why would that concern you?"

"I should like to study it," Mary said.

"Whatever for?"

"Because I wish to understand the argument that is being made against me. Then I might be some help to my mother in attempting to combat this vile propaganda against us both."

Catherine tilted her head, as if she was deciding whether Mary's desire was foolish or admirable. Then she crossed over to her desk and opened a drawer, from which she drew the offensive pamphlet. She held it out to Mary.

"I don't see what good this will be to you, though, my dear," she said as Mary took the folded parchment. "After all, you're far from Scotland."

Mary's jaw tightened. "Even so, I am Scotland's queen. I want to do my part in seeing to the welfare of my country."

"The best thing you can do for your country is to marry Francis and pop out a long succession of fine baby boys," Catherine said in a no-nonsense tone.

Heat rose in Mary's face. "I understand that duty, I assure you. But if I am to be Scotland's true queen, I should—"

"You shall never be Scotland's true queen," Catherine said sharply.

Mary drew in a startled breath. "What did you say?"

"You're unlikely, my dear, to ever set foot on Scottish soil again. Someone else will always rule in your name. First your mother, of course, and then Francis."

Mary felt as though she'd been splashed by cold water. But Francis wasn't like that. He was not some stranger who knew her only by reputation, who'd treat Mary as his property and everything she possessed as his, as well. Francis would be her partner. Her equal. He'd support her, and she him, as they always had. They would be there for one another, side by side until death parted them.

But Catherine had a point. Mary would stay in France. A woman's place, after all, was beside her husband. Francis would be her anchor. But an anchor was also, by its very definition, a heavy weight that kept you from going anywhere.

No. She would not be held down by anyone. Mary drew herself up to her full height, which was several inches taller than that of Queen Catherine. "I am afraid that you are mistaking my position for your own."

Catherine's sharp eyes narrowed. "How's that?"

"Francis is not my lord and master, nor will he ever be. He will not rule Scotland the way Henry rules France. I am a queen in more than just my name."

Unlike you. The words were unspoken between them.

Anger flashed in Queen Catherine's eyes. Mary had the good sense to be frightened. She decided to backpedal (although she wouldn't have understood the term *backpedal*, as bicycles hadn't been invented yet). She cleared her throat. "What I mean to say is . . ." *Merde*, what *did* she mean to say? "I don't believe any of this nonsense about a woman being incapable of ruling a country." She held up the pamphlet. "A woman is just as capable. Perhaps more capable. And it is you, Your Highness, who has truly taught me that. Your strength has taught me that I can be strong."

The corner of Catherine's mouth turned up in the ghost of a smile. "I am glad that you are to marry my son," she said at last. "He will benefit from your fire."

"I, too, am glad," Mary agreed. "And I hope that you and I can work together for the benefit of both our countries."

(This is a deft move that has been used by young women across the centuries. It's called the schmoozing of the mother-in-law.)

"Indeed," said Queen Catherine, and drew Mary to her and kissed her cheeks.

Mary made an excuse (again: so many things to do before the wedding, what was a bride to do?) and excused herself from the queen's presence.

"Can you send the Nostradamus girl to see me?" Queen Catherine requested as Mary was about to flee. "Whenever you get a chance."

"Of course. She is right outside the door, in fact," Mary said.

She went to fetch Ari. The poor girl's expression grew tense when Mary informed her that Queen Catherine wished to speak with her.

"Speak? Me? Now? Why would Queen Catherine want to speak with me? I have no idea. I don't often work for Queen Catherine. I hardly even see her."

She did protest too much, Mary thought.

"Maybe she wishes you to give her a vision," Mary said. "You should tell her the one about Sarah Connor and the man with the dark eyes. Perhaps she will know what to make of it."

At this, Ari went from white to a pale green. "Right," she said, and then screwed up her courage and knocked upon Queen Catherine's door.

Mary dashed (or rather strode quickly, as queens do not run) back to her room, still clutching the fateful pamphlet to her chest. She went immediately to her desk and read it over thoroughly, trying to ignore the way the hair on the back of her neck prickled when she looked at the drawing of her own beheading.

Scotland should no longer suffer under these deficient rulers, she read. *We Eðians must rise up and seize our natural place as the true leaders of our country. We will take on the hollow Verity queen. We will chase out the Verity regent. We will make a monarchy of our own, with strong Eðian men who will deliver strong Eðian sons.*

A sense of dread descended into her stomach. She pressed her hand there. Indeed she felt hollow.

But she was not truly a Verity.

And she was not a deficient ruler. And somehow she must prove it, if she was going to keep her country.

Starting, she supposed, with marrying Francis.

Mary crossed to the window and leaned out into the fresh air, and in that moment, she tried to simply breathe in and out and think of nothing else.

Breathe, she thought. *Just breathe.*

ELEVEN

Ari

"So, girl, tell me what you've learned of Queen Mary," Queen Catherine demanded.

Ari gulped and glanced around nervously, but there was no one to help her. It was just Ari and the queen of France. "Your Majesty, I am still working on ingratiating myself to Queen Mary, to gain her trust."

The queen frowned. "Well, what of Nostradamus's prophecy? Have you happened upon any news of a trap? A betrayal? Any new faces? Has anyone tried to sneak her nefarious biscuits?"

"No, Your Majesty. But I assure you I am ever vigilant, and I'm confident I will discover something soon."

"Very well. And have you, Aristotle, had any visions?"

Ari fidgeted. There was no way she was going to tell the

queen about the vision with the boy and the girl on the door. Or the one from this morning. Neither of those would impress Queen Catherine, Ari was sure. "I am still waiting for the right inspiration."

"Aristotle de Nostradame, I have not made you one of Mary's ladies-in-waiting to form some sleepover pillow-fighting, hair-braiding girl-clan. You remember our condition?"

The condition. The one where Ari found useful information for Queen Catherine or she would be exiled from the court to live a life of poverty and singledom.

"I remember," Ari said. "I will find something."

"Good. Now, there's one more thing. I need you to make two potions."

Ari perked up. Now *that* she could do. "What kind of potions, Your Majesty?"

"The first will be for Mary. The young queen is, as you might imagine, somewhat anxious about her upcoming nuptials. You will make something to ease her worries so that she may enjoy her wedding."

Ari nodded. She had just the thing in mind. The *Worries Be Gone* potion was quite effective, and she could make it with her eyes closed. "Of course, Your Majesty. I'll have it ready this afternoon. What else?"

"The other is regarding a more sensitive issue. I expect your utmost discretion."

"Always, Your Majesty."

"My husband"—the queen curled her lip—"King Henry, wishes to witness, personally, the consummation on Mary and Francis's wedding night."

A flush spread up Ari's whole body. How terrible for them!

"My son"—the queen smiled now—"Francis, has informed me he would rather this not happen. And as we both know, when given the opportunity to thwart my husband, I will take it."

"Did you have anything in particular in mind?" Ari asked.

"I leave that to you. Just come up with something that will make the king . . . not there."

"I will, Your Majesty," Ari said, having no idea how.

"Excellent." The queen put a finger to her chin thoughtfully. "If only there were a way to make him not *anywhere*."

"Your Majesty?"

"Nothing. Go on, now. The wedding takes place in four days' time. I expect results."

"Yes, Your Majesty." Ari curtsied and hurried down to her lab.

It was strange, she thought, hearing that Queen Mary was anxious about anything. Ari had always observed Queen Mary to be confident, secure. Fearless. One didn't have to be in her inner circle to see that.

Ari suddenly felt quite consequential, being needed by Mary like this. Before now, Ari had always been in her father's shadow—a second choice when the first choice wasn't available. An adequate alternative.

But Queen Catherine's requests for potions, watching over

Mary to ensure she remained safe from traps or betrayal (or, sigh, biscuits), and taking part in the upcoming wedding—it all made Ari feel different. She was first fiddle. She could contribute. She would make herself indispensable through her potions.

She could see her future as a trusted adviser to Queen Mary and King Francis. A critical appointment. A secure place to stay. (Of course, she couldn't actually see that future since, as we've discussed, her visions have been largely irrelevant up to this point. But still.)

When she rounded the corner into the palace's secret lab beneath the public lab, her heart sank. There, standing over a boiling pot, was Greer. She was green in the face. Literally, her face was a shade of green that Ari had never seen anywhere in nature before, let alone on skin.

"Greer!" Ari exclaimed. "What's happened here?"

Greer's bottom lip trembled as she stirred the pot. "Your father asked me to make a potion that would induce envy," she said. "This is my third attempt." Her eyes were drooping, and she was stirring as if the movement was purely mechanical. "I have not slept in two days."

"Greer, stop stirring the pot."

Reader, this was before "stirring the pot" was a cliché, so Ari meant it very literally.

Good grief. Ari had been gone for only forty-eight hours, and already the lab was falling apart.

Greer sniffed and obeyed. Ari grabbed two thick cloths and

used them to remove the pot from the fire, careful not to inhale the steam.

"An envy potion is way too advanced for you," Ari said.

Tears welled up in Greer's eyes.

"I don't mean that in a bad way," Ari said quickly. "It's just that an elixir like that requires a host of ingredients and precise measurements." And at least *some* spiritual gifts, Ari thought. "It's no wonder you wouldn't know how yet."

Greer let out a sigh of relief. "I envy your abilities."

Ari frowned. "Let me see your face." She put her fingers on Greer's chin and turned her head one way and then the other. "I can fix this. It will just have to wait a little bit. Why don't you rest while I take care of a few things?"

Greer nodded and sank onto a pile of burlap sacks full of oats. Ari was pretty sure the apprentice would be asleep in moments. Which she was.

Ari turned to her father, who was sitting obliviously at his desk, his feather quill quivering as he scribbled over a page. Next to him was a stack of more parchments, each one filled with nearly illegible writing. Only her father and Ari would be able to decipher it.

"Papa," Ari said.

He didn't seem to hear her.

Ari placed her hand over his, and slowly he stopped writing. He looked up at her.

"Galileo?"

Ari closed her eyes for a moment. "It's still me, Papa. Ari."

"Oh, right. Ari," said her father warmly. "Where have you been?"

"You remember, Papa. Queen Catherine asked me to watch over Queen Mary."

"Oh, yes. Well, Greer and I have been getting along fine without you."

Greer softly snored in the corner, the candlelight illuminating her green face.

"Papa, you must remember that Greer still has much to learn. And she hasn't shown any signs that she's gifted in the way we are. She's only meant to be an assistant."

"Oh, she's fine."

"She's green," Ari said.

"You're right. She's very new, but she is learning."

"No, I mean the envy potion literally turned her green."

Nostradamus glanced over at the poor girl. "Are you sure she didn't always look like that?"

"Yes, Papa. I'm sure. You must promise me to give her some respite."

Nostradamus sighed. "Very well." He smiled up at her. "You're a good girl."

Something in her throat squeezed. "Thank you, Papa."

"I am so proud of you," he said.

Her throat squeezed even more. "I—"

"It's very impressive, you discovering those moons." He

patted her hand. "And your idea that it is the sun and not the earth that is the center of the universe is quite brilliant. But a bit blasphemous. Be careful with that."

"I will, Papa," Ari said wearily. "Now don't you need to work on your quatrains?"

Her father loved to write all his predictions in rhyming verse. He had become well-known for his quatrains. Also, it was the best way to distract him.

"You're right." Nostradamus returned to his parchment and began scribbling again.

Ari went to the shelves and started gathering the ingredients for her *Worries Be Gone* remedy for Queen Mary. She wanted it to be perfect. It had to be calming, yet not calming enough that Queen Mary would become blasé about important political decisions. It had to be soothing, yet not so soothing that she would go right to sleep.

When the potion was mixed and simmering in her cauldron, Ari turned her attention to the second part of Queen Catherine's request.

How to make King Henry *not there* on Francis and Mary's wedding night.

Not there. *Not there.*

Ari had been pondering this ambiguous request for about an hour.

Her first instinct was to take "not there" literally. She

consulted the index of her "History of Beets" book for incantations related to *not being there, being gone,* and *unable to attend consummation.* (Even your narrators will concede that last one was a bit of a stretch.)

The book didn't offer anything obvious, so Ari looked through the samples she'd kept of some of the potions she'd made before. There was one called the Solution to Silence, to quiet overbearing personalities. She combined it with one called Toddler Tincture, which had been developed for the younger princes when foreign dignitaries visited.

"Greer, wake up." Ari shook her apprentice gently. "I need you to test something for me."

The poor girl was still groggy, but even an hour of sleep had done her much good. The dark green shadows under her eyes were less noticeable.

"Drink this." Ari handed her a small vial of the first iteration of the *Not There* potion.

Greer, still not quite awake, took the vial and sipped—and immediately disappeared.

Ari yelped. Greer yelped. Nostradamus didn't look up from his quatrains.

"Greer?" Ari asked hesitantly.

"What happened?" Greer's voice was high, panicked. "What's going on?"

Ari reached into the space Greer had just occupied, and she felt the girl's stomach. "You're invisible."

"You can't see me? I'm invisible?"

Suddenly, there was a loud thump, and Greer wasn't speaking anymore.

Darn. She must have fainted. Ari bent down and felt around for Greer's shoulders, then dragged the girl back to the oat sacks so she could get some rest and—more important—Ari wouldn't trip over her while she set about making the next iteration of the *Not There* potion.

She went back to the drawing board (which, at the time, was a literal graphite board for drawing) and made a list of different ideas that would cause the king to be "not there."

1. Invisibility. Too supernatural. Also, it would be creepy and he would still witness the consummation. She crossed it out.

2. A simple laxative. But then Henry would surely suspect Queen Catherine. The problem wasn't in the king's being there, necessarily, but the king *seeing* the consummation. So what if he couldn't see?

3. Something involving the king's eyes.

"That could work," Ari murmured to herself. "I'll go for the eyes."

After several trials and errors, Ari was ready to test out her latest iteration.

That is, she was ready for Greer to test it out.

Conveniently, Greer was now visible again. Ari gave her a sip from the vial, then watched as Greer's green face grew even greener—with nausea. Ari felt especially bad when Greer clapped a hand over her mouth and ran from the room. By the time she got back, Ari already had a new potion.

"One more, Greer," Ari said.

Greer shook her head and softly belched.

"I have a bowl for you right here, in case you need to, um, relieve your insides." Ari handed her a wooden bowl.

"All right," Greer said weakly. She sat. "But please, just a drop."

Ari took a glass dropper and squeezed a drop onto Greer's tongue.

Then she stood back and watched. "What do you feel?"

Greer wearily looked up at Ari, and then past Ari toward the wall. "Lady Livingston," she said.

Ari turned toward the wall. There was nothing.

Oh dear. Greer was hallucinating, either from too much testing or from the latest potion itself. Either way it was a failure. Or, as Ari liked to refer to failures: one step closer to success.

"Good day, Lady Livingston," Greer said, her words slurring.

Ari patted Greer's head. "Greer, Lady Livingston isn't here."

"Except I am." Liv's voice came from the doorway.

Ari whipped around.

"How long have you been standing there?" she asked, her voice more accusatory than she intended.

"About a second," Liv said.

"Oh." Ari smoothed her frizzy hair and rumpled dress.

"Maybe you could use some of that fabric wrinkle potion," Liv said, a twinkle in her eye.

"It's very humid down here," Ari explained, as if Liv couldn't tell. "Anyway, what can I do for you?"

"I thought you might like a dance lesson. Seeing as how the wedding is coming up, and you will be expected to dance with the rest of us at the celebration. . . ."

That sounded ominous. "I already know how to dance," Ari said. "Don't you remember?"

"Oh, I remember," said Liv.

"I can see through walls," announced Greer. She wandered around the room, open mouthed, staring at nothing. Then she wandered out of the laboratory.

Nostradamus looked up from his scribbling. "Did the green-faced girl just say she could see through walls? How interesting." He grabbed his cane and hobbled after Greer.

Which left Ari and Liv suddenly alone.

Ari found herself tongue-tied.

"Is it always like this down here?" Liv asked.

Ari shook her head. "It's just that I haven't been here to oversee things."

"Should I come back another time?"

"No, I have time," Ari said swiftly. She glanced at the *Worries Be Gone* potion still simmering over the fire. Potions became more potent with the application of heat. She had to make sure it never got to a full boil, and she should probably take it off soon.

But she had a few minutes.

She gave Liv her best curtsy. "Shall we dance?"

This is when she learned that the more formal dancing that would occur at the wedding celebration was very different from the hand-clapping, jumping, and circling she'd done with Liv at the tavern. Formal dancing involved a complicated series of steps and wasn't nearly as fun.

"I think I have two left feet," Ari said when she turned the wrong way yet again. (This was the first time, dear reader, that anyone had ever made that claim, and for a moment, Liv was alarmed, until she realized that Ari was speaking figuratively.)

"It takes practice," said Liv. She gazed around the laboratory, lingering on the sacks of oats where there was a Greer-shaped hollow. "So is this where you lived before coming to be with us?"

"No, we have quarters," Ari said, flushing hotly. "With beds."

"Everyone says that your father is a great man," Liv remarked as the two of them took a seat on the oats—the only place that two people could comfortably sit in the laboratory.

"He was," said Ari, then quickly corrected herself. "I mean, he *is*. He's a good father, although lately his health is not what it was. He suffers from gout, and arthritis, and . . ."

Something that was affecting his mind, but Ari didn't voice that concern.

"I'm sorry to hear that," Liv murmured. "My own father died a few years ago, and my mother has not been well, of late. It's difficult not being there for her."

"Where is she?" Ari asked.

"Back in Scotland," Liv answered.

"Do you have a large family?" It occurred to Ari that she knew almost nothing about Mary Livingston. She'd been gazing at her for a year, but they'd only had a handful of conversations.

"I have two brothers and five sisters," Liv said, the light dimming somewhat in her hazel eyes.

"You must miss them." Ari herself had five brothers and sisters, living with their mother in a house in Paris, but she could see them whenever she wished.

"I do miss them." Liv lowered her head, her golden hair tumbling into her face. "Especially my sisters. The situation in Scotland is worrisome, and it has been hard on them."

"How so?" Ari asked.

Liv tucked her hair behind her ear, glancing away. "My sister Janet has . . ." She fell silent.

"You don't have to tell me," Ari said. "It's not my business."

"But I'd like it to be your business." Liv smiled sadly. "She's fallen in love with the wrong person."

Ari's breath caught. The wrong person. Like Ari was assuredly the wrong person for Liv. "Society can be unforgiving," she said slowly.

"Yes," agreed Liv. "It can."

Ari wanted to take Liv's hand, or put an arm around her, to offer some form of comfort, and she was just working up the nerve to make her move when liquid hissed on the fire and she realized that the *Worries Be Gone* potion was boiling over. She jumped to her feet and quickly removed the cauldron from the flames.

The liquid inside was a dark pink color. Darker than it should be. "Oh no!"

Liv came to stand beside her. "What is it?"

"It's a potion for Queen Mary, to ease any wedding jitters."

"Oh, that's thoughtful of you," Liv said.

Ari didn't mention that it had been Queen Catherine's idea.

"Is it ruined?" asked Liv.

"No, it's fine," Ari decided. "It will just be stronger than I usually make it. Will you do me a favor and take it to Queen Mary?"

"You don't want to give it to her yourself?"

"I still have some work to do here," Ari said. "I have to . . . fix my assistant."

"All right," said Liv, her sunny disposition returning as quickly as it'd gone. "I'll take it to her."

Ari filled a vial with the pink liquid, sealed it, labeled it, and handed it to Liv. "Tell Queen Mary to take it twice a day, morning and night, although she may start this afternoon and then this evening. And with a potion this strong, she only needs a drop. Two at most."

Their hands brushed as she gave the bottle to Liv.

Liv studied it. "*Worries Be Gone.*"

"I like to call them names that make it easy to remember their purpose."

Liv arched an eyebrow at her. "If this works, Aristotle de Nostradame, you just might become Mary's favorite."

Ari blushed. "I'm not sure it's Mary's favorite I want to be."

Wow. She'd actually possessed the courage to say that out loud. And even more miraculously, Liv laughed.

"You're already my favorite," she said, and then she leaned in to *kiss Ari on the mouth.*

Ari had never been kissed before, but now she was kissing a girl, and she liked it. Her heart was pounding. Her stomach was full of butterflies. She didn't know where to put her hands, so she put them on Liv's shoulders. And then her cheeks. And then her shoulders. *Is holding a chin a thing?* But it didn't seem to matter. The kiss was like a question, soft and fleeting, and just as Ari was about to give her answer (also in the form of a kiss, possibly with more awkward hand placement) the door burst open and Greer and Nostradamus entered.

Greer's face was red *and* green. Ari wondered if she could still see through walls. "Your father has had another vision!" Greer said.

Ari's father hurried to his desk to write it down. "The young lion will overcome the older one on the field of combat in single battle. He will pierce his eyes through a golden cage, two wounds made one. Then he dies a cruel death," he said out loud as he scribbled down the words.

This one sounded serious. Thank goodness they didn't know any lions. Perhaps it was an Eðian thing.

"I should go," said Liv.

"But . . ." Ari couldn't think of an excuse to keep her in the laboratory.

Liv tucked the vial of *Worries Be Gone* into the folds of her dress.

"Just a drop," Ari said again.

"Just a drop," Liv repeated. "I'll see you soon."

Ari wanted to touch her, but she held back. "Save your next dance for me."

TWELVE
Francis

"Lady Beaufort!" Francis smiled his hardest. "It's so good to see you. Thank you for coming."

The pale, grandly dressed lady he was addressing abruptly stopped and looked at Francis. "Dauphin?"

"Yes, my lady." Inwardly, Francis sighed. Wedding guests had been arriving at the palace all afternoon. Mary was nowhere to be seen, while Queen Catherine and King Henry were likely on opposite ends of the palace, scheming up ways to destroy each other, so it had fallen to Francis to welcome everyone. By himself.

And no one seemed to know who he was. He supposed people expected him to look more like his father. Taller. Broader of shoulder. Rakishly handsome. Francis wished even more desperately for a growth spurt.

"I thought you'd be taller by now," said Lady Beaufort, and then she covered her mouth in a way that was supposed to make it seem like that comment had been a mere slip of the tongue, not a direct insult.

The next nobles to arrive were Lord and Lady Livarot, who were both somewhat round with tough exteriors, but Francis had found that inside, they were really softies. He greeted them warmly.

"Welcome to Louvre Palace," he said. "I trust your journey was uneventful?"

"Very, aside from the incident with the bulrush." Lord Livarot glanced at his wife. "Someone fell into a stream and got tangled in it."

"How dreadful," Francis replied. "Have you recovered, my lady?"

"Yes, yes." She waved away his concern. "The servants had to peel the plants off me, though. I thought I'd fall over from dizziness."

Next came Lord Roquefort, a pale man with skin so thin you could see the blue of his veins. He'd always been popular at court, in spite of his odor and odd appearance. Francis shook his hand, then subtly wiped his palm on his doublet.

As more and more guests arrived, Francis began to feel as though he'd been here for hours. Watches hadn't been invented yet, but if they had, he'd have been checking his every few minutes. As it was, he had to rely on the position of the sun.

The sun had barely moved.

"Good morning, son." King Henry came to stand beside him.

"It's a bit early for all these people to come to our palace, isn't it? What day is it? Monday, Tuesday, Thursday, Wednesday—there are no weekends when you're king."

Francis leaned away from the king, who still reeked of wine. "It's afternoon, Father. And these people are coming for my wedding." The hours were racing by, bringing him closer to the walk down the aisle . . . and the evening after.

The thought made his heart pound.

But his mother had promised to keep his father away from the consummation. How she would do that . . . he didn't know. He didn't *want* to know.

"Ah." Henry squinted up at the sun. "So it is afternoon. Well, some nights are later than others, I suppose. Being king means you're king at all hours."

That did not make Francis like the idea any more.

"Come along, son. I have a meeting with Mary's uncles. Now that you're getting married, you need to take part in these matters. They concern your wife, after all, and you'll be king after I'm gone."

Thank goodness that was a *long* time off.

Francis followed his father to a small (by palace standards) parlor where the uncles were already waiting. A decanter of wine sat on a low table, surrounded by trays of lemon tarts and other snacks.

"Your Majesty. Your Highness." Duke Francis stood and opened his arms wide, as though to embrace the king and his son, even though they were on opposite sides of the room.

Cardinal Charles rose a moment later and bowed low. "I've heard our guests are beginning to arrive."

"They are." Henry patted Francis's shoulder. "My son has been greeting everyone himself. He'll make a fine king one day. Pour a glass for me, will you?" Henry took a seat on one of the silk-upholstered sofas. "It's been *hours*."

When the uncles offered Francis a glass, too, he shook his head. "No, thank you. It's only been hours." He did accept one of the lemon tarts, though. Francis was no fool.

While his father and Mary's uncles made small talk, Francis focused on the sweet, flaky carbs, wondering if he should bring a tart for Mary, or if some had already been delivered to her room. They weren't biscuits, but Mary had a weakness for treats in general, and if he showed up at her door bearing a gift . . .

He was so thoroughly engrossed in imagining her smile (and then in imagining her biting into the pastry with a happy shiver) that he almost missed the conversation swing around to the purpose of this meeting.

"I've finished drawing up the papers for Mary and Francis to sign." The duke laid a folder onto the table. "Charles and I will meet with them before dinner."

What papers were those?

"Good, good. Let me see them." Henry took the folder and scanned the pages as though looking for something. "It all seems to be in order."

"May I see?" Francis set his plate aside.

The king passed him the pages. "I'm glad you're taking an interest in this, son. The future of France is in these pages."

Francis nodded and focused on reading the flowery script while his father and Mary's uncles continued their discussion.

"This wedding is the best thing that's ever happened to France," the cardinal said. "Soon, Your Grace, you will be king of an empire. France, Ireland, and Scotland will bow to you. Perhaps even England, if we can do something about Elizabeth Tudor."

Henry was nodding emphatically. "I've always thought I could be king of an empire. How the world would tremble before me."

In spite of Francis's lack of interest, his tutors had usually complimented him when it came to his understanding of treaties and other political documents. The language of these three pages was dense, but if Francis was reading it correctly, the gist was this: Francis and Mary's wedding would essentially make Scotland a French province.

Francis looked up. "Has everyone approved this?"

His question had interrupted the duke laying more praise upon the king.

Henry frowned, because he loved praise. "What is that, son?"

The weight of their glowers settled over Francis, and his voice came out small. "These documents put Scotland under the rule of France. What does Mary think of this? What of Mary de Guise?"

The cardinal snatched the papers away from Francis. "Of course everyone has approved the language. Our houses are united."

The de Guises were French, so on the one hand, it made sense for them to seek more power for the French monarchy. On the other hand, this didn't seem like it was good for Scotland.

Francis wasn't quite sure how to feel. He was French, and heir to the throne, so he should be pleased for his kingdom. But Mary . . .

"Francis," said Henry, "I'm sure you have other duties to attend to now."

In other words: *Get out and let me talk to my friends.*

Francis didn't waste time. He retreated into the hall. He stood in the intersection, thinking about where to go. He should find Mary. He should tell her about the documents her uncles wanted her to sign. But if her family was in agreement, and it was best for France, was it really any of his business?

Doubts in tow, Francis soon found himself at Mary's door. That was when he realized he'd forgotten to bring one of the tarts for her. "Droppings," he muttered. He was just about to knock when she emerged, her face paler than usual, and a heavy air about her. "Are you all right?" he asked.

"Of course." She twisted her ring and started walking down the hall. Francis followed. "I was actually just coming to find you. I'm sorry I missed breakfast this morning. Last night was just—"

"It was a lot," he agreed. "And you were far from the only one who didn't come. Father emerged from his rooms just twenty minutes ago."

"Did I miss anything good?"

"The strawberry crepes were delicious."

"I wish I could travel back in time and eat them! Unless you saved some for me?"

"Sorry," Francis said as they turned a corner, feeling even more guilty about the tart. "I ate yours too."

"You didn't!"

He flashed her a smile. "We are soon to be married. What's yours is mine, and what's mine is yours. Including breakfast."

"I'll remember that the next time— Eeek! What is that?" Mary stopped walking and pointed at the floor in horror.

Frantically, Francis followed her gaze and saw it: a mousetrap. "*Mon Dieu!*" he cried. "Who would put that there?"

"Get it!" Mary commanded as she climbed onto a bench along the wall. "Get it, Francis!"

Francis got it. He extinguished one of the tapered candles in a sconce, then gently touched the end to the fine cheese someone had baited the trap with. The bar snapped, making Francis jump back and Mary *eeek!* again.

"Stay there, Mary. I've got it." Francis took the corner of the mousetrap between his thumb and forefinger and carried it at arm's length. "Avert your eyes!"

"Just get rid of it!"

Francis carried the mousetrap to the nearest window and dropped it outside. Someone below shouted, and Francis ducked back inside before they could see him.

"It's gone, Mary."

"Gone gone?"

"It won't bother you again." Gallantly, he held up a hand to help her off the bench. "I have slain the mousetrap—"

"Don't even say its name!"

"And I will search the halls for any of its brethren that may have escaped."

"My hero." Mary stepped down from the bench and kissed his cheek.

Warmth spread through him. What he wouldn't give to *actually* be her hero. "I would also like to inform you that we will not be selling tickets to our wedding night."

She stared at him blankly.

"I've taken care of Thursday night," he explained.

"You have?" She tilted her head. "What did you do?"

"I asked my mother for help," he admitted. "You know how she is. She wouldn't miss the opportunity to thwart my father."

"That's very true," Mary agreed. "So she's going to take care of it?"

"We'll be alone," he confirmed, and his heart jumped into his throat at that thought. Just him and her. Alone. On their wedding night. Whatever would they do with this freedom? He could think of a few things.

"Well that's a relief." Mary started walking down the hall again. Francis wondered if they were going anywhere special, or if they were just walking. "Since we won't be observed, and it's not as though we need an heir right away—because Henry will live a long,

long time—we can just *tell* everyone we've completed our, ah, task. We could play cards instead."

"Right," Francis said faintly. "That sounds like my kind of night."

"Perfect. We'll have the best time. Just you and me."

Alone. Playing cards.

Francis stuffed down his disappointment. "There's something else I wanted to talk to you about."

"What is that?"

"There's someone I think you should spy on."

Her eyes brightened. "Oh?"

"Really spy," he clarified. "Not just for gossip."

She pursed her lips. "Go on."

He had to say this delicately. "I have reason to distrust some of our wedding guests."

"Who?"

Francis didn't want to tell her that it was her uncles, but there was pretty much no way around it. "Your uncles," he said.

"My uncles? We have nothing to worry about from them."

Francis told her about the documents they'd shown Henry. "It just seemed like a very good deal for France, and a terrible deal for Scotland."

Mary scoffed. "My uncles would never do anything that wasn't good for me. They look out for me. I'm certain the documents simply outline how France will protect Scotland."

"As a province?"

"As an allied sovereign kingdom." She slipped her arm in with his. "My uncles want what's best for me. For us. There's no need for me to spy on them, because I already know who they are and what they're about."

"They want to help France," he said. Why wasn't she listening to him?

"Exactly. What's good for France is good for Scotland." She said it like she didn't believe he'd have bothered to read the papers describing the future of both of their kingdoms.

True, he hadn't had very much time to study the documents, but . . . "I don't trust them. I think we should both read the documents carefully before you sign anything."

"You've been listening to your mother too much. She doesn't trust my uncles, either. But powerful families *can* help one another, even in the French court."

Francis pressed his mouth into a line.

"I trust them, Francis. And you trust me, right?"

"With my life." But why didn't she trust *him*? Why wouldn't she listen?

"Then trust my uncles, too. They love me and wouldn't do anything to harm me."

She sounded so certain, so unshakable. He hoped she was right.

THIRTEEN

Of course I'm right, Mary thought to herself all afternoon. Francis meant well—she knew that—but he didn't know the de Guises the way Mary knew them. All her life her uncles had been protecting her, seeing to her interests, because they could be there in her mother's stead. *My uncles can be trusted*, she assured herself. They were family. When Francis officially became part of her family, perhaps he would see it, too.

Even so, when Mary received a summons to her uncles' chambers later in the day, she felt a twinge of unease.

"Tell them I'll be there directly," she informed the messenger, who hurried off.

"Your uncles wish to see you?" asked Flem from where she was enthusiastically knitting and then unknitting and then reknitting the sock she was working on. "What for?"

Mary set aside her own project—a silk handkerchief with the words *Vous et nul autre* embroidered in the corner. It meant "You and no other." Mary was hoping to finish it before the wedding and present it to Francis. "My uncles apparently have some sort of document they'd like Francis and me to sign—an agreement to take place before our nuptials."

"I've never heard of such a thing," said Hush from the corner. "What sort of prenuptial agreement?"

"Something to solidify France's promises to Scotland," Mary said vaguely. Because she didn't actually know.

"That sounds like a good idea!" said Flem. Then she stared intently at her knitting for a moment. "I must have dropped a stitch somewhere," she grumbled. "Darn."

She passed the sock over to Hush, who would fix it.

Mary wished Bea was with her. Bea was the best at understanding the wording of laws and edicts. But Bea was halfway to Scotland by now.

The door opened, and Liv slipped in. She, like Flem, seemed to be in a merry mood. "Good day, my queen," she said with a quick curtsy.

"Where have you been?" Mary asked, but not in a cross way. They had all been running off the usual schedule since dinner last night.

"Giving our new lady-in-waiting some courtly dance lessons," Liv said.

"Ooh," said all the ladies at once.

"What happened with that?" Mary asked.

Liv's face went pink. "I don't kiss and tell."

"So you did kiss her," Hush whispered, smiling as she bent over Flem's sock and then handed it back to Flem.

Flem's head cocked to one side as she started to knit again. "What kind of girl's name is Aristotle?" she asked. "And why does she smell funny?"

"She's making potions all day," Liv said. "So she's around all kinds of strange ingredients." She remembered something and dug into the satchel she always carried with her. "Which reminds me. She sent this for you."

She produced a small vial and held it out to Mary, who took it and examined the label. *Worries Be Gone*, it read in neat handwriting.

"What is it?" asked Flem. "It is a bauble? I love baubles."

"It's to ease pre-wedding jitters," Liv said smoothly. "And calm the nerves on the wedding night."

Mary felt her own face redden.

"Oh," said Flem. "The wedding night." Then she suddenly scowled at her sock. "Hush! I did it again!"

"Give it here," said Hush patiently. "Well, that was awfully sweet of Ari," she said as she deftly fixed the mistake in Flem's knitting for the bazillionth time.

Mary agreed. It *was* sweet of Ari, and it sounded like something Mary could use, if she was being honest. But then she also remembered that Ari was a spy and had been summoned to speak to Queen Catherine alone after Mary had left her.

Mary handed the vial to Flem. "Sniff this."

Flem opened the vial and sniffed the contents deeply.

"I smell herbs," Flem said, and then sighed. "It's nice, actually, makes my nose feel all tingly. There's no poison."

"Of course there wouldn't be," Liv said. "Ari is a good person." She turned her attention back to Mary. "Ari said to take one drink, no more than two, morning and night, but it would be all right to take some right away today, if you feel that you need it."

"Thank you," Mary said as Flem handed the vial back to her. Then—because she'd just remembered that she needed to go to her uncles forthwith, and that made the sense of unease flare up again, she took a long, single swig from the bottle. One drink.

The liquid left a warm sensation in her throat and then settled in her stomach. For a moment she got light-headed, but then, when the dizziness passed, she realized that the tension was gone from her shoulders. She felt like she'd been dozing in the sunshine. A bit sleepy, perhaps. But . . .

"So?" Flem said eagerly.

She glanced up to find the Marys watching her intently.

She smiled. "I feel good." Better, she added silently. The dark cloud that had been hanging over her since reading that awful pamphlet was beginning to break up, the sun peeking through.

"Good," said Liv. "I told you. Ari knows what she's about."

"So you're feeling all right about the wedding, then?" Hush asked. "Still excited?"

"Yes." It was what she'd always wanted, after all. "I'm the happiest woman in the world."

"And what about the wedding night?" Flem blurted. "How do you feel about what's going to happen then?"

"Flem!" Hush poked at her with a knitting needle. "That is not an appropriate question to ask the queen."

Mary shook her head. "I'm not worried about that." She and Francis weren't going to be consummating anything Thursday night. They'd agreed on it. They were going to play cards, and they'd worry about heirs later.

Mary did love babies—she loved to hold them and kiss them (as that was part of her job description, as a politician), and she loved how their heads smelled—but she also liked handing them back to their mothers when they began to cry. When she pictured herself and Francis together, married, she always pictured them walking in the gardens, perhaps, or lying on the white bearskin rug in front of a fireplace in Francis's bedroom and talking. (What did you think they would be doing? Get your mind out of the gutter, reader. Mary and Francis used to spend hours when they were children sitting together on the white bearskin rug. Completely innocently. Talking. Making each other laugh.)

Anyway, Mary didn't imagine them with a baby.

Not yet, anyway.

She took another sip of the potion. Liv had said one drink, no more than two. So this was two.

"I'd be worried," Flem said. "I know the men do most of the work, and you're supposed to simply lie there and think of England until it's over, but still . . ."

"This from the girl who can't wait to be married," Liv pointed out.

Flem sighed. "I know. But who knows? Maybe it would be fun."

"Flem!" Hush chastised in an uncharacteristically loud voice, which would have been a normal volume for anyone else. "Please do stop talking."

Unbidden, the oddly specific image of Francis on the bearskin rug sprang to Mary's mind, lying back, his head pillowed by the crook of his elbow, gazing up at her with warm blue eyes, a strand of his golden hair curling charmingly over his forehead. He was wearing a simple white nightshirt, open at the throat. His lips curved into that fleeting smile she knew so well.

She blinked a few times, coughed, then examined the vial that she was still clutching in her hand. That was a *good* potion. She tucked the vial into the pocket of her dress and rose to her feet. "I'm off to my uncles," she announced.

The Marys all jumped up as well, except Liv, who had already been standing.

"Shall we come with you?" Hush asked.

"No, I'll be fine seeing myself there," Mary said. "Sit," she said to Flem. "Stay."

She was almost to her uncles' chambers when she came upon Francis, who was clearly headed the same place from another direction. He smiled when he saw her, as usual, but his eyes were guarded. Still worried. She was tempted to offer him a bit of her *Worries Be*

Gone potion. But instead she took his arm wordlessly, and they stood together as the guard announced them.

"Mary, my girl!" Uncle Charles boomed the instant he saw her. He grabbed her hands and drew her to him so that he could kiss both of her cheeks, his beard tickling her face. "You are a glowing bride, already."

"Thank you, Uncle," she said, blushing, but she wasn't sure if this was because of the potion or the compliment. "I am glad to see you." She shifted to kiss Uncle Francis (but not her Francis) and then took Francis (her Francis) by the arm as he stepped in between them.

"You're a lucky man, my boy," Uncle Charles said to Francis, clapping him on the shoulder.

"I know," Francis replied.

Aw, thought Mary. *Wasn't that a nice thing for him to say?*

The duke gestured to chairs near the fire, and the four of them sat. For several long minutes they made small talk, which for her uncles always meant gossiping about the queen of England.

"We've heard that she's appointed an equal number of Eðians as Verities to her Privy Council. And she's called for a new Parliament to reflect an equal split, as well," said Uncle Francis.

Uncle Charles snorted. "It's heresy. She should be burned at the stake."

"She's probably an Eðian herself," Uncle Francis mused, as Mary had heard him do many times. "Her mother—that heretic Anne Boleyn—certainly was. They say she could transform herself into a cat."

"Could she?" Mary shivered. She'd never been fond of cats. For obvious reasons.

"It's bad enough that there's a woman on the throne of England—no offense, my dear," said Uncle Charles, "but for the usurper to be an Eðian as well, it's simply unbearable."

"Intolerable," agreed Uncle Francis.

"Outrageous," said Francis (Mary's Francis, this time) with a faint smile. He met Mary's gaze. "A woman *and* an Eðian. The most horrifying combination of all."

"Indeed." She glanced away before she could smile. He was so funny. So clever.

"However . . ." Francis paused for effect. "We had a hand in putting this 'usurper' onto the English throne, did we not?"

Uncle Charles's face reddened. "It was the king who made that blunder—no offense, Your Highness," he said to Francis.

"None taken," Fiancé Francis replied coolly.

"Not that I truly blame him. It was Edward Tudor who came to ask for Henry's aid in deposing his sister Mary. You have to admire the sheer cheek of the boy, to petition the king of France to be an ally to England. And how was Henry to know that once they'd prevailed at the battle, King Edward would give up his throne? Who could have seen that coming?" Uncle Charles scowled. "Only a coward would forsake his God-given appointment to the monarchy and abandon his throne in such a way."

Beside her, Mary heard Francis suppress a sigh. She knew what he meant. All this talk of Eðians and England was tiresome.

And the subject never failed to get her uncles worked into an ireful state.

She manufactured a smile. "I believe that Elizabeth has proven herself to be a shrewd political mind. It seems like she has a plan for everything. It's been four years since Edward abdicated, and her position on the English throne is stronger than ever. Or at least that's what I hear."

At Mary's instruction, Bea had been collecting information concerning Elizabeth during her travels. Mary found herself wildly curious concerning this other queen across the channel. She was impressed, in spite of herself, sometimes, by all that Elizabeth had been able to accomplish.

Sigh. Elizabeth wasn't a mere figurehead. She had real power.

"Bah," said Uncle Charles, waving his jeweled hand dismissively. "It's you who should be sitting on the throne of England, Mary. You have a much stronger claim than some Eðian bastard. You're the rightful ruler."

"Perhaps," Mary said lightly. "But I am also a woman, am I not?" *And an Eðian*, she added silently.

The corner of Francis's lip twitched in what she knew was a smile.

"Yes, of course, my dear." Uncle Francis patted her hand affectionately. "But you are the perfect woman, with impeccable breeding, and a natural queen. Mark me, but someday"—he smiled, as if the thought gave him great joy—"someday soon, I hope, you will find yourself Queen of All of It: Scotland, England, France, and Ireland. And after that, who knows? You could be the beginning of a great dynasty that will encompass all of Europe."

Something like irritation flashed in Francis's eyes. Mary agreed. It did seem a bit far-fetched, if you asked her—QUEEN OF ALL OF IT—but she had to admit that she didn't hate the idea.

The uncles exchanged a meaningful glance and then stood. "Which brings us to why we sent for you," Uncle Francis said. "I summoned you both here to go over some quick paperwork regarding your wedding. It's a rare thing, you know, a sovereign of one country marrying the future sovereign of another, and we want to make sure there is no confusion about the way things will be after you're wed."

The sense of unease promptly returned to Mary's stomach. "Yes, that makes good sense, Uncle," she said softly. "We should all be on the same page about the way things will be."

He ushered her to sit at a long table, and then Francis (her Francis) to sit beside her. Uncle Francis spread several pieces of parchment on the shining wood in front of her and then pointed to the bottom of the last page.

"Sign right here, my dear," he said.

She could feel Francis tense beside her. She blinked up at her uncle. "I should like to read it first."

"Of course."

She peered at the document. Droppings, the words were written so small. She rather felt that she should ask for a magnifying glass. "Goodness!" she exclaimed. "This is very fine print."

"It's a standard prenuptial agreement among monarchs," said Uncle Francis. (Even though he'd previously told her it was rare. Which is it, Uncle Francis?)

Uncle Charles started to sharpen the quill and ready the bottle of ink. Mary reached into her pocket and slid out the vial of *Worries Be Gone*. She uncorked it and took a deep drink, then returned it to her pocket. Three drinks would probably be all right. Was it three? Maybe it was only two. . . .

Francis touched the back of her hand. "What was that?" he whispered.

"Nothing to worry about," she whispered back. (See what she did there?)

She felt dizzy again, then warm. Almost on its own volition her body leaned toward Francis (sigh, her Francis) until her face nearly brushed his. "Your eyes are so wonderfully blue," she said softly. "It's my favorite color."

He drew in a sharp breath. "Mary . . ."

"So are you ready to sign?" boomed Uncle Francis.

Fiancé Francis's eyes dropped to the page on the table again. He coughed and pointed at a particular passage. "Here," he murmured. "Read this part. It says—"

"It says Scotland will be under France's protection, forever," filled in Uncle Charles.

Francis's protection. Forever. That sounded nice.

"No." Francis's jaw tightened. "It says that this treaty will be forever binding, no matter what agreement you make with the

Scottish parliament or any other leaders of Scotland, either before or after the wedding. This treaty will nullify and supersede any other treaty you could make."

Nullify and *supersede* were very complex words. Mary was sure she knew their meaning, but she found that at the moment she didn't remotely care. Francis was obviously worried—his brow was rumpled adorably—but Mary couldn't bring herself to worry, too. He really could use some of the *Worries Be Gone*.

"That section is only a formality," Uncle Francis clarified. "Of course Scotland would never have any reason to suggest a treaty that would conflict with this one. The Scottish parliament desires France's protection, too."

Her Francis pointed to another place on the parchment. "What about here, where it says that if Mary doesn't produce an heir, Scotland must pay France a million—"

"But of course I'll produce an heir!" Mary sat up. "I'll produce many heirs. Fine heirs. You'll see." She fanned herself. She was so hot. "Won't we, Francis?" She gazed imploringly at Francis. *Mon Dieu*. Francis was so hot, too. Her insides gave a strange quiver. "You want to, right?" she asked. "Make heirs? With me?"

Francis's wonderfully blue eyes were now very wide. "Yes," he rasped.

Mary was becoming vaguely aware that she was not behaving properly. Perhaps she'd taken too much of the *Worries Be Gone*. (Reader, she'd definitely taken too much. Ari had said *one drop*. Two at most.)

155

She cleared her throat daintily. "So we don't need to worry about the part about heirs." She grasped the quill Uncle Charles handed her, eager to complete this assignment and flee to her chambers before she embarrassed herself further. "Where do I sign?"

Uncle Francis pointed to three separate places on the parchment, and Mary quickly but carefully inscribed her official signature (*Mary the Queen*), mindful of her penmanship.

"Excellent," said Uncle Charles. "The dauphin should also sign. At the bottom. Here." He pointed.

Francis (her Francis) looked torn. Confused. And still wildly attractive.

"Mary, are you sure?" he murmured.

"France will protect Scotland," she said matter-of-factly. "You'll protect me, won't you, Francis?"

"I'm trying to." He closed his eyes for a moment. "Yes," he said at last. "France will always protect Scotland."

Then he took the quill from her and signed his name.

It was hours later, after the potion had nearly worn off, that Mary realized what she'd done.

She'd signed something without even reading it.

(Yes, dear reader. Your narrators are here to tell you that by signing that prenuptial agreement, Mary, Queen of Scots, had made a grave error. She hadn't actually read the terms. It was the sixteenth-century equivalent of hastily checking the agree box so you can just use the app right away. But we shouldn't be too hard on Mary. The *Worries Be Gone* potion Ari had mixed for her was awfully strong. And Mary had taken much more than the recommended dose. It was just a mistake—a huge, and we mean *colossal,* mistake. Now back to Mary.)

Alone again in her room, the last warm fuzzy of the potion ebbed from Mary's system. She pressed a hand to her head. "I may have just made a huge mistake," she said.

But what could she do about it now?

She bit her lip. Maybe it wasn't too late. Perhaps she could return to her uncles' chambers and read over the treaty again. She'd read the fine print this time. And pay extra-special attention to the parts Francis had pointed at.

She closed her eyes and groaned, remembering how she'd been fawning over Francis and thinking about heirs, and the producing of, instead of actually listening to what he was trying to say.

She was a fool.

Her shoulders straightened. She must go back and read the treaty straightaway. And if Francis was right to be suspicious of its contents (and she had the niggling feeling that he was right), she'd destroy it.

She didn't wait a moment longer. The light flashed, and she scrambled free of the heavy folds of her gown before they could even fall to the floor. Then she scurried straight into the hole in the back wall.

Two lefts and a right and a thousand tiny mouse steps, and Mary emerged into her uncles' receiving room on a bit of molding near the ceiling—a space just wide enough for Mary-the-mouse to fit upon and gaze down at the room below.

What good luck! she thought. The room was empty.

Droppings! she thought two seconds later. The table was empty, too.

No treaty. She didn't see it anywhere.

She'd have to go down and become human and search for it. She couldn't exactly rifle through a bunch of papers as a mouse.

She hesitated. She had one unbreakable rule when it came to being the mouse: she never, *ever*, changed back and forth into her Eðian form anywhere but inside her own room, with the curtains tightly drawn and the door locked.

That was how she had stayed undiscovered for so long.

That was how she'd stayed alive.

Turds, she thought.

This was clearly an emergency, and it called for emergency rules. Mary sensed—deep down—that it was vitally important for her to find that treaty.

Fine. Emergency rules. Which she was making up at this very moment.

She started to edge her way down the molding, but she hadn't taken two mouse steps when the door of the chamber opened and Uncle Francis strode in, followed by another person.

And the other person was . . . Liv.

"Go on, then, my dear," her uncle said. "I don't have much time for you."

"Yes, Your Grace," Liv answered, more meekly than Mary had ever seen her. "The queen was in a somber mood today."

"Is she upset about the wedding?" her uncle asked. "Does she wish to avoid marrying the dauphin?"

"No," Liv said firmly. "She loves Francis. I found that pamphlet written by John Knox in her desk. Perhaps she is worried about Scotland and her mother."

If Mary had been human, she would have flushed hot to think of Liv rifling through her desk, but as she was a mouse, she only gave a tiny, inaudible squeak of outrage and then kept listening.

"She also sent a letter to her mother today. With Mary Beaton as the carrier."

Mon Dieu, Mary thought dazedly. *She has told him that Bea is an Eðian. Perhaps he knows about us all.*

Uncle Francis sighed. "I disapprove of my niece having any contact with Eðians—as you well know—but even I cannot deny that the bird-girl is useful, for now. I occasionally employ members of that filthy race, myself. They make excellent messengers." He smiled knowingly at Liv. "And spies."

"May I go now, Your Grace?" Liv asked in a flat voice.

"Oh, don't be so sour-faced. I only ask this of you because I must know how the queen is doing at all times. She must be protected. Sometimes even from herself."

"Yes, Your Grace." Liv straightened. "May I go?"

Her uncle's eyes narrowed. "There's nothing else I should

know about? I would hate to discover new information from another source and find that you kept something from me."

He said it kindly, but Liv stiffened like he'd threatened her. She shifted from one foot to the other. "Mary has been assigned a new lady-in-waiting, sent by Queen Catherine. She is undoubtedly a spy." There was no trace of Liv's affection for Ari in her voice now. "Today the new lady gave Queen Mary a potion, and Mary drank it."

Mary's breast burned with shame. She *was* a fool.

Uncle Francis was frowning. "I did notice that she had a vial of something earlier. What does the potion do?"

"It eases her worries," Liv said. "It seems harmless enough."

"Ah," said Uncle Francis, stroking his beard thoughtfully. "Well. That's all probably nonsense, and could possibly be some form of heretical witchcraft, but it doesn't matter. It seemed to make Mary complacent enough. Encourage her to keep taking it. Is that all?"

"Yes, Your Grace. That's all." Liv shuffled toward the door.

"What is the girl's name?" Uncle Francis called after her.

"Your Grace?"

"The new lady-in-waiting?"

"Oh." Liv's lips pressed together. Then she blew out a sigh. "Aristotle de Nostradame, Your Grace."

"An offspring of Nostradamus," mused Uncle Francis. "Definitely a heretic, then. Thank you, my dear. I will see you next week. Keep up the good work."

Mary's tiny jaw clenched. She knew she shouldn't be surprised.

People had been betraying her all her life. It was part of the queen gig. But she'd never in a million years have dreamed that Liv would betray her. Liv, her oldest friend. Her confidante. Her sister, in so many ways.

She wanted to rage. To scream. To throw things, break them. But she was a mouse, so she had to hold it in until she could become human. She resolved never to take that blasted potion again and never to trust anyone, not even her best friends, apparently, not even her own family—except for her mother, of course.

And Francis.

Francis had been right all along.

FOURTEEN
Ari

Ari could see through walls! She'd tweaked the *See Through Walls* potion a bit (because you never knew when an accidental potion could come in handy), and when she'd thought she had just the right proportions, she'd tested it out herself.

Now she was wandering around the palace. She'd watched the cook sneeze into the chicken dish that would be served for dinner. (Ew! Wash your hands and stop touching your face!) She'd seen Mary's uncles in their chambers toasting each other over something. She'd seen King Henry doing . . . well, she'd seen him. In chambers that were not his own. She couldn't unsee it.

She was starting to understand why walls existed.

But she could still see through them, so she might as well do the job that Queen Catherine had sent her to do, which was to spy on Queen Mary.

At first, Mary's chambers appeared empty. Then Ari looked lower—much, much lower—and spotted a flurry of movement near the back wall.

It was a mouse.

The palace was apparently being overrun by rodents. This was the second time this week Ari had seen a mouse in a queen's bedroom. She'd have to speak to housekeeping.

Then there was a flash of light and suddenly the mouse was gone and in its place stood Mary. In the flesh. Quite literally.

Queen Mary.

A mouse.

Was Mary.

Mary was a mouse.

Ari couldn't move, except to avert her eyes momentarily while Queen Mary pulled on a dressing gown. Then the queen let out what could only be described as a roar of rage that Ari could hear even through the thick stone between them. She picked up a pillow from her bed and hurled it toward the wall.

Ari ducked. Then she remembered she didn't have to, because there was a wall in the way. But the queen was glaring in her direction. Maybe, thought Ari, the queen could see her, too!

But no. Queen Mary had turned to glare in the other direction now. She stamped her foot. (It was most unqueenly.) Then she stamped her other foot. Then she stamped both feet. Then she screamed again and threw more pillows and raked all the papers off her desk onto the floor.

She was having a bit of a temper tantrum, Ari observed,

which was strange, but it wasn't the strangest thing that was happening.

The strangest thing was obviously that Queen Mary was a mouse.

And a human.

And a mouse.

Which meant she was an Eðian.

A mouse Eðian.

Tall, queenly Mary was a mouse Eðian.

Ari put her hand against the stone wall and tried to catch her breath. What to do. What to do? She'd never even known an Eðian, let alone seen one transform right in front of her. Well, behind an invisible wall. It didn't make any sense. Mary was supposed to be a Verity queen. A protector of the true human form.

But she was a mouse. This was brand-new information.

Information that Queen Catherine would be most interested in knowing.

Ari should run right away to tell the French queen. But she wasn't sure she should run while under the influence of the *See Through Walls* potion, so she sat down on the floor in the hall instead, her mind still blown. Mary was about to marry Prince Francis, which meant someday (far in the future, but still) Mary would be the queen of France. An Eðian queen, ruling a Verity kingdom.

Didn't Ari owe it to *her* queen, her country, and her father to report what she had seen?

Ari rubbed at her eyes. She, along with the rest of France,

had been raised to believe Eθians were abominations. But she was so far removed from any Eθians, she'd never really had to think about them.

Until now.

Revealing this news could reward Ari with everything she'd ever wanted. It could secure her future.

But revealing it would also destroy Queen Mary. Her station wouldn't matter. At the very least, she'd be imprisoned. Probably tortured. But more likely, she'd be burned at the stake. Or (gulp) beheaded.

Could Ari sentence her to that fate?

"Ari?" a familiar voice said.

Ari looked up to see Liv standing in front of her. For a moment Ari forgot her problems, because Liv looked so unhappy. Her hazel eyes were rimmed with red, as though she'd been crying. Her face was pale. Ari scrambled to her feet.

"Are you all right?" Ari asked.

Liv nodded quickly. "I'm fine," she said hoarsely.

But Liv was clearly not fine.

"Is it me?" Ari's heart jumped into her throat. "Is it what happened earlier? I'm sorry if—"

"It's not you," Liv interrupted. "What happened earlier was wonderful. I shall never forget it."

Ari felt a stab of worry so sharp she wished she'd brought some of the leftover extra-strength *Worries Be Gone* potion. Of course it was wonderful that Liv thought what had happened earlier was wonderful. But "I shall never forget it" is the kind of thing one says when something is never going to happen again.

And Ari really, really wanted to kiss Liv again.

Liv touched her arm. "What happened to you? Why were you sitting out here on the floor?"

Oh. Ari turned back to the wall in time to see Queen Mary try to rip the curtains from around her bed but get caught in them instead. It seemed like she could use some help. And the *Worries Be Gone* potion, obviously. Ari wondered briefly if she'd taken it yet.

And then Ari went right back to freaking out, because that's what you do when you find out that your fake boss is actually a traitorous mouse.

"What are you looking at?" Liv followed Ari's gaze to the wall and then back to her face. "What about that painting bothers you so?"

Ari squinted until she could see the painting hanging on the wall. It was of a woman, sitting in front of a pastoral scene, a mysterious smile on her lips. All the courtiers were so enthusiastic about it, which was why it was hanging outside Queen Mary's chambers, but Ari could never understand what the fuss was about.

It was also very small.

"I'm not sure, exactly. I'm not an art critic," Ari said. "But you'd think such a masterpiece would be bigger." She grabbed Liv's wrist and pulled her over to an alcove where there was a little more privacy. They sat on a bench.

"What is it?" Liv asked. "Tell me."

Where to begin? The queen is a mouse. The queen is a *mouse. The queen is A MOUSE!* This was obviously the place to begin.

But she couldn't.

"Things," Ari said. "So many things. I—" Ari stopped midsentence.

Liv tilted her head. "Use your words, Aristotle."

Ari tugged at the collar of her dress. "I just . . . I only . . . Liv, did you know that there are *animals*?" Ari whispered the last word.

"Where?" Liv whispered back.

"I mean . . ." Ari gestured wildly. "Everywhere! Here. There." She pointed in all sorts of directions, *except* toward Queen Mary's chambers.

"Of course," Liv said slowly. "But mostly, they're outside."

Ari blew out a breath. What to do? What to do.

"Please use words," Liv said. "Any words."

Ari glanced in the direction of Mary's chambers. She slapped a hand over her eyes.

Liv pried Ari's hand away from her face. "You're frightening me. Has one of your potions gone wrong?"

"My potions never go wrong," Ari snapped.

Liv took her hand back, and Ari blew out some more breaths.

"I'm sorry. I do make mistakes. But I usually learn something from them." Like today's potion, which led her to learn Queen Mary was a mouse. Which felt like a whole new mistake. Ari folded her hands in her lap.

"The point is, there are *Eðians*." She whispered that last word again.

Liv stared at her blankly.

"You know," Ari continued, still whispering. "People who can turn into animals."

"I know what Eðians are."

"I mean, there are so many questions in this ever-changing world in which we live in," Ari said, sounding strangely preachy. "So many uncertainties." This was not going well. "But one truth we should all know is that humans are not supposed to turn into animals, right?"

Liv's brows furrowed, and she frowned. "I guess," she said tentatively.

"I mean, weren't you raised that way?" Ari's voice was high and squeaky. Like a mouse. "I didn't worry about it when I was younger"—meaning, dear reader, up until ten minutes ago—"but it just occurred to me, they are out there. The *truth* is out there."

Liv patted Ari's knee. "I understand, it's a scary world. But we're in here."

"But what if the truth is *in here*, too?" Ari exclaimed.

"Listen, Aristotle, I'm not exactly sure what you're getting at, because there is probably . . . truth . . . everywhere. But the clash between Eðians and Verities is not the only truth *I* know."

"What other truth do you know?" Ari asked in a small voice.

"I know there are good people everywhere. I know that we are here, in this place, for a reason. I know that here, with the six of us, we have a family. We take care of each other. Haven't we taken care of you?" Liv smoothed her hand over Ari's hair. "Haven't you taken care of us?"

Ari nodded, her heartbeat slowing. It was nice to have someone else making sense of the world for her.

"Queen Mary is the heart," continued Liv. "She will watch over us, as we watch over her. There is nothing to be afraid of. We are home. The truth may be out there, or in here, or all around, and it may be scary. But the only truth we need is each other. No matter how we came together, never forget, we are the lucky ones."

That sounded good. But a lady like Liv had a secure future. Ari was going to have to fight for hers. She had to pick a side. Mary's. Or Catherine's.

What to do? she thought. *What to do.*

FIFTEEN
Francis

Thwack. An arrow hit the target dummy.

"Are you nervous about tomorrow?" Henry III asked. (This Henry was Francis's nine-year-old brother, not the king or any of the five thousand other people named Henry. We know. It's a lot.)

"No," Francis lied, and then he felt bad for lying. "A little. Have you seen all the preparations?"

"I did!" Charles IX (Francis's ten-year-old brother, not the cardinal) loosed another arrow, which hit the dummy in the throat. "I've been helping Father with the ships."

The ships. Francis shuddered. Why did there have to be so many boats involved with his wedding? That was weird.

"Father said you're going to be making babies all the time

now," Charles IX said. "He said you're going to have fifteen babies by the end of the year."

"First of all," Francis said as he nocked an arrow and aimed for the dummy's heart, "babies take a bit longer than that." It was April, after all, so even if they started tomorrow—which was expected, of course, but unlikely—a baby wouldn't appear until after the new year.

Francis loosed the arrow. It sailed past the dummy and into the grass.

"It's a good thing we're not at war," Henry III observed. "You can't even hit Bash."

"Bash?" Francis lowered his bow. "Do you mean the dummy?" He looked across the yard where the dummy stood, just a stuffed burlap sack the boys had constructed with sticks for arms and legs, and a slim wooden board holding up the target that served as a head. Someone had painted a smile on its face and given it piercing blue eyes.

"Don't call Bash a dummy!" Charles IX said. "You take that back."

Francis looked between his younger brothers and the dummy. "Why did you name it Bash?"

"Because we bash him with our arrows. Sometimes our swords." Henry III rolled his eyes. "But don't talk bad about him. Bash is our friend."

"Yeah," Charles IX said. "He's like the older brother we never had."

Francis scowled. "I'm your older brother."

"Exactly," Henry III said.

Francis started to protest, but just then Mary stepped outside, her auburn hair blazing red in the sunlight, a sky-blue gown swirling around her ankles. Francis's heart skipped a beat at the mere sight of her. Even though he saw her every day. It was impossible to forget how she'd looked at him the other day, all heat and fondness. She'd never looked at him like that before, not once, and Francis found he'd been thinking about it a lot.

Like, every hour.

Both Henry III and Charles IX sighed in admiration.

"She's so pretty," Henry III said.

"Way too pretty for you," Charles IX said.

"And nice," Henry III said.

"Way too nice for you," Charles IX said.

"What do you know about anything?" Francis's throat was tight. "You're only children."

"I know if you don't want to marry her," Charles IX said, "then I will. I'll be king, once you die."

Mary's gaze swung toward them, and she and Francis locked eyes. A smile turned up the corners of her mouth, making him smile in return as she strolled across the yard.

Francis started thinking about how close her face had been the other day, right after she'd taken a swig from that vial and signed the paper.

"Good morning," Mary said.

"Good morning," all three boys said in unison.

Francis blushed. "We're just having a little practice before breakfast. While it's still cool out."

"May I?" Mary nodded at Francis's bow, which he gave to her without hesitation. She lifted the bow and nocked an arrow. (All the movies and shows where the boy stands behind the girl and shows her how to shoot an arrow—or swing a golf club, or any number of things boys think girls need help with—hadn't been invented yet, but even so, Francis had the urge to adjust her stance and shift her shoulders and maybe get a whiff of the rose-petal soap she used.

Mary released the arrow and it struck Bash in the nose.

Both younger boys clapped. "Francis couldn't hit the target," Charles IX said.

Mary looked at him. "Is that true?"

"I couldn't bear to harm dear Bash."

"Who's Bash?"

"They named the target dummy Bash."

"He's cute." Mary looked at the boys. "Why did you name the target dummy Bash?"

"Mama said we weren't allowed to name him Francis," Charles IX said.

Francis's mouth twisted. "I'm not sure how I should feel about that."

Mary stepped close to Francis and touched his hand. "Might I speak with you privately?"

"Of course." Francis took the bow and left it on a bench. "I'll return in a moment," he told his brothers, but they didn't seem to notice that he was leaving.

"Let's pretend we're fighting Eðians," Charles IX said. "We'll both be knights, and the Eðians are coming at us from the other side of the battlefield."

"Ahh!" Henry III raised his bow and shot poor Bash in the chest. "Take that, evil Eðian!"

Francis cringed and walked with Mary away from the epic battle taking place behind them. "I'm sorry about that," Francis said. He wished there were a way to talk to the boys about Eðians that wouldn't get all of them in trouble, some way to make them understand that Eðians weren't bad. But the one time he had brought it up, both of them had gone straight to Henry (the king), and Francis had been forced to sit through hours of lectures about how there was no place for an Eðian sympathizer in French court.

He wouldn't make that mistake again. It could put Mary in danger. Her ladies, too.

"You have nothing to be sorry for," Mary said softly. "I know you walk a very fine line with them."

He forced a smile. "You shouldn't have to hear it, though. We are royalty. We must not spew hate so freely."

"I agree, but we are in precarious positions in a dangerous world. We have to be careful about when and how we speak to others regarding such things. France is a Verity kingdom, but that may not always be true. One day, common Eðians may rise up and overthrow the Verities."

"Speaking up shouldn't fall to the common Eðian. If royalty cannot express their opinions without fear of consequences, what must others risk?" Death, he knew. They risked death.

Mary sighed and gazed northwest, toward Scotland. "I don't have a solution," she said, "but I do know that in other parts of the world, Eðians have risen up and declared themselves just as deserving as anyone else. The same may happen in France, and when you are king of France, and I am queen consort of France, we will do what we can to make lives better for Eðians here."

"That may be some time off," he said. "My father will live a long time yet."

"Then we'll have plenty of time to prepare."

Francis just walked along with her, trying to ignore the sounds of his brothers bashing on Bash the Eðian dummy / the brother they never had. "Is there something you wanted to talk about?"

"Yes." Mary halted and looked at him, her gaze steady. "About the other day, when we were talking in the hall."

Francis waited for her to finish that sentence.

"I'm afraid I might have been a bit"—she pressed her eyebrows together—"dismissive. But I want you to know that I value your insight and I take your concerns seriously. I shouldn't have behaved in such an unbecoming manner."

Francis smiled. "I'm glad you said that."

"Were you very angry with me?"

"No, of course not." He touched her hand. "I could never be angry with you. It did hurt a little, but I also know that you think the world of your uncles and that my suggesting they may not have your best interest at heart would be difficult to hear."

Her eyebrows drew closer together as she nodded.

"Has something happened?" he asked.

She touched the amethyst ring. "I just found out that someone I trusted—someone I consider family—hasn't been honest with me."

His eyebrows lifted. She must be talking about her uncles. He felt a flash of relief. "What are you going to do?"

"I don't know. I was angry at first." (To which your narrators would say, um, UNDERSTATEMENT much?) "But now I just feel sad. What would you do?"

Francis thought for a minute. "If I still cared about them, I'd find a kind way to remove them from my presence."

She nodded thoughtfully. "Yes. I shall think on that." She smiled. "I'm glad we talked about this. This situation has made me realize how much I value your honesty and forthrightness. Growing up as a queen, I've always had to be suspicious of those around me, but with you—we are equal. We are meant to be together."

Francis's heart thundered. "I think so, too."

"In some ways, everything will be different after tomorrow."

"Yes," he said softly. "But you and I will be the same, won't we? The way we feel about each other?"

"That's right." A spot of pink appeared on each of her cheeks. "Unrelated to the wedding—do you still have that bearskin rug? The one that we used to sleep on in front of the fire?"

Francis blinked. Where had that come from? "Yes," he said slowly, remembering the night years ago that he'd awakened in his room to find Mary there, sitting on the rug and looking into the fire. He'd climbed out of bed to sit with her, letting her talk until she curled up and fell asleep. She'd come to his room regularly after that, and they'd play cards or trade gossip, but after a while she'd had to stop; her uncles had said she was too old to go sneaking into his room, but Francis had left the rug there like a relic of their childhood he could not bear to disturb. "I still have it."

A smile touched her lips. "That's good."

Francis skipped breakfast. Instead, he informed his father that he was riding out for the day and wouldn't be available for any of the wedding minutiae.

There was something far more important that Francis needed to find.

The ride was relaxing, and Francis, for all his shortcomings as the future king, was a good rider. He enjoyed the sun on his face, the breeze tangling through his hair, and the sense of the ground flying beneath him. He went on like that for a while, down the roads and away from Paris, reveling in the feel of not being judged—not being found so *lacking*—until he came to a stretch of wildflowers growing along the roadside.

Then, breathing heavily from the exercise, he reined in his horse and dismounted.

It wasn't hard to find what he wanted: they were white flowers with a bright yellow center, a kind of primrose. Francis produced a length of wet fabric (to keep the flowers fresh), and a sharp knife. He thought about the light in Mary's eyes when she'd said they were meant to be together. And by this time tomorrow, they would be. They'd be together forever.

Francis knelt in the grass and cut the first cowslip for Mary.

SIXTEEN ⸌Mary

Mary gazed at her reflection in the mirror. Her gown was undeniably gorgeous, a shimmering white, embroidered with silver thread and sparkling with diamonds, topped with a train of bluish-gray velvet. Her long auburn hair fell in waves down her back. From her throat dangled a large jewel-encrusted pendant bearing a blue diamond the size of a walnut—a gift from her soon-to-be father-in-law, engraved with his initials: *HV.*

Mary lifted her hand to touch the diamond. The girl in the mirror felt like a stranger to her, an impostor.

"Here are your mother's earrings," Hush said, holding out her hand, where, nestled into her palm, was a pair of drop earrings fashioned from Scottish pearls. Mary de Guise had received these earrings from her then soon-to-be husband, James V, on the day of *their* wedding, and she'd sent them along with her daughter when Mary traveled to France, so certain Mary de Guise had been that Mary would marry Francis someday.

And now someday was today. Her wedding day.

But her mother wouldn't be here to see it.

"Let me do that," Hush said. Mary turned her head so Hush might fasten the pearl earrings onto her ears. Normally it was Liv who handled her jewels, but Mary had sent her on an errand, just to get her out of sight. It had been four days since Mary had discovered Liv's treachery, and the pain of it had not eased. But she had taken Francis's advice and now had a plan for how she would deal with Liv, a course of action that she hoped would be the best for both of them.

She gazed again into the mirror. Her mother's earrings were the perfect accent. But she would have rather had her mother than the earrings.

"No one has heard from Bea?" she asked.

Hush and Flem shook their heads mournfully.

"I'm sure she was simply delayed," Hush murmured.

Mary nodded. Of course, this was what she would like to believe. She hoped Bea hadn't been intercepted. If the uncles knew that Bea was an Eðian, who else might know? Mary clenched her fists for a moment, thinking about how Liv must have told the uncles. She'd put Bea in danger. And perhaps all of them.

"She's probably flapping wildly back to us as we speak, bearing a congratulatory letter from your mother," Flem said. "But if she were here, she'd tell you not to worry about her and enjoy yourself today."

A knock came at the outer door. Flem went to answer it and returned with the two younger Valois princes: Henry III and Charles IX.

"You look so pretty, Mary," Henry III said, gaping up at her.

She smiled and ruffled his golden hair.

"You should marry me instead of Francis," Charles IX said.

She laughed and bent to kiss his cheek. "Now I shall get to be your sister, won't I?"

"We have enough sisters," grumbled Charles IX.

"Francis sent us to give you this." Henry III drew a bouquet from behind his back and thrust it at Mary. It was a simple gathering of white flowers: cowslips.

Mary's breath caught. Francis had been listening when she'd rambled on and on about what she'd wanted her bouquet to be.

"He spent all day yesterday picking stupid flowers," Charles IX said.

And he'd picked them himself.

Mary had a bouquet already, made from marigolds—because the marigold was what she'd randomly chosen to be the emblem of her royal crest when she was eight years old and thought yellow flowers were very elegant. But of course she would set the marigolds aside now, and use Francis's bouquet.

She handed the flowers carefully to Hush, who went to put them in some water to keep them fresh until the wedding. Then she crossed to the armoire and retrieved something from the top drawer: the silk handkerchief she'd embroidered.

She knelt to give it to Henry III. "Tell Francis that the flowers please me greatly, and give this to him as my token in return."

You and no other, it read. She hoped he'd understand how much she meant it.

She kissed the princes again and sent them back to the groom.

A moment later Liv and Ari burst into the room, both dressed in silk gowns, blue like all of Mary's maids of honor.

Mary's jaw clenched at the sight of Liv. But she reminded herself that she had a plan.

"Oh dear," said Hush. "Let's do something with that hair."

Ari nodded, breathless, but first she pulled two vials out of her cleavage. She'd been skittish lately, nervous around Mary and the ladies. Mary couldn't imagine why.

Ari glanced between the potions, reading the labels. "This one reads *Worries Be Gone*, doesn't it?" she asked Liv blearily.

"Yes."

Ari held the vial out to the queen. "I made you a new batch," she panted. "Much milder than the first. And remember, you only need a drop."

"Thank you," Mary said, and took the vial, but she didn't intend to partake of any mysterious potions today. That had gotten her in enough trouble last time.

"What's the other potion for?" Liv asked.

Ari's face went red. "Something else. Totally unrelated to the wedding." She quickly stuffed it back in her cleavage.

Flem's head tilted to one side the way it did when she heard someone in the hallway. "They're coming to fetch us now!" She squealed excitedly. She would have been wagging her tail if she'd had it available. "Are we ready to go to the church?"

Mary took a deep breath and let it out slowly, which was difficult, what with her corset laced extra tight to ensure that her figure would be impeccable.

"Let's not forget the final touch," Liv said, and went to retrieve Mary's crown—crafted especially for today. It was pure gold and studded with diamonds, pearls, rubies, and emeralds. The huge sapphire at its center flashed in the light as Liv placed it gently on Mary's head.

Her ladies all drew in an awed gasp.

Mary struggled to keep her head up. The crown weighed (according to our exhaustive research) an approximate butt-ton, and it made Mary's neck ache immediately. Droppings. She was going to have to wear this crown *all day*.

But it was fine. She was the queen, after all.

"You look radiant," murmured Hush.

"You are . . ." Ari seemed at a loss for words. Or perhaps she was still out of breath.

"Splendiferous," Flem supplied for her.

"You look like you're ready to take on the world," Liv said.

Mary closed her eyes and tried to think of Francis.

"I'm ready," she said.

* * *

I'm not ready! Mary thought about an hour later. The journey to Notre Dame had gone by in a bumpy, jumbled blur as they'd ridden in a carriage through Paris, every street and alleyway and window filled with onlookers, all craning to see the queen on the way to her wedding. At the cathedral there'd been even more people crowded into the square, shouting at her, cheering, calling her name. And now she was standing at the end of a very, very long aisle in the cathedral with its high walls and vaulted ceilings and stained glass windows everywhere. She was clutching the arm of King Henry, who was to walk her down the aisle. And she was silently freaking out.

"You look ethereal, my dear," the king was blathering on obliviously. "Even if you didn't bring a country with you, my son would be lucky to win such a prize. Why, if I were a younger man, I myself might . . ."

Mon Dieu. She was going to barf.

Or she was going to slap the king of France.

Or she was going to faint, because she couldn't breathe. Because corset.

"Won't you smile for us, my dear?" Henry said, glancing at her ashen face.

But her lips felt like they were made of wax. All at once she knew with absolute certainty that this was the moment that would seal her fate forever. The aisle represented a path that she was embarking on, a series of steps, starting now, leading to the end of her life.

The music started, and the crowd rose to its feet, all turning to gaze at her in awe.

Mary tried to look past them, down the aisle, to Francis. But she couldn't see him. He was too far away. She found she was trembling.

"Walk, girl," the king said into her ear. "I have no wish to drag you."

Her pride flared. "Mind that you don't forget, Your Majesty, that I am also a queen. I will not be rushed, even by you."

He grinned almost boyishly. "That's my girl."

She straightened and moved decisively forward. Behind her, Liv and Flem tried to match her sudden strides, holding the corners of the velvet train.

"Look at her crown!" she heard a courtier exclaim.

"I've heard the sapphire alone is worth half a million francs!"

Step.

Step.

"What a regal bearing she has."

Step.

"She's a hundred times more beautiful than a goddess of heaven!"

Step.

"How perfect she is!"

"How divine!"

Step.

"Her person alone is worth a kingdom."

The crowd stared at her raptly, hungrily, as if they might

suddenly rush forward and devour her, but Mary kept her gaze focused straight ahead. She could finally see Francis, flanked on one side by his brothers and on the other by her uncles.

At his expression, she almost laughed out loud.

He looked miserable. His face was pale and drawn, his arms clasped tightly behind him, a sheen of sweat shining on his brow beneath his simpler (probably lighter—ha!) crown. He must have been boiling under the mountain of layers he wore: the white undershirt with its stiff ruffled collar, topped by an ornately embroidered golden doublet, topped by an ermine-trimmed coat of heavy blue velvet. He was also wearing silver-threaded, puffed trousers (what we, your narrators, would describe as "pumpkin pants") and fine white tights. But the pièce de résistance was the shoes, which were heeled so that he would appear to be as tall as Mary as they stood at the altar.

(Your narrators here again. It turns out that men were the first to wear high heels, which proves our theory that all torturous contraptions worn now for the sake of beauty were first invented and then discarded by men. But, let's be honest, those heels made Francis's calves look amazing.)

Francis swayed slightly. Mary caught and held his gaze as she continued toward him, step by step. *Eyes up*, she mouthed, and found her smile again, and hurled it at her fiancé like he was drowning, and she was throwing him a life preserver (even though life preservers hadn't been invented yet). She even managed to arch an eyebrow at him playfully, like this entire charade could be simply a game to them.

His blue eyes softened. The corner of his mouth twitched.

That's when Mary knew that they really were going to be fine. Everyone else in the room faded away for her, every face, every voice but that of her uncle Charles, the cardinal, murmuring, "Dearly beloved, we are gathered here together . . . to join this man and this woman . . . ," and even then, she was only half paying attention.

And then they got to the part with the vows:

"I take you to be my wife."

". . . to be my husband."

". . . and pledge to you that I will be faithful and loyal . . ."

". . . forsaking all others."

". . . keeping faith and truth in all matters between us . . ."

"In sickness and in health."

"Until death us do part."

"With this ring, I thee wed," she said at the end, taking his clammy hand and sliding the ring onto his finger. "With my body I thee worship, and with all my worldly goods I thee endow."

Her uncle declared them man and wife, unable to resist gleefully adding that Mary would someday be queen of both Scotland *and* France. And then he said, "You may kiss the bride."

She'd completely forgotten that they were supposed to kiss.

The last time she'd kissed Francis had been after they'd danced, when she was five years old. And that, as it happened, had been the first and last time she'd ever been kissed on the lips.

He turned toward her, a silent question in his eyes.

She gave a slight nod. Yes. Of course. It was expected.

He tipped her chin up (in the shoes, he was as tall as she was now) and paused in just a moment's hesitation before he touched his lips to hers. It was meant to be brief and perfunctory (a church kiss), but his mouth lingered on hers. His hand stayed at her face, his thumb still brushing her chin gently, his fingers coming to rest beneath the dangling pearl earring. Her own hand rose, of its own accord, it seemed, and buried itself in the golden curls at the back of his neck.

After a time she became aware of a noise. A roaring. She suddenly realized that it was the crowd.

She stepped back almost drunkenly, bringing her fingers to touch her tingling lips, fighting the urge to grab her husband—yes, her husband, now—and pull him close again.

So that was kissing.

Francis glanced down, face flushed, the corner of his mouth turning up in a slight, half-embarrassed smile. Her uncle led them from the altar, Francis and Mary holding hands for just an instant before they were pulled apart again, swept off to make their separate ways back to the palace, and the party that awaited them there. And the wedding night.

SEVENTEEN

Ari

Ari was exhausted. All day yesterday she'd been perfecting the *Not There* potion that Queen Catherine had ordered for the king. Then she'd been up half the night working on the *Not There* antidote, and testing variations of both on poor, poor Greer. (She'd given Greer the day off today, and promised to bring her some wedding cake.) Then this morning she'd tried to deliver the *Not There* potion to Queen Catherine, who, to Ari's dismay, insisted that she wanted nothing to do with "poisoning my dear husband" and informed Ari that it was her job to somehow slip said potion into the king's drink at the opportune moment.

To which Ari thought, *merde*. What to do? What she wouldn't give for a vision telling her how to accomplish this herculean task.

Then she'd had to put on a terribly uncomfortable dress and

run straight to Mary and the rest of the ladies and off they'd headed to the church, where she'd walked ahead of the queen, sprinkling rose petals and struggled to keep her eyes open during the vows.

(This was before coffee, dear readers. Although our research did reveal that in the ninth century, an Ethiopian goatherd named Kaldi noticed how excited his goats became after eating the beans from a coffee plant. So, really, it was before coffee was available in France, which we think is inhumane. Anyway, back to the wedding.)

Finally, *finally*, the ceremony was over. But Ari still had hours to go before she could rest. After the big to-do at the cathedral, the wedding party (with King Henry and the dauphin on horseback, Queens Mary and Catherine following after in a golden litter, and Ari and the other ladies-in-waiting in a series of coaches behind them) toured the streets of Paris. It wasn't a long journey from Notre Dame to the Louvre, but the Duke of Guise had changed the route, making it longer, to maximize the exposure of Mary to the crowds of adoring subjects.

At first, everywhere they went, the heralds leading the entourage threw gold and silver coins into the crowds. For a few minutes, it seemed heavenly, like riches were falling from the skies. And then the inevitable pandemonium broke out. Commoners pushed and elbowed their neighbors to grab a share of the spoils. So many observers suffered from being trampled and pushed to the ground that eventually even the peasants were begging the heralds to stop throwing money, which was probably a first in history.

(Again, we've done the research, and indeed, this was the first time in history peasants had requested that money *not* be thrown.)

Finally the caravan made its triumphant return amid cheers and a showering of even more rose petals. From there the party proceeded to the grand banquet, which was too large for any one hall. In total, it spanned across six great halls, which housed the most important foreign ambassadors, magistrates, dignitaries, and nobility, with the most influential of the guests nearest the main hall, and the next influential a little more distant and so on and so forth.

The tables in the main dining hall were set up in a giant U shape, with Mary and Francis at the head of the dais. The uncles were seated on Mary's side, with King Henry, Queen Catherine, and Diane de Poitiers on Francis's side. The rest of the guests sat along the two legs running perpendicular to the wedding party, with the Marys and Ari in the seats closest to Mary, after her uncles.

Dancers and ribbon twirlers performed in the middle of the U while servants on the outside kept wine goblets full as they presented course after course of the most exotic and delectable foods Ari had ever seen or tasted.

"This is so exciting," Flem said for the millionth time. "The food, the wine, the dancing, the food!"

"You mentioned the food," Liv said.

"Yes, but that's only because there's so much of it!" Flem exclaimed, eying a delicious-looking tidbit on someone else's plate, even though she had a plate of her own.

The ladies, even Ari, giggled. Ari had never seen the Marys so excited about anything. She wished she could wholeheartedly join in the excitement, but Ari had more important things to worry about.

Like the stupid potion for the stupid king. Which Queen Catherine wouldn't give to him her stupid self.

"I can't wait to see the mechanical ships," Liv said.

"There's going to be a ship?" Ari asked.

"Six," Flem said.

"Six ships?" Ari repeated. "But we're in Paris. In a dining room. Indoors."

"So?" Liv said.

"So, I'm no geographer, but there are no bodies of water near us large enough to accommodate a ship."

"Not just one ship," Flem reminded her. "Six."

"How does this make any sense?" Ari asked.

Liv smiled, her eyes doing that twinkle that they did more and more often. "Just you wait, Aristotle de Nostradame. Just you wait." Under the table, Liv reached for Ari's hand. She found it and squeezed it. Ari couldn't believe she would make so bold a move, but she squeezed back, and felt a thrill all the way down to her toes.

But she still had to figure out how to get the potion into the king's drink, which would be difficult, considering that everyone was looking at the king and he hadn't set his goblet down once.

King Henry stood and raised the cursed goblet. "To Mary and Francis. And to the future of France, and Scotland, and a French empire that will soon reach to the farthest deserts and the tallest mountains and . . . the . . . other land stuff out there."

The guests raised their glasses. "To the land stuff!" they repeated right before they glugged.

"And," King Henry continued, "to the truly amazing mastermind behind this most celebratory . . . celebratory of occasions. Who happens to be"—he paused dramatically—"myself!"

"To the king!" Glug.

"And to this blessed union, which I will have the honor of overseeing tonight, for I would like to witness the creation of the next great heir to the throne!"

Queen Catherine shot Ari a pointed look, and Ari nodded quickly. She could do this. She had to do this. She would figure this out. Hopefully without getting caught and beheaded. (There was a reason, after all, that Queen Catherine refused to do it herself.)

The guests raised their glasses again but were not sure which part of the king's toast to repeat, so it came out as a sort of jumbled mess.

"And now, it's time for dancing!" the king exclaimed. "Everyone—dance and make merry with all of these wonderful things that your king has provided. And by king, I mean me!"

The crowd of guests cheered again. A band of musicians began to play a lively song. The king rose and extended his hand to Diane de Poitiers, who followed him away from the table to where people were lining up to dance.

Ari's gaze fell on the king's jeweled goblet, which he had left at the head of the table.

"Now's the opportune time," she murmured to herself.

"The opportune time for what?" Liv asked.

She'd apparently murmured a little too loudly. "For dancing," Ari said quickly. "We should dance. After all, you spent so much time teaching me how."

"Very well," Liv said merrily. "Let's dance."

Ari turned away for a moment and fished the vial out of her cleavage as she got to her feet. She grabbed Liv's hand and walked her over to where people were starting to bow and twirl. Ari was grateful that she did know the steps, as, keeping in time with the music, she and Liv danced around the room. With each pass, Ari led them closer and closer to the wedding party's seats, particularly toward where the king had been sitting.

Just one more pass and she would be close enough to—

"What are you doing?" Liv asked, spinning Ari away.

Ari bit her lip. "What do you mean?"

"I know you know this dance, but you're purposely messing it up. Why?"

"I can't say," Ari said awkwardly.

Liv stopped dancing and crossed her arms, and Ari was equal parts terrified and endeared by her pout.

She straightened up. "Liv, is there any way you would trust that I am trying to help Francis and Mary? If I don't succeed, Queen Catherine might just kill me. And if I do succeed, King Henry might kill me."

Liv's brows furrowed. "I can't tell if you're joking or not," she said.

"Me neither. I just . . ." Ari gulped in a breath. "I just have to put something in the king's drink. Right now. Nothing that will hurt him," she added quickly. "Not permanently, that is. I have an antidote."

Liv grabbed both of Ari's hands, and with the sincerest of smiles, she said, "I know what it's like to be in a difficult position. You don't have to tell me details. I'll help you."

Ari smiled, and Liv returned her smile, and quickly it became a secret game.

The dance floor was quite crowded by this point, and it was difficult to navigate, through dance, to the king's spot. But Ari was determined, and Liv proved to be a dedicated partner, and after many misses, one particular pass led them straight to their destination. In a movement one could only catch if one knew to look for it, Ari emptied the contents of the vial into the king's goblet.

She did it in the nick of time, too, because a moment later the king returned to the table. "Bring out the cake!" the king bellowed. "Also, bring me more wine!"

Ari breathed a sigh of relief as she watched the king take a long drink.

"Promise me that one day, you'll tell me what we just did," Liv said, her face glistening with sweat. She was breathing so hard, her corset was barely holding her chest in.

"I will," Ari promised, but she was suddenly preoccupied remembering how it felt to kiss Liv's lips, to feel her arms around her. And she was wondering when she could do all that again.

"Let's go congratulate Mary," Liv said. She took Ari by the hand and drew her to Francis and Mary's place at the table, where they were feeding each other cake.

"Your Majesties," Liv and Ari said in unison, dropping into curtsies. It was the best curtsy Ari had ever done.

Francis and Mary looked up. Francis smiled. But Mary did not seem particularly pleased to see them.

"I just wanted to say how honored I am to have been part of your wedding, Your Majesties," Liv said. "I wish you all the happiness in the world."

"Thank you," said Francis sincerely.

Queen Mary was silent for a moment. Then she said, "I wish you happiness as well, Lady Livingston."

Ari felt Liv stiffen beside her. Even Francis looked surprised at the use of Liv's formal name, and the coldness of Mary's tone.

"And to that end," Queen Mary continued smoothly. "I am pleased to say that I have found a match for you. I was planning to tell you later, but I suppose now is as good a time as any."

Liv's smile faded. "What?"

"Now that I am married, it is time for me to think of my ladies and your futures. You have been such a good friend to me all of my life. I would like to return the favor."

Liv fell back a step, her mouth opening. "But, Mary—"

"You mean, Your Majesty," Mary said.

Liv's face filled with color. "Yes, of course, Your Majesty." Liv glanced at the other Marys, who were all watching with similar expressions of shock. "But I would wish to remain in service to you, Your Majesty."

"I understand. You have always been so loyal and obliging. Which is why I am choosing to secure your future first, out of all my ladies. You do not have to thank me or try to change my mind. It is done."

"What do you mean, it is done?"

Mary gestured to a finely dressed man across the room. He wasn't particularly unappealing. He had two arms and two legs and two eyes. So what if those words were all Ari could come up with to describe him.

"That is the Duke of Shetland, from Norway," Queen Mary said. "He has recently lost his wife. He will see that you are well cared for for the rest of your life. I suggest you pack warmly, because he has regaled me with tales of his homeland, and the stories are mostly about how cold it is."

Ari felt her own chill spread through her body. This couldn't be. It couldn't.

"Your Majesty," Ari said, wondering what in the world she could say to stop this. She closed her eyes and pressed her hand to her forehead. "I'm seeing a future in which the Duke of Shetland is not well."

"Not well?" repeated Mary.

"He could die at any time," Ari said quickly.

They all swiveled around to inspect the duke again. At the moment, he was dancing. Or at least it was supposed to be dancing.

Some would call it bench-pressing one of the ladies in the air, his large arms pumping.

"The sickness will come on quite suddenly," Ari stammered. "Without any warning."

Mary's mouth twisted into what was meant to be a smile. "He seems well enough now. And if some tragedy were to befall him, Liv would find herself a rich and titled widow."

"But, Your Majesty," said Ari.

"This is a gift for my dear friend," insisted Mary. "She will leave in two days."

Liv drew herself up straight. "Queen Mary—"

Mary held up a hand. "I have appreciated your service. And I hope you will appreciate my gift to you. You are dismissed, the both of you. Enjoy the party. Eat some cake."

Liv staggered off as though she'd been run through with a sword. As Ari began to follow, she heard Francis say, "What was that all about? You're really sending Liv away? But I thought—"

"It's a kind way to remove her from my presence," Mary said.

A kind way? thought Ari, still too shocked to be properly indignant. She sank into her seat next to Liv.

"Did she actually just tell us to eat cake?" she sputtered.

"I'm not hungry," Liv said.

Before they could even begin to talk about it, King Henry was standing in front of the hall again.

Ari hoped there were not going to be more toasts. The *Not There* potion should be taking effect any moment now.

"My son Francis," he said, "and my other sons, Charles and Henry, and the de Guises, and you there, Prince Condé . . . follow me to the grand parlor for an even more exciting part of the evening."

The six men of royal blood exited the room behind Henry. After a few moments had passed, Mary stood up and addressed the crowd again.

"Ladies and gentlemen, please join us for a most spectacular journey."

Right then, servants rolled out long canvases along the floor. They were painted blue and white, and they resembled waves on the ocean. Other servants opened certain windows, which propped up the waves and made them appear as if they were in motion.

"The tides are coming our way, and so are the esteemed ships of the Argonauts." Queen Mary gestured to the doorway, where a large mechanical ship was approaching, swaying this way and that.

"See?" Flem said over Liv to Ari. "Ships!" Then she frowned. "I hope this doesn't have anything to do with your vision about the door." She eyed the door that the ship was moving through.

The crowd whooped and hollered at the sight. Ari felt seasick. She had no idea how it was moving; perhaps they had used a design of the late Leonardo da Vinci's? He was always inventing mechanical things that seemed to defy all earthly laws.

At the helm of this ship was Francis's youngest brother. He stood at the ship's wheel, turning it this way and that and occasionally looking out through a telescope.

"Alas, I do not see my golden fleece in this room. Crew!" Several stewards appeared on deck. "On to the next island!"

Ari hoped this meant there would be a lull in the entertainment during which she could talk to Liv, but as the ship left, an entire army of court jesters, jugglers, and flamethrowers overtook the dining hall. Ari had to take care to watch, lest her eyebrows be burned off.

In this way, ship after ship came sailing in, each captain talking about a golden fleece, adding some embellishing to the script, tales of islands they had been to and wars they had fought to get this far. And in between, an endless procession of performers. As the third ship left, a cavalcade of . . . poets swarmed in. This was Ari's chance. She leaned over to Liv. "You can't go away."

Liv sniffed and dabbed at the corner of her eye. "If that's what Mary has decided, I must. The final step for a lady-in-waiting is to find a suitable position in marriage. I am lucky." She sniffed. "Lucky she chose me first." The tears started to fall from her eyes. "Please excuse me."

Ari stood to follow her.

"No, don't cause a scene," Liv protested. "Your place is here with the queen. I will return."

"No." Ari reached for Liv's hand, but for the first time, Liv didn't take it. She hurried out of the room.

The fourth ship came and went. The fifth ship carried Francis at the helm, and although he blew a kiss to his new wife, and she a kiss back, he turned and sailed away as well.

When the sixth and final ship arrived, King Henry was at the helm. He held up his scope, peered this way and that, and finally landed on Queen Mary. "Ah, there she is. My golden fleece."

Ari was disgusted. The king had reduced Queen Mary to nothing more than an object to bring him power.

"Join me, my daughter-in-law. And together, we will unite France!" Cheers went up. "Scotland!" More cheers. "England!" More cheers. "Ireland!" More cheers. "And eventually all of Europe!"

This brought the wildest cheers of all.

But Ari couldn't bring herself to cheer. She watched numbly as Mary went to the ladder on the side of the boat and began to climb.

The queen was nearly to the top when a gut-wrenching scream silenced the room. Even the ship stopped tilting.

The horrible sound was coming from the king.

"My eyes! My eyes! I cannot see."

Guests looked around, wondering at first if this was part of the show. Ari didn't have to look. She knew exactly what was going on.

"My eyes! Catherine! I've been blinded!"

The plea for his wife was the first sign that something was terribly wrong.

Queen Catherine rose up. "Guards. Guards! Call for a physician at once. The king is ill."

"Is there a doctor in the house?" called out Ari, knowing there was no doctor who could help. Guards and servants scrambled in and out of the room. Within a few moments the court physicians arrived, for they were never far away, especially during colossal events, and this was by far the most colossal event the palace had seen in decades.

They held candles in front of King Henry's eyes. They covered one eye with a black patch and looked into the other. Then they switched eyes.

"What is it?" Queen Catherine asked.

Ari had to commend her for her acting abilities.

"Your Majesty," the head physician said. "We cannot see anything that would cause His Majesty to lose his vision."

"And yet, I can't bloody seeeeee!" the king called out in agony.

"I told you to stop doing *that* so much," said Catherine.

The entire room went quiet.

Normally Ari would have felt a sense of triumph. Her potion had worked. She should have been glad, proud even. But Mary was taking away Ari's brightest beacon, and she had done it so callously, without one bit of concern for Liv's feelings. As if all of Liv's years of service had earned her nothing except a loveless future in a sunless place.

It wasn't right, Ari thought. Liv couldn't get married. Not now.

EIGHTEEN
Francis

By the time Francis and Mary retired to his rooms, Francis was thoroughly torn between wanting to crash into bed (to sleep) and wanting to stay awake as long as possible so the day might last forever.

The door of Francis's chambers closed behind them. His shoulders sagged in relief. He was concerned about his father's sudden and completely unexpected blindness, but surely it would wear off soon. Just not too soon.

Beside him, Mary gave a small sigh that meant she was thinking the same thing. Francis smiled at her tremulously. Finally, they were (gulp) alone.

"Oh good, you're here."

They spun around to find the Cardinal of Lorraine sprinkling water on the bed.

"What are you doing?" Mary asked in alarm.

"Anointing your bed with holy water so that the consummation of your marriage will be pure." He said it like this should be
obvious. "Unfortunately, King Henry will not be here to observe,
and he has forbidden anyone else from observing in his stead.
However, I—and a few others from the house of Guise—will be
just outside the door. The kingdom must be assured that an heir is
on the way, you understand."

Francis and Mary exchanged glances. "Of course," she said,
before Francis could protest.

"I'll be right outside," the cardinal said. "Shout if you need
anything. I will hear." Then he was gone, and Francis and Mary
were alone.

Mary shuddered. "What a barbaric practice. Also, he wet the
bed. Who'd want to lie in the bed when it's damp?"

Francis glanced at the door. "What are we going to do? He's
going to camp out there all night if he thinks we haven't—you
know." Not that Francis didn't want to sleep with Mary. That is
to say, he did—sometimes desperately. But definitely not with an
audience, even if that audience was only listening. He didn't even
think it would be possible for him to do such a thing when he knew
someone was judging and measuring his worth as a husband and,
by extension, a king.

"You're right," Mary said. "We need a plan. How can we play
cards if someone's waiting for"—her cheeks flushed—"you know."

Francis knew.

"Maybe we should have eloped," he mused.

"Maybe you should never say that again, because that wedding was spectacular. Have you seen my gown?" She gestured down at herself.

Francis had seen it. "Didn't you feel self-conscious at all, with everyone looking at you?"

"Of course not. I was perfectly calm the entire time." Mary tilted her head. "Did *you* feel self-conscious?"

"Pretty much always," he said, "but to be honest, I got the feeling that no one noticed I was there. You were the star. You were the one everyone wanted to look at." Francis studiously avoided looking at the bed. And thinking about the bed. It was wet, anyway, he reminded himself. (Reader, it wasn't *that* wet.)

Mary's cheeks glowed with a blush. "You thought I was the star?"

"I've always thought so." And then he wondered if he'd had too much wine at the banquet, because that was something he defi nitely should not have said out loud. "What I mean to say is, you've always been the queen of Scotland, but today you were a bride, too, and the bride is always the star of the wedding, isn't she?"

Mary smiled again, her fingers grazing the massive jewel at her chest. "We do have one problem."

Francis's heart plunged downward. "What is that?"

"It took all of my ladies to dress me. I certainly can't get out of this by myself, and no matter what we do tonight, I need to be wearing something that's not my wedding gown."

For a moment, Francis envisioned helping her out of her dress.

He imagined the scent of her skin, the softness of her hair, the draw of her breath. He was supposed to help her, wasn't he? That was why they'd been left here together: so they could not wear clothes.

But no matter how much he might enjoy helping her remove the layers and layers of her wedding gown, that would signal . . . something. And they'd agreed that they would play cards tonight.

"You're right," he said. "The dress looks like a lot of work. I'll have your ladies summoned."

An odd look crossed Mary's face, like she'd expected him to say something else. "If you ask my uncle to send one of my ladies, will they think we're not . . . you know?"

Francis still knew.

"I'll tell him that I don't want to fumble and accidentally ruin the dress. It's too precious to risk me tearing out a button by accident. Anyone would believe that." Even Francis, although he knew that he would have been as careful and gentle as humanly possible.

Her lips parted, like she had something to say about that, but then she nodded. "Have them send for Liv—" Her expression darkened, as if she'd just remembered something unpleasant. "No, Hush. It'll have to be Hush."

"What happened with Liv?" He studied her face, worry crowding his heart.

"I don't want to talk about it tonight. This is our night." She pressed her lips into a line as she checked the curtains and the lock on the door. "You know what? Don't send for anyone. I can escape this myself. I will need a change of clothes, though."

Francis tilted his head in confusion while Mary climbed onto the bed, shoes and all, and then disappeared in a flash of light. A small mouse darted out from the yards of fabric before they touched the bed, and Francis lunged to whisk her to safety as the jewelry and heavy crown followed.

"You could have given me some warning," he said as he placed her on the footboard. "We can't have you getting crushed to death by your own crown."

Mary squeaked.

"That's true. You have indeed"—gulp—"undressed without help."

Before she could see how red his face was turning, he hurried to his wardrobe and looked through it for something that might fit Mary. He didn't have any dresses, which left pants as the only option. He held up a few of the clothes she'd admired before—the blue doublet and so on—but she gave annoyed squeaks and shook her head. (Which looked very silly coming from a mouse, and not very queenly, not that he would ever say such a thing to her.)

"Then all I have is a nightshirt."

Mary-the-mouse nodded.

"Good point," he said. "We will be going to sleep eventually." He dug through his armoire and produced two nightshirts, then laid one out on the bed for her. "I'll be in the other room."

When Mary-the-mouse scurried over to the clothes, Francis retreated into the next room and hurriedly changed out of his wedding attire, careful to fold the handkerchief she'd embroidered for him. *You and no other.* The words made his heart pound. Did she mean it? Did she see him that way?

Tracing his fingertips over the neat stitches, he tried not to think about Mary on the other side of the door, turning back into a human and donning the shirt he'd left her.

His. Shirt.

On her.

He swallowed hard and splashed cool water on his face. Then he waited for Mary to call him back. And waited some more. And waited. He rinsed his face again. What was taking so long?

"Francis?" Mary's voice was muffled by the door, but fortunately he'd been paying very close attention. He stepped back into the bedroom to find Mary human again and relocating the wedding gown and all the accompanying jewels. The white fabric of his shirt hung loose over her shoulders, giving him a glimpse of her smooth skin, and because she was taller than he, the hem fell to her knees rather than the middle of her calves, so whether Francis wanted it or not (reader, he did), he had a heart-stopping view of the graceful curves of her legs and delicate ankle bones, all the way down to her perfect toes.

It was getting really hard to breathe.

"Help me move everything off the bed. I have an idea."

Francis was having ideas, too.

"All right," he managed to say, scooping jewelry into his hands. "What's this plan of yours?"

"Uncle Charles is going to stay outside that door until he's satisfied we've—"

"I know," Francis said, suddenly feeling far less excited now that he remembered that a person was just outside. "What do you propose to do about it?"

"We'll get on the bed," Mary said, which made Francis instantly revert to his previous state, "and jump and yell."

Francis paused. "Like when we were children?"

"Not quite like when we were children." She finished arranging the dress on a chair. "We'll have to make it sound convincing."

"Oh." Francis deposited the jewelry and turned to face Mary. "Do you think that will make him go away?"

"There's only one way to find out." She took his hands and dragged him to the bed. "On you go."

Francis climbed up, uncomfortably aware of how little they were wearing as he offered a hand to her. He tried (and failed) to avoid noticing the view down her shirt.

Francis grabbed a pillow.

"What's that for?" Mary asked, adjusting her balance as the mattress shifted beneath them.

"Protection," Francis said quickly. "In case we fall."

"I'm not afraid of falling." Mary shifted from side to side for a moment, and then she jumped, forcing Francis to jump, too, or risk *actually* falling. A moment later, they were both jumping and laughing, making as much noise as they could possibly make. With each bounce, Francis felt his worries lift away. It was his wedding night, after all, and even if they weren't going to . . . you know . . . they were together and having fun.

Panting, Mary asked, "How long do you think we need to keep this up?"

"I'm not sure." According to his father, the event took hours. Francis assumed that was an exaggeration, and Mary already looked tired. She was breathing heavily and her eyes were weary from the long day. "Are you ready to stop?"

"Keep going!" she yelled. Then, softer: "Say something encouraging."

"This is the most fun I've ever had in my life!"

Mary laughed and kept jumping. "That's not really what I meant." Then she raised her voice again. "Incredible!"

"Fantastic!"

"Sensational!"

"Marvelous!"

"Outstanding!"

"Superb!"

"Magnificent!"

"Splendid!"

By then, they were both laughing too hard to keep going, and they collapsed onto the bed in a fit of giggles.

Francis struggled to catch his breath and turned to look at Mary.

She was gazing up at the ceiling, her skin flushed and her eyes bright, a smile illuminating her whole face. "That was fun," she said, turning to look at him, too. "I'd forgotten what it felt like, just having fun with you."

Their hands were so close together. All he had to do was move his fingers a small bit, and they would be touching. He could take her hand, like they used to do all the time, but now, in this context, it might mean something else, and he didn't want her to think he expected anything. One day they'd need to do this for real, because kings and queens had to produce heirs, but tonight . . .

He tried not to notice the way his nightshirt slid down her shoulder. He failed. So then he tried not to notice the way the fabric laid over the curves of her chest. He failed again. At that point, he had little choice but to find the pillow and hold it over himself once more.

"What are you thinking?" Mary whispered.

"About how fun that was," he lied. And then he felt bad for lying. "About the day we'll do this for real."

Her eyebrows raised. "Oh?" Then, embarrassingly, she noted the pillow and seemed to recognize what it was for. "*Oh.*"

He sat up and hugged his pillow, staring at the armoire. "Kings and queens don't usually sleep in the same room." Catherine and Henry actually slept on opposite sides of the palace now, and at this point, no one expected the king to even visit his wife. "It would be understandable if you wanted to return to your quarters now that we've—"

"I know." She climbed off the bed and padded barefoot to the door. She slid the bolt free and peeked out, but whatever she said, he couldn't hear. A moment later, Mary returned and touched his chin. "Eyes up, Francis."

He looked at her to find her with her arms stretched toward him. With her hair loose and wild from all their jumping, she looked like some kind of goddess of the sky.

"Come with me," she said. "Bring your pillow, if you want."

"What are we doing?" He followed her to the bearskin rug in front of the fire, the same one she'd asked about yesterday.

"You promised me a game of cards." She settled onto the rug, her legs tucked neatly to the side. Firelight glowed across her skin. "And I don't intend to let you back out of that."

A smile tugged at Francis's lips as he found the deck he'd left on the mantel ages ago. "As you wish, my queen-dauphine. What game would you like to play?"

"Whichever game I will win at."

"Ah, yes," Francis said, and smiled. "That would be all of them."

NINETEEN

Mary

Mary woke on the bearskin rug. It was dim inside Francis's chambers, as the drapes were still drawn, but there was a thin beam of light cutting across the floor now, and she could hear birds singing outside. It was morning. She stretched out her hand and gazed at the shining gold ring on her finger.

So. She was married.

The wedding had been an undeniable success. All in all, it had been as wonderful a wedding day as Mary could have imagined for herself.

With cowslips. She smiled and turned onto her side, and there was Francis, lying on his back with one arm cast over his head, his eyes closed, his dark gold lashes fanned against his cheeks. She shifted closer to him and propped herself onto her elbow to watch the rise and fall of his breath as he slept. Her chest felt tight, looking at his dear face, as familiar to her as her own, but it seemed different now—a man's face, perhaps, instead of a boy's.

He was her husband. She would make him happy, she resolved right then and there.

She couldn't stop staring at his slightly parted lips, remembering the way they'd felt against hers. She could lean over now, so easily, and kiss him again. It would be as natural a thing in the world to do: a wife kissing her husband. She wanted to so badly that her entire being seemed to ache.

But if she kissed him, he would surely wake, and then what would he do? In her mind she saw him as she had when she'd taken Ari's potion, smiling up at her, his blue eyes warm and inviting. She suspected there could be a lot of kissing, after that.

Then things between them would change, forever.

They were friends now, dear friends, best friends. They would become more.

But *more* meant heirs to her throne, and his.

She didn't know if she was ready for more.

His eyes fluttered open, pinning her.

"Hello," she said almost shyly.

"Hello," he murmured. "Did you sleep well?"

"Yes." Her back was a bit stiff from the hardness of the floor, but she'd slept more deeply last night than she had in weeks. "And you?"

"Quite well." He sat up slowly and stretched. "Although

perhaps next time we should try the bed." He froze. "I didn't mean . . . I mean . . ."

"Of course," she said, stifling a smile. "We will naturally be expected to . . ."

"Visit one another," he finished for her. "At night."

"For the sake of appearances," she said.

"But last night didn't go so badly, did it? We survived."

"Thanks to you," she admitted. "It was fun."

He nodded. "So would you like to . . ."

". . . visit you again?"

"Just to keep up appearances," he said lightly.

"Yes, of course. To keep up appearances. Perhaps tonight, even?"

"Excellent. Hopefully this time there won't be anyone listening at the door." Almost absent-mindedly he lifted his hand to tuck an errant strand of her hair behind her ear, his fingers brushing her cheek.

Mary was suddenly aware that all she was wearing was a nightshirt. His nightshirt. "I should . . . return to my chambers soon. I have many things to attend to today."

His hand dropped. "What things?"

"I must see if my lady Bea has returned, with news from my mother." She rose quickly, went to the door, and peered out. At her feet she discovered her purple robe, neatly folded. And beside that, a curled-up spaniel.

"Good morning, dear," Mary said.

"Bark!" said Flem. In an instant she had scampered into Francis's room and was jumping and shimmying around him, yipping excitedly.

Mary snatched up her robe and retreated back into the room, closing the door. When she turned around again, now sufficiently covered, she found Flem enthusiastically licking Francis's face.

"Well, this is a bit awkward," he said, trying to politely keep the dog (who he knew quite well was actually a girl) off his lap.

"Down, girl!" Mary said, mortified. "Come."

Flem ignored her. Possibly because Francis had begun to scratch behind one of her ears. Which made one of her legs beat at her side just so.

"I'm sorry. In that form it's hard for her to show proper restraint," Mary explained. "And she likes you."

"Bark!" said Flem approvingly.

"I'm glad to hear it," Francis said.

Then the dog/girl proceeded to sniff at his crotch.

"FLEM!" Mary's face flamed. "Come here at once!"

Flem reluctantly returned to Mary's side, tail wagging.

"I'm so sorry," Mary said.

Francis rubbed at the back of his neck, smiling sheepishly. "It's all right."

"I should . . ."

"Yes. But I'll see you later?"

"Of course." She was struck by the urge to cross the room and hug him, to thank him, just for being himself, but with Flem there it felt like too public a display. So Mary simply smiled. "Good day to you, husband," she said.

He gave a formal bow, which looked quite silly and adorable with him only wearing his nightshirt.

"Good day to you. Wife."

"You should really exhibit better manners," Mary chided as the queen and her dog walked back to Mary's chambers. "That was embarrassing."

"Yip!" said Flem.

"Things will change—they have changed, I mean, now that Francis and I are wed. I'll be visiting his chambers frequently, I imagine. Perhaps, in time, we'll even share the same rooms." Her heart quickened at the thought. They might even share the same bed. It would be unusual for a royal couple not to keep separate chambers, but not unheard of.

Flem gave a lusty howl.

"It's not like that," Mary said. "We didn't actually . . . you know."

Flem whined.

"Well, we couldn't very well do it with my uncle standing right outside, could we? Did you know, he actually anointed Francis's bed with holy water? And he was listening! I could just picture him with his ear pressed against the door."

"Growl," said Flem.

"Right? So we bounced around on the bed a bit, like children,

217

so my uncle would think we were . . . you know . . . doing our duty, and then we played cards, and we talked." Mary was grateful that Francis hadn't brought up any serious topics, like Liv again, or the treaty with the uncles. "It was nice."

"Woof!" said Flem.

"And we'll get to . . . you know . . . eventually. I think. But we won't really need heirs until Francis is king, and that's years away. So we have loads of time."

As if on cue, King Henry stumbled out of the dining hall with his arm slung around an uncomfortable manservant. The king had apparently recovered his sight. "I see horses!" he bellowed. "I see banners! I see trumpets and cheering!"

"You *see trumpets*, Sire?" asked the servant.

"Oh, I hear them, too. Mark me, it will be the greatest jousting tournament the world has ever known!"

Clearly the king was on to his next lavish "vision."

Mary and Flem dashed into an adjoining hallway before Henry could spot them. Then they ran all the way back to Mary's room. Once inside, they came upon Mary's ladies already assembled: Liv and Hush, that is. Mary's heart sank. Still no Bea. And where was Ari?

Mary swallowed. "How are you this morning? I trust that you all enjoyed yourselves at last night's festivities?"

In a flash, Flem was a girl again. "Some of us enjoyed ourselves more than others," she said, looking pointedly at Liv, whose face remained totally impassive.

"It was a beautiful night, Your Highness," said Hush. "One we'll always remember."

Mary twisted the gold ring on her finger—a replacement, now, for the amethyst one.

"She and Francis just played cards all night," Flem reported a bit glumly. "But they seemed cozy enough this morning."

"Manners, Flem," Mary warned, and Flem dropped her eyes to the floor with a suppressed smile.

Once her ladies had dressed her, and Hush was seeing to her hair, Mary's gaze flitted again to the window and the empty perch.

"No one has seen Bea?" Mary asked.

"No," Liv answered softly. "And we've had no other word."

"I could go sniff around for her," offered Flem.

"All right." Mary couldn't imagine that Bea would be close enough that Flem would catch her scent without leaving the palace grounds, but there was no harm in her trying. "But please be careful, dear."

"I'm always careful." The light flashed.

But that was exactly what Bea had said before she disappeared.

Liv opened the door for Flem the spaniel to run out.

"And where is Ari?" Mary asked when the dog was gone.

"I don't know," Liv replied softly. "I haven't seen her this morning."

Mary reasoned that Ari was probably off stewing over the impromptu announcement of Liv's impending nuptials to the Norwegian lord. It was unfortunate that Liv and Ari must be separated.

But it was necessary, Mary thought grimly. They'd all known the day would come when Liv would have to marry a man—even Liv herself had always seemed resigned to the idea—but now, because of her disloyalty, that day would have to come sooner rather than later.

"The rest of you may go, as well," Mary said. "We could all use a day of rest."

"Thank you, Your Majesty." Hush placed one last pin in the simple knot at the base of Mary's neck, and took her leave.

But Liv lingered. "I'd prefer to stay, if I could. There are some things I'd like to discuss."

Of course Liv would want to talk about it.

"Not now," Mary said lightly. "I'm going to write a letter to my mother and send it the old-fashioned way. At the very least we can find out if Bea ever made it to her." But it would take a very long time, weeks, perhaps months, to receive a reply.

Liv swallowed. "I know you're worried about Bea. We're all worried. But—"

"Perhaps she was betrayed," Mary said smoothly. "By someone whom she thought she could trust."

Liv's face grew pale, her eyes wide as they met Mary's cold gaze. "Mary. I—"

"How long have you been spying on me for my uncles?" Mary asked.

"Only a few weeks," Liv answered in a quavering voice. "I swear I didn't mean to . . . I never . . ."

"What exactly do they have over you?"

Liv bowed her head. "My sister has gotten into something of a scandalous situation. She's fallen in love with an Eðian. If anyone were to find out, the entire family would be ruined."

Mary tamped down any sympathy. She had to be hard. She had to be a queen. "You could have come to me about it."

Liv shook her head wildly. "I wanted to, but your uncles said if I told you. . . ."

"Do they know about . . . the mouse?" Mary asked.

"No. They do not even suspect that you might be . . . They think of Eðians as a different class from themselves. And I would never tell them. I promise I am still your friend, Mary."

Mary's eyes burned, but she didn't allow herself the luxury of tears. She swallowed hard. "I can no longer trust you, so I can't have you with me anymore," she said sadly. "Now, please go. You have your own wedding to plan for."

Liv took a breath like she meant to argue but then thought better of it. She nodded. "Yes. All right."

When she was gone Mary wiped at her eyes and took a deep breath. Then she went to her desk and began to compose a new letter.

Dear Mama . . . She paused. How would she even describe the wedding to her mother? There was so much. And how would she slip in a question about Bea that only her mother would be able to decipher?

"Why are you being so cruel?"

Mary looked up, startled. Ari had come into the room, standing with her fists clenched by her sides.

"Cruel?" Mary asked. "Cruel to whom?"

"To Liv. You're marrying her off to a stranger."

Mary rubbed at her temple. She had a headache coming on, and Excedrin hadn't been invented yet. "I am doing what's best for her."

She really thought she was. Of course, she was furious at Liv, but she wasn't being vindictive. Mary had chosen a good match for her, a man who Mary felt could be well suited to her headstrong friend, who would provide for her and even care for her, perhaps, in a place where she'd be safe and far away from the influence of the de Guises.

"What's *best* for her is to stay here with . . . you," Ari said.

Mary sat back and eyed Ari appraisingly. "Perhaps," she said slowly, with authority, "you don't know Liv as well as I do."

"I probably don't, but I know that she loves you," Ari burst out. "She is loyal to you, and true. She said you were a family, and you would take care of us, always. And now you're throwing her away!"

Mary blinked back more sudden infuriating tears. She drew herself to her full height and leveled Ari with a steady queen-like gaze. "Liv knows how things are done here, and you do not. It is expected that I should arrange marriages for my ladies. That is why their parents agreed to part with them so long ago, so that they might marry well and bring honor and fortune to their families back in Scotland." This was all true, although it was more customary to arrange these marriages to men within the French court, so that the ladies could remain by Mary's side. But that wasn't prudent with Liv, now. She couldn't be trusted, Mary told herself again. She must be sent away. "That is the promise I made to them, and I will see my ladies wed to men I deem appropriate for them. All of my ladies. I suppose that now applies even to you."

Ari's face drained of color. "But, Mary, I beg you—"

"You are being too familiar, Ari, to come to plead with me on her behalf. I know you are fond of Liv, but she has accepted my decision. So should you."

Ari was scowling now. Her fists opened and closed again helplessly. Then, without another word, she spun and fled the room. The door banged shut behind her.

Mary let out a breath. She didn't want to send her best friend away, but what could she do? Her uncles were using Liv to spy on her.

She bit her lip. Her uncles' actions were so underhanded it was hard to see them as anything now but villains. On the other hand, if they had wanted to depose Mary as queen, or harm her in any way, they could have easily done so at any time. It even made a kind of sense that they would employ one of her household to observe her and report back to them, so that they would always know exactly what was going on in Mary's life. But it still hurt.

She couldn't trust anyone but Francis now, which made her feel lonely. She cleared her throat. For a few minutes she tried to concentrate again on writing a letter to her mother, but her mind kept wandering back to Liv. Finally she sighed and set aside the quill.

She would go speak to her uncles. Perhaps, if she got it all out in the open, she could find a solution that wouldn't involve sending Liv to a foreign country. Perhaps, if she gave the uncles a chance to explain themselves, she could release Liv from the hold they had over her. And then perhaps Mary could forgive her, and they could all move on.

They were a family, as Ari had said. And Mary had promised to take care of them. And so she meant to.

At her uncles' door she stopped, suddenly nervous. She would have to be cautious with her words—revealing that she was aware that Liv had been informing on her but not revealing how she had come to this knowledge, making sure all the while that it was clear that Liv herself hadn't told her.

It would be tricky.

It might be outright impossible. Her uncles were shrewd and discerning men.

Her fist hovered in the air in front of their door, but she did not knock.

She heard them talking, inside. About the wedding.

"It was lovely. It went off even better than we planned," Uncle Charles was saying.

"It was perfect," agreed Uncle Francis. "She was perfect."

Mary swallowed. That word—*perfect*—had been applied to her so often: the perfect child, the perfect queen, the perfect girl. It was a heavy word. She rather hated it.

"And now we're moving smoothly along. She and Francis are made for each other. You should have heard them last night. Their coupling was unusually enthusiastic."

Mary's face burned. She pressed it to the cool oak door. Which helpfully allowed her to better hear this mortifying conversation.

"Good, good," said Uncle Francis. "I'd be surprised if she's not expecting within a month or two. Everything is going along swimmingly. And as we've already seen, the boy will follow Mary's lead."

"The seed has been planted with the king, as well. He just announced the 'epic royal joust' a few moments ago in the throne room." Uncle Charles sighed heavily. "The man is insufferable, but nothing if not predictable. He feels he needs to reassert his manhood after his show of infirmity at last night's dinner."

"And what was that about, I wonder?"

"I do not know, but I suspect Queen Catherine had something to do with it. She's constantly scheming to wrest away some power for herself. Thankfully we won't have to deal with her too much longer."

Mary's scalp prickled. What did they think was going to happen to Queen Catherine?

"And what of Montgomery?" asked Uncle Charles. "He's still on board?"

"Montgomery will fall in line. Anyway, let's to Mary to offer our congratulations."

Mary scrambled away from the door and then walked quickly, nearly running but not quite, back to her chambers. Then she threw herself into her chair by the fire and picked up her embroidery, her mind racing. She might be a queen, but she was beginning to feel like a pawn. But what could she do about it?

When her uncles arrived, she did not mention Liv, or that she had discovered anything out of the ordinary. She just smiled and nodded and continued being perfect.

As she always did.

TWENTY

Ari

Ari paced the empty laboratory. Mary was as bad as the rest of them, she decided. The Queen of Scots had proven herself to be as vindictive and manipulative as everyone else in the palace. Sending Liv away—without cause! Without reason!—was just plain mean. Within two days, Ari had gone from finally feeling like she had friends, a place where she belonged, to . . . this. This nothingness.

She had to *do* something. Liv was set to leave for Norway tomorrow. But what could Ari do about it? Queen Mary was one of the most powerful people at French court.

Ari stopped pacing. She did happen to know someone else just as powerful as Mary. *More* powerful, some might say.

Queen Catherine. The *actual* queen of France.

Ari took a drop of her *Worries Be Gone* potion (she'd started

227

keeping a vial on her at all times, what with her stress levels now constantly through the roof) and marched herself toward Queen Catherine's chambers. Along the way, she heard the hubbub about King Henry's upcoming jousting tournament. The entire palace was talking about it.

"All the best knights are participating," a lady said.

"I heard the king himself will ride," said another.

"Fifty livres on the king's victory," laughed another. "I'm sure to win that."

Ari agreed. The king was bound to win, if only because he was the king. That was the way of royals: they always got what they wanted.

But not this time. Ari would get *her* way.

When she reached the queen's chambers, the guard announced her arrival.

Ari walked in, keeping her spine straight, her voice steady. "Your Majesty, I—"

"Oh, good, it's you. I'd like you to make a new concoction for me. I heard one of your potions turned a girl green. I'd like to put in an order."

Ari swallowed. "Actually, I've come to ask you for a favor."

Queen Catherine narrowed her eyes. "I do not make a habit of doing favors for servants."

Ugh. Royalty. They were all the same. Ari clenched her jaw. She had to be strong. "A trade, then," she said. "I know something you don't know. But before I tell you, I need something in return. Queen

Mary has recently betrothed one of her ladies-in-waiting, Lady Livingston—I'm sure you know her—to a Norwegian lord. She doesn't wish to go, and I thought perhaps that you might intervene."

The queen let out a little snort of laughter. Not the nice kind of laughter. "You mean to bargain with me?"

"Um," Ari said.

"You work for me, serf."

Ouch. *Serf* hurt. But it did remind Ari of her place. She was not a real lady. But she didn't care. She had to do something for Liv.

"I mean, please, Your Majesty," she said. "I'm not asking for myself."

Queen Catherine's voice went low and dangerous. "You will tell me what you know. This is not optional. I am your queen."

Ari gulped. Then she gulped again, for good measure. "After all I've done for you—" she started, but the queen lifted a hand to silence her.

"How about this bargain?" The queen clapped as if this was a fun game to her. "You tell me the information that you think I would like to know, and I let you keep your fingernails attached to your fingers."

This was not going how Ari had hoped.

"Ooh!" exclaimed the queen. "Would you like to try my very uncomfortable rack I just had installed in the dungeon? I could call the guards right now. Or a hot poker. I haven't used one of those in ages. Or—"

"Queen Mary is a mouse!" Ari blurted.

Catherine froze. "What did you say?"

"I said . . . I said Queen Mary is a . . ." Why did the word *mouse* suddenly not sound right? Mouse. *Mouse.* House. Cows. Language was a strange thing. "Queen Mary is a mouse. Some of the time. That is to say, she's an Eðian."

There was a long moment of silence. "A mouse, you say." The queen poured herself a goblet of wine. "This would've been good information to have before . . . I don't know . . . *yesterday*? When did you discover this?"

Ari lowered her head. "Um, yesterday. Or the day before. Or the day before that. I can't remember. It's a blur."

The queen took a long drink. She glanced at the corner, where the dessert tray with the biscuit had been. And at the tiny hole the biscuit-stealing mouse had disappeared into. She turned back to Ari, a terrifying gleam in her eye.

"I sent you to watch over Queen Mary and ensure she had no secrets that would endanger the kingdom," she said slowly. "Now you tell me, *after* she has married my son, that she has the most perilous secret of all, which would destroy her and gravely injure the reputation and security of my son and the French crown."

"But I did give you that potion to prevent the king from witnessing the consummation last night," Ari pointed out.

"By *blinding* him and creating a scene at my son's wedding." Queen Catherine shook her head. "Aristotle de Nostradame, your services are no longer required at my court. Pack your things and leave the palace at once."

Ari's heart turned black and then burned to ash, and then

she wasn't breathing. She had always known her position as Mary's lady-in-waiting was temporary, but she'd hoped it was a rung on a ladder to becoming an official adviser. She couldn't be *fired*, on top of losing Liv . . .

"No!" Ari shouted. "No, you can't fire me!"

The queen jerked back and put her hand to her heart. "Excuse me? Were you *hoping* to find yourself in the dungeon, after all? I could provide actual fire."

"No," Ari rasped. "No, but my father—"

"Your father hasn't given me an accurate vision in months. You and I both know that he's lost his touch. He is no longer of use to me, so he, too, must go."

"But, Your Majesty . . . What will I tell Queen Mary? I can't simply—"

"I will deal with Mary." The queen smiled grimly. "Now get out of my sight."

"Please," Ari said.

"Leave. Or die," the queen said.

Ari fled the queen's chambers. She felt as though she were caught in the middle of a horrible dream.

She'd gambled and lost everything—not only her love and her job, but her entire future.

Numbly, she returned to the laboratory. This time her father was there, working on his quatrains again, mumbling incoherently to himself. For a moment she just stood and watched him scribble onto the parchment. How could she tell him? What would he think of her when he heard what she'd so foolishly done?

She started to move about the laboratory, wrapping up glass vials and stacking cauldrons. After a time, Greer appeared in the doorway. "What are you doing?" her assistant asked.

"Packing," Ari answered.

"Are we going somewhere? Where?"

A lump rose in Ari's throat. "I don't know. Queen Catherine is angry with me. She has ordered me to leave the palace. You should . . ." Her eyes met Greer's. "You should go immediately and find another position."

"I see," Greer said softly. Then the girl began to cry, not a gentle flow of tears but a loud, wailing sob. She clapped her hands over her mouth and ran from the room.

"How's that?" came her father's voice from behind her. "What's this about the queen?"

Ari crossed to kneel in front of her father. Then she told him the entire sordid story, including every detail (except the detail about Ari kissing Liv in this very laboratory—right over there, in fact). For once, her father seemed to be fully listening. His filmy blue eyes focused on her intently, and when she was finished, she was confused, because he smiled.

"Papa? Did you hear what I said?"

"Of course, dear child. But do you realize what this means?"

"Um, it means we're fired?"

"It means that my visions were correct. You just fulfilled the third of them."

"Huh?"

"Deadly biscuits. Traps. Betrayal," he counted off on his fingers. "There was that deadly biscuit in the queen's chamber," he said.

"Was it deadly, though?" Ari asked.

"Hush, child. Then we saw a mouse—a literal mouse!—eating said deadly biscuit, and the queen responded by ordering that mousetraps be set all over the palace to combat the rodent infestation. Literal traps! And now you've discovered that Queen Mary is herself a mouse. And you told the queen. There's the betrayal." He patted her hand excitedly. "Don't you see? It all came true. And that means that I've still got it!"

He jumped nimbly to his feet with an energy she hadn't seen from him in years. "I'm going to need more parchment!"

"That's wonderful, Papa, but did you hear the part where we have to leave the palace?"

"Bah!" he said. "That's not going to happen. Trust me. I know."

"You know?"

"It's Queen Catherine's favorite threat. Besides, there's still the thing with the lions."

"The lions?" Ari couldn't decide if he was now completely lucid or if he'd lost his mind altogether. "But what about the queen?"

"Queen Catherine won't always have power over us," he said distractedly. "Can you order me more ink, dear child?"

"But, Papa . . ."

"You know what I'm craving right now? Biscuits. I bet you

could get us some biscuits, now that they're safe. I've quite missed them."

"But, Papa, let's get back to the queen," Ari said. "How does she not have power over us? She's the queen of France."

"Only while she's married to the king of France," her father pointed out.

Ari frowned. "You predict that she'll divorce Henry?"

Nostradamus's nose wrinkled. "Good gracious no, child. Divorce is only something people do in England."

He wasn't making sense. The only other way for Catherine to stop being married to the king of France was if Henry were to—"You think the king will die?"

"He dies a cruel death!" Nostradamus said cheerfully.

Ari shook her head. It was a preposterous idea. Everyone knew that the king was as healthy as a bull. "Don't be silly, Papa," she said. "The king's going to live forever."

TWENTY-ONE
Francis

"The king is dead."

Francis swayed on his feet. He'd misunderstood the physician's words, surely. The king wasn't dead. The king was as healthy as a bull, aside from his raging alcoholism and the variety of poxes and other downstairs problems that likely plagued him. Everyone said he'd live for years and years. *Everyone* said it. All the time.

"Francis?" Mary touched his shoulder. There was a murmur of stricken conversation behind her, but Francis barely heard anything over the pounding of his heart. The worried faces lined up outside the medical tent were starting to blur. "Eyes up, Francis."

Eyes up? His eyes had been up all day, watching the tournament with the rest of the royal household. "Watching," we should say, because Francis had never been all that interested in sports that could maim someone for life.

Or kill someone.

Like the king.

There was no way the king could be dead. Yes, he'd insisted on jousting in the tournament, because what a show *that* would be. Yes, he'd lost the first bout. Yes, he'd insisted on trying again (that first one had been a warm-up and therefore didn't count). Yes, both Catherine and Diane had tried to talk him out of it. Yes, the king had gotten his way and the Count of Montgomery had been ordered to rearm.

But Francis hadn't been truly watching any of that. He'd been, as he had all day, watching Mary. Gazing, more accurately, and thinking about how later she'd come to his rooms and they'd talk for hours until they fell asleep. They wouldn't even have to sneak. Because they were married!

Then he'd squirmed and pulled his doublet so that the hem lay over his lap. Not for any reason, of course. Just because it was more comfortable like that.

He'd very quickly gone back to admiring Mary's profile, the way afternoon light shone through her auburn hair, and how she held herself as though she were a queen.

She *was* a queen. And she looked the part every moment of every day. How was he ever supposed to be like that?

Fortunately, he would have a lot of time to practice, because King Henry would live a long, long time.

Except the royal physician was now saying the king was dead.

The words were a roar in Francis's ears. The world started to spin. Time stuttered, and it was hard to say how long he'd been standing here, swaying here, resisting those four awful words.

But they kept burrowing inside him, deeper and deeper, like a song he couldn't shake.

The king is dead.

That couldn't be right.

Sure, the second match hadn't gone Henry's way. Francis hadn't been watching, as we've established, because he'd been completely distracted by the way Mary was breathing. So elegant. So steady. So, well, breathy. Then, completely out of nowhere, she'd gasped. (Mary had actually been watching the match.) Francis had delighted in this, because Mary had a delightful gasp, but then everyone else had gasped, too.

Then he'd followed all the eyes to the joust, just in time to see the king fall from his horse. His armor had clanged against the hard-packed dirt, the horse had bucked, and the Count of Montgomery had dismounted and thrown off his helm. Squires and physicians had run onto the field, obscuring Francis's view of the king, but the gist was this: the lance had struck King Henry's chest, then slid up under the visor of his helm, where it splintered into the king's face. They said the shards could have pierced his brain, but they wouldn't know for sure for a few more days.

Grimly, morbidly, Francis had envisioned sitting at his father's bedside with the rest of the family, praying for the king's eventual recovery. Then he'd imagined his mother sweeping in with some kind of cure concocted by Nostradamus and Ari, and all the tiny slivers from the lance would dissolve into harmlessness, leaving King Henry with a scar worth bragging about.

But the king had been carried into the medical tent an hour ago. Francis had been waiting outside with Mary, Charles IX, Henry III, Queen Catherine, Mistress Diane, Cardinal Charles, Duke Francis, several of Mary's ladies, and a ton of other people who thought they were important enough to loiter nearby. This— the king dying within the hour of his accident—wasn't supposed to be how it happened.

"The king is dead," people murmured. The words rippled through the crowd. "The king is dead."

Then, horribly:

"Long live the king!" someone called. "Long live the king!" And before Francis realized, it had become a chant.

The king is dead. Long live the king.

It was the most confusing thing in the whole world, because the king was *dead*. How could he live any longer?

Francis's breath caught in his chest, rattling there as his vision grayed out, then back in. Faintly, he saw ladies helping Queen Catherine to one of the nearby benches. Someone fanned her, like more air would help. Mistress Diane was weeping not far away. She held her hands against her chest as she spoke hurriedly to her ladies. Without the king's favor, she would have to leave court.

"Francis?" Mary squeezed his arm. "Francis, you have to say something. Everyone is waiting."

Hadn't he been screaming this whole time? It seemed like he should have been.

"Help him sit," the Duke of Guise said. "The dauphin is too pale."

"Just breathe," Mary whispered. "Breathe through it. Do not sit. Do not cry. Do not reveal anything of what you feel inside."

What? Sitting was probably the best thing he could do right now.

That chant was still going, though: *The king is dead! Long live the king!*

"You must show strength," Mary whispered. "Stand straight up, just for right now."

The king is dead! Long live the king! The chant went on and on, the Duke of Guise and the Cardinal of Lorraine the loudest of all. Then, as though this were some kind of waking nightmare, they knelt right there in the muck. Mary's uncles first, followed by her ladies, Francis's younger brothers, and out and out until everyone around him was bent in submission. Even Mary herself had lowered into a graceful curtsy, her head bowed.

No. No no no.

At once, he understood why Mary hadn't wanted him to sit yet. And he understood the apparent contradiction in the chant, because it wasn't a contradiction at all.

The king is dead! That part was about King Henry.

Long live the king! That was about Francis. *King* Francis now.

He swayed as gray fogged his vision again. He tried to breathe through it, tried to blink it away, but suddenly he couldn't tell up from down or even hear the chanting he knew was still going on.

Help, he tried to say, but no sound passed his lips. He'd already fainted.

TWENTY-TWO 〔Mary〕

"Give him space," Mary said. "Please."

A handful of courtiers lifted Francis, limp as a rag doll, but they didn't seem to know where to put him. Not in the medical tent, obviously. Because the king's body was in there.

Henry's body, Mary silently corrected. Because now Francis was the king.

Oh, dear. She was feeling a bit faint, herself.

Catherine rushed over. Her face was pale as paper, but her expression was calm. "What has happened?"

"I don't know," Mary wanted to answer. It seemed so impossible to her. The king—Henry, not Francis—was the most vivacious person Mary knew. Say what you will about him, but Henry had definitely tried to live his life to the fullest. An hour ago he'd been laughing and bellowing out orders and guzzling wine and sweating under the sun. And now . . .

"Has Francis . . . fainted?" Catherine asked.

Mary didn't like something in the queen's—the former queen's—tone. There was an underlying criticism in it, of Francis being weak. Mary straightened. "He was overcome. It's too much for any man to bear. The death of his beloved father. And the sudden weight of the crown."

She was being metaphorical, of course. It would be days before Francis had to wear the literal crown.

"Your Highness," grunted one of the courtiers. Oh, yes, they were still carrying Francis. "Where should we take him?"

"Over here," she said, and directed the men to a shaded spot under a willow tree. They laid Francis gently in the soft grass. Mary dropped down beside him. She smoothed his hair and stroked his cheek. His eyes fluttered, then opened. He gazed up at her warmly for a moment, and then he remembered. His brow rumpled.

"Mary," he murmured. "I had the most horrible dream." He gazed up at her. "No. It wasn't a dream."

"It wasn't."

"He's really dead."

She nodded mutely. "I'm so sorry, Francis." Tears burned her eyes. Henry, for all his faults, had been a father to her, too. The only one she'd ever known. But she didn't allow herself to weep on her own account just now. Francis needed her to be strong.

"How did such a thing happen?" Francis whispered. "I wasn't looking."

"It was Montgomery," Mary said, and then her blood ran cold.

Montgomery. Her uncles had been talking about Montgomery only yesterday. *Montgomery will fall in line*, is what Uncle Charles had said.

Montgomery would fall in line for what?

Her breath caught. Had Montgomery killed the king on purpose?

But Montgomery had protested, hadn't he, when the king wanted to joust with him again? He'd been reluctant.

Hadn't he? Or had he merely been *acting* reluctant? Had he known that protesting a rematch would only make Henry more determined to have one?

Had Montgomery been working at her uncles' behest? Had Uncle Charles and Uncle Francis (gulp) assassinated the king?

And why would they do such a thing?

Mary knew why. Her uncles always worked for Mary's benefit. And killing the king would be to her benefit. An hour ago, she was the queen of faraway Scotland. Now she was the queen of Scotland *and* France.

"Mary," Francis said.

"I'm here." She grasped his hand. "You must . . . you must get up now. You must show everyone that you're all right."

"I'm not all right. Mary, I don't want to be . . . I can't be—"

"You mustn't say that," Mary said. "You must be king."

His jaw clenched. "Fine."

She helped him to his feet. He didn't let go of her hand. "Stay with me," he said. "Please."

"Of course." This was her place, by Francis's side. It had always been her place.

The next few hours went by in a blur. They retreated back to the palace, where they withdrew into Francis's chambers, allowing no one entry but her ladies. Francis passed the time sitting at the window, staring out at nothing. Or staring into the fire. Or staring at Mary, which made her nervous.

Because deep down, she really was starting to wonder if the king's death was somehow her fault.

There was a knock at the door. Hush went to open it, and there were Mary's uncles. They were trying to look solemn, but they couldn't help it. They were nearly grinning. She stepped out into the hall to speak with them.

"How is the king?" Uncle Charles asked.

Mary's chin lifted. "He's shaken, naturally. None of us could ever have expected King Henry to be killed so suddenly. It's quite a shock."

"Yes, it's a great tragedy," said Uncle Francis. "Everyone expected that Henry would live for years and years to come." He exchanged a knowing glance with Uncle Charles. "But tragedies do happen."

"The important thing now, dear," said Uncle Charles, "is for you to be there for Francis. You have the benefit of years of experience in being the monarch of a country. He listens to you in all things, so you must tell him what to do. You must guide him."

Mary swallowed. "I suppose."

Uncle Charles patted her head like she was a dog. (Nothing against dogs, of course, some of our favorite characters are dogs.) "I have no doubt that you are capable of handling this great responsibility. You are the queen of two countries now."

"And perhaps, quite soon, a third," added Uncle Francis. Meaning England, of course.

Mary suddenly felt very tired.

"We must have the coronation as soon as possible," said Uncle Charles. "And be sure that you are crowned alongside your husband, so that you will present a united front."

"I don't wish to think about the coronation right now," Mary said stiffly. "This is a time of sorrow, of mourning. I am here to comfort Francis. That is all."

"Of course," said Uncle Francis. "We'll talk later about the arrangements that must be made."

She bade them farewell and shut the door.

She closed her eyes. She wished with all of her heart that she could write to her mother. What would Mary de Guise advise her to do now? But Bea still hadn't returned and her mother hadn't even received Mary's other letter yet.

Mary was on her own.

Except for Francis. She hurried back to his side.

"So what's the all-important news from the hall?" Francis said.

"What?"

"You went into the hall. What happened there?"

"Oh. I spoke to my uncles. They send their deepest condolences."

Francis rubbed at his eyes. "They must be distressed, to know that I am now the king. I don't think they've ever liked me."

"Actually, they—"

She almost told him about what she'd overheard them saying yesterday, concerning Montgomery. About her suspicions. Her doubts.

But Francis had enough to deal with.

"They do like you," she said, instead. "They seem quite optimistic, in fact, at the prospect of you being king. And they said I must help you, in any way I can. Which of course I will. You're not alone, Francis. We can bear this burden together."

She reached and took his hand. He squeezed it.

"Yes, thank you," he said. "I don't know what I would do without you, Mary. I really don't."

She twisted her wedding ring around her finger. Her uncles were cunning. They had tricked her. They had spied on her. They'd blackmailed her dearest friend. (Right then all of her anger toward Liv melted away, and Mary resolved to break off the engagement with the Norwegian lord. She needed her friend. She needed to forgive her.) But the question remained: would her uncles stoop to regicide?

She bit her lip so hard she tasted blood. Yes. Yes, they most certainly would. The mention of Montgomery could not be a coincidence.

Her uncles had arranged for the king to be murdered.

All for her.

TWENTY-THREE

Ari

"Papa," Ari said, gently touching Nostradamus's shoulder. "Papa, wake up."

Her father opened his eyes. "Galileo?"

Sigh. "It's still just Aristotle, Papa. You have to get up now. It's time to leave.".

"Leave?" Nostradamus's bushy white eyebrows furrowed. "But I'm quite comfortable here, thank you."

"Queen Catherine has expelled us from the palace. You remember, Papa? And now all our bags are packed, and we're ready to go back to Mama and the house."

If they were still at the house, which the crown had always paid for.

If they couldn't stay there, she didn't know where they'd go. There wasn't a lot of available, affordable housing for a famous ex-prognosticator, his failure of a daughter, wife, and five other children. Ari had heard that Calais was nice this time of year.

Nostradamus sat up. "I told you, Catherine cannot expel us if she's no longer the queen."

Ari nodded. "Yes, but last I checked, Catherine still is the queen, Papa. So we must go."

There was a knock at the door, and Greer slipped inside, her expression grave.

She'd been out job hunting all morning.

"Did you have any luck?" Ari asked. She gulped. She was going to miss Greer. Who else would be willing to try every single one of her potions? "Do you need me to write you a recommendation?"

The ex-assistant shook her head. "No. I— No one's told you, have they?"

"No one's told us what?" Ari tried to exchange glances with Nostradamus, but he just looked expectantly at Greer. "What's happened?"

"It's the king," Greer said quietly. "He's dead."

"See?" said Nostradamus. "I told you so."

Ari sank down onto the sacks of oats as Greer related exactly what had happened to the king. It was not good. It was also exactly as her father had predicted. Ari was a little jealous.

"Congratulations," said Nostradamus to Greer when she'd finished speaking. "You're hired again. Now can you make me a cup of tea?"

"Yes, sir." Greer flashed a relieved grin. "Thank you, sir.

Right away." She started digging around in the stacks of boxes to find the teacups and a pot to boil some water in. Ari stoked up the fire, her mind reeling.

What a week she'd had. Dancing with Liv, drugging the king of France, betraying Queen Mary. Well, those last two made it seem like Ari was a villain. But she wasn't.

She would wager there was a 99 percent chance that she wasn't the villain of this story. Of course, that depended on Queen Catherine being the good guy, considering Ari had been working for her. And really, Ari couldn't think of one person who would define Queen Catherine as being the good guy, not even Ari.

The ugly truth was, Ari had blinded the king, and then the king had died in a jousting competition because a splinter of wood had pierced his eye.

It felt, in some ways, like her fault.

Greer got the tea started. Ari stood over the pot, watching the water boil. She loved how a watched pot boiled. She found it comforting that some things in this world were so predictable.

"You should go to Francis," her father said after the tea was poured.

Ari choked on a swallow of tea. "To Prince Francis? Why?"

"He's the king now," Nostradamus pointed out. "He could use you as an adviser and prognosticator."

Ari's throat closed. "But, Papa, I am not skilled at prognostication. I don't know what I'm doing."

Nostradamus cleared his throat. "Neither did I, when I first started. And yet, that, in itself, is another lesson to learn. Fake it until you make it. Here's a secret, Aristotle," he said. "I am never certain about any of my prophecies. Sometimes I'm right. Sometimes I'm wrong. Sometimes I think that whatever I say will come to pass, simply *because* I said it. That is the nature of the job." He held his hand out, and Ari took it. "All you can do is your best, and pretend that your mistakes are purposeful."

"That sounds like we're frauds," Ari said.

"Everyone is a fraud," Nostradamus replied.

Ari squeezed his hand. "That's not what I wanted to hear."

"I know," her father said. "No one likes the truth."

A kitchen maid appeared at the doorway to the laboratory. She must have been new, because she addressed Ari as "Lady Aristotle." Then she added, "The queen summons you."

Besides the fact that Ari hadn't gotten used to the word *Lady* in front of her name, she was also confused as to the rest of the request.

"Which queen?" Ari asked.

"There is only one queen now," the servant said. "Queen Mary."

Ari dabbed her cheeks with a towel and tried to smooth her hair. She was in no mood to deal with Queen Mary, but she desperately wanted to see Liv. Because Liv was supposed to leave today. For Norway.

"Good luck," said Greer. "Job hunting is the worst."

"She doesn't require luck," Nostradamus pronounced. "She is

a Nostradame. We make our own luck. In that cauldron, right over there." He smiled at Ari. "Go, my child."

Ari had no choice but to obey.

Ari's path to Queen Mary's chambers unfortunately took her right past Queen Catherine's chambers. There was no way to avoid it. She would just have to move quickly.

As she neared Queen Catherine's door, she heard a crash, followed by a stream of incoherent yelling.

"This is unacceptable!" The queen's raging carried through the heavy wooden door and echoed down the hallway. "I will not relocate. These are my rooms!"

Ari's eyes widened. Someone had dared suggest that the queen move out of her rooms? That seemed . . . foolish. But then she remembered what her father had said, that the queen was only the queen while she was married to the king. And now the king was dead.

Queen Catherine was no longer in power.

Just then the door opened and a maid came running out. Ari caught a glimpse of broken dishes, curtains askew, and some sort of red liquid on the floor. Hopefully it was only wine. Then the queen came into view, her eyes wide and hair wild.

Ari watched as the queen (the dowager queen, is what she would be called now—the official title for the wife of a dead king) sank into the chair at her desk. All the fury seemed to leave her. She put her head into her hands and began to weep quite brokenheartedly. Ari's breath caught. Her heart squeezed in spite of itself. She was inclined to dislike Catherine, considering all that had happened, but she also realized that the queen was a woman who'd just lost her husband. Granted, the queen had hated her husband. But she must have loved him once, too.

The queen let out a scream. It was mournful at first but grew into a bellow of rage. Then she swept all the contents of her desk onto the floor. (Poor Ari. This was twice now that she'd witnessed a royal temper tantrum. It was never a pretty sight.) Ari tried to slowly move back from the door.

At the movement, the queen turned swiftly and spotted Ari. "You." Her lip curled into a derisive snarl. "What are you still doing here?"

Ari didn't answer. She picked up her skirts and ran past the door. She didn't look back until she reached Queen Mary's chambers, where she stood outside the door, her fist raised, waiting for her heartbeat to slow.

"Do you wish me to knock for you?" Mary's guard said.

"No," Ari retorted. "I am perfectly capable of knocking. I am just taking a moment. Haven't you ever needed a moment?"

The guard looked confused. Ari realized that she herself had never uttered those words, either. For non-ladies and non-lords, there really was no such thing as "taking a moment." You worked all day until exhaustion took over. Rinse. Repeat.

Nevertheless Ari took her moment. Then she knocked.

Thankfully Mary's chambers were in a much calmer and more

composed state than Queen Catherine's had been. Mary was seated in her usual place by the fire. Beside her, to Ari's surprise, was Francis. He was gazing out the window and didn't seem to notice Ari's arrival. Hush was standing over the queen, her fingers deftly twisting Mary's hair into three intertwining braids. Flem was in the corner muttering over a knitted sock.

But Ari's eyes went straight to Liv, who was sitting on Mary's other side doing embroidery. Ari's breath caught at the way Liv's hair reflected and refracted the sunlight streaming through the window. She almost expected to see a rainbow prism on the opposite wall. She couldn't imagine a Paris court without Liv.

"Oh, good," Queen Mary said as Ari stepped fully into the room. "You're here."

"Your Majesty." Ari curtsied stiffly.

"Where have you been?" Mary asked. "Obviously I am in need of all of my ladies at such a time."

"I'm sorry, Your Majesty. I would have been here before, but Queen Catherine has dismissed me."

Mary frowned. "Dismissed you?"

"She has ordered me expelled from the palace."

"She can't do that. You're *my* lady-in-waiting."

"But—" Ari bit her lip. Queen Mary still didn't know that Ari had come here to spy on her, that Ari had truly worked for Catherine.

"But what?" Mary asked.

"But Queen Catherine is the one who hired me to work for you."

Mary glanced over at Francis. He was still looking out the window. Mary kept her voice low. "Catherine is no longer queen of France. I am. And I say you're not dismissed. You work for me now, and only me. Is that clear?"

It was clear, Ari realized sharply, that Mary knew exactly why Ari had come to work for her. And it was clear that Mary expected Ari's loyalty now. But Ari still wasn't feeling inclined to be loyal.

"Why?" she asked. "Why should I?" Her gaze fell on Liv again, but Liv didn't look up. She gazed at her needlework, smiling a little. She didn't look like a person about to be shipped off to Norway.

"Perhaps I should make myself clearer," Mary said. "None of my ladies are dismissed. And none of my ladies will be leaving my side. You are all too important to me now."

Ari's heart raced. She had so many questions. Wait, scratch that. She had only one big question. "So you're not sending Lady Livingston away?"

"No," Mary said. "I've informed the Duke of Shetland that he cannot marry Liv. I need my friends about me now."

Relief poured through Ari, and she nodded. "All right. Yes, then. I will work for you. What do you need? A potion? I can make everyone a potion that will ease the grief."

Francis got to his feet, suddenly agitated. "We've no need of any more blasted potions!" he exclaimed.

This was not going how Ari had hoped.

He tugged at his collar. "Lord, I can't even breathe!" He

strode forward and grabbed at Ari's hand. "Give me a vision. Tell me what else will happen. I must know."

"Oh, Sire, I cannot," Ari said, struggling to free her hand, but Francis didn't release it. "It doesn't work that way. I'm so sorry."

"Everyone's sorry," Francis said. "But sorry doesn't help me. You could. Please. Tell me the future."

"Francis," Mary said slowly. "Please let go of my lady."

But Ari had pressed her other hand (the one Francis wasn't clutching) to her forehead. The floaty feeling came over her again. "I see a man dressed all in black armor and robes, with a black mask over his face," she intoned. "He breathes strangely. He bears a sword made of red light. He says the force is strong with you. He wants you to know the power of the dark side. He says you have a sister." She blinked a few times. "Oh. I don't know what that was about. Forget I said anything."

Francis let go of Ari's hand, stunned by her pronouncement. She took several steps back.

Mary made Francis sit down again.

"A red sword made of light?" he scoffed. "And everyone already knows I have three sisters. What kind of fortune-teller are you?"

"It's not an exact science," Ari said miserably.

"I liked that one," Liv said softly. "It's been my favorite vision of yours so far."

Ari beamed.

"Please, have a seat," Mary said to Ari. "There's a free chair next to Liv."

This was going better than Ari had hoped. But she had just sat down next to Liv when the guard announced another visitor, and Catherine swept into the room. She was perfectly dressed and coiffed, with no trace of her earlier meltdown, her face freshly powdered and her eyes sharp as always.

The guard cleared his throat. "The dowager queen, Your Majesties."

Catherine lifted her head regally. "You will refer to me as the Queen Mother. As I am the mother of the king."

As her piercing gaze passed over every person in the room, Ari wished she had her invisibility potion. But Catherine ignored her (for the moment). Instead, she went directly to Francis.

"My darling boy," she cooed. "How are you?"

"Terrible," he answered petulantly. "What else could I be?"

Ugh, thought Ari. *Royalty. As if becoming king was such a bother.*

"Of course you are," Catherine said. She licked her palm and smoothed down a flyaway curl of Francis's hair. "But don't you worry. Mother is here."

Ari'd had no idea that Catherine was so maternal. Generally she preferred to leave parenting her children up to the servants, as far as Ari had seen.

"Thank you, Mother." The tension eased from Francis's shoulders. "Thank you for coming." (Everybody wants their mommies during a crisis. Even kings.)

"Of course," Catherine said. "You're my son. My favorite offspring. My pride and joy. I will always be here for you. Whatever you need."

Ari caught Mary, the queen of France and Scotland (and maybe one day, England) subtly rolling her eyes.

"Well now that you mention it," Francis said. "I would really like to have a glass of warm milk. I've been having such trouble sleeping, of late."

"Right away, darling." The queen snapped her fingers at Flem, who was so startled that she dropped her knitting. "You there. Fetch the king some milk. Be quick, girl."

"Yes, Your Maj—" Flem caught her mistake. "Your Mother-liness," she amended, and dashed out the door.

Mary sighed.

"Now I want the two of you to relax," Catherine said. "I have come to relieve you of all of your burdens. Leave everything to me."

"Oh good," said Francis.

"Which burdens?" asked Mary.

"Oh, you know, all those tiresome day-to-day chores that you needn't be bothered with right now. You two should focus on getting each other through this tragedy, and working on your new marriage. Now more than ever, for instance, we need an heir. And I will take care of the rest—the laws that the crown must make to keep the kingdom running, and the silly things like royal proclamations and tax collections and the affairs of the royal treasury."

Mary straightened in her chair, suddenly alert. "That sounds like you wish to be Francis's regent," she observed.

"Well, now that you mention it, that seems . . . wise. You two being so young and inexperienced in politics and me being, well, myself. I mean, whatever I can do to help."

"That would be very helpful, Mother," Francis said.

Merde. Ari felt a chill. She didn't know whether to be terrified or awed by Catherine's deft maneuvering of the situation. But one thing was very clear: Catherine was still clutching at power. If she could not be the queen of France, she would rule through Francis.

But Mary wasn't having it. "That will not be necessary," the Queen of Scots said firmly. "Francis and I will be more than able to fulfill our duties as the king and queen."

"But—" Catherine began.

"You have served this country well for many, many, *many* years," Mary interrupted. (Oh snap, say your narrators. Mary just interrupted Catherine de Medici. And called her old.) "And now it is time, we feel, for you to be allowed a much-deserved rest. In fact, I have settled on a castle in the South of France that would be perfect for you to live out your retirement."

There was a long moment of silence. Everyone seemed to be waiting breathlessly for Catherine's reaction. The dowager queen lowered her head as if thinking. Then she smiled.

"Of course. Whatever you deem best, my dears," she said. "Indeed, I thought you might say that. I will take my leave, but first, I've brought you a gift."

Ari cringed. If she knew Catherine (and Ari felt like she did know Catherine) this was going to be ugly.

Catherine snapped her fingers, and the maidservant she'd brought with her stepped dutifully forward, bearing a small wrapped box.

"Oh, you're too kind," said Mary stiffly. She took the box and opened it. Then she gasped and dropped it onto the floor. As the box overturned, a mousetrap bounced onto the carpet, making a sharp snapping sound as it went off.

Mary stifled a shriek. She pulled her feet up onto the chair, her face draining of color. She glanced desperately at Francis, who leapt up.

"Mother, what is the meaning of this?" Francis demanded. He quickly bent and shoved the trap back into the box.

"A reminder," Catherine answered coolly. "You're a king now, my dear, and there are . . . rats all about us. You will need protection from the vermin of this world."

Ari felt sick. This was her fault. This was all her fault.

Francis's hands shook as he passed the box to Liv, who'd sprung up to take it away. Mary still looked shaken. Catherine smiled at her.

"Now that you understand me fully, you'll be a good girl, and do what you're told."

Mary put her feet back on the floor. Her dark eyes flashed with the contrariness that even Ari had already come to know. "I will not be threatened by you," she said. "I am the queen."

"For now," Catherine said lightly. "Things are changing so quickly these days."

"I am not—" Mary began, but Francis stepped forward.

"Mary and I are grateful to have your guidance, Mother," he said. "For however long you wish to stay."

Ari's heart sank. Catherine had won.

TWENTY-FOUR
Francis

Francis's coronation was to be held in Reims, where all the kings of France's past had been officially crowned. Unfortunately, the moment the royal party arrived at the city gates, a soaking downpour appeared completely out of nowhere, leaving everyone looking like drowned rats. Or mice, in some cases.

"Get the king inside!" cried Duke Francis.

"Before he catches his death of cold!" cried Cardinal Charles.

"Or ruins his outfit!" cried Queen Catherine.

Because of the surprise rain, which absolutely no one had predicted (what was the point, Francis thought irritably, of paying people to see the future when they never saw anything remotely useful?), the Duke of Savoy caught a fever. As he was one of the highest-ranking guests, the entire production had to be delayed.

"Seems like someone should have dragged *him* inside, too," Francis noted that Sunday afternoon. Mary nodded solemnly but seemed too distracted to joke around with him. "I mean, it makes sense to delay a coronation if the man about to get crowned king is the one who fell ill. But that's not the case. I'm perfectly healthy. And yet, the coronation is delayed, all because of someone else. Now all the medals we gave out will have the incorrect coronation date."

"Perhaps they will be collector pieces one day, more valuable than if they'd had the correct date," Duke Francis replied.

"Or we can have new medals made," suggested Catherine with a side-eye at Mary's uncles. "I always find it bad luck to print the date on anything before the fact."

Francis was rather beginning to feel that he was in a tug-of-war between his mother and Mary's uncles. And Francis was the rope.

"Either way, I'll be soundly mocked, I assume," Francis said. "It will be as bad as that fiasco with the portrait."

He was referring to a time when, about a year ago, Catherine had commissioned a portrait of the dauphin by the famous artist François Clouet, who had somehow managed to make Francis look like a sickly, sulking seven-year-old.

Catherine tsked. "Nothing could be as bad as the portrait. Everyone thought you were going to die."

"I almost did. Of embarrassment."

"Nobody remembers that anymore. You're king now. Or you will be, tomorrow."

But in truth, Francis didn't mind the coronation being post-poned. It gave him more time as Not King, even if everyone was calling him king because of the whole continuity-of-the-monarchy situation, which was very, very important to some people. Like, all of France, apparently.

But even with all the delays (which Francis was trying not to see as bad omens, even though everyone kept saying what bad omens they were), tomorrow arrived. The day of the coronation. The day he officially became the king of France.

It began with Francis putting on a gown.

Now, Francis didn't have anything against gowns. He rather enjoyed when Mary wore them. But Francis was made to put on this gown over his shirt and trousers, which seemed like an excessive amount of clothes. Moreover, everything was made of white silk, and as everyone knows, wearing white silk is asking for trouble.

"There's no tomato sauce on the menu, is there?" he asked the attendant.

"No, Sire."

"None in the building?"

"Not as far as I know, Sire."

"What about on the way there?"

"No tomatoes on the streets, Sire, but are you worried about mud, too? It has rained recently."

Immediately, Francis was deeply worried about the mud. (It was better than thinking about the long years ahead of him. As king. King of France. Because his father had died.)

But the white silk (and Francis) made it to the cathedral without incident. Trumpets blared and a choir began singing an anthem.

Mary took his hand. "It'll be all right."

"Don't jinx it," Francis said.

The rest of the event simultaneously went very quickly and took forever (according to our research, about five hours), and frankly, it was all sort of a blur for Francis. He was anointed with special oils, there were songs and readings of scriptures, more songs, and a litany. It was just . . . a lot. Francis had practiced, so he knew basically what to do (but between you and us and Francis, he zoned out for most of it).

Finally, the actual crowning. He was presented with the usual scepter and ring, and of course the ridiculously heavy crown, and then he took the throne.

Cardinal Charles bowed and shouted, "*Vivat rex!* May the king live forever!"

In thunderous reply, the entire congregation joined in. "*Vivat rex!* May the king live forever!"

It was a bit dizzying, all that noise, the heat, the weight of the crown on his head.

When it was over, Francis was relieved. And terrified.

He was king.

As guests filed out of the cathedral, stretching their legs and rolling their shoulders after sitting still for so long, Mary came to stand next to Francis. "Well," she murmured softly, "that was awkward."

Indeed, it was. In fact, the history books would later agree, saying, "Overall, it was perhaps the most awkward and least convincing coronation day in French history."

To which your narrators must wonder, if five hours of ceremony and singing and anointing isn't enough to convince people, what the heck is?

At last, Francis, Mary, Queen Catherine, and the rest of the coronation party were walking out of the cathedral, more than ready to climb into the carriages that would take them to nice, soft beds. Yes, walking, because even though Francis had just been crowned king of France (he was trying very hard not to think about it), he still had to do regular things like walk places. It just seemed so much more mundane now, given all the majesty and celebration of half an hour ago. Already, the coronation seemed like a dream. Not a good dream, but a dream, nonetheless, and suddenly, Francis understood a thing about his father that he never had before.

Perhaps King Henry had so many "visions" of parties and festivals and celebrations because he wanted that feeling again. Henry, from what Francis could tell, had *liked* the feeling in the cathedral, the singing and anointing and various expensive outfits, and every needless event he'd thrown since then had been an attempt to regain that emotional high. Including, he realized with a deep sadness, that jousting tournament. His final vision.

Francis was sure he'd be a very boring king by comparison. But perhaps easier on the royal treasury.

"How do you feel?" Mary asked quietly. She'd been quiet ever since that horrible showdown in which Francis's mother had, in effect, blackmailed her. And there was even more on Mary's mind, he knew. Her ladies trailed behind her, all except Bea. She was still missing. And there had still been no word from Mary's mother.

But let's make it about Francis again, shall we?

"I feel"—Francis heaved a sigh—"tired. Hollowed out."

"You did well today," she said.

He hadn't completely humiliated himself by forgetting lines or freezing up, although the weight of the crown had nearly toppled him over on more than one occasion.

"You're the king now." Catherine strode up beside them. "You cannot afford to be tired."

"I don't see how that's possible, Mother. Aren't kings allowed to sleep?" His father had slept all the time. Well, "slept," possibly. But he didn't want to bring that up to his mother.

"Only when their power is secure."

Ugh. His mother was being insufferable. He still couldn't believe that she'd given them a mousetrap as a gift.

"I've just been formally crowned," Francis said. "Surely—"

Catherine shook her head. "Your power is slightly more secure than it was yesterday, but we still have so much work to do."

We. Because his mother was now his regent.

"Aren't you glad that I have been a reigning monarch for many, many, *many* years?" she said, smiling at Mary.

Mary's shoulders were up near her ears. Her jaw tightened.

She placed her hand on Francis's arm. "You always have my support," she murmured.

Catherine sniffed. "You have done very well to allow your mother to help you rule your country, my dear Mary. Francis could take a lesson from that."

Mary's fingers tightened over Francis's arms. "My mother may assist me, but she—as well as the whole of Scotland—knows that I am queen."

"Not that Knox fellow," Catherine quipped.

Thank God they'd reached a line of carriages by then, resplendent with gold filigree and fine white stallions. Francis wanted to hug the horses.

"Your Majesties!" Duke Francis jumped out from behind the carriages, smiling as they approached. "Congratulations once again. You'll make a fine king. All of France will sing your praises."

A creeping discomfort crawled down Francis's spine. This was the same way the Duke of Guise had spoken to Henry, and the same way he always spoke to Mary. Francis didn't want to be anywhere near the uncles, but he supposed it would be impossible to avoid them now that he was king.

Catherine didn't try to hide her sneer as the Duke of Guise bowed comically low, with respect so exaggerated it made Francis recoil.

"Your Highness. Nephew." He said it with a serpent-like smile. "The House of Guise would be honored for the royal family to join us in the Château de Blois. We are all family now, aren't we?

It would send a message of unity, if you were to stay with us for a time."

Francis rubbed at his eyes. The Château de Blois was over a hundred miles south of Paris. It would take them a week to get there. "I don't—"

"The king doesn't wish to travel so far from Paris," his mother answered for him. "He should return to the Louvre, where there is much he needs to attend to."

She meant much *she* needed to attend to.

"But surely he deserves some measure of rest after all he's been through," argued the duke.

"That's right." Mary swept forward, as though she thought traveling all the way to the Loire Valley was a great idea. "Thank you, Uncle. We would be happy to stay in your home for a while. Wouldn't we, dear?" She smiled at Francis.

Merde.

"Good, good." The duke smiled again. "I've already made all the arrangements. We can travel there tonight."

"Very well," said Catherine. "But if Francis is going, then I am going. I am the Queen Mother, after all. I follow my son."

Francis sighed. "I'd much rather—"

No one seemed to hear him, though, not even Mary. She'd decided that they were going, and before he even realized, Francis was in the carriage.

Just what he wanted after five long hours of coronating.

As the carriages rolled south, leaving Reims behind, Francis sank into the cushioned bench with a sigh. He was king now, which should give him a certain measure of control over his life—a few more choices—but the crown might as well have been a collar. What he wanted mattered even less now than it had before.

What he wouldn't give for those halcyon days of being nothing but a dauphin.

It took well over a week to reach the château. They had stopped in Paris so the servants could pack more clothes and immediate necessities; everything else would follow in a few days. Francis and Mary left the carriage only to stretch their legs, and then they were always whisked right back into the compartment.

The land was charming here, with sweeping hills, orderly vineyards, and lush orchards. They passed by several châteaus, each more elegant than the last, until finally they arrived at their destination, with so much fanfare it was embarrassing.

The townspeople had decorated the streets with Francis's sun emblem, in celebration of his arrival, and he'd heard the cheering long after the carriages had deposited him and his court at the doors to the royal apartments. They seemed genuinely excited that the new king and queen had chosen (ahem) to come here of all places, and Francis wasn't halfway to his rooms when he was informed of a feast tonight, in his honor.

After that, he raced upstairs to avoid any more social interaction. That had been useless. He'd found a schedule placed on one of the many tables in his rooms, detailing where he was to go, what he was to do, and—most important—what he was supposed to wear.

Francis blew out a breath and, alone for the first time in a thousand years, walked to the window where he could see the Loire River rushing by, the townspeople still celebrating in the streets, and the stars beginning to appear on the horizon.

As for the rooms Francis had been assigned, they were lavishly decorated. A massive fireplace stood along one wall, and the canopied bed was large enough for ten of him. Truly, the château was marvelous. Stately. Fit for a king. It was easy to see why Mary had wanted to come here.

Francis wished these beautiful rooms didn't feel so much like a cage. But tomorrow, he'd begin the business of ruling a kingdom. Well, more likely it would be Catherine. And Mary. And her uncles. They were the experts, as they kept reminding him. And as he'd already seen, Mary was more than ready to put herself in charge.

A soft knock came against his door. Mary.

He started to call, "Come in," but the door opened before he could finish, and Mary stepped inside.

Could he not even control his own door?

Obviously he wanted her to come in, but she hadn't even waited out of politeness.

Was this what his life would be like now? Caught between what Catherine wanted and what Mary's uncles convinced her she wanted? The years stretched long before him. He would be a king in name only, the instrument through which his mother and wife ruled France.

Without waiting for an invitation, Mary took a seat near the fireplace. "Something is on your mind." (She was incredibly perceptive, that Mary.)

Francis looked into the crackling fire.

"Francis." A note of irritation touched her voice. "Tell me, what is on your mind?"

He could tell her. He could say all the things he'd been thinking, tell her all the frustrations he'd been feeling, but what would that accomplish? Truly, he didn't want to fight. Not with her, his wife, and one of the few allies he had.

He already knew how such a conversation would go. He'd say she'd spoken over him after the coronation. She'd reply that she'd known he was too tired to decide. He'd ask why she hadn't considered he was also too tired to travel to the Loire Valley. She'd inform him that they were already here now, so there was no point in discussing it further.

Instead of fumbling his way through that argument and all her superior logic, Francis just slouched into a chair and gazed beyond Mary, into the fireplace.

"I just keep asking myself why," he said finally. "Why Father decided to hold a tournament. Why he felt the need to participate. Why he was so proud that he had to compete again."

Mary's expression melted into compassion. "Oh, Francis."

"I wasn't ready," he said. "Father should still be king. He should not have participated in that joust."

Mary didn't respond.

"And what of Montgomery? Everyone said he would be dealt with, but no one has told me anything about where he is."

Her eyes shifted downward.

"And why would the man agree to joust with the king, anyway?" Francis shook his head. "I know, I know, he couldn't exactly turn down his monarch. But still, that should have made him more careful. People die in jousting tournaments." Francis's voice broke. "My father died. My father. And"—he drew a shuddering breath—"I just don't understand why."

Finally, Mary met his eyes. Her voice was soft but steady as she said, "I think I do."

TWENTY-FIVE

Mary

Francis stared at her. "What do you understand?"

Mary swallowed. At some point in the past five minutes she'd realized that withholding things from Francis hadn't protected him. "I know why your father died," she murmured. "At least, I think I do. My uncles made it happen."

He went still. "*What?*"

She told him everything: the conversation she'd overheard, especially that bit about Montgomery, the jubilation of her uncles now that Henry was dead, their advice that she should tell Francis what to do and guide his every decision. By the time she stopped talking, Francis's blue eyes had gone completely cold. He jumped to his feet and started to pace.

"The audacity you'd have to have, to kill a king," he said, and gave a hard, humorless laugh. "Your uncles are monsters."

She closed her eyes against the wave of shame. "I don't know for certain that they were responsible, but . . ." Her gut told her they were. "If they did it, they did it for me," she confessed. "Oh, Francis, I'm sorry. It's my fault."

He scoffed. "You didn't tell them to murder my father, did you?"

"No, but . . ."

He raked a hand through his hair. "Then it's not your fault. But—" Suddenly he turned on her. "Why didn't you tell me before?"

"I . . . I should have," she admitted. "I didn't want to burden you with anything more."

"Burden me? Why, because you didn't think I could handle it? Because you think I'm weak, like everyone else does?"

Her eyes widened. "No. No, of course not. I just—"

He pointed at her, scowling. "I told you your uncles were up to something. I told you so!"

He was right, but nobody likes an "I told you so," even in French. Mary scowled right back at him.

"That was about the prenuptial agreement," she protested.

"Oh, you don't think that's connected to what they're doing now? What they did to my father?"

She regretted telling him. She understood that it had been the right thing, because he should know the truth about his father's death. But it was rude to throw it back in her face.

"I don't know," she said sharply.

"Well, perhaps we should find out," he said. "*Now* do you think it might be wise to spy on them?"

"Yes!" she said. "Why do you suppose I agreed to come to Château de Blois? I thought I might be able to discover what my uncles are up to here, at their home."

"About that." Francis was still frowning deeply. "You didn't— you never—if you had only told me about your suspicions earlier, I would have . . ." He dragged his hand down his face, then sighed. "Fine. I can see why you might have wanted to come here. But if your uncles are really our enemy, Mary, you've just brought us into the lion's den."

"Oh, like Paris is any better?" she countered. "Your mother brought a mousetrap into our chambers!"

"She's bluffing," said Francis. "Fine. So she might know that you have a mousy side, and that's a definite problem, but—"

"And how does she know that?"

"I certainly didn't tell her. Perhaps you weren't careful enough."

Mary remembered, uneasily, the incident in the queen's bed-chambers. Deadly biscuit, indeed! "It doesn't matter how she found out. You know what happens to Eðians in this country. My royal blood won't save me."

Francis shuddered. "My mother would never really do that. She only cares for my welfare."

Mary stared at him. "Have you even met your mother? She's evil!"

"Your uncles are evil, too!" he yelled back.

"Yes, but—" Mary took a deep breath. "Fine. I will take care of this," she said firmly. "I will discover the truth about my uncles, one way or another."

"And you'll tell me about it," Francis said pointedly. "Immediately."

"And you will smooth things over with your mother," she said.

"I will try," Francis agreed.

Mary twisted her ring around her finger. "And then we can decide what to do."

But Francis didn't seem satisfied. "Perhaps—just this once, probably—I should decide what to do, without your help. Alone."

Her breath caught. "Francis."

"Clearly there's a conflict of interest for you in this situation. Considering your uncles killed my father so that you could be the queen."

"I'm sorry," Mary gasped.

"Don't be sorry," Francis said. "Be sure."

He sounded, she thought, as a king should sound. She would almost have been proud of him if she hadn't been so hurt by what he was saying.

There came a frantic barking at the chamber door. Flem, obviously, bearing some sort of news.

Francis grabbed his jacket where he'd flung it on the back of a chair. "I need to take a walk. Clear my head."

He opened the door, and Flem darted past him, panting

heavily. He gave a quick, perfunctory bow to Mary, so formal that it stung her, and exited to the gardens.

Mary sank onto the bed. A few days ago he would have wanted to take a walk with her. But they had just had their first official fight as a married couple. He was cross with her. Maybe he even felt like he could no longer trust her. And given what she'd told him, Mary couldn't exactly blame him.

She became aware that Flem was still barking at her. She'd hardly ever seen her friend so excited, not even when the mailman came. Mary got up, bolted the door, and pulled the drapes over the windows. It felt risky, undergoing an Eðian transformation here, in an unfamiliar setting, after all that had happened. There were undoubtedly secret passages here, too, and possibly peepholes or other Eðians sent to spy. But Flem seemed desperate to tell her something.

"All right, dear, out with it," she said when she'd secured the room as best as she could.

There was a burst of light. She held out her robe to Flem, but the girl seemed too agitated to take it.

"I've found Bea!"

Mary gasped. "You found her?"

"I found her scent, at least. I was sniffing around near the cellar, and I caught it. She's here. I'm sure of it."

If Bea was here—if she had been here, at her uncles' château, all this time—perhaps Liv was not the only one of Mary's ladies who was in the employ of her uncles. Perhaps they all were.

She reached out and grasped Flem's arm. "You're not a spy for my uncles, are you? If you were, I'd understand. They're very persuasive. But I need to know. I need you to tell me."

Flem cocked her head to one side. "What are you going on about? Of course I'm not spying for your uncles. I patently dislike your uncles, particularly your uncle Charles. Pardon me, my queen, but I've always quite wanted to bite him in the arse."

She was telling the truth. Mary felt it. Also, she knew Flem to be a terrible liar. Every time she tried to be deceitful she got this guilty look on her face and refused to meet a person's eyes. "You say you caught her scent by the cellar?"

"Yes. I'm certain it's Bea."

Mary nodded. "Show me where."

A few minutes later a woman dressed in a dark, inconspicuous robe and hood made her way to the cellar stairs holding a large basket. If anyone had seen her (which no one did) they would have thought her a washwoman, perhaps, bearing a basket of laundry. They would not have thought, *Now there goes the Queen of Scots—oh, and France now, we guess.*

Mary moved quickly down the stairs. In the cellar she found the usual cellar stuff—tubs of onions and potatoes, some salted meat, a large stash of ale, that kind of thing. She put the basket down, and Flem, in dog form again, hopped out and started to sniff around. After only a few seconds of investigating, the dog darted into a corner of the room, where there was a door. Upon opening it,

Mary discovered yet another set of stairs, this one descending farther down, under the building. It was a black hole down there. Flem whimpered. Mary lit a candle, and without hesitation, followed the stairs into the dark.

What she found was a dungeon. There was a line of cells, each closed off by a door with a barred window at the top. Piles of chains upon the floors. It smelled of excrement and fear. Mary's stomach turned at the prospect of what might happen in this place.

But it was empty. No prisoners at the current time. No Bea.

Flem whimpered again.

"I know," said Mary. "But can you smell her?"

The dog traversed the corridor, nose to the ground. At the last cell on the right, she scratched at the door. Mary found it unlocked. She turned a slow circle in the cell, noting scratch marks on the walls, and dark stains on the floor, but there was no sign of her missing lady-in-waiting.

Flem didn't seem discouraged. She bounded over to the back wall and then pointed as she might have done if she'd treed a fox. (Although Flem never participated in foxhunting, which we as your narrators highly disapprove of, because of the poor foxes and especially if they might possibly be Eðians.)

"There's nothing here," said Mary.

"Bark!" said Flem.

"What, you think there's a secret door here somewhere?"

"BARK BARK!" said Flem.

"Shhh! Someone might hear you!" Mary admonished.

"Bark," said Flem much more quietly.

Mary scanned the wall for a seam, but it looked like a simple stone wall. Still, she knew that appearances are often deceiving, and she trusted Flem. There must be a secret latch or switch.

It was the sconce, she discovered, the iron fitting meant to hold a candle, attached to the wall. (Of course it was.) She should have known right off—it was much too nice and clean for a space like this. And who would care if a prisoner had a candle to see by?

Mary firmly pushed the candle back, because everyone knows that's how it works, and it gave way easily, and right before her eyes the stone wall swung open, revealing the secret passage.

"Eureka!" Mary cried. (We doubted that this was her exact word, as how would Mary know about a town in Oregon, but as it turns out, *Eureka* is Greek for "I found it," and was first uttered by the mathematician and inventor Archimedes sometime between 300 and 200 BCE. And Mary had studied Greek. So she did, indeed, exclaim *Eureka!* when she opened the secret door.)

"Bark!" said Flem approvingly.

This is going very well, Mary thought. It was a bit of welcome excitement, given the drudgery and sorrow of the past few days. Francis had made her feel so badly about herself, but here she was solving a mystery, finding her friend, and gathering evidence against her uncles. It was turning into quite the productive day. Maybe later she and Francis would even "kiss and make up" and he'd apologize for being so mean to her.

They reached the end of the passage, where there was a huge and heavy (and imposingly locked) oak door.

"Droppings!" muttered Mary. She pushed against the door with her shoulder, but there was no possibility of forcing it. "Damned English oak!"

"Bark!" said Flem quietly. "Growl! Bark! Growl!"

"I know," Mary said irritably. "But it's locked. I'm no good at picking locks, are you?"

"Whine," said Flem.

"Usually I don't have to bother with locks," Mary said. "I just slip underneath the door."

"Bark!" said Flem.

Oh. "All right," Mary said, removing her cloak, folding it neatly, and placing it at her feet. Emergency rules it was, then. "Stand watch, won't you?"

Flash. She was a mouse. She was under the door in no time, as a mouse. Mary glanced around, sniffing. The room was deserted.

Flash. She was a person again. She turned and unlocked the door, admitting Flem and allowing herself access to her clothes.

Sometimes it was so handy, being a mouse.

She pulled the cloak around her and fumbled about the room for a light. It would have been easier to see in the darkness as a mouse, but she didn't want to change back and forth needlessly. She located a candlestick on a desk—she was in a study of some kind, perhaps—and searched the drawer for a match.

"Whine," said Flem.

"Be patient," Mary said. "I'm trying my best." At that moment her fingers closed around a matchbook. She held it up and stuck a match triumphantly, lit the candle. Smiled.

Another light flashed. Flem (as a girl) tapped her on the shoulder.

"Mary," she whispered. "Oh, Mary, look."

The walls were lined with cages, each one filled with animals: a rabbit, a fox, a badger, a parrot, a seagull, a lizard, even a cage containing a large glass bowl, which held a goldfish. Which seemed a little extreme.

Mary and Flem stared, openmouthed, in horror. Eðians. They must be.

There was a feeble croaking sound from one of the cages, and Flem rushed toward it. "Bea!" she cried.

There was a sad-looking raven, half-starved, from the look of her. Her feathers, which were normally a glossy, well-groomed black, were dull and mottled with dirt. Her eyes hardly seemed to recognize them. But it was Bea.

"Find something to break the lock," said Mary between clenched teeth.

It turned out they didn't need to. There was a key in the desk drawer. They unlocked Bea's cage at once and drew her out, Mary holding her gently in her arms, stroking her feathers.

"I'm so sorry. I should have thought to look for you here. I should have come sooner."

Francis had been so right. She should have been spying on her uncles weeks ago.

Flem was moving around unlocking all the cages. Her uncles would know someone had been here, but Mary didn't care. Most of the E∂ians stayed in their animal forms and scurried off without a word. But others remained for a moment. Lights began to flash. The fish became a man, who gurgled his thanks. The parrot became the old court jester who'd been reported drowned in the Seine years ago, his body never found. He was emaciated and battered-looking now. The seagull became a haggard-looking woman. Mary wondered if this was the woman who had been caught with John Knox's pamphlet.

The woman bowed to Mary. "My thanks, Your Highness," she said in a quavering voice with a strong Scottish brogue. "Perhaps we have misjudged you, in Scotland."

Mary was surprised and a little dismayed that the woman recognized her. "Perhaps you have," she said. "Do you know what has happened with my mother?"

"No," said the seagull woman. "I've been down here for weeks." Then she staggered toward the door.

Mary turned her attention back to Bea. "Oh, my dear. Are you all right?"

"Croak," said Bea weakly.

Mary stroked her wing. "Stay as you are. I'll carry you out."

She should have stayed for a few moments longer and poked about for more clues, evidence about the death of the king, perhaps, or some idea of what the uncles were up to now. But she was too eager to get Bea out of this terrible place, so she and Flem (as a dog again) hurried back along the secret passage, through the empty dungeon, into the cellar, up the stairs, and through the halls of the château until they reached Mary's chambers, where they rushed in and laid Bea upon the bed, bolting the door behind them.

The flash of light from Bea's transformation was more of a flicker. Flem hurried to cover her up, not out of modesty, but to warm her. The girl immediately started to shiver and shake. Mary threw herself down beside her and wrapped her arms about her friend, while Flem ran to the fireplace to build the fire up to a roar, then went out to get some food.

"I knew you would find me," whispered Bea. "He caught me, coming back to you. He had a net, and a man outside your window. He seemed to be expecting me."

"I'm sorry. I'm so sorry," Mary said. "Who was it? Was it—"

"Your uncle Francis," Bea said. "He said he was sorry, too, but he couldn't have you knowing. Not just yet. He said you had enough to think about, with your wedding and the king's impending trag-edy." She shivered. "What tragedy did he mean?"

"The king is dead," Mary answered. "He was killed in a jousting . . . accident." But it hadn't been an accident—this much was crystal clear now, if her uncle had known it was about to hap-pen. It was true, then. Her uncles had murdered the king. "What didn't he want me to know?"

"Your mother," Bea rasped.

Mary's heart became a chunk of ice. She couldn't breathe. "What about my mother?"

Bea's dark eyes filled with tears. "When I got to Scotland, I couldn't find her. She wasn't at the castle at Edinburgh, or anywhere. She's gone."

TWENTY-SIX

Ari

"Oh, Ari. I am glad you're here." Queen Mary breathed a sigh of relief at the sight of her. The queen's eyebrows were furrowed, and her normally pretty brown eyes were red and puffy.

"What's happening?" Ari asked. "What do you need?"

Queen Mary gestured toward her bed, where a girl with long black hair was resting under a blanket. It took a minute for Ari to realize that it was Mary Beaton, Queen Mary's missing lady.

Bea looked emaciated and weak. Liv was sitting beside her, holding her hand.

"What happened to her?" Ari asked.

"We're not exactly sure." Liv exchanged glances with Queen Mary.

"Do you mind?" Ari pulled back the blanket to get a better

sense of the condition of the patient. Bea had been starved—that much was immediately clear. Her skin was so pale it was almost gray. Her heartbeat was steady, but faint, and there was a worrisome wheeze to her breathing. But most concerning of all were the bruises up and down her arms, some new, some fading to yellow.

"Who did this to her?" Ari asked, aghast.

"My uncles," Mary answered grimly. "Do you think one of your potions could help her?"

Ari felt a dart of pain when she thought about her fully stocked laboratory back in Paris, and her father, who was there, too, and who might have better known what to do. But she nodded, still staring at Bea, who was asleep, although her eyes fluttered.

"Yes. I'll find something." Ari hoped there were the right herbs in the kitchens.

"Good." Mary tenderly smoothed a strand of Bea's hair from her face. "Please be quick."

Ari hurried to the kitchen to gather ingredients for a health and wellness tincture. The kitchen staff were bustling about preparing for a feast in Francis's honor. Ari spotted the cook who appeared to be in charge.

"What do you want?" the cook asked.

"I need radish, bishopwort, garlic, wormwood, helenium, and cropleek." Ari was out of breath.

"Who died and made you queen?"

"The order comes from the queen," Ari said, mustering as much authority in her voice as she could.

The cook waved her ladle. "Which queen?"

"The queen of France!" Ari exclaimed. "I am the queen's lady, and the queen demands it at once!"

The cook tsked but jerked her head toward a door in the back. "You'll find most of what you need in the larder, but for the cropleek, you'll have to go to the cellar."

It would have been easier for the cook (who knew her way around the kitchen) to retrieve the ingredients, but Ari wasn't going to argue with her any more than she had to. Plus, the cook had the feast to prepare for.

"Also," Ari said more timidly. "I'll need a pestle and mortar, and a pot. And a fire. And butter, celandine, and red nettle."

The cook rolled her eyes but snapped her fingers at a kitchen maid, who must have been used to such commands because she flew into action.

"Anything else, *Your Majesty*?" the cook said sarcastically.

"That will do," Ari said. "Except the pot should be copper. And I'll need a straining cloth."

As the maid went upstairs to get her part of the ingredients, Ari made for the cellar. She had just located the cropleek when she heard voices, coming not from the stairs, but from another room in the back of the cellar. Male voices. Angry voices.

"All the prisoners?" yelled one of them.

"Yes, my lord," answered another voice pitifully.

My lord. So it must be one of the uncles doing the shouting. Ari froze, her heart pounding in her chest. There was no way to make it to the stairs, so she did the only thing she could think to do: she climbed into a half-filled barrel of what turned out to be cabbages and pulled the cloth cover over the opening.

"Even the fish?" yelled the uncle.

"There was an empty bowl, my lord. Even the water was gone."

"I told you," said another voice. "We should never have held any of them prisoner. The only proper way to deal with Eðians is to put them to death."

Ah. This was the other uncle now, clearly. The cardinal. A chill went down Ari's spine. It was so dangerous for Mary to be here. Especially if the uncles knew about Mary's—cough—mouse problem. But surely they couldn't know.

"I agree, Your Grace," said the pitiful voice. "Put them all to death, I say."

"We're wasting time talking about what we should have done," said the first uncle. "What we need to know now is who freed the prisoners? And what do they know?"

"It was undoubtedly Catherine de Medici," said the cardinal. "She has spies everywhere, you know."

Ari gulped and slid farther into the cabbages.

"I cannot believe that you allowed that conniving woman to come into our home."

"It's not as though I could help it," said the duke. "She goes where the king goes."

"But why must she? The entire point, my dear brother, was for us to be in charge of the king."

"Clearly our work here isn't done," said the duke irritably. "We must persist with Mary. When we control Mary, we control Francis. And if Catherine has the bird-girl, it will only be a matter of time before she learns of what's happened in Scotland, and perhaps even our part in what befell the king."

"We must act first, then," said the cardinal. "We must separate Mary and Francis from Catherine immediately. And then move up our plans for England."

"You, boy," ordered the duke. "Return to the workshop to see what else might have been stolen."

"Yes, my lord," said the pitiful voice, and Ari heard him scurry away.

"You're going to have to deal with him, too," said the cardinal. "He knows too much."

"One murder at a time," answered the duke. They walked toward the stairs, so near to Ari's barrel that she could smell the cardinal's musky cologne. "For now we must take care that dear, sweet Mary never comes to know what happened to her lady."

Ari held her breath as they exited the cellar. Then she let out a sigh and peeled off a leaf of cabbage that had gotten stuck to her cheek. When they'd been gone for several minutes, she climbed out of the barrel and retrieved the cropleek. There was no time to waste. Bea needed her help, and Mary needed to know what Ari had heard from the uncles.

Her heart was still beating fast, but a tiny thrill shot through her. Finally, she had a way to be useful to the queen. To prove her loyalty. To make up for what she'd done.

Twenty minutes later, she was standing over a boiling pot, watching her tincture turn from an earthy brown into a deep red.

"That smells like the inside of a horse stall," the cook remarked.

"It tastes like feet, too," Ari said.

"What does it do?"

Ari tore a piece of fabric into several strips. "It helps where help is needed."

"Well that's vague, isn't it?" the cook said.

Ari finished stirring the pot. Then, one by one, she dipped each torn strip of fabric into the elixir and placed them all in a basket. "Gotta go."

As she was racing out of the kitchen, she heard the cook say, "If it goes on the skin, how do you know it tastes like feet?"

Ari returned to Queen Mary's chambers to find Mary pacing, Liv stroking Bea's forehead, and Hush and Flem frantically moving about the room, packing things into saddlebags.

"Ari's here now, Bea," Liv said, glancing up. "She's going to help you."

Ari carried her basket to Bea's side, and together she and Liv draped the fabric over Bea's arms and legs and heart and head. Ari smoothed the one over Bea's head and closed her eyes, saying a silent prayer.

When she opened her eyes, she saw Liv looking at her with a

hopeful smile. The fire must have been extra warm because Ari's cheeks began to burn. She recalled, in a flash, the feel of Liv's lips against hers.

"What will it do?" came Mary's voice from above them.

Ari blushed. "It will help her body absorb nutrients three times faster when she eats and drinks. It will soothe any pain, and it will mend any wounds. In essence, she will recover more quickly, Your Majesty."

"My goodness," Queen Mary said. "If it does all that, why didn't we use it on King Henry?"

"There are some things you can't come back from." Ari winced at her own words. "Speaking of King Henry, there's something you need to know. I was in the cellar and heard your uncles talking. Something about what 'befell the king.'"

At the mention of the uncles, Bea shuddered.

"I know," said Mary. "My uncles conspired to kill him."

Oh. Drat. "Well, what about what happened in Scotland? I heard—"

"You mean with my mother? Bea told me." Mary's mouth pressed into an angry line. "She's missing."

Ari was turning out to be a terrible spy. Mary probably already knew that the uncles were planning something in England, too. She glanced around. "Are we going somewhere?" she asked, noting the saddlebags.

"We are leaving tonight," Mary said.

"Should I pack my things?" Ari asked.

Mary shifted uncomfortably. "I'm afraid not. My ladies and I must travel in a particular way, and it wouldn't . . . accommodate you."

What was that supposed to mean?

"So you don't want me to come?" Ari said.

"I need you to stay here to look after Francis." Mary glanced away. "He's going to need your help."

Tears pricked at Ari's eyes. "But, Your Majesty, I want to be one of your ladies." Now more than ever, she wanted it, and not only because it meant staying with Liv. All right, maybe it was all about Liv.

Mary shook her head. "You can't. I'm sorry, but you're not suited for this journey."

This must have something to do with Eðians. "You can trust me," Ari insisted.

"It's not a matter of—"

"I know your secret," Ari blurted out.

"Ari, perhaps you should—" Liv attempted to intervene, but Mary was curious now.

"And what secret would that be?" she asked.

Ari leaned close to the queen, in case any of the other Marys didn't know what she was about to reveal. "I know that you're a mouse," she whispered.

The queen drew back sharply. There was a revelation in her eyes, like she'd just discovered something about Ari, not the other way around. "It was you," she said at last.

"Me?"

"You're the one who told Queen Catherine." Mary's voice was ice-cold. She made no attempt to lower it. The other Marys must all know.

Ari stared at her toes. She was suddenly aware of Liv's gaze on her. She swallowed. "Yes. I saw . . . never mind what I saw. The point is, I shouldn't have told Queen Catherine anything. I was upset about Liv. And the queen threatened me with the rack or maybe a hot poker. But I want to make up for it. To help you."

"Oh, I think you've done quite enough," said Mary. "You're dismissed."

She turned, as if to put her back to Ari and her betrayal, but Liv caught her arm. "Mary," she murmured. "You forgave me. And you know how persuasive Catherine can be."

Mary sighed. "Very well. I un-dismiss you, Ari. But you must still stay behind and look after my husband."

"Yes, Your Majesty," Ari mumbled.

This had not gone how she'd hoped.

"Thank you, Ari," Queen Mary said. "That will be all."

In the corridor Liv caught up with her.

"I'm fine," Ari said, holding up a hand, even though she was starting to cry.

"I'm sorry," Liv said.

"You have nothing to be sorry about. If it weren't for you, I'd be fired. It's just . . ."

Ari sighed and sat on a bench. "I don't know where I belong." She put her head in her hands and squeezed her eyes shut so they would stop their stupid crying.

Liv sat next to her. She rubbed Ari's shoulder. "Us leaving has nothing to do with you."

Ari shook her head. "Nothing ever has anything to do with me. Why do I even bother? I'm never needed."

Liv put her arm around Ari and held her close. "You saved Bea. Of course you're needed."

Ari scooted away from her. "But you're leaving me behind. And it's like you don't care." She shook her head. "I mean, it's like none of you care."

Liv moved closer to her. "We care. I care. You know I do," she said. "It's . . . complicated."

Ari gave a frustrated laugh. "That's what my papa says when he wants me to stop asking questions."

"This is bigger than our own problems," Liv said. "We're going to Scotland, to look for Mary's mother. But we have to sneak out, before someone tries to stop us."

"Like the uncles," Ari said.

"Or Catherine," Liv added. "Or even Francis."

"But why can't I come with you?"

Liv wet her lips almost nervously. "Remember that night we danced at the wedding, when you asked me to trust you?"

"Yes," sniffed Ari.

"I'm asking you to trust me now. We would take you if we

could." Liv put her arm around Ari again, and this time, Ari sank into her. Liv pressed her lips against Ari's head, and then once, gently, to her lips. "I promise," she said. "We're not going away forever. This will all make sense one day."

Ari sniffed. "I hope so."

TWENTY-SEVEN

Francis

Francis endured the feast alone.

Not totally alone, we should say, because Catherine was there. But her support was almost more trouble than it was worth, because three times he'd had to prevent her from tipping the contents of a small vial into someone's drink. Plus, all these people talking to him, various nobles angling for favors . . .

And Mary wasn't here. Clearly, she was getting him back for their fight. He could almost hear her now, saying that if he didn't want her help, then he could be king without her.

It seemed like a very childish, unqueenly thing to do.

But mostly, he missed her. After his walk, which didn't make him feel any better, he'd gone back to his rooms to find she'd left. (That made sense, he supposed, as she had her own rooms.) But then she wasn't at the feast her uncles had planned for their arrival, which seemed strange. And even stranger, her uncles had left the feast partway through, which suited Francis fine because he was having a very difficult time being in the same room as the men who'd possibly had his father killed. But even so, every single thing about the last week felt wrong. And strange, as we mentioned.

After he escaped this latest public humiliation disguised as a social function, Francis headed toward Mary's rooms. He hoped she was all right. Perhaps she felt ill after their fight earlier. He certainly did.

As he reached her door, Francis decided that he would apologize. He needed Mary, even if she did sometimes forget to ask his opinions. They could work it out. That was what married couples did, right? Besides, they had all of France and Scotland to hold together. If they couldn't keep their marriage together for even a month, then what chance did their kingdoms have?

Heart in his throat, Francis knocked. There was a rustling inside, muffled voices, and then Mary Fleming answered the door, her eyes wide.

"Your Majesty!" She curtsied, and just over her shoulder, Francis could see that Bea had returned. She was sitting in front of the fireplace, cradling a cup of tea in her hands, and wearing several strips of cloth draped across her forehead and arms. Liv and Hush were wrapping rounds of cheese into cloth before tucking them into a saddlebag.

A saddlebag?

Mary—Francis's Mary—looked up as she pulled a fur-lined

cloak from her wardrobe. "Francis. What are you doing here?" Her expression was drawn, her cheeks pale. She looked unwell.

At once, Francis realized what she was doing.

Packing.

Leaving.

She had one foot out the door already, metaphorically speaking.

Francis blinked a few times, trying to make sure he saw what he thought he saw. His wife. Packing to leave. After a fight. About coming here.

Just . . . what? What was wrong with her? Why was she doing this to him?

"Were you just going to leave?" he asked softly. Abruptly, movement slowed around the room. The Four Marys stopped what they were doing and looked to Queen Mary for instruction, but her eyes were on Francis as he asked again, "Were you just going to leave without me? You dragged me here because of your uncles, and now you're abandoning me to them?"

Fury filled Mary's eyes. "You want to come in here and accuse *me*?"

"I think we'd better leave Their Majesties alone," Liv said quietly, letting the pack she was holding fall to the bed. The Four Marys, even poor Bea, evacuated the room without another word.

The door shut behind Francis, trapping him inside with his wife.

"Well you *are* leaving, aren't you?" Francis tried, and failed, to keep from raising his voice. "We had one fight. One. I was coming here to make up. But now you're leaving. Over a single fight!"

"You think this is about you?"

Francis threw up his hands. "I suppose you're going to tell me now that it isn't? The timing is just a coincidence, you changing your mind about wanting to come here? This was your decision, Mary. Yours alone. You didn't ask me. And you kept your uncles' part in my father's death a secret until it was convenient for me to know."

"You think it was *convenient*?" Color rose in Mary's face. "Since when are you convenient?"

A shock hammered through Francis, numbing him to the fingertips, but Mary didn't give him a chance to respond.

"Anyway, this isn't about you. This is about my mother."

How did Mary de Guise fit into any of this? "You brought me here, against my will, because you said your uncles had my father assassinated. And now somehow your own mother, another de Guise, is the real concern? What makes you think she doesn't have something to do with the murder? She wants you to have all the power in the world, too, doesn't she? And it's *convenient* for your ascension to the French throne if my father is out of the picture."

Mary gave a gasp of outrage. "You really think that of me?"

"Maybe I think that of your family! They don't have our best interests at heart. They don't have Scotland's best interest at heart."

"You take that back." Her fists clenched at her sides as she stalked toward him. "There may be a few bad apples in my family, but we all love Scotland. My mother has been caring for my kingdom all my life. You cannot claim—"

Francis dragged his hands down his face. "Your family is manipulating you, can't you see that?"

"My mother is *missing*," Mary said. "She is missing, and I'm going to find her."

"What are you going to do? Turn into a mouse and listen for court gossip?"

She looked shocked. "That's just mean, Francis. You're being so mean lately."

"I'm not. What's mean is you trying to leave me."

"This is my mother. I have to go after her."

"My father just died."

"And he will be avenged, I'm certain. But right now, my mother needs me."

"What about me?" Francis cried. "*I* need you. After all, who will make decisions if you're not here?"

"Your mother, of course!" She glared down at him. "Maybe you would understand my situation if you were *actually* the king of a country."

"I am the king," Francis said. "And as king, I forbid you to go."

"You forbid me?" Her voice was dangerously quiet.

"I do."

"As the king of France?"

"Yes." He swallowed hard. His heart pounded in his ears. If there was one thing he knew about Mary, it was that she defied orders. Even as a child, if someone had told her to eat her chocolate cake, she'd turn up her nose and demand strawberry. Mary *hated* being told what to do, and she never *ever* listened after that.

All that is to say, Francis had made a mistake. A huge one.

Mary let out a sharp laugh. "You forbid me. As the king of France. Oh, Francis, you don't even know how to be king. You don't even *want* to be king."

Red tinged the corners of Francis's vision. How dare she say that? How dare she throw that back in his face? "I *am* king," he said.

"If you have to remind someone," she said, "then you're not really king at all."

"You say it all the time," he retorted. "But you haven't actually been queen of your country, have you? Your mother has been running it this whole time. You've been here, in France, dressing up and going to parties, making bad deals with your uncles. Well, guess what, they're murderers. I told you not to trust them, but you did anyway."

"Get out," she growled. "Get out of my rooms. I can't look at you right now."

"Gladly. I can't look at you, either."

Which was saying a lot, given how much time Francis usually spent looking at Mary.

Without another word, Francis opened the door, waited a beat for the Four Marys to duck out of the way as though they hadn't been listening to every word, and then stormed down the hall.

TWENTY-EIGHT *Mary*

Mary escaped the château under the cover of darkness. First the queen loudly insisted that she needed some fresh air, so she took a "walk in the garden," Bea as a bird again tucked into a sling around Mary's neck, and Flem as a dog at Mary's side. Then they slipped out the back gate, headed for a barn nearby, where Liv had arranged to meet them with their bags.

Once in the barn, Mary dressed as a servant boy. They powdered Flem's fur in soot, so the white bits of her coat would be less visible in the dark. Bea remained in the sling. Ari's tincture had done wonders for her, but she was still weak.

"I know I've said this already," Mary said gravely, when they were ready to depart, "but I will say it again. This journey will be long and arduous, and undoubtedly dangerous. I know that you are loyal friends to me, and that opinion will not change if you decide to stay behind."

"Bark!" said Flem, a determined bark, which Mary interpreted to mean that Flem was going with her, no matter what.

"I'm going, too," Hush whispered, and showed her quiet smile. "Without me your hair would be a mess, and we can't have that."

"All right." Mary gazed down at Bea in the sling. It had already been decided that Bea should come along, as it certainly wasn't safe for her at the uncles' château.

So it was down to Liv.

When they'd talked before, when Mary had informed Liv that she was no longer going to be sent away to Norway, they'd both started crying. And then they'd both said they were sorry at the same time. And then they'd hugged, and Mary had felt like something had been righted in the world. In spite of everything, it was good to have her best friend back.

But she wouldn't ask Liv to risk her life and position yet again.

"You can say no," she whispered.

Liv shook her head. "I'm with you, Mary," she said fiercely, putting a hand on Mary's shoulder. "Please believe it when I say you have my undying loyalty. Until the very end."

"I hope it won't come to that," Mary said. "But thank you." She glanced around them. It wouldn't be long before her absence was noticed. They should go. "Shall we, ladies?"

Liv and Hush removed their clothes and folded them into the

saddlebag. Mary adjusted Bea's sling. There was a bright flash—two combined flashes, in fact—and when the light faded, Mary was the only human standing there. At her feet sat a white ermine with a black-tipped tail (an ermine, dear reader, is a small weasel, also known as a stoat). And a few feet away stood a shining dun-colored mare with a pale blond mane.

They didn't waste words. (Well—they couldn't talk, so that helped.) Mary hurriedly saddled the horse and attached the saddlebags, a mere three bags to hold everything they'd need, which was the lightest she had ever traveled. Flem was placed into her own special saddlebag, where she could feel the wind in her ears and loll her tongue out as they went. Once Liv and Flem were properly outfitted, Mary scooped up the stoat and settled her into the sling with Bea, where they could ride comfortably against her chest.

Then she swung herself up into the saddle.

Her heart was beating like a drum. Her breath was already coming in gasps. She was risking everything in this moment. Her marriage, certainly. Her crown.

But she had to know, firsthand, what had happened to her mother.

And since her uncles (and apparently her husband) wouldn't allow her to make the journey officially, she'd have to do it in secret.

"Let's go," she murmured.

Liv moved swiftly out of the stable. One of Mary's footman bowed his head at her and closed the door behind her.

"Godspeed, Your Highness," he said.

The earth seemed to fly beneath them as Liv ran. Mary held on tightly.

She didn't look back.

They headed along the Loire River until they hit Orleans, where they found an inn in which to rest through the night. In the morning, Hush became a girl and donned Mary's servant-boy clothes, and Mary became a mouse and rode in Hush's pocket. They rode hard north for two days, skirting Paris, bound for Calais, where Bea became the human of the group and sought out one of her contacts, who arranged passage across the English Channel.

On the boat they all became human again and had some supper.

After they ate, Mary stared off across the water, toward England, toward Scotland, toward what felt like her destiny.

But then she turned around and gazed back at France.

"I'll see you again," she murmured to herself.

"Of course you will," whispered Hush from beside her. (Liv, Bea, and Flem were all sleeping again, Liv because it was exhausting, running and running all day, Bea because she was still recovering from her captivity, and Flem because, well, Flem napped a lot.)

"Of course," Mary repeated, twisting her wedding ring around her finger.

"Should you have said goodbye to him?" Hush asked gently.

Mary sighed. "No. He would have tried to stop me."

Francis would see this as a betrayal, of course. He'd think she had abandoned him. This wasn't how things were supposed to happen. Married people had fights. That was normal. But Mary and Francis had fought once, and then again, even worse the second time, and now Mary was sailing off to a different country.

My country, she reminded herself.

What he'd said about her not being a real queen had stung. But this was her chance. She was going to her country to sort things out. To be a ruler, for once.

But leaving Francis, no matter how mad she was at him still, felt wrong.

"I'll be back," she said to the wind, to the water, as if they could carry her words to him. "I promise. I'll be back."

TWENTY-NINE

Ari

Ari breathed in the familiar scents of the Louvre gardens, sewage in the streets, and body odor. After a long week of travel, made longer by the constant bickering between Queen Catherine and Francis, she was finally back in Paris. But as glad as she was to be home, Ari felt as though she'd lost direction. She'd lost Queen Mary, and Mary's ladies, whom she had come to consider as friends. Mary had told her to look after Francis, and Ari was trying, but it wasn't like she could become *his* lady-in-waiting. That would be considered inappropriate, obviously.

But she reminded herself that she hadn't lost her father, or Greer, both of whom would be waiting for her in their laboratory. All she had to do was get there.

She stepped out of the royal carriage, where she'd been trapped with Francis and Catherine for the entire journey, and looked up at the palace. Almost there.

"I'm not holding court today," Francis said behind her. "And you can't make me."

Ari cringed.

"You will," Catherine announced. "We—and by *we* I mean *I*—have too much work to do. You've spent long enough moping about Mary."

Ari tried to scurry away, but she still hadn't learned how to scurry in the fine dresses she was forced to wear, and the royals were out of the carriage before she could vanish into the palace basement.

"Perhaps you should be more alarmed about Mary's departure," Francis said.

"Oh, I am," Catherine replied.

That was true. The morning after Mary left, when her absence was finally noted, the uncles had ordered the entire château locked down and searched, from cellar to stables. Everyone had been questioned, especially Ari, but she hadn't betrayed Mary's confidence—not again. She hadn't said a word when the uncles cornered her, and before they could properly threaten her, Francis had swept her away into his household, effectively protecting her from the de Guises. Catherine had been a different matter, of course, because she loomed over Francis's every move, but Ari had kept to the background as much as possible and let Francis do the talking. Or grousing, depending on your point of view.

No, he didn't know where Mary was.

No, he didn't intend to send guards after her.

No, it *wasn't* necessary, because after a search of her rooms, it was clear she and the other Marys had left of their own volition. They would turn up when they were ready.

Then Francis had declared they would leave the château immediately.

"I'm going to bed," Francis announced now. "I'll hold court tomorrow. If I feel like it."

"But, Sire." Cardinal Charles popped out of the carriage behind them. "It's only three o'clock in the afternoon."

"My son is tired," said Queen Catherine, abruptly changing her mind to oppose Mary's uncle. "He should rest."

"We'll see him at dinner, then," said the cardinal. It was strange, Ari thought, seeing this man without Duke Francis, like coming across a single, lonesome shoe without its mate. The cardinal had insisted on returning to Paris with the king, as he was needed to be the king's "spiritual adviser." (Ari shuddered, remembering this "spiritual" man speaking so lightly of torturing and murdering people. Including King Henry.) Duke Francis had stayed behind at the château, saying he'd be along to Paris shortly after he "took care of some things." Ari wondered if "some things" included the plan for England she'd heard them talking about in the cellar.

"I wouldn't count on seeing me at dinner," said Francis. Without another word he strode away. Ari tried to stride after him, but Catherine caught her arm.

"Just a moment, girl," the dowager queen said.

"I swear, I don't know where Mary went," Ari lied smoothly.

Catherine scrutinized her face for a moment. "That's interesting. But not why I wanted to speak with you." She glanced over at Cardinal Charles, who was lingering nearby. "Don't you have some prayers to get to?" she barked.

"Yes, I shall pray for you, especially," the cardinal replied in a nasty tone. "I'm praying for your soul right now."

"Do it somewhere else." Still holding Ari's arm, Catherine pulled her into one of the garden courtyards. "I may have been hasty in dismissing you, Aristotle."

Ari blinked at her. This might be the closest anyone had ever come to receiving an apology from Catherine de Medici. "It's all right," she murmured. "Queen Mary hired me. Officially, I mean."

"But Queen Mary is gone."

"And I have no idea where."

"Yes, so you say. But I have thought of a way you can help her."

Blink blink. Queen Catherine's "help" was usually designed to help only herself. But Catherine was in power again, so Ari didn't dare outright refuse her. "What can I 'help' you with?" *Merde.* Now she was using air quotes.

"I wish you to make a potion."

Double *merde.* Not another potion. But some part of Ari was immediately intrigued. "What potion?"

"Given what you told me about Queen Mary and her 'little' issue, if she does return to court—"

"She will," Ari said. Liv had promised that they wouldn't be gone forever.

"Of course," said Queen Catherine. "So when she returns, we must ensure that her secret remains secret."

On this, Ari was surprised that she agreed. "Yes," she said slowly.

"But secrets do have a way of getting out. You discovered her secret after only a week of watching her."

"Yes, but I had—" Ari stopped herself. What would Queen Catherine do with a *See Through Walls* potion? "Never mind. You're right."

"If someone were to accuse Queen Mary of being"— Catherine glanced around to make sure no one was nearby; she lowered her voice—"an Eðian, it would be Mary's word against whoever accused her."

Ari's brow rumpled. "But what could I do about that?"

"You could make a potion to transform a person into an animal." Catherine said this like it was the most obvious of conclusions. "That way, if conspirators accused Queen Mary, we could arrange for them to be 'revealed' as Eðians, themselves."

Ari bit her lip thoughtfully. She didn't want to do any favors for Catherine, but this actually seemed like a clever idea. It was a way to help Mary, and by extension, Liv. And it was a tantalizing challenge. Could she really make a potion to turn a person into an Eðian? It sounded like fun to try. (Maybe not so fun for Greer.)

"If I do this," Ari said carefully, "and I can do this, I want an assurance that my position here at court, and my father's, will never be in question again."

The corner of Catherine's mouth turned up in a hint of a smile. "Well played. But I can't promise you that. I'm only the Queen Mother, after all."

"Then make your own potion," said Ari, turning away.

"Wait!" Catherine caught her shoulder. "I wasn't finished. I'm sure the king would be most grateful if you could protect his wife. He could provide you that assurance."

"All right," said Ari, trying to not smile herself. "I'll give it my best shot."

It was exhilarating to be back in the laboratory. Ari spent a few minutes greeting each piece of her equipment.

"Hello, giant cauldron," she called tenderly. "Good afternoon, favorite vial! We meet again, dear fireplace."

"Uh, I'm here, too," said Greer.

Ari threw her arms about her. "Oh, yes. I have missed you most of all."

A throat cleared from behind her. She turned to see Nostradamus looking up from his quatrains.

"Hello, Galileo," he said.

Sometimes she wondered if her father was messing with her. But she went to him and hugged him, too. "Hello, Papa. I'm back."

"I predicted you would be. And you have restored our position here, as I also predicted. Now you have an important task to complete." Nostradamus stroked his long beard in a satisfied manner.

Ari had a shivery feeling. She did not like being the subject of any of her father's prophecies. "Yes, well . . ."

"Better get to it," he said. "No time like the present. Unless you're me, of course, in which case it's the future."

"What task?" asked Greer, a note of trepidation in her voice.

Ari grinned. "We're about to have a lot of fun."

Greer already looked a bit green.

THIRTY
Francis

Francis wasn't very good at being king.

Day one back at the Louvre: two farmers had declared ownership of the same land. One planted grapes. The other planted apples. Catherine sided with the apple farmer, but Francis, who wouldn't have minded a glass of wine about that time, and knew that wine came from grapes, proclaimed that the grape farmer should keep the land. Later, one of his attendants located the actual records, which revealed that Catherine had been right. The apple farmer truly owned the land.

Day four: seventeen new parents arrived to ask Francis to kiss their babies. Francis, whose wife had just left him for another kingdom, started crying. The babies cried. The parents cried. Everyone was crying.

Day seven: Francis stared into the middle distance while Catherine held court.

Day eleven: a handful of courtiers approached him to request a festival or celebration of some kind. King Henry would have held three by now, after all. *I don't care*, Francis thought, but he'd accidentally used his outside voice. The courtiers immediately decided to interpret that as permission—he didn't care if they went ahead and did what they wanted.

Day fifteen: Francis was dragged to one of those parties. He didn't have a wife to dance with, so he didn't dance with anyone. Instead he got into a huge fight with his mother.

"You need to try harder," she chided him over dessert. "Or, at all."

"I am trying," he said. Like now, he was trying to eat a sticky bun.

Catherine tsked. "Oh, darling. We must not tell lies."

So she was calling him a liar now. That was rich, coming from her. "How's this for the truth?" Francis said. "I never wanted to be king. I've been dreading it all my life."

She glanced around. No one was looking at them, but the room had gone quieter. "Tough luck," she replied softly. "You are king."

"Yes, I am," he said.

"So act like it," she muttered.

"Are you sure that's what you want? Because I thought you wanted to rule the country."

"All I want is what's best for you," she said. "And for France, of course."

"And you think I'm not what's best for France."

"I think you're very young and inexperienced."

"So it's better to be old and corrupt."

The room got even quieter. Catherine gasped in outrage. "What did you call me?"

"Old," he said. "And corrupt. And you're right. I am the king, and it's time for me to act like one, and kings don't need their mothers hovering over them."

Catherine went very still. "We'll speak more on this later," she said after a moment, and then swept away from him into the crowd.

Francis refused to let his shoulders sag in relief.

"Get me the Nostradamus girl," he heard his mother snap to a servant as she went out the door. He hoped Ari wasn't in trouble now.

The room stayed silent a moment longer, then returned to a normal volume as everyone hurried to discuss what had transpired. Like Francis wasn't even there.

Even so, it felt good, standing up for himself. This was the best he'd felt in weeks. Unfortunately, it also felt like a terrible mistake.

Catherine didn't speak to him for days, which made ruling the kingdom . . . tricky, to say the least, with both of them acting like the other wasn't there.

She'd proclaim one thing. He'd contradict her a moment later.

He'd declare something. She'd undermine him with her next breath.

The nobles complained about the public bickering, how no one knew what to do anymore, the chaos this was causing throughout the kingdom, but Francis couldn't bring himself to stop. If he stopped, Catherine won.

One evening, about a month after they'd returned to Paris, Francis was writing a letter to Mary. He wouldn't send it—that would be too dangerous for her—but it helped him feel better, imagining he was talking with her, getting her advice on how to handle the situation he found himself in now.

A knock sounded on the door, and without waiting for his reply, Catherine entered.

Francis quickly flipped his paper over. "What do you want?"

"To make amends, my dear." Catherine motioned for a maid to set a tray on the table. A pot of tea and plate of biscuits rested there, making the room smell heavenly. "I've brought a peace offering."

"Why?" he asked suspiciously.

"I've been thinking about our argument the other day," Catherine said. "And I've been thinking about what's best for France. Our infighting is not good for the kingdom."

On that, Francis could agree.

"So I thought I might come here and discuss the issues," she went on. "Perhaps we can find some common ground. No more fighting about apple farmers."

A knot in Francis's chest loosened. "All right." He turned his chair to face her. "Have a seat."

The maid poured two cups of tea, then left the room. Catherine pushed one toward him. "Let's start big. What's important to you? Where do you see France in five years?"

Well, for one, he saw France with both monarchs present, perhaps with an heir on the way. But he didn't say that. Not to Catherine. "I can start sooner than that," he said. "I want Montgomery punished."

Catherine nodded. "I can agree with that. He's in our dungeon now, awaiting trial. We will ensure he is brought to justice."

"And anyone else who's responsible for Father's death." He wanted to tell her that Mary's uncles had been behind the murder, because Catherine would make them pay—and then some. But telling her the truth might put Mary at risk. Catherine already knew that Mary was an Eðian; if she knew that Duke Francis and Cardinal Charles had assassinated Henry to prematurely put Mary on the French throne . . . No, Catherine would not let that slide.

"Yes," said Catherine. "Those responsible for Henry's death must be held accountable."

Francis fought off a faint smile. Maybe his mother wasn't *so* bad. They could get along—when she wasn't being unreasonable and power hungry.

(Which was, dear reader, all the time. But okay, Francis.)

"What else, dear? Think big. Think beyond our family. Think like a king."

Francis swallowed hard. "Well, I have had something else on my mind. . . ."

Catherine nodded encouragingly.

"Criminal justice reform—for Eðians."

Her eyebrows rose. "What do you mean?"

"I think it's time that we decriminalize being an Eðian. They're just people, like Verities." And it didn't hurt that accepting Eðians would keep Mary out of danger . . . if she ever returned to Paris.

Catherine looked pensive. "That would be an enormous overhaul of our system," she said at last. "It would take time. Years, perhaps."

"You did ask for a five-year plan," Francis reminded her.

"Yes." Catherine's smile was strained. "I'm not sure this is something that we could reasonably expect to do in five years, but that doesn't mean it's not worth trying. It may take longer, but we could make incremental changes to prepare the kingdom."

"I don't like waiting," Francis murmured.

"One of the benefits of being old," Catherine said with a wry smile, "is accepting that things worth doing take time."

"So you think my idea is worth pursuing?"

"Yes, of course." She plucked a biscuit from the plate and took a small bite. "You are the king, after all. It's difficult for me to pass the reins of the kingdom to someone else, but you were right when you said that you must learn. I just hope that you'll allow me to help."

"And by help you mean *help*, not take control of everything?" he asked.

It looked like it pained her, but at last, Catherine gave a single, decisive nod.

Finally. She was listening to him. Maybe he'd be able to pull off this king business after all.

"Here." Catherine nudged his teacup. "Before it gets cold."

Hesitantly, Francis picked himself up and went to the table to sit across from her. "Thank you, Mother. You don't know what this means to me."

"You're my son. I want you to succeed." She sipped her tea.

Francis sipped his. It smelled odd, like coriander mixed with chamomile, but tasted all right. He took another sip, and then reached for a biscuit. He wished Mary were here. Mary loved biscuits. He would eat an extra one for her.

Francis sighed. "I hope Mary's all right."

"I'm sure she is," Catherine said. "Now, tell me more about your five-year plan."

"I want to build a university with the largest library on the continent, where everyone can study no matter their station." Francis had no idea where that had come from, but it sounded like a fine plan.

"Well, that certainly is ambitious. But what will we do if the peasants learn to read?"

"I think we'd be better off—

FLASH.

White light enveloped him, and then everything went dark. From somewhere far, far away, he heard Catherine say, "I'm sorry, darling, but I'm afraid you left me with no other choice."

THIRTY-ONE ᶜMary

At the exact moment of Francis's lights-out (as he would later call it), Mary, Queen of Scots, was approximately 679 miles away from Paris. She and her ladies had arrived in Edinburgh, Scotland. They had not gone straight to the palace, however, but stopped at an inn on the outskirts of town, much as you do before you're about to see someone you want to impress—you stop at the restroom first to fix your hair. Or, in Mary's case, have your lady-in-waiting fix your hair.

Everyone was a bit on edge. Ever since they'd crossed into Scotland the journey had been rough, to say the least. There'd been groups of disgruntled Scots on the roads, accosting anyone they suspected as a Verity. "Show us your animal," they'd insist to the people they stopped, which was uncomfortable, but of course, doable, for our group of Marys. Even now, in what Mary had assumed would be the safety of Edinburgh, there were rumblings of discontent. People with pitchforks were standing around in clusters that very distinctly resembled mobs.

"I'm sure everything will be fine," Mary said as Hush combed out her tangled and somewhat frizzy auburn tresses—it'd been a while since she'd had access to shampoo. "My mother has probably been found by now, and she's working to get my kingdom in order again, and this whole trip will have been for nothing."

The other Marys exchanged glances and murmured unintelligible things like, "Of course, you're right, whatever you say, Your Majesty, et cetera."

"Then we'll have a nice visit." Mary sighed. "I haven't seen my mother in so long. I wonder if she'll even recognize me."

Hush set down the brush and started to plait Mary's hair.

Bea paced nervously near the window. She'd fully recovered by now and had spent most of the days flying out ahead of them, scouting, or talking with other bird-type E∂ians, and at no time had she heard anything, one way or another, as to the whereabouts of Mary de Guise.

Below, in the street, someone bellowed, "Down with the queen!" not because they knew that the queen was anywhere nearby, but because that seemed to be the sentiment of the general population.

Yes, reader. Largely thanks to the smear campaign that John Knox had been waging against Mary all year, things were pretty bad. And Mary only knew the half of it. The pamphlet had been just the beginning. . . .

"Of course she'll recognize you," said Flem, always the optimist. "But she will also be amazed at what a beautiful, graceful woman you've become."

"On that note, let's get you dressed and looking like a queen again," said Liv.

"Or maybe not the queen," Bea said quickly. "But a woman—yes."

Mary held up her arms, and Liv pulled a dress over her head. It felt strange. They'd spent the few weeks dressed as boys—the only way to travel safely from one country to another in the sixteenth century—and the feeling of skirts swishing around her ankles seemed foreign and suddenly stifling.

"Don't be nervous," Liv said.

"Oh, I'm not nervous," Mary said. "I'm simply eager to find out what's happened. I'm sure all will be perfectly well."

"And at least we're not in England anymore," Flem piped up.

Yes, there was that.

England, too, hadn't been what Mary expected. First off, nobody in England seemed to be able to understand what she was saying, although Mary had been assured by all of her previous tutors that her English was quite excellent. Secondly, there seemed to be a strange disagreement among the people in England over whether Britain was actually a part of Europe. This became apparent on Mary's first day in England, when, as they disembarked the boat at Dover, they were accosted by a man who insisted that they pay him.

"You've come from France, have you?" the man had asked. (At least that's what Mary thought he'd said, as she couldn't understand him very well, either.)

"Not that it's any business of yours, sir, but yes," she'd replied.

The man had nodded. "There's a tax," he'd informed her. "Anybody leaving Europe has got to pay it."

"But England is a part of Europe, is it not?" Mary had argued.

The man had shaken his head. "Not anymore, it's not. We voted to exit from Europe five years ago."

Mary had never heard of this, but it sounded like a terrible idea.

"So pay up," the man had said.

"Maybe we can make a deal," Mary had suggested.

But no deal had been struck, because Mary had decided that this man was a simple highwayman, and given Liv the signal to kick him and run away.

It had all been quite confusing. Mary had decided that she didn't really care for England, as a country.

Too much rain.

Entirely too much tea. Biscuits that weren't actually biscuits, like what the cook at the Louvre made, but cookies. And not nearly enough wine.

And what were these chips that people were constantly offering her?

326

Mary had been most eager to get out of England. And now here they were. Arrived. In Scotland. A place she still thought of as "home," even though she hadn't set foot on Scottish ground in many years.

But when she thought about the word *home*, the image of Francis also floated up in her mind.

She twisted her ring around her finger. She wished he were with her. He'd be nervous about this, too (and yes, she was nervous, no matter what she claimed), but then her role would be to help Francis feel more confident. She'd say, "Eyes up," to him, and then she'd remember to hold her head high, herself.

She wondered what he was doing now. (Gosh—if only she knew.)

"We'll find her," Liv said, assuming that Mary's pensive silence concerned her mother.

"I know," Mary replied. "That's what we've come to do. And so we will."

"I demand to be taken at once to Mary de Guise," said Mary an hour later, at the entrance to Holyrood Palace.

The guard squinted at her. "Oh, you demand it, do you? And who are you?"

"I'm her daughter. She'll wish to see me immediately."

The guard scoffed. "Her daughter. Mary de Guise has no daughter but the one who lives in France, and you're not—"

"I am the Queen of Scotland, England, and France," said Mary, straightening to her full height. (Never mind that Elizabeth was currently queen of England, where she claimed to be the reigning monarch of England, Scotland, and France.) "I am your queen, in fact. Now announce me to my mother, before you irritate me further."

If you have to say you're the king, she remembered from her fight with Francis, cringing inwardly, *then you really aren't one.*

Sigh. She even missed Francis's mad face. He'd been so very angry at her the last time she'd seen him, and with good cause, she supposed. It seemed like so long ago, she could hardly remember what they'd quarreled over. Oh, right. Her leaving to search for her mother. Which she was still doing, right now.

She supposed he was even angrier with her now that she'd abandoned him. He'd do that funny little hop he did whenever he was truly angry. The one that always made her want to smile.

"Wait here," said the guard.

She was about to tell him that queens did not wait, unless they wanted to, but he had already shut the door. She glanced around at her ladies, who all looked nervous for a different reason. Bea, most of all.

After a moment the door opened again, and James Stuart, the Earl of Moray, stepped out.

"Mary!" he gasped in amazement, and then looked around to see who had noticed them and ushered Mary quickly inside. "What are you doing here?"

"Is that any way to greet your sister?" she said, leaning to kiss his cheek.

Half sister, technically. James was her older half brother, the bastard son of her father, but Mary considered him a whole part of her family. When she was a small girl she'd called him "horsey" and rode around on his back while he'd whinnied and bucked (but not in an Eðian way, of course) to make her squeal with laughter.

Now she found him a rather dour-faced man with a weak chin and an even weaker smile.

"I'm surprised to see you, is all," he said. "I didn't know you were planning a visit. And . . . why?"

"I need to see Mother," she said. "Is she here?"

A strange expression crossed his face, guilt, perhaps, and sorrow.

"So it's true, then," Mary said softly. "She's gone missing."

"Not just missing," said James. "Your mother is dead."

Afterward (Mary couldn't have said how long, as time got fuzzy for a while) Mary got through it all by doing what so many people do: she threw herself into work.

"I'd like to take a tour," she told James. "Now, please."

"Of the palace?" he asked.

"Yes. And then of the city."

"You've been traveling so long," he said. "Surely you should take a few days to rest."

"And after that, I'd like to travel the country," she continued as if he hadn't spoken. Rest sounded like the last thing she needed. "The people should know that I am here, quite well in both body and spirit and capable of serving as their queen after my mother's . . ."

She still couldn't say out loud that her mother was dead. James had shown her the grave of Mary de Guise, and told her about how the sudden onslaught of "the Affliction" (a kind of catch-all illness of the time, like dropsy or consumption) had spirited her mother away in the span of a few days, so quickly that the doctors had hardly been called before she passed. But it seemed to Mary that this must all be a great misunderstanding. Her mother could simply not be dead. She was only still missing. She would return. She would be found. But until then . . .

Mary cleared her throat. "The people will want to meet their queen, and I wish to meet them, as well."

"The people aren't in a very good mood," James said.

"Yes, I noticed," said Mary. "We shall have to remedy that."

"I don't know if that's something you can remedy," James said.

"Well, I can certainly try. I refuse to cower in the castle, if that's what you're suggesting I do. No, thank you. A queen must be bold and decisive."

James's expression became resigned. "Very well. I will make the arrangements. But I do not believe it to be a good idea, in truth. You have enemies here, Mary. It's not safe to parade about the country unguarded."

"So guard me," Mary said, her brow rumpling. "I'm aware of what's being said about me. I've even seen the pamphlet. But why should these people really be my enemies? What have I done but give my body and soul over to the interests of my country?"

"We're in the middle of an Eðian rebellion," James reminded her.

"Yes, but why?"

"You are a Verity monarch," James said plainly.

Well. That was a matter of opinion.

"And you may be of Scottish blood, but you've lived your entire life in France, which causes many to see you as a foreigner."

"I am a Scot!" Mary protested hotly. "It's right in my name."

"You even speak Scottish with a French accent," James pointed out.

"I do not!" She glanced at her ladies, who were standing beside her looking very uncomfortable about this conversation. "Do I?"

"No, Your Majesty," they murmured in unison, but they didn't meet her eyes.

Oh. Droppings.

"And to top it off, you're a woman, which many people—but not me, I assure you—believe are not fit to be the rulers of countries," James said softly. "So, to sum up, you're a female, Verity, foreigner—the embodiment of all that the people dislike and distrust."

This felt like a very unfair assessment.

"Nevertheless, I am the queen," she said.

There you go again, she thought, imagining Francis laughing at her. *Insisting that you're queen.*

"If I have enemies, the only way to bring them over to my

side is for them to get to know me better," she said, her chin lifting. "And to do that, I must meet and speak with them. Then they will see my merit as their monarch."

"Perhaps," James said doubtfully.

"Name one," she said impulsively.

"Name one what?"

"Name an enemy of mine. Someone nearby, who I could meet today."

James rubbed at his chin. "Uh, well. There are so many . . . it's hard to pick just one."

"Name one!" she demanded.

"All right, all right," he assented. "John Knox. He really, really hates you."

"John Knox is in Edinburgh?" Mary suppressed a shiver when she thought of the pamphlet. Even the name of John Knox caused her heart to beat faster. But she forced herself to scoff. "How can he hate me if he doesn't even know me?"

"He hates the very idea of you," James said.

"Invite him to the palace this afternoon. I wish to speak with him."

James shook his head. "That's a bad idea. I can't let you do that."

The Marys cringed. Even Mary herself had misgivings. But now she was committed.

"Invite him," Mary insisted. "I will win him over. You'll see."

* * *

John Knox was a tall, gaunt man with the worst beard in the history of bad beards. (We checked this, dear reader, and it's legit—John Knox had a terrible black beard that smelled of rotten eggs and occasionally had a fly flutter in and out of it, and we don't want to think about it anymore.)

He definitely hated Mary. He seemed to consider her gender to be the most serious of her offenses.

"I've even written a book about it," he said as he stood before her in the throne room. "I wrote it largely in response to that heretical witch, Elizabeth, taking the throne of England, but it could also be applied to you. It's called *The First Blast of the Trumpet against the Monstrous Regiment of Women*. Monstrous, of course, meaning in this case, unnatural, and regiment meaning, not a section of armed forces, but 'rule.' In other words, women should not be rulers."

"And why not?" asked Mary stiffly. She'd expected this, but still, it was unpleasant to hear. She rather wanted to have Knox thrown into the dungeon and wash her hands of him. But that would surely not accomplish her goal of winning over the Scottish people.

"God, by order of his creation, has deprived woman of authority and dominion," he explained matter-of-factly. "The weak should never govern the strong, and everyone knows that women are naturally weaker than men. Their sight, then, in the ruling of a country, is but blindness, their strength, weakness, their counsel, foolishness, and their judgment, folly. They are guided by wild fits of emotion, and lack the ability to reason."

Mary wished he'd tell her how he really felt. Or not.

"But doesn't God, as you say, dictate the line of succession? Didn't God make me the queen?" she reasoned. "And does not your holy book say that you must accept those in authority that God has put over you?"

Knox tutted like she was a silly, ignorant child. "You know nothing about God, being that you are a Verity."

She rubbed at her eyes. "Is there a different God for Verities and for Eðians, then?"

"No," answered Knox sagely. "But the Verities, in denying the sacred animal form inside of all of us, cannot understand the true nature of the divine."

Mary really, really wished that she could tell him that she was an Eðian. It would be so easy. She could change, right this instance, into a mouse. But that would be revealing her greatest secret and getting herself into hot water with a whole other group of enemies. Like her uncles, for instance.

"What animal are you?" she asked. She would have guessed something like a badger or a wolf. "Can I see?"

Knox stroked down his terrible beard. "The animal form is, as I said, a sacred thing, not to be flashed about at the whim of a teenage girl."

She propped her head in her hand. She wanted to point out the way that, earlier that week, his followers had been demanding that very thing of passersby on the roads. But him changing would also mean that he'd disrobe, and she had no desire to see this man without his clothing.

"If there is a sacred animal in all of us," she said after a moment, "then doesn't it exist also in Verities, no matter their beliefs? So we are really not different."

"What we believe is everything," Knox said, shaking his head. "Verities believe that the animal magic should be suppressed and hidden. Which is against God's will. Hence all Verities are eternally damned and will burn in hell. I'm sorry, madam, but that also means you. You are beautiful, I find, and well spoken, and witty—"

"Why, thank you," said Mary. Perhaps he was warming to her.

"But you will still burn. And you should not be ruling a country."

Mary sighed.

Knox wasn't done. "As long as you insist upon sitting on the throne, you will be cursed. That is why your mother was struck down, as well."

Mary stood up abruptly, her face filling with heat. "You have no right to say such things about my mother," she said.

Knox shrugged. "I have every right. You are the one who has no rights."

She wished she could have come up with the perfect reply to this—the exact right words that would put this insufferable man in his place. But instead she was overtaken by a wild fit of emotion, which only seemed to prove his point.

She called for her guards, and had John Knox thrown into the stocks for the rest of the day, to remind him of who was in charge of this country and who was not.

"I am the queen," she whispered to herself. "I am the queen."

THIRTY-TWO

Ari

Ari walked through a field outside of Paris, a basket of fresh-cut herbs on her arm. It was good to be out of the confines of the palace just for a morning. Ari had been working awfully hard for weeks, brewing away in the laboratory. But she'd given the *Embrace Your Inner Animal* potion to Catherine yesterday. She was free. The air was cool, but the sun beamed warm on her skin. Even the birds were singing.

Just then, a bird dove at her head.

Ari shrieked and dropped her basket.

The bird dove again. It was a mockingbird. Ari swiped at it with her hands, but it floated up and out of reach. Then it dropped something on her head.

Ari froze. Slowly she reached up and felt whatever was now lodged in her hair.

Oh good. It was just a bit of parchment.

The mockingbird gave one last loud squawk and flew away.

That was weird. Ari stared down at the parchment. It was almost like the bird had deliberately brought it to her.

Like a message or something.

She turned it over, and her heart skipped a beat when she saw her name—just Ari—written on the other side.

It *was* a message. She tore it open.

> *We have arrived at our destination safely. I miss your face.*
> *Liv*

Ari pressed the parchment to her chest. Then she yelled, "What if I want to write back?" at the trees where the mockingbird had vanished. There was no reply.

But Liv had written to her. She was safe. In Scotland. And she missed Ari. Specifically, her face.

Ari floated on a cloud back to the palace and down to the lab.

"Hello, Papa," she nearly sang out to her father at his desk. "Hello, Greer," she said to the guinea pig sitting glumly next to him.

(That's right, dear reader. It'd been a hard few weeks for Greer. She was currently—and not exactly voluntarily—embracing her inner animal. Which was, appropriately, we think, a guinea pig.)

Greer made a noise that was a cross between a squeal and a whistle.

"Hello, Ari," her father said slowly.

Ari was in such a good mood. She began to dance around.

"Really, Aristotle," her father said. "Must you be so jubilant? You're bound to break something."

"That's impossible, Father," Ari said, mid-twirl. "I know every inch of this laboratory." She promptly ran into a cart and knocked over a cup of white powder. "Wait, who put that there? No matter— look what I received!" Ari held up the parchment from Liv.

"Aristotle," Nostradamus said in a sterner voice, and that's when she realized something was wrong. "You haven't said hello to our guests."

Ari whipped around to follow his eyes. There, at the back of the room, stood two armed guards. She hadn't even noticed them before.

"Oh, hello," Ari said, her heart now dropping into her stomach.

"Queen Catherine has graciously sent these men to guard us," Nostradamus said tightly. "It's for our own protection. From our vast number of enemies," he read from the cards that came with the guards. "And, most importantly, from ourselves."

This was obviously bad. Ari's mind whirled. She had delivered the potion Catherine had requested, on time, and it did exactly what the dowager queen had wished it to. So why were they in trouble?

Greer-the-guinea-pig made a rumbling noise, her tiny body vibrating with the sound. Ari hoped the potion wasn't about to wear off. She wasn't sure yet exactly how long the effects would last. She guessed it would be somewhere between a day and a week. But it would be difficult to explain if Greer changed back now.

Ari forced a smile to her lips. "Thank you, sirs, for watching over my father. But I'm here. We don't need protection."

The guards just stared at her.

"I suppose I should go talk to the dowager queen," Ari said.

"Yes, I believe she is expecting you," said Nostradamus. "But be careful. I've seen a long, arduous road stretched before you. It could be metaphorical. Or it could not. Who's to say?"

Gosh, Ari hated it when her father predicted long, arduous roads, metaphorical or not.

"Yes, Papa," she said.

"Be well, daughter," he said as she reached the door.

It sounded ominously like goodbye.

The walk to the queen's quarters felt long. Ari tried to reassure herself that the guards meant nothing. She and her father did important work in the laboratory. Perhaps they did require protection. Or Queen Catherine simply had a few questions regarding the potion. Surely between last night and this morning, there'd been no time for her to use the potion on anyone. Besides, Ari really hadn't made that much, so she assumed that it would only be used in case of an emergency. Which couldn't have happened between last night and this morning. Could it?

Ari knocked on the door. "It's Ari, Your Majesty."

One of the queen's ladies opened the door, and Ari was

relieved to see that this lady was most definitely human and not an animal.

"Ah, Aristotle. I've been expecting you. Leave us, Jane," Queen Catherine said.

Her lady left and closed the door.

"Your Majesty, I was hoping to speak to you," Ari said. "Regarding the guards you sent to the laboratory?"

The queen gazed down at her fingernails. "Yes? What about them?"

"Why did you send them?"

"To protect my investments," answered Catherine.

Ari gulped. "Are you not pleased with the potion I gave you yesterday? It does work, I assure you."

"Yes, I know," said the queen. "That potion worked wonders."

Ari felt the color drain from her face. "Worked?"

The queen walked over to her desk, where there was a small wooden box with holes punched into the lid. She carefully lifted it, and as she did so, Ari was sure she saw the top of the box vibrate and push against the small gold latch at the side.

She instantly had a bad feeling about this. "What's that?"

"This is a most precious cargo, and one in which I am entrusting to your care."

"My care?"

The queen carefully set the box down in front of Ari and then went to her desk, where she opened an intricate wooden chest in which Ari knew she kept many of her own tinctures. She pulled out a medium-sized jar and thrust it into Ari's hands. "These should be enough."

Ari held the jar to the light. Through the distorted glass she saw a bunch of tiny black things flying about.

The queen smiled. "You must travel to Calais at once, and you must do it discreetly, and if I were you, I would dress like a boy."

"Your Majesty, please tell me what is going on."

"This is our new arrangement. You protect what is mine. And I will protect what is yours."

Ari's hands started to tremble. "You mean my father."

"Yes. That's how this works."

This was going much worse than Ari had hoped. "What are you going to do to him?"

"Nothing," said the queen brusquely. "Assuming you do what I ask."

Ari felt strangely disconnected from her body. She saw herself nodding. "All right. What's in the box?"

The queen unhinged the latch. "Ari, may I present, His Majesty, the king of France."

What? Did she mean Francis? *Mon Dieu*, what had she done? "That's the king? But he's a—he's a—" She felt a little faint and swallowed down some bile.

"He is," the queen confirmed. "But never fear. This is for the good of the country. *Vive la France!*"

THIRTY-THREE
Francis

I'm a what? Francis thought loudly.

No one answered.

What am I? he thought again, but his voice was trapped in his head. No one heard him. Instead, a loud, croaking noise emerged, rattled around him, and echoed inside his box.

He considered jumping over the edge of the box and escaping into the room—perhaps he could find the passages Mary had used in her mouse form—but he had a suspicion that would only enrage Catherine, and that would be bad for everyone.

"Well. This is a most interesting development." The thunderous voice from above belonged to Ari. It was so, so loud. Not only that, but her face was huge, looming over the entire box. She was a giant.

No, Francis was very small. Puny, one might say. He'd figured that out last night when his mother had fished him out of the folds of his clothes and shut him in this box before he could try to run away. And he *would* have run away, if he could have, because he hadn't recognized her at first. His vision was weird, multidirectional, and tinged blue, like something about the very structure of his eyes was different.

As if trapping Francis in a box hadn't been enough, Catherine had stabbed small holes into the lid, startling him each time. Spears of light permeated the gloom, but Francis couldn't see what had changed about himself. He couldn't turn his head to see his body, so whatever he was, it was a complete mystery.

Except . . .

"Watch this," Catherine said. He was pretty sure that was his mother's voice, anyway. It had a different quality than before, but he supposed his ears were different now, too. Did he even have ears? He couldn't feel them.

Metal scraped on glass. Buzzing. Sharp, frantic movement.

Before Francis even realized, something warm and wiggly filled his mouth. Then he swallowed it.

He didn't know why he'd swallowed the fly. Perhaps he'd die.

The lid settled on the box again, leaving him in the dark except for the spots of light from the breather holes. Their voices were muffled as they continued their conversation.

"Incredible," Ari breathed. "But why?"

"Why is none of your business. You just do what I tell you to do. For your father's sake."

Francis was starting to think his mother might be evil.

"Ah." Ari sounded uncomfortable, but Francis had bigger—rather, smaller—problems to worry about right now.

What am I? he tried to shout, because it felt like the most important thing to know at this moment. He should probably be worried about the whole *take the king to Calais* thing, but that seemed like a problem for five minutes from now.

"Once you've left Paris," the queen said, "I will announce the king's untimely demise."

WHAT? Francis squeaked.

"There, there, my dear." Someone—Catherine, probably—patted the box. Her fingers boomed against the lid, and her rings rapped like claps of thunder. "It's for the best. And the funeral will be a grand affair, just as extravagant as any of your father's parties." She tsked.

"Your Majesty?" Ari asked nervously.

"This is no time to be squeamish, girl. Your kingdom needs you. And when the news of Francis's death reaches Calais, you will be just as sad and brokenhearted as the rest of the people. I'll say that Francis died of an ear infection, which will surprise no one. As a baby, he had ear infections every week. Even now, people see him as somewhat sickly, because that ill-fated portrait. I'll have the artist flogged again, I think, for misrepresenting my son. But I'll also thank him, because that image is turning out to be useful."

"This is all most alarming, Your Majesty," Ari said.

"Yes," Catherine agreed. "And poor Francis, taken so soon after my late husband's departure from this world. But Francis cannot remain king, and in order for Charles IX to ascend to the throne, Francis must be dead."

And that was why he was trapped as an Eðian of some sort? Francis had heard that Eðians (or the religious type of Eðians, anyway) believed that there was an animal inside of every person, a true representation of who the person was. Francis had always scoffed at the notion. Mary was nothing like a mouse, after all. Her Eðian form was useful to her—she'd become what she needed to be, to survive.

But this was different. He hadn't wanted to change. And what the heck had he changed into?

He'd spent all night trying to revert back into a human (with only a slight fear of bursting through the wooden box around him), waiting for that flash of light to surround him again, but no matter how he strained (and oh, he strained—his eyeballs hurt from all that straining), he stubbornly remained a mystery animal. But he tried again now, as his mother and Ari continued quietly talking. And again. To no avail.

"Do you think he can understand us?" Ari asked as he lay panting at the bottom of the box, totally exhausted from not becoming human.

"Of course he can! He may be a"—the box shifted, and Francis couldn't hear what his mother said over the thunder surrounding him—"but he still has his mind."

The box stilled for a moment.

"You've been given your instructions," Catherine said. "And I've had a bag packed for you. I'm trusting you with my son's life. And your father's."

"I will take care of him," Ari promised hoarsely. "I will guard his life with my own."

Francis's heart twisted. What was happening? He'd been poisoned, that was obvious. And now he was being sent away, his throne usurped.

It had all been an act, last night when his mother had come to ask him about his ideas. All along she had intended to give Charles IX the crown and make herself regent, because she *would* have to be regent, as Francis's brother was still only a child.

Francis groaned as his box changed hands.

"Be strong, my son," Catherine said.

Francis wanted to call out to her, but again he made that awful noise. He still had no idea what he was, beyond a creature that was happy to eat flies and couldn't turn its head.

Before he knew it, his box was in a bag of some kind, and being carried out of his mother's rooms. Out of the palace.

Everything that happened next was wildly uncomfortable. Whatever creature he was, it was not suited to being kept in small boxes.

He was bounced and jostled from side to side, and Ari must have known it, because she kept saying, "Sorry, sorry." A short time later, the jostling changed from the two-legged gait of a human to the four-legged gait of a horse.

What was the plan? They were going to Calais, he knew, but

what about after that? Did they have lodging? What about food? Ugh, food. Francis was already hungry again—so hungry he'd have eaten another fly, if one had been offered. But what he *really* wanted was a fly.

What?

No, he wanted a nice juicy fly.

No! Not a fly.

He had to stop thinking about flies.

Instead, he bounced around his box and wished Ari would stop and *talk* to him.

It was a miserable trip. Francis had to admit that being fake-dead was worse than being a king, at least when it came to exerting any measure of control over his life. Where he used to have choices about what to wear, when to eat, even whether to get out of bed that day, now he was just carted around, his feelings about all of this totally overlooked.

He must have slept, but it was hard to tell how long. He had no idea where they were or how far they'd ridden. It was all just. the. same.

Terrible.

Eventually, Ari must have remembered he needed to eat, because she dismounted the horse and took the bag with his box. Air rushed in through the breather holes, and a moment later, the lid was up and a fly was, ah, flying by. Francis ate it without thinking. Then he ate another. And another.

All this eating of flies. It was so unlike him.

"What a very good king," Ari said softly. "Such a good frog."

Frog?

FROG?

Francis made the noise again, the sound that he finally recognized as a *ribbit*.

What kind of king turned into a frog? That was only for princes. Except he wasn't king anymore, was he? He was a frog, maybe forever.

Perhaps the Eðians were right, he thought desperately. Maybe this was Francis's true form—his nature, the very essence of who he was—a pitiful, croaking, slimy frog. And one thing was certain—it wasn't easy being green.

RIBBIT.

RIBBIT.

RIBBIT.

Light suddenly flashed around him, and then Francis was sitting on top of the box, human again (yay!) absolutely naked (oh no!).

"Ack!" Ari averted her eyes.

This was worse. This was much worse than being a frog. "What the—"

Flash! Francis was a frog again.

"Ribbit," he said, sitting inside the box once more.

"Oh, thank goodness," Ari said. "I wasn't sure how I'd get you all the way to Calais like that."

"Ribbit," Francis said miserably.

"I only have one horse," Ari explained. "And enough people food for me." She shrugged helplessly. "Your mother gave me firm instructions. I'm not to deviate. I'm sure she'll know if I don't do exactly what she says."

She proceeded to carry Francis across the countryside like a piece of common luggage. Then, it happened again.

Flash!

Francis tumbled out of the box and onto the road, bruising his royal elbows and knees. "What the—!"

Abruptly, he was a frog again, and Ari was just in time to scoop him up before he made a quick escape to the nearest river to eat bugs in peace.

They ran and ran. Francis stayed tucked away while Ari carried him to the city as fast as she could.

"Don't change," she was saying. "Don't change, don't change, don't change."

She was in luck. They made it to . . . well, Francis didn't really know where they were, what with being stuck in the box, but apparently Ari was happy about it because she dumped him out of the box with all the ceremony of overturning a sack of apples.

Francis tumbled out and then *flash!* White light flared around him.

"WTF!" he shouted, a quick abbreviation in case he changed back and didn't get a chance to finish his thought. Then he spotted a wedge of cheese hanging out of a saddlebag and shoved it in his mouth.

"What does that mean?" Ari asked.

Francis started to cover himself with the box that had been holding him for the last who knew how long, but it didn't matter. He changed back, and the box nearly killed him.

But we'd like to inform you that right here, this very moment, was the first ever use of the phrase *WTF*, which stands for, as we all know, "what the frog."

THIRTY-FOUR *Mary*

"These were your mother's apartments," James said as he finished showing Mary around Holyrood Palace. "And now I suppose they're yours. I'm sure your mother would have wanted you to have her things."

Mary gazed around the northwest tower. She expected to find these rooms full of her mother's presence, somehow, but it simply looked like an old castle tower, furnished in the same way as most rooms in most palaces, if she was being honest. Holyrood was also a bit shabbier than any palace she'd ever lived in before—it was large, but not enormous. There were not as many windows as the Louvre, which left the rooms a bit dark and gloomy. Or perhaps that was just the Scottish weather.

"It smells like her," Flem remarked as the Marys began to take stock of the situation, inventorying the dresses in the armoires and how they might need to be altered to fit Mary—which wasn't much, as it turned out that Mary de Guise and our Mary were nearly the same size, even down to their shoes.

"It smells like my mother?" Mary said.

Flem nodded. "She smelled of oranges and cloves and fur—mink, perhaps, from those capes she wore. I always enjoyed her scent, even as a child."

Mary couldn't remember what her mother had smelled like. At the moment she was having trouble remembering what Mary de Guise had looked like. When Mary tried to picture her mother's face—all she could call up was a painting.

She sighed. She had communicated in letters to her mother all her life, received advice and admonishment, even poured her heart out through the stroke of her quill at times. But she hadn't truly known Mary de Guise.

And now—she was slowly starting to accept this—her mother was gone. And Mary was expected to take her place. She was to wear Mary de Guises's gowns and jewels and literally step into her shoes.

Was she ready for such a responsibility?

And what would that mean for her duties back in France? What would that mean for her marriage? For Francis?

She hadn't thought any of this through before she'd left Paris. She'd been so focused on finding the answers to the mystery of her missing mother. She hadn't considered what would happen if that mystery was solved.

She crossed to the window. Below stretched the private gardens, green and well kept, at least.

"Can I get you anything?" James asked. "I know this can't be easy."

At least James was kind to her. It made her feel like she had some family left.

"A few butts," she said after a moment.

He looked taken aback. "Butts, Your Majesty? I'm afraid I don't know what—"

"For the garden," she explained. "Archery butts?" Archery had always been calming for her. And Francis had been so dreadful at it, but he'd always made it fun to practice.

James smiled and nodded. "Oh yes, archery. Thank God. I thought you meant—"

At that moment they heard drums in the distance.

James's smile faded. "I should go. We might all need to practice some self-defense very shortly. The Eðians are a little worked up."

"I could go with you," Mary said. "I could—"

James held up a hand. "No, that's fine. My . . . advisers and I will take care of it."

The way he said the word *advisers* was strange. Mary had the sudden, terrible feeling that James could be plotting to take her crown, too. Or maybe she was just under a lot of stress and imagining things. Or maybe it was James who was stressed. On account of the violent mob who seemed about to attack at any moment.

Perhaps she shouldn't have thrown John Knox into the stocks.

"Very well," she said. "Thank you, James."

He bowed and took his leave.

Mary went over to the desk in the corner and began to look through her mother's papers. There was nothing that could be remotely helpful in quelling a rebellion. All she found were a few lists of things Mary de Guise had wanted to do (she was the original bullet journaler, we discovered). A sketch of a starling. A design of a very pretty pair of jeweled shoes.

Mary took up the quill and ink and considered what she would say, if she were to write a letter to Francis. She *should* write to him. There was so much she wanted to tell him.

She carefully wrote out the first two words: *Dearest Francis,* and chewed her bottom lip for a moment, thinking.

What could she say that would even begin to make things right?

I'm sorry?

I wish you were here?

Help—I'm now officially the queen, and it wasn't what I bargained for. People are being so mean to me, and it's not remotely fair?

She laid down the quill. No. None of that would do.

She opened the desk and slipped the nearly blank piece of parchment inside. She could come back to it later, she told herself. But as she was about to close the desk, she was struck by an image—a memory, perhaps, from when she was very young—of her mother sitting in this exact spot, showing her how this drawer in this desk had a false bottom. To open it, one only had to push on the side of the desk . . . here.

There was a soft click.

From across the room, Flem cocked her head to one side. "What was that?"

Mary didn't answer. She was too busy opening the *secret drawer*.

In which there was another letter.

From her mother—she instantly recognized the elegant slant of Mary de Guise's handwriting.

And it was for her. Mary knew this because it opened with *My clever girl*, because her mother had still thought of her daughter as a girl, and still thought of her as clever, even though Mary no longer felt that she was exactly either of these things.

She swallowed hard, unfolded the letter fully, and continued reading.

> *My clever girl,*
> *I am writing this in great haste, so please forgive my unsightly penmanship.*

Mary smiled. Perhaps she had not fallen far from her mother's tree. She continued to read.

> *If you have found this letter, I fear that you are in danger, and my heart seizes with more worry for your well-being than it could ever possess for my own. It has recently come to my attention that you are soon to be married to the dauphin of France, as we*

always planned. My heart was glad to hear it. I know that you and Francis are dear friends, and I am of the opinion that it is wise, when entering a state of matrimony, to consider your spouse a friend first, before all other things. Not that I have much experience in that matter, as I myself, having been twice married, found neither husband particularly friendly. But I have better dreams for you, my daughter, of being more than just an accessory to the stature of your husband. You will find your own greatness in this world, of that I am sure.

Mary heaved a sigh. She certainly wasn't feeling any greatness.

Naturally your uncles are pleased to be solidifying the alliance between our two countries. They are drafting up an agreement that they wish you to sign regarding France's obligations to Scotland, and Scotland's to France, upon the advent of your marriage. In many ways it is a standard agreement, but when I read the document myself, I found a troublesome section. It states that if you perish, or if you and Francis do not produce an heir within a certain period of time, Scotland will in essence become the property of France.

Now Mary felt rather sick. That blasted treaty. Mary had almost forgotten all about it. Her mother had immediately seen the treachery of it. Why hadn't Mary?

Why hadn't she listened to Francis, for once? Why did she always have to be contrary when people told her what to do?

She kept reading.

I am a Frenchwoman, as you know, and loyal to my family there, but I am also, after these many years, a Scot. This agreement would be devastating to the interests of Scotland, and, by extension, to you, as the rightful ruler of Scotland. Therefore I wrote immediately urging you to refuse to sign this document, but found my messengers cut off from me and the letter destroyed. I do believe that your uncles are acting for your benefit, but also for their own. Through you they wish to dominate and control all of England, Scotland, and France. I cannot in good faith support this course of action, and as I voiced this opinion to my brothers, they made it clear that if I am not with them entirely, I am against them, and from now on will be treated as an enemy. There is unrest here in Edinburgh, an uprising of Eðians, which means, ironically, that I find myself besieged on two sides. Which of my enemies will prevail against me now, I cannot say.

I can say that I will always be on your side.

I wish you all the best on your wedding. But I hope you will not sign that document. Beware your uncles, my dear. They are unprincipled, dangerous men. I can only hope that you will somehow find a way to escape their clutches and take your rightful place in this world, without aligning yourself with their schemes.

Your loving mother,

Mary de Guise

Mary laid down the letter and pressed a hand over her mouth. Her mother had been murdered, she was certain of that now. But who had done it? The rebel Eðians? Or her uncles?

But another, more pressing matter had come to her attention. She stood up.

"Your Highness?" came Hush's soft voice from beside her. "Are you all right?"

Mary brushed a tear from her cheek briskly. She turned to her ladies, who were all staring at her with concern.

"Pack my things again," she ordered. "We have to go."

"You're going where?" James repeated in exasperation.

"Back to France," Mary answered simply.

"But you just got here," he said.

"I know that. But now I must return to France."

"But with your mother gone, shouldn't you stay and rule Scotland?" he said, clearly flummoxed.

She shook her head. "I cannot. But I hereby appoint you, my dear brother, to serve as ruler in my stead."

He stared at her, mouth open. "But I—"

"You've been doing fine so far," she said.

At that moment, something rattled the windows. A voice screamed out "FREEEEEEEDOOOOOOM!" and there was a distant, roaring cheer.

"So carry on, as if you never saw me here," she said. "I'm very sorry, James, to leave you in such a position. But I really must go."

He gazed after her helplessly as she turned and, her ladies trailing her, left the palace. Out the back door. Into the empty garden.

"Shall we, ladies?" she said. She was dressed as a boy again.

Her heart was beating in time with the drums that were growing louder outside.

"If that's what you command," said Bea.

"Of course. Let's go back to Paris," said Liv cheerfully. (She had her own reasons, you'll remember, for wishing to return to France.)

"But why do we have to hurry back, if I may ask?" asked Flem. "I'd rather been hoping you'd find me a husband here. A good Scottish one with a title. We're none of us getting any younger, you know."

"I know, Flem. I know. But now is not the time." Mary didn't want to explain that she'd been a fool, and had signed that dratted agreement, and if she didn't return to France and produce an heir with Francis, like, *toute suite* (which in French means "right freaking now"), Scotland was going to be in big trouble.

"DOWN WITH THE VERITIES!!!!" someone yelled.

Way more trouble than it was currently in.

Which was a lot.

"I came to find out what happened to my mother, and now I know," she said simply. "Now I must return. I miss my husband."

She did miss him. Every day she thought of Francis—every hour, practically, what he might be doing now, if he was getting along all right without her. On the one hand, she hoped he was, of course. But she also hoped that he missed her, too, that he realized how much he needed her. So they could forgive each other about that horrid fight and get into the business of making an heir.

Right freaking now.

Her face filled with heat. It seemed so silly now, how shy they'd been about it, how naive. The way they'd acted like they had all the time in the world.

She remembered them jumping on the bed.

Francis lying on the bearskin rug, his face flushed with sleep, his blue eyes laughing up at her.

That spectacular kiss on their wedding day.

So this is going to be fine, she thought. Maybe even more than fine.

It might be a little awkward when she appeared at the palace again and said, "Oh, I'm sorry, dear, for my sudden disappearance, but I'm back now. Let's go make a baby."

But that was just what they'd have to do.

For Scotland.

"Uh, Mary?" Flem said.

Mary cleared her throat. "I'm sorry to ask you to travel again so soon. But I need to get back. I've already been gone too long."

"Yes, Your Majesty," said Bea, and without another word she became a raven and fluttered into the sky over their heads. Flem nodded glumly and then barked. Hush flashed into her stoat form. Liv dropped the three overstuffed saddlebags she'd been lugging onto the ground and bent to fold and put away the others' dresses.

"All right," she said, when she was ready for the change herself. "Stand back, Your Majesty." She flashed Mary a dimpled smile. "I'm glad to be going home."

"I know." Mary grinned back.

She was helping Liv out of her dress when a voice called after them.

"MARY! MARY, WAIT!"

The two girls turned to see James puffing down the palace stairs. He ran up to them, then bent over his knees and caught his breath.

"James, you can't talk me out of it," Mary said impatiently. "You'll be a fine ruler by proxy. You'll see."

"No, it's . . ." James gulped in a breath. "I've had news . . . Big news . . . News that . . . concerns you."

"What news?" Mary asked, frowning.

"About . . . the king . . . of France. He's dead."

Mary scoffed. "I know all about that already. Henry died in a jousting accident. That was weeks ago. Really, James, you need a better Eθian message network if you're only hearing about it now."

"No." James straightened. "Not Henry. Francis."

"What?" Liv asked sharply. "That cannot be."

"What . . . cannot be?" Mary still did not understand. She had a feeling of time slowing, like she'd been thrust into a deep pool and was staring up at her brother through hazy water, only half hearing him. Because she couldn't have heard him correctly.

"King Francis is dead," James said, his eyes full of pity. "According to my source, it was caused by an ear infection. He's always been a bit sickly, right? There was that dreadful portrait."

Mary began to tremble all over.

"You're saying King Francis died of an ear infection," Liv said slowly. "When?"

"Yesterday. My source flew here the moment it was announced. The rest of the world will know in a few days, at most."

Liv turned horrified eyes to Mary. "Oh, Mary," she murmured. "I'm so sorry. Mary? Mary?"

But Mary didn't hear her at all. She had fainted dead away.

THIRTY-FIVE

Ari

Queen Catherine had been very specific in the directions she'd laid out for Ari. She had given her money. "Not much," she had said, because she wanted them to have the "authentic" peasant experience. But when she handed Ari the bag of coins, the poor girl could barely lift it.

"I'm afraid if I give you more, it will make you stand out," the queen had said.

She had also given Ari a detailed map to the hovel she was now standing in front of. It was a small white structure with a rectangular footprint and a thatched roof.

Ari tied her horse up near some tall grass. "Eat up, Beau," she said. The horse hadn't come with a name, but Ari felt it distinctly rude to ride astride an animal without calling it by a name, so she named it Beau, which meant "handsome."

During one of Francis's human moments, he'd mentioned the horse was a mare, but she'd kept the name Beau anyway.

Francis was on the ground beside her. After he'd nearly been squashed by the box earlier, she'd decided it was better if he remained unencumbered by tight quarters.

"Shall we look inside?" Ari said.

Francis ribbited. The interior of the hovel was quite empty, other than a hearth with a fireplace, a small table with two chairs, and a bed in the corner. Just the one bed. Ari blushed, but she'd think about that later.

With a flash, Francis turned into a man. Ari whipped a sheet out of her satchel and held it between herself and Francis.

"Wrap yourself up, Your Majesty," she said. It was a phrase that up until a week ago she'd never have imagined herself saying. But she was getting used to it.

Francis took the sheet and wrapped it around his lower half. "You don't have to call me that. I guess I've been deposed." He sat on one of the chairs.

"That's going to take some getting used to, if I ever get used to it." Ari thought grimly about her father and Greer. Would Ari ever see them again? She had a feeling the answer was no. But what choice did she have?

Francis's pale face also looked paler than usual. "I'm famished," he said.

Ari instinctively reached for the jar of flies and then stopped. "I'll get some more human food soon."

"Where are we?" he asked.

"Calais."

"I know. But why?"

"Well, that's not what you asked. I don't know why. But your mother was very specific in her instructions."

"My mother." Francis scowled and looked away. "I've been poisoned and kidnapped."

"I suppose," Ari said slowly. "But when Queen Catherine tells you to do something, you do it."

Francis continued scowling.

Catherine had given Ari a letter for Francis to read, but Ari decided now was not the right time, because she'd read the contents, and there was no way Francis was in the right state of mind to understand and process it.

Maybe she'd wait until he was a frog again.

"So, what now?" Francis asked. "Did my mother's instructions include what in the world we're supposed to do here?"

"Well, first off, I think I should go get supplies," Ari said. She'd always dreamed of advising King Francis, but the dreams had never really involved her grocery shopping.

"Did she give you any money?"

Ari opened one of the satchels and hoisted the giant bag full of coins onto the table. The table legs creaked under the weight.

Francis's eyes widened in horror. "That's it?"

Ari snorted. *Aristocrats*, she thought. "It's more than enough for our needs."

"Yes, but for how long?" Francis asked, clearly panicking now.

"In our current situation, this amount of money would last two or three lifetimes."

"Just how long are you going to keep me here?"

Ari sighed, feeling sorry for the former monarch. "I don't know. It's not like Queen Catherine can bring you back from the grave."

Francis was quiet for a moment. "And what about Mary?" he said at last.

Ari hesitated. "Well, she's gone to Scotland."

"Yes, but won't she hear that I'm dead?"

Ari bit her lip. "Try not to think about that right now. After all, we just got here."

He walked over to the bed and threw himself on it, draping an arm over his face.

Ari took her chair over. She awkwardly patted his knee. "There, there," was all she could think to say.

"Oh, what do you know of it?"

Ari closed her eyes for a moment. "Well, I, myself, am also separated from . . . someone. Multiple someones. I wouldn't be here myself, but your mother has taken my father hostage."

"It's the worst feeling in the world," Francis moaned.

Ari was beginning to think he could be a bit dramatic about things, because he'd said traveling by horse as a frog was "the worst thing in the world" and eating a fly just as he turned human was "the worst thing in the world."

But about this, she believed him.

"If Mary were here, I'd know what to do. Mostly because she'd tell me. But still. That's all I want. Mary here. And for me not to be a frog. And not to be kidnapped."

Ari winced. Yes, she would definitely wait to read him the letter.

A little while later, Ari was wandering the Calais market, where the news of the king's death was everywhere. Flyers were posted on every community board, and mournful sentiments touched everyone's lips (along with the occasional, "Well, he never seemed very kingly anyway"). She bought bread, cheese, dried meat, lard to cook with, and several different herbs and spices, and every time she went to pay, the merchant would give her the change and say, "The king is dead, long live the king."

For entertainment purposes, Ari imagined saying, "He's not dead. He's a frog."

Then she remembered that her father had predicted a frog on the throne of France and her mind was blown for a little while.

But then she tried to focus on what she and Francis would need for nourishment. Most of her cooking had been of the concocting-potions variety, but she was sure that given enough practice, she would get the hang of it. As she meandered through the busy streets and alongside the canals, she tried to picture this as her new home. Where she would live in a hovel. With the former king of France. As brother and sister. Indefinitely, or at least until they received further instructions from Queen Catherine.

If they ever did at all. Ari couldn't understand it. She knew the queen was ambitious. And she knew the queen adored playing tricks on her enemies, and even some of her less-likable allies. But how could a mother cast off her child so easily? Take away his kingdom? And turn him into a frog, on top of all of that?

And then there was the letter . . .

Ari reached into her pocket and touched it, to be sure it was still there. And then her fingers found the small piece of parchment next to it. Liv's message. Ari wondered if she was safe, and if Liv thought of Ari as much as Ari thought of her, and if they'd ever see each other again.

Too many ifs. Ari wanted nothing more than to write a message back. But she didn't know any bird-type Eðians who could deliver it. Or any Eðians at all, apart from a certain frog.

"Watch it, lad!" A man hauling a cart of barrels ripped her from her own thoughts.

One of the barrels was labeled *verbena*, and suddenly Ari knew what to do next.

"Excuse me, monsieur, but do you know where the apothecary is?" Ari asked.

The man jerked a thumb behind him. "Half a block, on the right."

Ari scurried off and found the place, but once inside, she was deeply disappointed with the lack of supplies. Who didn't have mugwort? What was this, the fifteenth century or something?

This would never do.

If she were going to make her own laboratory, a *real* laboratory, she would have to go in search of the ingredients herself.

She returned to the hovel with fresh food and other items that would keep for a long time, and a blanket and some straw that could make do for another bed. Probably for her, as Francis would undoubtedly insist upon the real bed.

Francis was on the real bed now, in frog form. She wasn't sure if frogs' faces were permanently sad or if it was just Francis's face.

Then she noticed the fireplace. Where it had once been empty, now there were two logs, neither of them touching the other, both placed flat on the stones. There was no tinder, no kindling. But pieces of flint and iron were lying sadly to one side of the hearth.

Ah. It seemed as though Francis had tried to light a fire, his first, from the looks of it. Now she understood the super-sad frog face.

"It's all right." Ari turned to Francis. "You had the right idea. But you have to chop the larger pieces of wood into kindling and tinder, and light those first. I'll show you how."

She opened the fly jar next to his face and his tongue whipped out and snatched a fly. He ate it fast enough, although he seemed thoroughly unimpressed by the experience. Ari fed him another one. He ate it, too, and then turned his body around with a *ribbit* that sounded distinctly like a *humpf.*

Ari pulled a folded parchment out of her pocket. "Now that I have your attention, Your Highness, I have a letter from your mother."

Francis did a full-body turn back toward Ari.

Ari unfolded the letter.

"'My dearest boy,'" Ari started.

It was met with a ribbit that sounded like a belch.

"'You are probably confused and angry right now. But I can't worry about that.'"

Ari really wished she could edit the letter, but if she tried to make it nicer, it wouldn't sound like Catherine. Plus Francis could read.

"'I have to worry about the future of France instead of a son who clearly doesn't want to be king and is not suited for the job. So, in a way, I am granting your deepest desire. You will not be king, and you will have all those choices you so desperately wanted.'"

Francis licked his eyeball. Ari had to assume that was the frog in him, and not something Francis had secretly always wanted to do.

The next part of the letter was the part that Ari was dreading reading the most.

"'Rest assured, dear Francis, that the kingdom is in safe hands. You are to live out your days as a peasant. Ari will see to your needs. Do as she says, for she was barely more than a peasant when we took her in. She'll know what to do.

"'But you must remain hidden, for at least the next three to five years, until you have faded from the memory of your subjects. Few of them would recognize your face, of course, but there was that one unflattering portrait going around.

"'I shall try to visit you. But I shall be very busy running the kingdom.

"'And don't worry about Mary. My sources tell me that she is in Scotland, where I think we can both agree that she belongs, and it will be easier for everyone if she believes you are dead as well.

"'You may disagree with my methods or my decisions, but of all the new choices available to you, changing this course of action is not one of them.

"'Your dear mother,

"'Queen Regent Catherine, Mother to King Charles IX.

"'PS: Accept it.'"

THIRTY-SIX
Francis

Francis was in no way going to accept it.

Of course, he was currently a frog, so for the time being, he gave a loud croak and tried to convey his utter displeasure at the note his mother had sent. If Ari interpreted his mood, she didn't respond.

"I've been thinking about some rules." Ari folded the note and placed it on the bed beside Francis. "Your Highness."

Francis gave a quiet ribbit. He didn't want to think about rules. He wanted to mope about Mary, who he was never going to see again. Because she thought he was dead.

"Rule the first," Ari began. "No leaving the hovel."

Francis blinked at her. She'd left the hovel already today.

"You, I mean," Ari clarified. "You're the former king of

France. Even if the people won't recognize you, you still *act* like a royal. And you're supposed to be dead—"

I'm not supposed to be dead, Francis thought, but he was currently a frog, so the words came out only as an annoyed "ribbit." *I don't want to be dead, real or pretend.*

At that very moment, a knocking came at the hovel door. Ari leapt to her feet and opened the door just a crack. "Yes?"

"Midnight vigil for poor dead King Francis," said a woman. "It's BYOC."

"BYOC?"

"Bring your own candle."

"Ah," Ari said. "For poor dead King Francis, you say?"

"Died of an ear infection," said the woman. "A dreadful thing, so soon after his father. But long may Charles the Ninth reign."

"Indeed," Ari said weakly.

"Well, I'm off to the next hovel. The vigil will be at the lighthouse, if you want to come. And remember, BYOC."

"Thank you," Ari said, and shut the door. She came back to where Francis was still sitting on the bed, a frog, decidedly not dead. "That is why you can't be seen around town. That exactly."

Francis gave a sad little croak.

"Well, yes, I'll probably go to the vigil," Ari said. "I need to make friends around this place, and she seemed nice enough. I suppose I've got to find a candle. . . ."

"Ribbit?" Francis asked.

"No, you can't go. You're a frog." Ari folded her arms over her chest. "Rule the second: no spending money."

Francis gave a deep croak, and his throat expanded. Well, that was new.

"I'm in charge of the money." Ari nodded to herself. "This is the only money we have, and I won't have you spending it on silks or hunting hounds or whatever you royals like to buy." She continued nodding, agreeing with herself. "Yes, I'll have to manage the money, because I don't see how you'd be able to keep us living within our means. Unless you wanted to get a job, that is."

Francis licked his eye.

Not on purpose. That was just how frogs do.

"Right," Ari went on. "And you can't get a job because of your face, not to mention that my potion is still in your system. You might not be able to control you form until it wears off all the way."

Francis blinked at her. He couldn't get a job because he might turn into a frog or, more likely, because he had no commoner job skills. He also couldn't spend money because he couldn't be trusted and he couldn't get a job. They would almost certainly go broke within a matter of days. Hearing all of this, it really sounded like Catherine de Medici was actually trying to kill him, just slowly and from a distance.

"Rule the third," Ari said. "No sending letters to the palace or anyone else you used to know. This is basically witness protection."

Francis gave a confused croak.

"True, you haven't witnessed anything you shouldn't have," Ari agreed. "And you haven't helped solve a crime. But the rules are the same. Your old life is over. You're my frog now. I mean my brother."

Francis sighed.

He was a peasant. He'd never been a peasant before. He'd never lived in a hovel before. Or even set foot in one, for that matter. But here he was, a frog, a peasant, and living in a hovel.

Ridiculous.

"Look on the bright side." Ari went to the fireplace and began piling logs and kindling.

To Francis, everything was a bright side, seeing as how his frog eyes were very sensitive to light.

"We won't have a bug problem. Not in this house."

"Ribbit," Francis said, and ate another fly.

Somehow, Francis had gone from Mary controlling his life, to Catherine running the show, and now to Ari. She managed the hovel with frightening efficiency, giving him simple tasks to complete while she went out every day to rebuild her laboratory.

The tasks had to be simple, because Francis was still turning into a frog without warning, but he was spending more and more time as a human now, so that was an improvement. Ari had purchased clothes for him, a tunic and trousers, both so drab and rough he felt like the fabric might scour the skin off his bones. When he'd complained about it, she'd asked if he wanted something made out of silk.

"Yes," he'd replied. "Silk would feel so nice."

Then she'd rolled her eyes—at the king! Well, the former king—and said, "You'll have to get used to the clothes the rest of us wear. This is the life of a peasant."

"Being told what to do by the person who controls the money?" He was whining and he knew it, but he missed the fine breads and cheeses, the silk bedsheets, and the rich tapestries.

"Yes," she said. "The person with the money makes the decisions."

Francis had frowned, but she hadn't left much room for arguing. Mostly because she'd left the hovel shortly after.

That had been this morning, and he'd spent his day completing the chores she'd given him—sweeping the floor, cleaning the chamber pot, and washing the walls—and rereading his mother's note again and again, committing every brutal word to memory.

He kept getting stuck on the part about Mary. Maybe it *was* better for Mary that he was "dead." She could focus on ruling Scotland without feeling obligated to him. To their marriage.

And maybe it was better for France, too, with Charles IX as king and Catherine as regent. She had the knowledge and experience. She had the drive and determination to rule the kingdom. She *liked* that sort of thing.

Francis, however . . .

Francis scowled and scrubbed at the wall, but it still looked dirty. How could he accept this? How could he just move forward with his life, as though he'd never married Mary, or been crowned king, or endured the tragedy of losing his father? He knew he must have been a most disappointing heir and king, but he *had* been good at being married to Mary (aside from that one—all right, those two fights), and maybe he could have learned to be a good king, if he'd been given the time to mourn his murdered father. Or if he'd had better guidance. Neither of his parents set great examples when it came to running the country. But he *could* have been king. A decent king, maybe. Perhaps.

He picked at the dirt under his fingernails. (This was the first time he'd ever had dirt under his fingernails, and it was more annoying than he'd anticipated. How did peasants live like this?)

Maybe . . . Maybe he should go back to Paris. What was stopping him? What could Catherine do to stop him, if he marched into the throne room and announced that he wasn't dead after all? Commoners might not know his face, but the nobility certainly did, given all the social functions he'd been forced to attend.

Francis imagined doing just that—marching into the throne room and taking back his crown—but what if the nobility liked Charles IX and Catherine better? Francis didn't have an army to support him, just his name, and right now it wasn't worth very much. Heck, even his memorials were BYOC. If Francis went back to Paris now, like this, Catherine would ensure he disappeared again—to an even less desirable place than this hovel.

And if he somehow succeeded in taking back his crown . . . then he'd be king. Was that what he wanted?

Francis dropped the soapy rag and leaned his forehead

against the damp wall. "I think I might be having an identity crisis."

Your narrators don't think that was the only crisis he was having at that moment.

After a few more days, the final dregs of the potion wore off, and Francis finally stayed Francis. That is, he didn't turn into a frog again after a few minutes, or an hour, or three hours. By the time he'd been a human for two days without accidentally turning into a frog, he felt like things were finally looking up.

This morning, Ari had congratulated him on his humanity and then gone out to collect wild herbs. Over the last week, Francis had been watching her laboratory grow, trying not to get in her way as she worked on drying and grinding various ingredients. It seemed like she was settling in for the long haul, though, and that was . . . distressing. Did she really think they were going to live here as brother and sister for the rest of their lives? They would starve on the meager sum of money that Catherine had sent. *Starve.*

More than anything, he missed Mary. He missed her laugh. The way she smelled. Even the way she told him what to do. She was very good at it, after all. Throughout the day, he found himself wondering what she was doing, hoping she was safe, curious if she liked living in Scotland.

If only there were a way to find out.

Well. There was.

It would involve breaking Ari's rules.

This was the thing about the sixteenth century: the internet hadn't been invented yet. Social media wasn't there to give instant updates on a person's life, or show off what they were eating, or their hair on a day they felt particularly pretty. But gossip moved at lightning speeds, even without the internet, because some Eðians could fly.

These lines of gossip had always been available, even in Verity-controlled France. He just had to be willing to look. And here, in this old port city that both England and France had been fighting over for years, there would likely be plenty of people talking about Mary, Queen of Scots.

Francis might not be able to show his human face outside the hovel, but he did perhaps have another disguise now.

If changing into a frog had been more than Ari's potion. If he was an Eðian.

Francis had never spent much time wondering what his Eðian form would be (if he believed that everyone had an Eðian form, which he didn't), but maybe he'd secretly hoped to be a majestic steed. Or some kind of big cat, like a lion or tiger. He would have been happy with a bear, too. But a frog? That just wasn't what Francis hoped was inside of him.

Still, a frog could be useful right now. It could move through the small spaces in the city and listen for Mary's name.

If he was an Eðian. If he could change into a frog at will, like Mary could. But how?

Mary had made it look so easy: she just wanted it enough, and poof, she was a mouse. Or a human.

Francis closed his eyes and thought froggy thoughts. Flies. Hopping. Lily pads.

Nothing happened.

All right. This would be harder than simply desiring to change shape.

He closed his eyes again and thought about what it felt like to be a frog. Small, yes, but he'd had powerful legs, ready to leap tall buildings in a single bound. The weird sight, the occasional need to lick his own eyeballs, the lack of ears . . .

He knew exactly what it felt like to be a frog. He could almost feel it now. Almost, almost.

There was a flash. And then a ribbit.

Francis leapt for joy. Then he hopped toward the door and hesitated. He wasn't sure what Ari would do if she knew he was sneaking out. She'd be angry, he was pretty sure.

But he had to find out about Mary.

So, for the first time in what felt like a very long time, Francis defied the rules someone else had set for him. They could tell him what to do all they wanted, but he was his own frog now. He squeezed himself under the hovel door and began hopping and hopping toward the busiest parts of Calais.

Waterways and canals crisscrossed the town, giving Francis a lot of options when it came to traveling. (He couldn't hop along the roads. He might get stepped on!) He started toward the lighthouse, jumping from stone to stone, keeping to the edges of the canal where he knew he was safe-ish. There were fish and other creatures swimming in the water, and while he wasn't certain what ate frogs, he was sure that something did. He wasn't about to become anyone's meal.

But he did snack on several flies, mosquitoes, and other insects along the way. He didn't want to admit it, but he was rather becoming accustomed to the taste. And they were filling, at least while he was a frog, which was probably the most important thing, since his mother had sent them into exile with next to nothing.

The town was bustling. Long legs stretched above Francis as he hopped along, his nonexistent ears perked and listening for Mary's name. What he needed to find was a place where Eðians congregated, where the bird-types gathered and traded gossip.

He paused not far from the lighthouse, water rushing on either side of the rock where he sat. He nabbed a few bugs, watching for birds behaving strangely. Or birds at all, because it wasn't just fish he had to watch out for. Creatures of the air probably ate frogs, too.

With the water crashing around him, Francis listened for Mary's name in the hum of voices. He kept an eye on the buildings he could see over the edge of the canal, watching birds flit from windowsills to balconies. And he kept the same eye on the surface of the water beneath him, in case any hungry fish came up from the deep. Because frog eyes.

But he heard nothing useful. The voices were too indistinct, too obscured by the sound of water. He'd have to get closer, find somewhere else to stake out.

Francis hopped up toward the canal's ledge—and went face-first into the stone wall. His entire body went stiff as he stuck there for a moment, then peeled off and dropped into the water, where he sank like a rock.

Fortunately, his frog self took over, and he began to breathe through his skin. Then, as the shock wore off, he started to rise.

Suddenly, movement in the water. A fish darted at him.

Francis kicked, catching the creature in the nose, and swam as fast as he could for the surface. But the fish was not deterred; it reoriented itself and wriggled toward him.

If Francis had been human at that moment, he would have been sweating. But because he was a frog, and he had the instincts of a prey animal that wanted to live, Francis swam as fast as his flippered feet would allow, kicking with all his might until he broke the surface of the water.

He threw himself onto a rock, and the fish sailed past without catching him, then dove back into the water to search for a different lunch.

Francis sat on his rock and caught his breath. His little heart was pounding hard as he looked for a better place to hop over the canal wall. He'd have to practice jumping if he ever wanted to try a leap like that again.

Finally, he found a set of wooden stairs on a small dock, and—keeping a wary eye out for human feet—he took them one at a time and found himself at a crossroads. Literally.

Traffic was everywhere. Carts and carriages careened past,

while people on foot hurried between them. Everyone was moving as fast as they could, certainly not looking out for a small frog on the edge of the road, waiting for an opportunity to cross. (Pedestrian lights and crosswalks hadn't been invented yet.)

Francis went forward, then back, then forward two lanes, then back one. Whew, this was scary.

Then, it happened. Suddenly a voice rose up over the din: "Make way for the Duke of Guise! Make way for the Cardinal of Lorraine!"

Francis would have gasped, if he'd been human. As it was, he gasped through his skin. And then, if he'd been human, he would have—well, honestly, he would have ducked behind someone taller and avoided meeting their eyes, because the last thing he'd ever wanted in his life was conflict. But now . . .

Now he was a frog peasant. Now he'd lost not only his kingdom but also his wife. Now he knew who was responsible for the murder of his father.

These men.

And now they were here, in Calais. Doing *what*? More murder?

His whole froggy body vibrated with rage as he looked for the Duke of Guise and the Cardinal of Lorraine, but even with his weird frog eyes, he couldn't see their faces.

A grand carriage rolled forward, heading toward the docks. Clearly, it belonged to Mary's uncles, as it was decked out in gold inlaid with more gold, and a little bit of gold just to keep things interesting. Of course that was how they traveled.

Francis had to get to them.

He didn't pause to think about why, or what he'd do. Instead, he coiled his froggy muscles and—with all his might—leapt onto the nearest wagon. But it was going the wrong way.

He hopped to the opposite side, grateful to see another wagon going the right way. He started to jump, but then noticed there were children in the back of the wagon. It seemed like a bad idea to get stuck in there with them.

So he waited, then made the long, heart-stopping jump to the next wagon—because he was going to lose sight of the de Guise carriage if he waited any longer. He sailed through the air and landed in the back of the new wagon with a small thud, scatting bits of hay everywhere.

Two yellow eyes opened within the hay, and an orange cat slipped from lying down to crouching. His tail lashed.

Francis would have shrieked, but frogs couldn't, so he just gave a terrified *croak* and jumped away as fast as he could. He should have gone with the children.

The cat pounced, landing exactly where Francis had been seconds before. He leapt again, and again, and heaved himself onto a wagon passing by, which was going just slightly faster than the wagon he had just been on.

The cat yowled and hissed, but Francis was ahead of him now, and pretty soon, the new wagon was catching up to the carriage.

Francis steeled himself and made the final jump, letting the frog instincts do all the work. (If he'd thought about it too hard, he would never have attempted such a move.)

He landed on the back of the carriage, rolled, and settled on the roof. His heart was pounding, but he could hear the two men talking inside. Just the sound of their voices made Francis see red, and if he hadn't been a frog just then, he might have tried to strangle them.

"It's hardly the ideal situation," Duke Francis was saying.

"Nothing here is ideal. We've lost France."

Because he was "dead," Francis realized suddenly. These men had possessed a measure of control over Mary—but without Francis, she was nothing to France, nothing but a ward who'd stayed here for years and years and now had no way to repay the kingdom.

Without Mary on the throne, the uncles must have been expelled from the Louvre. Catherine would have gotten rid of them as fast as she could. And now they were here, doing . . . what?

"With Mary in Scotland," Cardinal Charles said, "we still have a chance at England. All we have to do is put her on the English throne."

Francis's heart jumped at the sound of Mary's name. She *was* in Scotland. She'd made it. But—

"I know," said Duke Francis. "I know. We can still have England. The boy is on the way to Scotland as we speak. But we are French. France should belong to us."

"Perhaps once Mary is on the English throne, we can take back our own kingdom." The cardinal's voice was light. "But first, England."

"In five days' time," Duke Francis said. "Elizabeth's throne will be Mary's."

At once, Francis—our Francis, the current frog—understood: Mary's uncles, the same men who'd assassinated King Henry, manipulated Mary, and basically ruined his entire life, were going to murder Elizabeth, the queen of England.

And frog or no frog, Francis had to stop them.

THIRTY-SEVEN *Mary*

Mary opened her tear-swollen eyes. The palace was silent. In the three days since she'd learned of Francis's death, everyone had been moving about Mary quietly, carefully, as if she were a delicate glass vase that, at the slightest disturbance, might shatter into a thousand pieces. (We're not counting the first evening, when they'd almost had to flee for their lives because the Eðian rebellion had been attempting to burn down the castle, but James had somehow managed to muster enough force to drive the Eðians back and, with Mary's help, come to a tentative peace with John Knox. But after the emergency was over, Mary had been able to return to her wallowing in grief.)

For three days, she hadn't left her room. She'd hardly left her bed, in fact. She had not eaten or slept beyond a few fitful stretches, and when she woke, she was crying, as she had been when she'd gone to sleep.

She closed her eyes again. Francis's face—that face as familiar and dear to Mary as her own—floated up in her mind. That smirky little smile he had. The smattering of gold fuzz that had appeared on his face in the past few months, just above his lip and along his jawline. The tiny glints of gold and green in his otherwise storm-blue eyes.

She swallowed against a pain in her throat. Francis was still dead today. And he would be dead tomorrow, and the day after that. He was dead, and the last words she'd said to him had been in anger, and she hadn't even given him a proper goodbye, and now it was too late to make it right. He was gone. *I am already shattered,* she thought, tears slipping down her cheeks and into her wet pillow. *I am lost.*

(Sigh. We as your narrators would like to take a moment here to acknowledge how much bad luck / terrible news / anguish in general Mary had been going through lately: the deaths of her father-in-law, her mother, and now her husband, all in such a short period of time. It's a lot—too much, maybe, and we wish history had been kinder to Mary, Queen of Scots, but it just . . . wasn't. These things happened, and they sucked. But we'd also like to remind you that—in our story, anyway—Francis is very much alive at this moment, if not exactly in the best mood himself, and Mary is bound to find that out eventually. Spoiler alert.)

There was a tap on the door, and the Four Marys slipped in, Flem bearing a tray with bread and cheese.

Mary rolled onto her side and faced away. "I'm not hungry." Her body felt empty, hollow, and she had no desire to fill it.

"Come, now. It's time to get up," Liv said more firmly.

Mary turned and stared at her reproachfully. "Why should I?"

"Because you must be strong," answered Liv.

Mary was tired of being strong. She had always been the strong one, because Francis had needed her to be strong. But being strong hadn't saved either of them, in the end.

"Your brother is insisting upon seeing you today," Bea informed her. "He says it's important."

Nothing is important, Mary thought.

"He doesn't need me," she murmured. "I've done nothing for him but make a mess of things."

And for Scotland, she realized, her heart sinking even further. Francis was dead, so now there would be no heirs. Therefore, according to the prenuptial agreement that Mary had so foolishly signed, Scotland now belonged to France.

She hadn't told James about that yet.

"If you've made a mess, then now it's time to clean it up," said Liv.

Mary shook her head. There was nothing she could do about it now. She'd signed. It was over and done.

"Francis would want you to go on, you know," Flem said.

"He'd want me to never have left him in the first place," Mary said.

"You're right," murmured Hush, glancing meaningfully at the

other Marys. "You must stay in bed. Rest. James can wait."

Mary sat up. Without Francis, it felt like her life was over. But Mary still wanted to have a life. She had never been one to give up entirely.

If she was going to survive this, she was going to have to get up. Collect herself. Figure out how to outsmart and outmaneuver her enemies, who were all around her now: John Knox and the Eðians and Catherine and her insidious uncles and even, possibly, James. (He seemed like a nice enough fellow, but you never really know, do you? Her uncles had seemed like nice enough fellows.)

"Fetch me one of my mother's gowns," she said. "As fine a cloth as you can find."

Bea hurried away to look for one.

Flem smiled and bounced on the balls of her feet and went to locate Mary's shoes.

Liv crossed to the vanity and started to dig about in the drawers for suitable jewels for Mary to wear.

Hush nodded and approached eagerly with a hairbrush. "I'm glad you're all right," she murmured. "Now you'll show them that you're still the queen."

"Oh, I will," Mary said. "I'll show them."

The Mary, Queen of Scots, who entered the throne room of Holyrood Palace an hour later was an entirely different Mary than the one who'd first come searching for her mother a week before. That Mary had been, without a doubt, one of the most beautiful women in the world—at least in the top five, if there is a way to truly judge such a thing.

This Mary, the orphan, the widow, was a bit thinner, certainly, than she had been before, and there was a new, sad awareness in her large brown eyes—a knowledge of all that one could lose in this world, all that one could regret. We, as your narrators, would like to add that Mary's grief did not make her more beautiful. She had dark shadows under her eyes, which were still quite puffy from crying. She had a few stress-related "spots," as she would have called them, marring her chin and forehead. She hadn't bathed in days, so she didn't smell fantastic, and her hair was pretty greasy, even though Hush had done her best to fashion it into something suitable. She appeared, quite frankly, frail and exhausted.

She looked like a girl having the worst week of her life.

But she also looked determined to get through it.

"Ah, Mary." James jumped from his chair the moment she was announced. "I'm so glad to see you up and about."

She gave him a wooden smile.

"I have someone here I'd like you to meet," he said, and gestured at a figure who'd been sitting beside him, a young man who Mary had never seen before, who rose eagerly to his feet.

"May I present Henry Stuart, Duke of Albany and heir to the Earldom of Lennox," James said.

Mary extended her hand, and the young man kissed it gently. "Your Grace," he said.

She gazed at him steadily. "I have heard of you, I think." It was so hard to think, really, her head was so muddied by the pain of losing Francis.

"Only good things, I hope," he said.

She didn't remember what she'd heard, only that she should know his name. If only because it was Stuart, which was also, well, her name. "Are you my cousin?"

"Yes. Your first cousin, in fact. You can call me Henry, if you wish."

"I do not wish," she answered. "Being as how I find there to be entirely too many Henrys to keep track of."

The corner of his mouth quirked up. "Then you can call me Darnley," he said. "Everyone does. Or any other name that you wish to call me. I'll answer to 'hey, you,' if you'd prefer. I'm your servant, madam."

So. He was charming. He was also handsome, she realized dully, taller than she was (which was saying something) with red-gold hair, shrewd gray eyes, and a finely chiseled face.

But if he was her first cousin that meant that he was in direct line for the thrones of both England and Scotland. And a man. He had the right parts to be considered a "proper" monarch. Mary's heart began to pound. Had this guy come here to replace her as Scotland's ruler? Had James called him here? She glanced between her half brother and Darnley as they spoke to each other, trying to assess their relationship. They seemed friendly, definitely. But what did that mean?

"Isn't that so, Mary?" James was saying.

She blinked at him. "I don't know," she confessed. "I wasn't listening."

James looked mildly embarrassed, but Darnley's gaze was kind, sympathetic, even. "You've been through much these past few days," he said. "I was sorry to hear it."

"Were you?" she replied sharply. "Or have you come to usurp my throne now that you find me brought so low? Because I assure you, my lord, I am no meek and cowering woman to be pushed around by the likes of scheming men. I am the rightful queen, and you would do well to remember that."

There I go again, she thought in dismay. Insisting that she was the queen. Francis would laugh if he could see her now. (Reader, we don't think Francis would laugh, actually.)

"How could I forget?" Darnley said smoothly. "When your every movement, your every word and breath, is queenly."

"I don't know what that means," she said. "Have you come for my throne, or haven't you?"

He shook his head. "I haven't. I have no desire for a throne, and never have, although I do understand well enough what it's like to have titles and the responsibilities of birth thrust upon me. I have merely come to see if I might be of service to you, as part of your family, during this difficult time."

"Oh," she said. He seemed so earnest that she couldn't help but believe him. "Well, then I'm sorry if I was impolite just now."

"Don't be. I completely understand," he said.

They were silent for a moment, both at a loss for what to say next. Finally Darnley cleared his throat. "I will take my leave, Your Grace. I am sure you are tired, and I do not wish to impose upon you further. But perhaps, if you're feeling better on the morrow, we can take a walk together. I would like to get to know you and see how I can help your cause."

She nodded mutely. Darnley kissed her hand again and left.

Mary wandered over to the throne and sank down upon it. "What do you know of him?" she asked James.

He shrugged. "Very little, I'm afraid. His family is Scottish, but they were exiled by your mother for supporting the English during the Rough Wooing."

Mary shivered. The Rough Wooing, as it was called, had occurred when she was little more than a babe, when England's King Henry VIII had decided that Mary should be wed to his son Edward VI. When her mother betrothed her to Francis instead, Henry VIII had flown into a rage and declared war on Scotland.

It had been a difficult time for everyone, and Mary had always felt rather guilty about all this blood spilled on account of her.

"But he could be useful to us," James said. "He hails from a family of respectable Verities, but he is also in favor with Elizabeth, the English queen."

"Do you think he's come to challenge me?" she asked.

He shook his head with a knowing smile. "No."

"Why has he come, then?"

"Who knows, really? Maybe he just wanted to get a good look at the infamous Mary, Queen of Scots."

"Infamous?" she sniffed.

"Or perhaps he is interested in the Four Marys. He is known to be somewhat of a ladies' man."

She gasped in outrage. "My ladies are not his business!"

"Your ladies are renowned the world over for their great beauty. Second only to you, my queen," James added wisely. "And Lord Darnley is unmarried and seeking to reestablish his ties with Scottish families. He needs a good Scottish wife, one who will bring him prestige and fortune. I imagine that suitors will begin to arrive here regularly, when word gets out that you're to remain in Scotland."

"Oh," Mary said, feeling rather stupid. "And would Darnley be a good match for one of them?"

"He's a bit too puffed up for my taste," said James. "But he's a pleasant enough fellow. And seeing as he's your cousin, of royal blood and all, I can't see you finding a better match for your ladies than he."

"I shall consider that," Mary said thoughtfully. It would be a good time to find matches for her ladies, as she needed to begin to build support in Scotland. But the idea also unsettled her, especially when she thought about Liv and the ordeal with the Norwegian lord. It felt so frivolous, thinking about marriage. Arranging matches. Planning weddings.

But it could be an excellent distraction from her own dilemma.

Or it could be a constant reminder of Francis and all that Mary had lost.

Involuntarily she touched the golden ring on her finger. Francis's ring.

"You have lost your husband," James pointed out, like Mary had somehow misplaced Francis the way a careless child loses her doll. "You are therefore vulnerable, as an unmarried woman, and Scotland, too, is vulnerable. Best to find new allies, wherever you can."

Sigh. James didn't even know the half of it. She still had to tell him about the prenup that made Scotland a French province. And she would. Later.

"Perhaps you were right and he *has* come to challenge you for the throne of Scotland," James mused.

"*What?*"

James laughed. "He's not going to oust you, Mary. We—I mean, *I*—won't let him. I've held on to the throne for you all this time, through thick and thin, and I will keep holding it."

"Yes." Lord, he was going to have a fit when she told him about the treaty. "Thank you, James."

He raised his goblet of wine and drank from it deeply. "You are still the queen, and I say, long may you reign."

"Who was that man in the throne room earlier?" Flem asked when Mary and her ladies had retreated back to Mary's chambers. "He was a fine creature, wasn't he?"

"Flem, you're incorrigible," Bea admonished.

"What? I can look, can't I? He smelled good, too," Flem

continued. "And did you see that cleft in his chin? He's delicious, that one. I could have licked his face, that's for sure."

"Who was he?" Liv asked, rolling her eyes at Flem.

Mary startled at the question. "He was my cousin, apparently. Lord Darnley."

"Ah, a handsome lord," sighed Flem.

"It's funny that you say that," Mary said with a ghost of a smile. "James suggested that perhaps he's here because he wishes to marry one of my ladies."

Flem's mouth dropped open. "Oh! That's wonderful news!" She squealed, but then fake glared threateningly at the other Marys. "I saw him first. I call dibs."

"Flem!" cried Bea. "Be quiet, won't you?"

"Why?" Flem asked, cocking her head to one side exactly as she did when she was a dog. "We must all get married to this lord or that one, someday. If I must be married, I'd prefer a husband who's handsome and rich and well spoken."

"We'll find out what Darnley's intentions are soon enough, I think," said Mary, finding it hard to be stern and deliberate when Flem was dancing about squealing and flouncing her curls. "If he indeed wishes to be wed, perhaps we can arrange a match."

"We should find out more about him," advised Bea.

"Yes, and come to know his disposition and his character," Liv said a bit grimly. Mary felt a twinge of guilt.

"Yes," agreed Hush in a whisper. "Looks aren't everything, you know."

"Oh, tosh." Flem waved them off. She turned to Mary imploringly. "It would be an honor to marry your cousin. Then we'd be even more like sisters."

"I'll think about it," Mary consented.

"Do think about it," Flem said. "And please do pick me!"

THIRTY-EIGHT

Ari

"I said no!" Ari exclaimed.

Francis threw up his hands in exasperation. "But Mary's uncles are plotting to assassinate Queen Elizabeth in two days!" They'd already been arguing for three days. Time was wasting.

Ari started angrily chopping some sprigs of pennyroyal. "I know, but—" She carefully put her chopping knife down and sighed. "I know you're frustrated with our situation. But it's safe here. We just have to find something, or some way, for you to feel useful."

Francis's face turned red. "I'm tired of playing it safe! I've done it my whole life and look where it has gotten me. My father was murdered. My wife is gone. My kingdom was stolen, and I'm a frogging frog!"

"That's another thing," Ari said. "You can't even control when you change into a frog!"

"I've done it three out of five times successfu—"

His voice cut off, and with a flash, Francis turned into a frog. *Poor little guy*, Ari thought.

"Emotions, Your Highness." She sat next to him and practiced calm breathing, hoping it would rub off on him, and waited. Sometime later, there was another flash and Francis was human again.

Ari turned her head and handed him one of the several sheets she had stashed around their hovel. "Welcome back."

"Ribbit," human Francis said.

Ari gave a small laugh as he scooted toward the wall and pressed his back against it.

They both sat there for a moment, two lonely people who might just spend the rest of their lives together, wishing they were somewhere else.

"I may not have the frog thing totally down, Ari, but I refuse to stay the same inconsequential person I've always been." He stood and began pacing. "I will not simply sit back and take it. Not anymore."

"I understand," Ari said. And she did. She knew what it was like to feel inconsequential. Maybe she and Francis had something in common after all.

"Those damn de Guises have ruined my life. They think they can murder and manipulate their way to the top. Well, I'm not going to let them do that."

Ari stood and went back to chopping. "What do you propose to do about it? It's not like your mother is going to help you."

Ari couldn't believe the harshness of her own words, but Francis simply shrugged. "You're right," he said. "But I'm in a perfect position to help by myself. Isn't there a certain freedom in everyone thinking you're dead?"

"You may have gotten better at controlling your Eðian form, but three out of five times isn't good enough."

"You could come with me."

Ari nearly chopped a finger off.

"Why not?" Francis asked. "We make a pretty good team, don't we? You keep things running, and I do the chores."

Ha, Ari thought. Sure, they made a good team. She went out every day, gathering herbs, searching the nearby woods for harder-to-find ingredients, picking up food, making breakfast, lunch, and dinner, rebuilding her laboratory. And Francis completed the tasks Ari assigned him to keep him occupied. But apparently he still had time to sneak out of the hovel, gallivant about the town on his own, and then hatch a plan to single-handedly stop an assassination attempt on the queen of England, an Eðian stronghold that also happened to be the nemesis of France.

Keep him out of trouble, Queen Catherine had instructed.

It wasn't going well, so far. But there was one thing she knew for sure.

"I can't just up and try to rescue the queen of England. It would be treason," Ari said.

Francis scoffed. "Treason? You're with the king of France."

"Former king of France! The queen gave me specific instructions. I only had to do three things. Keep you hidden in Calais. Keep you safe. Keep you from spending money."

"I don't recall her saying to keep me from spending money."

Ari slapped her forehead. "That one goes along with keeping us both alive." She took a few deep breaths.

"I'm sorry, Ari, but I have to go. And you have to come with me."

Ari lowered her head. "I have more to lose than you do," she said quietly. She thought about her father. "If the queen finds out—"

"She's not the queen," Francis interrupted. "She's only the regent. And she's not even going to be that much longer. I'm going to save Elizabeth. And then I am going to Scotland to get Mary, and bring my wife back to France. And then we are going to reclaim my throne."

This all, except for the first part, was new information to Ari. "Oh, is that all?"

"That's all. Well, maybe solve world hunger in the process," Francis added thoughtfully. He grabbed her hand. "If you help me, I promise that when I have my crown again, you and your family will always have a place in my court."

Catherine had underestimated Francis, Ari thought. She hadn't seen any strength in him. But Ari saw it now. She also saw that this could be the solution to both of their problems. After all, Liv was in Scotland, too.

"All right," she said, and smiled breathlessly. "I'll help you. I'll go." She began to move swiftly around the room, tucking various vials into a small chest. "I just want to bring a few things that could come in handy." It would be a shame to have to start her laboratory all over again *again*.

Francis grinned and pulled three satchels from under the

bed. They were packed, bulky with the few clothes she and Francis owned and a good portion of food and other supplies.

"I guess you anticipated my answer," Ari said with a laugh. "I'm the one who's supposed to be able to see the future."

"I've come to know you a little," Francis said. "But speaking of the future, *have* you had any visions that could help us?"

Ari hadn't. She doubted she would now, but it was worth a try. She held a sprig of peppermint in front of her nose and let her eyes roll back. Miraculously the world melted away. "I see trouble at the castle gates," she murmured.

"Elizabeth?" Francis asked.

"I don't know. But there are guards. So many. We'll have to use trickery . . . Maybe a fireproof cloak? A wheelbarrow? Something about a pirate . . ." Ari's voice trailed off as she came to. "I'm sorry. That's not very helpful, I know."

"We have to go." Francis hefted the bags. "Pirates or no pirates. First, we should hire the best ship in the harbor—"

"Absolutely not. We can't afford that."

Francis huffed. "I counted the coins last night. I think we can just make it."

Ari shook her head. "No! We have to make the money last for the rest of our lives."

"Not after I get back my crown, remember? Then we'll be living like royals again."

Oh. Right. But they were still going to need money when they got to England, Ari reasoned. They shouldn't blow it all on one fancy trip across the channel. "Here's what's going to happen," Ari said firmly. "You're going to turn into a frog, and I'm going to buy passage on the cheapest ship I can find. I'll buy a ticket for one. You'll be a frog. And then, when we get to Dover, we'll look for the public carriages heading to London—"

"Public transportation?" Francis looked aghast. Ari assumed he'd never traveled via public transportation, not once in his life.

"It'll get us there," Ari said, "and it won't throw us into utter destitution."

Francis dragged his hands down his face, but Ari was sure it was simply for dramatic effect. "Fine," he said at last.

Ari shut the chest with her potions in it and snapped the clasps into place. "Come along, frog prince. We don't have all day."

Francis glared at her, but there was a burst of white light and he changed into the frog. Good. At least he was listening to her. No more of this insisting that they'd need a bigger boat.

"What's the frog for?" asked the inspector at the docks, peering into Francis's box.

"I'm an apothecary," Ari explained.

"What's that mean?"

"A potion maker." When the man still looked confused, she went on. "I could make you something to help your gout. Or constipation. Or even an unsightly rash." She couldn't help glancing at his neck.

The man blinked. "What's that have to do with your frog?"

"Oh." Ari smiled tightly and shut the box. "I like fresh ingredients."

She could feel Francis shudder.

"Don't worry," she whispered as they walked away. "I've never used fresh frog legs." Not specifically the legs, but he needn't know that.

Soon enough, they'd finished crossing the channel, and before they disembarked, Ari found a small cabin where Francis could change back into a human and get dressed.

Moments later, they were standing on the docks, looking for where to go next.

"There!" Ari pointed at carriages lined up on the road. "Surely one of those will take us straight to London."

But Francis was looking elsewhere, at a small sign tacked to one of the message boards. The paper was decorated with dozens of sketches of animals, everything from a horse to a bird to a ferret. "Look at this." She followed as he drifted closer to read the text in the center.

It was in four different languages, including French. It read:

Attention!
Are you an Eðian refugee fleeing persecution in your Verity country? Do you need assistance settling into England to live a life without the threat of your imminent and untimely death?
Well, you're in luck! Queen Elizabeth has a plan for that. Refugees are welcome. Come to the House of Rescuing Subjugated Eðians, located at 27 Market Square.

Francis pointed. "Look! It's a sign!"

"Yes." Ari tilted her head. "It certainly is a sign." Like, a literal sign.

"We need to go there right now," Francis said. "They know the queen. They can get word to her, especially if they have lots of Eðians going in and out. There must be someone who can carry a message for us."

"I don't know . . . ," Ari started.

"I don't have to be the one to stop Duke Francis and Cardinal Charles. Not personally," Francis insisted. "All we need is for the queen's guards to prevent them from entering the palace. Besides, public transportation is so slow."

Ari pressed her mouth into a line. Francis was still talking like someone who had the protection of being in a position of power. "Who are these people, anyway?" she asked. "What assurances do we have that they work for the queen? There's not even anything about being an official department or ministry. It just said House of Rescuing Subjugated Eðians. Do you know what that shortens to?"

Francis tilted his head. "No . . ."

Ari pointed to the English version. "Look. It says HORSE. What kind of official government agency shortens to HORSE?"

Francis shrugged. "I think we should try it. We can catch one of these carriages to London after, if they refuse to take the message or it seems like they might kick us in the heads. But we can't know if we don't ask."

Ari sighed loudly. "Fine, but you're carrying the trunk the

whole way there. The last thing we need is for anyone to recognize you. You're supposed to be dead."

"Fortunately, I look nothing like myself." Francis was still wearing his scratchy peasant clothes, and Ari had to admit he was really doing a good job of not looking like the king of France. Plus, he was in a completely different kingdom now.

They walked to the House of Rescuing Subjugated Eðians. It was a big building, made of white stone, but the thing that really struck Ari was just how many books waited in the lobby when she stepped in.

"I think we found a library," Ari said. "Are you sure you got the address right?"

But they had. There was a line of people winding up to a desk. It was impossible to see the person sitting there, thanks to the precarious tower of books, but Ari caught a woman's voice, and a flash of red hair. In a room off to the side, a chestnut-haired man spoke with a family—or a group Ari assumed was a family. Only two were human. The other three were a duck, a kitten, and a small black bear.

"Next!" called the woman behind the desk. The line shuffled forward. There were at least ten people ahead of them.

"Let's skip the line and demand an audience," Francis said, but Ari laid a hand on his shoulder.

"We have to wait our turn. We're no one important here, remember?"

"But our message is important."

She nodded. "I know, but we're still incognito. Plus, all these others need help, too."

So they waited as a boy with a wolf friend went ahead of them, then a sparrow, and a fox. All were directed into different rooms to speak to their new advocates. Finally, Francis and Ari were next.

"Hello!" said the small, red-haired woman behind the desk. "Welcome to HORSE. I'm Jane. How can I help you?"

THIRTY-NINE
Francis

Francis lurched forward. "I need to send a message to the queen right away. It's a matter of life and death. Namely, her life."

Jane's eyes widened. "What? What do you mean?" She spoke perfect French, which made Francis realize he hadn't switched when he'd meant to.

"I mean," Francis said, sticking to French since she clearly understood, "I've come across some information. Queen Elizabeth is in danger. You must get word to her at once."

Jane tapped her desk a couple of times, then sighed. "Gifford!"

The man in the other room excused himself from the group of Eðians he was talking to, then approached the desk.

"Gifford, I presume," Francis said in English.

"Call me G."

"Ah. Very well. G." What a strange name that was.

G turned to Jane. "You bellowed, my love?"

"Yes." Jane stood. She was tiny, as short as a child. "This young man says he has information. He says that Bess is in danger."

G frowned at Francis. "And who are you? How did you come by this information?"

"I'm—"

"No one," Ari said. "He's no one important."

Jane blinked a few times. "No, I know who you are."

"No, you don't," said Francis.

"Yes, I do. You're King Francis. You're supposed to be dead."

Francis and Ari exchanged uneasy glances.

"Um," said Francis.

"I knew it!" Jane cried. "I thought you looked familiar. I recognized you from this book I read." She started to pry a book out of the tower on her desk. G raced to steady the rest of the tomes, to stop them from falling. "It's called *How to Recognize Monarchs in Five Easy Steps*. It has pictures. The one of you . . ." Her mouth twisted into a frown. "Well, it's not very flattering, I must say."

"None of them are," Francis said.

"Ha!" Jane pointed. "You admit it. You are Francis."

"You'd already figured it out!"

Ari was just shaking her head at him. "This is embarrassing."

Jane grinned as she looked around the lobby. It was empty, but she waved them to another room. "Come into my office where we can have some privacy." She placed a small sign on her desk, which read, "Be Right Back."

They all moved into the small room, and Francis gave them the short version of everything that had happened leading up to his arrival at HORSE.

"So your mother turned you into a frog," Jane said thoughtfully. "And now everyone thinks you're dead. And these de Guise people want Queen Elizabeth dead."

She and G looked at each other, and G nodded.

"I'll raise the flag," he said, then left the room.

"I know something about becoming queen against your own will," Jane said quietly, after a few minutes of uncomfortable silence. "Not everyone who sits on the throne is meant for it."

Ari sat up straight. "Wait, you're—"

"Jane Grey. Well, Jane Grey Dudley. Gifford is my husband." Jane smiled. "Yes. I do have some experience in the area of escaping the throne—and imminent death—by discovering the Eðian inside."

"As do I." A young man walked in, trailed by G. The newcomer nodded to Francis. "Edward Tudor, at your service."

Francis was reeling. "You're here, too?"

"Of course." Edward smiled. "I've heard a lot about you, Francis. I was sorry to hear about, well, everything."

"It's been an ordeal," Francis admitted. "Lots of scheming."

"Assassination attempts." Edward quirked a smile.

"Some successes on that front," Francis said soberly.

"You being a frog at French court is hardly ideal," G said.

"Far from it," Francis agreed.

"And there's been weddings," Jane added.

"Just the one," Francis said. "And I mean to win her back."

G touched Jane's shoulder. "We need to help them."

"Of course," Jane said. "Edward, will you—"

"Yes." Edward glanced at G. "I'll fly to London immediately. Francis, I can carry you, if you wish."

"Oh, no," said Ari. "He stays with me. He was put in my care, and I won't let him out of my sight."

"You and Jane and I can follow behind," G said. "We'll be there soon after, if we hurry."

"I don't like it, Francis," Ari said.

Francis nodded. "I know. But I release you from your obligations to me. My mother had no right to demand that you give up your entire life to take care of me, and I certainly cannot ask you to do even more. If you want to return to France, then you may."

Ari's brow furrowed, but after a moment, she said, "I'm still going with you."

"Oh good," Jane said. "Let me just tell everyone here that we're going to be gone for a while. HORSE can run itself, of course. I just like to be here. It makes me feel useful."

"Jane likes feeling useful," G said. "Almost as much as she likes books. Edward, Francis, we'll be along shortly. Just get to Bess in time."

Francis and Edward went upstairs and into a room with a

413

large window and open wardrobe, which was filled with several different kinds of clothes.

"Just leave your things here," Edward said. "There will be more on the other side. I have a room— Well, you'll see it. For now, just"—he waved his hands—"go ahead and change. I'll carry you there."

"Won't that slow you down?" Francis asked. (No, Francis wasn't having second thoughts. Why do you ask?)

"Do you want to wait here?"

"Definitely not."

Both former kings vanished into white light.

Frogs were not meant to fly. Jumping, sure. Even jumping long distances. But flying? Nope. If they were in the claws of a raptor, they were most likely dead.

Francis would have screamed if he could have. As it was, he just ribbited a lot as the world zoomed below. Everything was tiny, trees and roads and waterways. Francis felt paralyzed, unable to move as the air rushed by him. He knew the wind was cold, but the only thing he felt was terror.

Just as the River Thames was coming into view, it happened. Light exploded around him. Francis—human, naked, and frozen to the bone—plummeted toward the earth, taking the kestrel with him.

Francis screamed.

Edward screamed.

The wind screamed.

Frog, frog, frog! Francis thought. The trees were getting closer, bigger, and the ground had never seemed quite so deadly.

A part of Francis knew that he should let go of Edward, so that he didn't kill them both, but he couldn't make his fists unclench, and it also seemed impossible to let go of the thing that could fly.

Come on, frog! Francis thought.

The ground rushed toward him as they dropped below the tops of the tallest trees.

Flash!

Francis became a frog again, but he'd come untethered from Edward's talons. He kept dropping, faster and faster, and then he was heavy for a moment as talons closed around him and dragged him upward, toward the clouds again.

Francis thought perhaps Edward would want to land and take a break, for both of them to catch their breath (even if they'd have to be naked for it, which would have been deeply uncomfortable), but the former king of England kept flying, faster and faster toward London.

At last, the city stretched before them. Francis caught glimpses of houses and boats and bridges spanning the river, and then, the Tower of London. Edward dove toward an open window in the White Tower and deposited Francis on a pile of blankets in the corner.

Both boys became human, and while Edward hurried to find clothes in the wardrobe, Francis huddled in the blankets and shivered. (Frogs, as we know now, are cold-blooded, and don't generate their own heat, so Francis's body temperature had dropped a *lot* while he was flying.)

"Here you go." Edward, dressed now, dropped clothes next to Francis. "Are you all right? You really had me scared there."

"Y-Yes." Francis couldn't stop shivering. The idea of flight had seemed fun back in Dover, but he was completely over it now. "I'm still learning to control my form."

Edward gave a sympathetic frown. "This is new to you, isn't it?"

"I didn't even know I might be an E∂ian until a few weeks ago. I've been practicing, but . . ."

"I understand." Edward walked toward the door. "I'll give you some tips later, when we have time. Get dressed. We'll check the throne room first. She's probably holding court."

Francis shoved his legs into the trousers, his arms into the shirt. The clothes were nice—not so fine as what he'd worn all his life, but they weren't scratchy by any means—and fit decently well. He and Edward were of similar size.

A minute later, both of them were rushing through the halls, down the stairs, and into the throne room.

It was packed. Elizabeth was indeed holding court. Nobles stood elbow to elbow, watching their queen. She had the bearing of a monarch, all straight shoulders and sober intensity. Her gown was voluminous, and a white ruffle collar encircled her neck. Queen Elizabeth was exquisite, the undeniable image of what a queen should be.

"I know," Edward murmured to Francis as they made their way through the crowd of courtiers. "She was made for this."

Francis just nodded. He couldn't help but wonder what Mary would think, if she could see Elizabeth here, sitting upon the English throne. Mary had always been told she had a claim, but it was hard to imagine anyone but Elizabeth sitting here.

"It is a puzzle box, Your Majesty." A voice twisted through the court. Francis couldn't see the owner yet, but the accented English, the slimy tone—it all sent a shiver through him, totally unrelated to the chill that clung to him after the flight. "I ask you, do not try to open it now. It will take time. Attempt the puzzle when you need to clear your mind after a long day of ruling."

"We thank you." Elizabeth's voice was strong, somewhat monotonous in her royal speech. "We will delight in this gift."

"In spite of all the upheavals in France," the man said, "our friendship with England is unshakable. The House of Guise wishes nothing but the best for England, and for you, its rightful queen."

Finally, Francis and Edward pushed into the fore of the crowd, just in time to see a golden, bejeweled box pass into Elizabeth's hands. And before her stood a man in de Guise livery. He was a messenger, possibly the son of some lesser member of the house.

"Stop!" cried Francis, forgetting to switch to English as he darted toward the queen.

"Guards!" Elizabeth's eyes went wide.

"Bess, wait!" Edward shouted, but it was too late. Three guards materialized from the background and grabbed Francis.

"Release him!" ordered Edward. "Bess, tell them to let him go."

"Who is this?" Elizabeth asked, and then looked at Francis. "Wait. You are familiar."

"Francis Valois." Francis tried to wrestle away from the guards, but they were stronger than him. He settled for standing up as straight as he could. And speaking in English. "The rightful king of France."

"You're supposed to be dead." The messenger glanced from Francis to the box that rested on Elizabeth's lap. "What are you doing here?"

"Stopping you from assassinating the queen of England."

Gasps rippled through the audience.

"What do you mean?" asked Elizabeth, then turned to the young man. "My lord Claude, explain yourself."

"There is nothing to explain," said Claude. "I've come simply to reestablish our friendship—"

"Lies!" Francis shouted. "You lie!"

"Release Francis," Edward told the guards. "He's on our side."

Francis wouldn't have gone *that* far, but it would do for now.

When the queen nodded, the guards let go.

Francis approached the queen. "Your Majesty, if I may examine this so-called gift?"

Queen Elizabeth handed it over. She still looked the part of a queen, but Francis didn't miss the slight tremor in her hands, the faint worry in her eyes as she exchanged looks with Edward.

Francis's hands were shaking, too, as he took the box. His trembling was more visible. Even so, he looked straight at Claude and said, "I won't let your family murder another monarch." Then he threw the golden puzzle box to the marble floor. The wood cracked open, and a snake—a viper—slithered out.

Alarm spread through the audience as everyone backed away. The viper was an Eðian, certainly, because it whipped around Claude protectively.

"Guards, seize them both!" Elizabeth commanded, and they moved immediately toward the young man and the snake. One held a basket, ready to trap the creature.

As the assassins were captured and taken from the throne room, a sense of relief washed over Francis. He'd done it. He'd saved the queen of England. The viper Eðian wouldn't be able to lie in wait and bite her while she slept tonight.

"Well," said Elizabeth. "This was certainly exciting. Now, let's discuss who is trying to kill us, and why."

FORTY

"How are you?" Darnley asked as he and Mary strolled through the orchard. It was a nice day, one of the few Mary had seen since arriving in Scotland. The sun was shining, birds were singing in the trees, and there was only the faintest smell of smoke from when the castle had burned earlier. "You look better than when I last saw you."

"I'm as well as can be expected, I suppose," Mary said. She did look better, much better, in fact. She'd bathed and eaten and slept a bit. But she'd been oddly numb for the past few days. No more tears for Francis. No moments of anguish at the thought of him. No painful, unbidden memories. She had been going about her day on what she would have called autopilot, if autopilot had been invented yet. Or autos. Or pilots.

"I can only imagine how you're suffering," said Darnley. "I

was in love, once. It ended badly, and it was years before I fully recovered."

"Oh, it wasn't like that with Francis," Mary said quickly, but saying this felt false, like a bald-faced lie, in fact. She touched the ring on her hand. "I mean, I'd known I was going to marry him for as long as I can remember, and I loved him dearly, but it wasn't what the poets write about. It wasn't *love* love."

"I see," said Darnley. "Have you ever been in *love* love?"

"No," she said stiffly after a moment, but again, this felt wrong to her.

"We're not supposed to find that kind of love, you and I," Darnley remarked. "We're supposed to do as we're told, and marry whom we're told, and behave how we're told. Love is a luxury we can't afford."

She nodded. "Indeed." It felt odd for him to be talking about the improbability of love when at any moment she expected him to ask about marrying one of her ladies-in-waiting. She was planning to put forward Flem, if he asked. Seeing as how apparently Flem had fallen in love with this man at first sniff.

"I've led a charmed life," he continued. "I know I am fortunate to have the wealth and privilege I've enjoyed. But just once I'd like to simply be who I am without all the pressure to be so—I don't know—perfect. You know?"

She did know. All too well. "Oh, so you're perfect, are you?" she challenged, trying to lighten the mood. "And modest too, I see."

He smiled. "I am. Perfectly modest. And people also tell me I'm pretty."

She laughed, which surprised her. She didn't think she should be capable of laughing. So then she frowned. "One of my ladies certainly thinks so," she said, to move the conversation over to her ladies.

"Does she?"

"Yes, she—"

"And what do you think?" he asked.

She blinked a few times. "Well. I find you pleasant to look upon, I suppose."

"Thank you," he said, as if her complement had been her own idea. "I happen to think you're stunning."

Oh dear. She was starting to understand that maybe it wasn't Mary's ladies he was interested in. Or maybe he was like this with all women. James had said he was a ladies' man.

"Actually, *you're* the perfect one," Darnley continued. "Everyone says so."

"Yes, well, everyone doesn't know me very well," she answered.

Darnley stopped beneath an apple tree and reached up to pick an apple. "They do say that you have one flaw. But it's a small one. Easy to overlook."

She gazed at him quizzically. "And what flaw is that?"

"You're contrary," he answered.

"I am not," she said instantly, then blushed.

"There's even been a poem written about it," he added, and then cringed, as if he had not meant to tell her about it.

"What poem?" she gasped. "By whom?"

"It's nothing much." He took a bite from the apple, revealing a flash of strong white teeth. "I don't know. Everyone in Scotland's been reciting it for weeks."

That didn't sound especially good. "How does it go?"

"Are you sure you want to hear it?"

"Is it . . . unflattering?"

"That depends on your interpretation, I suppose."

"Tell me," she demanded.

"All right." He tossed the apple aside and stood up straight, clasping his hands behind him and clearing his throat as though he were on a stage, in front of an audience, about to give a grand performance. "'Mistress Mary, quite contrary, how does your garden grow? With silver bells, and cockle shells, and pretty maids all in a row.'"

Her eyebrows squeezed together. "But I don't even have a garden."

"I think the garden is supposed to represent your reign over the realm."

She immediately felt foolish. "Oh. And the silver bells are—"

"The bells of the Verity Church, of course. And the pretty maids are your four ladies. As for the cockle shells, I don't know. I asked one fellow who seemed to think it meant that you'd left your husband for another man, which would have made Francis a cuckold, you see, but I've also heard that it refers to your expensive tastes, like for exotic food such as cockles."

(Your narrators here. Yikes, this harmless-sounding poem is actually so mean! In our research, we have found that the poem—or nursery rhyme, as it would become—possibly did refer to Mary, Queen of Scots. Cockles, for your information, are small mollusks—like clams. Which Mary was apparently quite fond of. Which, in some people's eyes, made her a snob.)

Mary tossed her hair over her shoulder irritably. "Oh, so everyone in the kingdom is saying that I'm a contrary Verity with an uncertain reign who's either a faithless cheater or an excessive spender completely out of touch with the Scottish people? That's a bit more than one small flaw, don't you think?"

His smile faded. "I apologize, Your Highness. I didn't mean to rile you."

"I bet it was Knox who wrote that poem!" Mary railed. "He'd happily see me run out of the country."

"But you haven't been run out of the country," Darnley said.

She gestured to the charred tower. "Not yet."

"You have friends in Scotland still. Allies."

She glanced around at the empty orchard. "Like who?"

"Like me," he answered simply. "I will be your ally, Mary. If you'll allow me to be."

She gazed at him appraisingly. "And what do you wish, in return?" She was starting to get some idea. "Have you set your sights on one of my pretty maids?" she asked, because she was still hoping this was about the Marys, any of the Marys but her. "Do you want me to line them up in a row for you? Because I can."

He shook his head. "No. I'm not after your ladies."

Droppings. "What, then?"

He didn't speak, but the way he looked at her, his eyes imploring, yearning, even, answered the question.

"No," Mary blurted out. "I couldn't possibly."

"I realize that we've only just met," he said gently. "I do not wish to rush you, or impose myself upon you during this time of great upheaval in your life. But you need protection—now, today— and I can offer you that. We could be ourselves with each other, at the very least, and in time perhaps you'd come to feel for me something like what you did for Francis. Not love, but comradery. Companionship. Friendship. Trust."

His offer wasn't unreasonable, she realized dazedly. Darnley was being generous, in fact. It turned out that he and Mary had much in common (like, cough, grandparents). He was fair company, pretty, as he'd humblebragged, but sharp-witted enough to keep up with her. He'd made her laugh. But the thing was: Mary was not ready to laugh yet. She was not ready to notice a man for his prettiness. She didn't want to—it felt disloyal. To Francis.

"I'm sorry. I can't," she whispered, and turned and fled back to the castle, leaving Darnley staring forlornly after her.

She hadn't been back in her chambers for more than a minute or two when she was summoned to the throne room again.

"No," she barked to the messenger. "Tell my brother that I am not to be ordered about like a common chambermaid. If I want to talk to anyone, *I* shall summon *you*."

"Yes, Your Highness," mumbled the messenger, and slunk away.

"Are you all right?" Liv asked softly.

"I'm perfectly fine," Mary said, and sat down in a huff. "Why does everyone keep asking me that?"

"How did it go with Lord Darnley?" Flem asked, even as Bea hissed out a warning for her to hold her tongue. "Did he ask for one of our hands in marriage? What was he wearing? Was he as clever and rich and handsome as he was before?"

"If you like him so much, you marry him!" Mary exclaimed.

Flem looked confused. "That's what I was talking about! I'd be happy to marry him, as I said. He's dreamy."

Mary clenched her teeth to hold in a scream.

"Look, dear, there's that troublesome squirrel stealing seeds from our bird feeder," murmured Hush. "Can you please go take care of that?"

"Oh, yes, I do detest that squirrel!" Flem cried, and darted off to spend the rest of the afternoon barking up a tree. For once, Mary was relieved to see her go.

Liv closed the door. "What happened? Did Darnley behave improperly toward you? Because if he did I'll . . ."

"No," Mary said quickly. "He was perfectly well behaved, which is rather the problem."

"Was your brother correct?" asked Hush tremulously. "Does he wish to wed one of us?"

"No." Mary sighed. "It's me he wishes to marry."

The three remaining Marys drew in a shocked collective breath.

"He proposed?" Liv gasped.

"Not in so many words," Mary admitted. "But he made his intentions clear enough."

Bea made a sound like an outraged croak. "But Francis just—"

"I know."

"You've only had a few days to process what's happened," Hush said softly.

"I know."

"You're expected to be in mourning for at least a year before it's appropriate to see suitors," Liv pointed out.

"I know!" Mary exclaimed, standing up and starting to pace. "Darnley knows that, too. He just . . ." She bit her lip. "He believes that I'm in danger now, and it would be safer for both me and for Scotland if I were to marry again, as soon as possible. He was quite nice about it, actually."

"How gallant of him," Liv said dryly.

"And how did you answer him?" asked Hush.

Mary rubbed her eyes. "I said no, of course."

"Of course," agreed Bea. "Because it's ludicrous, the idea that you would marry again so soon after—"

"I know," Mary said.

There was a knock on the door. The messenger, again. He looked sufficiently miserable about it. "Your brother says you really must come. It's a matter of national importance."

Mary snorted.

"I'm sure he wishes me to pick the royal china pattern, is all." There'd been a lot of that kind of thing since she'd arrived in Scotland and taken over for her mother. Insignificant busy work.

"There are some men who wish to see you."

Mary exchanged glances with her ladies. "Men? *More* men?"

"More suitors?" Hush whispered.

"How is that even possible?" scoffed Liv.

Mary straightened. "Fine. Let's go see. Fetch me my crown."

The men who wished to see Mary were not suitors, as it turned out. They were Mary's uncles.

Mary would rather have faced suitors.

"Mary!" beamed Uncle Charles. "Thank heavens you're safe. We've been sick with worry since you mysteriously vanished from our château in the middle of such a pleasant visit."

Uncle Francis (not her Francis, Mary thought bitterly) rushed forward and cupped her cheeks in his hands. "Whyever did you leave like that, child, without telling us where you were going? You know we could have helped you with anything you felt you needed." He glanced for a long moment at Bea, who was standing with the other Marys in the background. Bea's chin lifted, but Mary could tell she was terrified. All of her ladies (save Flem, who was still outside) looked frightened. Which was completely reasonable.

Mary stepped back from her uncles. Rage filled her, but her first instinct was to play along with them, to act as though she didn't know anything, to make small talk and be nice. She could behave, as she always had. It was the safest course of action. But the ruse was up. She was obviously the one who had freed Bea from their dungeon. And Liv, too, was still at Mary's side. Her uncles knew that she knew all about their treachery.

(Your narrators here: well. Not *all* of their treachery.)

"All my life, I trusted you," she began in a low voice. "I was such a fool."

James rose, looking worriedly at the other courtiers in the room. It was clear that Mary was about to make a scene.

"Perhaps this is a conversation that the queen wishes to have with her uncles in private?" he suggested, and the lords and ladies reluctantly left the great hall, murmuring to themselves. James glanced at Mary. She tilted her head to indicate that he and the other Marys should retreat, as well.

"You are upset, my dear," Uncle Charles remarked once everyone had gone. "Which is understandable. You've been through a terrible ordeal."

"Any ordeals I've been through have been at your hand," Mary said. "If my life has been a tragic story, then the two of you have authored it."

"Oh, don't be so dramatic," tsked Uncle Francis. "You're fine, aren't you? Ruling Scotland directly, as you always wanted to. Your mother would be so proud."

"Don't you dare talk about my mother!" Mary fumed. Then: "What happened to my mother? What did you do to her?"

"Our sister died of 'the Affliction,'" Uncle Charles said somberly. "We were as saddened as you to hear it."

"No." Mary shook her head so violently her crown tumbled to the floor. "I won't believe it. She learned of your plans, and she wouldn't go along with them, so you got rid of her somehow. And then you killed the king of France! You set all of this in motion! I always knew that you were ruthless men, but now I know you to be treasonous, as well."

Her uncles regarded her calmly. "Anything we did, we did for you, my dear. For your throne. For your well-being. As we have always done. Because we love you," Uncle Charles said.

"Did you kill Francis, as well?" Mary stormed. "I'll—I'll kill you if you killed him."

Uncle Charles scoffed. "Of course not. How could you believe we would do such a thing?"

"The moment Francis died, you lost France," Uncle Francis added. "If you'd had an heir already, perhaps we could have worked with that. But in that way you failed us. So of course we didn't kill Francis. There was nothing for us to gain by his death."

Mary gaped at them. That they would be so bold and unapologetic about their schemes was truly shocking. (We, your narrators, are not really that shocked.)

"It was the Medici woman," added Uncle Charles. "I wouldn't put it past her to murder her own child out of sheer ambition. If there was indeed foul play involved in the death of the young king, it was her doing. Not ours."

"Catherine would never harm Francis," Mary murmured, but her words lacked conviction. She thought of the way Catherine had smiled when she'd given Mary the gift of a mousetrap.

"Think about it. With Francis out of the way, Catherine is now the regent. She is, essentially, the ruler of France. It was as deft a political move as I've ever encountered," Uncle Francis said with an admiring sigh. "She's an evil, conniving witch, but she did manage to best us this time. Never fear, though. We'll find a way to recover France eventually. Maybe you could even marry the boy who's currently king—Charles. For now we must focus on you, my dear, and securing your position here in Scotland. And then we'll get England for you. We've had a bit of a setback on that front this week, but if at first you don't succeed, you know, try, try again.

"The first order of business should be to find you a new husband," added Uncle Francis. "A better one, this time. A good Verity, someone rich and powerful, hopefully a prince from Spain or Italy or, if we're feeling desperate, Bavaria."

Mary shook her head in dismay. "You are shameless, the both of you. How can you—"

"We are realists, my girl," said Uncle Francis. "And our family—which I would like to remind you is also *your* family—has survived so long because we are shrewd and unafraid of doing what must be done."

"And what must be done now"—Uncle Charles bent and retrieved Mary's crown. He crossed behind her and placed it back upon her head—"is for you to marry and produce an heir, as soon as possible."

"Let's see," said Uncle Francis. "Who do we know who's single?"

"I can find my own husband, in my own good time," Mary said furiously.

Uncle Charles gave an amused chortle. "Oh, can you? Do you have someone in mind, my dear? Do tell."

"Perhaps I'll marry—I don't know, Henry Stuart," she said. "Not that it's any business of yours."

Her uncles collectively snorted. "Lord Darnley? Oh no, dear, that would never do."

"Why not?" she asked. "He's of royal blood."

"He's a leech, at best. His family was exiled in disgrace years ago and has never recovered from the shame of it. He may possess some royal blood, as you say, but he is not a royal, nor will he ever be."

"He seems competent enough," Mary said.

Uncle Francis scowled. "No. You will not marry Lord Darnley."

"We forbid it," said Uncle Charles.

"I am not your puppet!" Mary screeched. "I will marry whom I please!"

Uncle Charles laughed again. "You can't really believe that. Are you done with your tantrum now? Because we have other business to discuss with you. About this John Knox fellow. The best way to be rid of him, we think, is—"

"I will be no part of your schemes. Not anymore," she said.

Uncle Francis crossed his arms. "Oh, dear. I would hate to have to threaten you, being as I'm so fond of you."

"You can't threaten me," she said. "There's nothing left I care about for me to lose."

"But that's not true, is it?" said Uncle Francis mildly. "You still have your ladies, and we all know how vulnerable they are. Especially the one with the unfortunate sister, and the Eðian bird-girl. And then there's your half brother. He's been somewhat useful, I admit, but he is ultimately expendable."

Mary's breath seized.

Uncle Charles patted her hand. "You'll be a good girl, I think. As you always are. Because that's how you survive. And how your friends survive, as well."

"Yes," Mary whispered miserably. "I'll be good."

But of course, Mary had no intention of doing what she was told.

Back in her chambers, the Marys, including Flem again, were waiting with grave expressions that meant they knew all that had happened. One of them—probably Hush, Mary guessed—had undoubtedly changed into her Eðian form and eavesdropped on her conversation with her uncles in the throne room.

Liv, especially, looked worried.

"What will we do?" Hush asked.

For a moment, Mary really didn't know the answer to that question. But if one of Mary's traits was being contrary—and yes, we're willing to admit that she was—she was also terribly, terribly stubborn. She was not about to simply let her uncles roll over her.

"My uncles forget that I am the queen, and therefore I am not powerless," she said.

"My sister—" Liv began.

"I can look after your sister. She need not be ruined," Mary said. "And I can expel my uncles from Scotland. While I was in France, it made sense for them to advise me, but I am no longer in France."

She'd never go back to France, she realized. She swallowed down a lump in her throat. "I have no further need of my uncles. They must go."

"What if they won't?" asked Bea grimly.

"I could bite them!" Flem offered.

"Thank you, dear, but no. I can handle them. I'll declare them enemies of the state and have them thrown into the dungeon if I must. I can align myself with other allies—" Something else occurred to her. "About that. Wait here."

She strode out of the room, across the palace to the guest wing, and stood for a moment outside of Darnley's door, considering whether what she was about to do was truly what she wanted.

It wasn't.

It was at this moment, in fact, that Mary realized what she'd felt for Francis had been every kind of love. The love a child has for a member of her family. The love a girl feels for her best friend. The thrill a woman feels when her lover puts his arms around her. With Francis, it had always been love. True love. *Love* love.

But now that love was gone. Francis was gone.

And Mary had to go on.

So she pinched her cheeks to give them some color, smoothed her hair and straightened her crown, and knocked.

"Why, Mary," Darnley said when he opened the door. "Are you all right? You look pale."

"I'm fine," she said briskly.

"To what do I owe the pleasure—"

"I will marry you," she said. "My answer is yes."

His mouth opened and then closed again. He smiled almost bashfully. "I haven't even asked."

"Nevertheless, that is my answer. Yes."

He took her hand and kissed it. "I am honored, truly. You are the most beautiful and elegant and clever woman in the world. I promise I will be a good husband to you, and a good king to Scotland, and I will keep you safe, and . . ."

She waved off his flattery and his promises. "I won't love you," she said plainly. She wanted to make this clear from the start. "I can't love you. As long as you don't expect that from me, we'll get along fine."

He nodded solemnly, still holding her hand. "I understand."

FORTY-ONE

Ari

Ari knew that if Francis had his way, they would have been on horses bound for Scotland, and Queen Mary, the moment after he thwarted the attempted assassination of Queen Elizabeth. She would have preferred that, too.

But in the English court, the deposed king of France was a long way off from having his druthers. And so, the night following their arrival in London, Ari and Francis were given quarters to sleep in, and fresh clothes to wear. Ari was grateful for the change of clothes, because she had smelled distinctly of horse. The clothes were of the boy kind, because that's how she'd been dressed when G and Jane had gotten her into the palace, and frankly she'd grown quite fond of them.

Officially, the queen was keeping Ari and Francis at the palace because there'd been several Eðian and Verity skirmishes on the road to Scotland. But unofficially, the queen had no intention of letting them leave without getting to the bottom of things.

Ari knew this, because Francis had actually tried to leave. He'd shown up at Ari's door with satchels packed. This was beginning to become a pattern with him.

"We're going to Scotland," he'd said.

"I'm right behind you," Ari'd replied, thoughts of Liv dancing in her head.

But it had turned out the queen's guards were right behind them as well, and when it came time to exit the castle, they kindly drew their swords.

"Are we prisoners here?" Francis had asked.

"Of course not," one of the guards replied.

"Then we are free to leave," Francis said.

"Naturally," the same guard said.

Francis took a step toward the main door, and the tips of all four swords came within an inch of his throat.

"So, we're prisoners," Francis said, glancing at Ari.

"Never," the main guard said again. He motioned behind him, and four more guards appeared. "Our palace is your palace. Our country is your country."

Ari furrowed her brows. She wondered if there was a breakdown in the translation of things here. Her English was rough, but it couldn't have been that rough.

"We wish to leave," Francis said.

"By all means," the guard said. He didn't move.

So they had turned back and gone to their separate rooms. That was last night.

They shouldn't have been surprised. Of course Queen Elizabeth wouldn't let them leave, at least not without an explanation for yesterday.

An explanation Francis and Ari were waiting to give her now.

It was morning, and they were in Queen Elizabeth's throne room, standing toward the back, watching masses of people—nobility, ambassadors, diplomats, relatives of relatives—all waiting patiently for an audience with the queen. Some were regional leaders who had come to report the latest on Eðian/Verity battles that were plaguing the country.

Ari could tell by the number of times Francis ran his hand through his hair that he was anxious to be done and on his way.

Patience came a little bit easier to Ari, who was thoroughly entertained watching the English court. She hadn't been there the day before, so this was her first time seeing *the* Queen Elizabeth. Not only that, she felt like she was witnessing an elaborate chess game, only nobody was really sure who was playing and which team they were on. So, it was a chess game where all the pieces were the same color, scattered about the board, with invisible hands moving them, and who knew how many teams.

Ari leaned toward Francis. "Don't you think this is like a giant game of chess, where—"

"Shhh," Francis said.

Ari crossed her arms. "Fine."

"I'm trying to listen," Francis said more gently.

Queen Elizabeth sat at one end of the room, the throne end, and at her right side was a man with a long gray beard. He leaned down to whisper in the queen's ear so many times Ari wondered how he hadn't thrown out his back. Most, if not all, of the people waiting to speak to the queen were men, and in addition to the ones there to report on the fighting, many of the others came with obvious marriage proposals. At least they would have been obvious had the gentlemen been free to say such things.

As it was, they usually went with something like:

"Your Majesty, I bring you warmest regards from my father, the duke of blah blah or the lord of blah blah, or your cousin blah blah, and I am at your service." Followed by a deep bow.

The bearded man next to the queen always followed their greetings with a lengthy ear whisper.

"Who is that man?" Francis asked Edward, who had stayed the night as well.

"He is William Cecil, the first Baron of Burghley. He is the queen's most trusted adviser." Edward shrugged. "He annoys me so."

"Why?" Francis asked.

"He always says things like, 'The queen is the head, but I am the neck that turns the head.'"

Ari tilted her head (wondering if someone was directing her neck, too). "Why are the men even trying to propose when there's so much fighting going on?"

Francis and Edward exchanged knowing looks. "It's all part of the same thing. Trying to retain control of the country," Francis said.

The queen nodded her head at her latest suitor, and then suddenly stood and waved her hand in a dismissive way. A page next to her stepped forward.

"Ladies and gentlemen, please clear the room," he said.

The line of petitioners dispersed, as well as most of the lords and ladies. Ari started to step away, but Francis grabbed her sleeve. Queen Elizabeth was gesturing for them to come forward.

Ari followed Francis toward the throne.

She gave her best curtsy, despite being dressed as a boy, and Francis nodded politely, as he was also a king (or at least a former king trying to reclaim his throne) and it would not be appropriate to bow. Ari couldn't imagine what was going through Francis's head, considering he had only recently been crowned king of France, Scotland, *and* England.

This was awkward.

"This is awkward," Queen Elizabeth said.

Ah! Ari was right. Maybe she was getting better at politics.

"You are our enemy," Queen Elizabeth continued. "And yet you saved our life." The queen was using the royal *our.*

Francis nodded. "And also I'm supposed to be dead."

"Yes, that adds to our current discomfort," Queen Elizabeth said in her stately manner. "I wonder, did you plan the assassination so that you could thwart it and ingratiate yourself to *us*?"

Ari snorted at such a suggestion, which she instantly regretted, because then Queen Elizabeth looked at her.

"And who are you?" she asked.

"Ari is my trusted squire," Francis said. "She has served faithfully by my side these past few weeks."

Edward came forward and gave a quick bow. "Bess, I believe their reasons for coming here are sincere. They crossed the channel dressed as peasants, and followed the signs to HORSE. If they had the support of France, there's no way they would have made the treacherous journey alone."

The queen leaned toward her brother and spoke under her breath. "Edward, how many times have I told you not to call me Bess in here?"

Edward smiled sheepishly. "Well, the room's practically empty."

"Still," the queen said.

"Yes, Your Majesty," Edward said grandly.

Queen Elizabeth sighed. "Let's adjourn to the grand parlor for some tea."

Ari and Francis followed behind Edward, who followed behind Cecil, who followed behind Queen Elizabeth. They entered a smaller room down the main corridor. It was smaller than the throne room but still larger than twenty hovels, and four or five times as high.

They sat around a table. "Cecil, send for tea and biscuits," the queen said.

After the tea came, things were a little more relaxed, but Ari could tell that Queen Elizabeth and Francis both had their guards up.

"You saved my life," she said, abandoning, for now, the royal we. "Why?"

Francis leaned forward. "Because the de Guises are evil."

"How did you come to know of their plan?" Cecil wanted to know.

"I overheard them talking," Francis said matter-of-factly.

"So the dead former king of France, who is also married to Queen Elizabeth's biggest rival for the throne of England, just happens to overhear a plot to end her life, and instead of letting it happen, he decides to travel here by himself and stop it?" Cecil leaned forward to match Francis's pose. "You see why we might find this very hard to believe."

"I understand," Francis said. "But can't you just thank us and we'll be on our way?"

Ari gasped and Edward gave an awkward laugh.

"You will not leave until we are satisfied that you do not pose a threat to the queen," Cecil said.

Francis folded his arms. "I'm not sure how we can prove our story to you."

"I am grateful for my life," the queen said.

"But we can't take you at your word," Cecil interjected. "You must see that."

Ari stepped forward, face flushed. Everyone was being so

stubborn. "You can take his word, because it's the word of a king. Francis came here to help you because these men had his father assassinated and he could not let the same fate befall another monarch. And he simply wishes to go to his wife, to protect her from the same threat, and return to France to reclaim his throne. Is that so much to ask?"

"I don't think so," Edward said mildly.

"You forget your place, girl," said Cecil. "You are speaking to—"

"Enough, William," said the queen, with a ring of authority in her voice. "She knows who she is speaking to. Edward says he believes them, and so do I, I find. What a different world we would live in if we as monarchs endeavored to help one another, as this king has done. So now I shall help you, King Francis, and perhaps that will ease some of the friction that has come between your family and mine for all these years."

Ari sagged with relief.

"Thank you," Francis said earnestly. Then he stood. "I am also glad for this chance for us to know each other better, so our countries will be better friends. But now we must go."

Ari and Francis stood to take their leave.

The queen gave her hand for Ari to kiss, which she did.

As they walked toward the door, Francis whispered to Ari, "Thank you for standing up for me. You, Aristotle de Nostradame, you are a loyal friend."

Ari smiled. It felt good to be of use.

Just as they were about to exit, a servant burst through the door. "Your Majesty, we have had a raven from up north."

"A raven?" Francis asked. "If a raven's come from up north, that means it's possible to get through the skirmishes. Perhaps I can send a message to my wife."

The servant was breathing hard. "It's the first one we've received in weeks. Eðian birds are being shot out of the skies. They're scared to fly."

Queen Elizabeth stood up. "What is the message?"

The servant unraveled a rumpled piece of parchment.

"It is news from Edinburgh. Mary, Queen of Scots, is engaged to be married to Henry Stuart, Lord of Darnley."

FORTY-TWO
Francis

The words echoed in the room. Mary was engaged. To some man named Darnley.

"That's not possible," Francis said. "She wouldn't."

Ari touched his shoulder. "Francis—"

"No." Francis jerked away. "She wouldn't get married again. Not yet. I've been dead five minutes. My corpse isn't even cold."

"Um," said the servant. "Should I be writing this down?"

"Please don't," said Elizabeth, settling into her chair again.

"I mean," Francis went on, "I know she didn't love me romantically, and I accept that. Really."

"We all believe you," said Ari.

Elizabeth was shaking her head in a way that suggested she didn't believe him.

"But we did love each other, in our way, and how could she get over me that quickly?" Francis threw his hands into the air. "I would never marry again, if she'd been the one to not actually die."

"I doubt she has much of a choice," Elizabeth said. "She is a queen. We are constantly being pressured to marry. For the good of the kingdom." She threw a sharp glance at Cecil.

Francis closed his eyes. That was true. It was why he and Mary had been engaged at such young ages. It was why Elizabeth had been presented with suitor after suitor. The goal was to produce an heir and preserve the family's power.

His breath caught. Heirs.

Mary was probably doing this because she felt she didn't have a choice but to wed again and produce an heir as soon as possible. To secure her throne.

The thought made Francis sick. Everything that he and Mary had put aside because they weren't ready, all that jumping on the bed and laughing, all their joking that they had forever before they had to worry about the heir part of marriage . . . He'd been so foolish. He should have told her right then how much he cared for her. How much he loved her.

His stomach turned as he imagined Mary sleeping, her long auburn hair fanned out, her breath soft and even—and she was lying next to another man.

This Lord Darnley.

"No." The word came out a deep growl. "I cannot permit this

to happen. Mary is my wife. She belongs with me." And he belonged with her. He had always belonged with her, and nothing—not even death—would change that.

Elizabeth looked up from her conversation with the servant; they'd been talking while Francis was having what probably counted as a complete meltdown.

"You are dismissed," the queen told the servant. Then, after the man had bowed and left the room, Elizabeth turned to Francis and said, "Sit. We must discuss this new development."

"What is there to discuss? I have to put a stop to this. Please. You have to let us leave for Scotland immediately."

Elizabeth just waited.

"This is outrageous!" Francis's stomach knotted. "I'm still alive. We're still married."

"She doesn't know that," Ari said gently. "She's only trying to do what is best for Scotland."

What if Mary went through with it? What if she actually married someone else and Francis never told her how he felt? What if he never got to apologize for the way they'd parted back in the Château de Blois? He would never forgive himself if he didn't make things right with her.

And if she still wanted to marry Darnley?

If she wanted an annulment, now that Catherine and Charles IX were ruling France?

The thought made him light-headed, and he staggered into the nearest chair.

"How can we stop this?" Francis said. "We must send a message immediately to let her know that I'm still alive."

"I'm afraid that's quite impossible," Elizabeth said. "You heard my servant. Eðian ravens won't fly. Knox's rebellions are growing more and more violent. We cannot risk another Eðian being captured, especially with sensitive information."

Francis closed his eyes. "There must be another way. If your wife were getting married to some strange foreign lord, you'd try to stop her, too. You know you would."

"That's fair," Ari admitted. "I would. I mean, I have."

"Unfortunately," Elizabeth said, "Henry Stuart isn't just *some foreign lord*. He is my cousin. Mary's cousin. He's in line for both the English and the Scottish thrones."

"Oh." Francis could hardly breathe.

Cecil jumped into the conversation again. "We must consider that she is making a play for Elizabeth's crown."

"But given recent events," Elizabeth said, "it seems just as likely that Darnley is her uncle's scheme, planted there to give them more control. She may yet come for my throne, but it will be the Duke of Guise and the Cardinal of Lorraine pulling her strings."

"Mary is no one's puppet!" Francis said—because he would always try to defend her, but he realized Elizabeth was probably right. It made sense that the uncles would be behind this.

"I know this Lord Darnley," Elizabeth continued, as though Francis hadn't said anything.

Francis looked up at her and leaned forward. "Tell me about him. Please. I have to know who I'm up against."

A faint, sad smile twisted Elizabeth's mouth. "I'm afraid that Darnley was one of my many suitors, some time ago."

"He sure gets around," Ari murmured.

"Why didn't you marry him?" Francis asked. If only Elizabeth had married that scoundrel, then he wouldn't be after Mary's hand right now.

"Because I never want to get married to anyone," Elizabeth said matter-of-factly. "But even if I were to marry, it wouldn't be to him. He presents himself as a good man, a kind and charming person who can both listen and speak, whichever the occasion calls for. He's charismatic, and I suspect there's a trail of broken hearts following in his wake. However . . ."

Francis leaned forward. "Yes?"

"Well, he liked to explain things."

Ari gasped. "No."

Elizabeth nodded solemnly. "Indeed. He once decided I needed to hear the entire history of my own family, as though I were not already aware of my ancestors' lives. I might have forgiven him as simply an interested party, but he misrepresented several key details." She sighed and waved that aside. "But more pressingly, he desires to raise his station. As I said, he is my cousin, and Mary's cousin, as well. Thus, he is in line to inherit both thrones. If he were to marry Mary, it would give him—and Mary—a claim to my throne. I cannot allow it. If she marries Darnley, I will have no choice but to respond accordingly. I will have to send soldiers north."

"Then we want the same thing: to stop this wedding." Francis was coming to admire Elizabeth. She was a strong monarch, one he would like to emulate, if he ever got his throne back. But most of all, she seemed like a reasonable human being, one who wanted to *stop* fighting and *start* mending relationships.

"It will be dangerous," Elizabeth said. "You could die."

But Francis stood, a strange calm coming over him. "Prepare whatever soldiers you want to send. We will leave immediately."

FORTY-THREE Mary

The second wedding day of Mary, Queen of Scots, began much as the first one had. Mary went about getting ready with a sense that everything would be changed after today. She felt strangely calm, considering. When she'd married Francis she'd been a tangle of nerves, worried about how well she'd represent herself (and Scotland) in front of all those people in the grand cathedral of Notre Dame, worried about how Francis would do under the pressure, and worried about the wedding night and what she and Francis would do together.

That former Mary (of only a few months ago, we should point out) seemed hopelessly naive to her now. She'd thought of her wedding as an ending to all of the waiting and promises she'd been given since she was a child. But today's Mary saw her wedding as a beginning, one in which she would take control of her destiny, wrest her future out of her uncles' hands, and make new alliances to secure her throne.

Speaking of the uncles:

"They wish to have an audience with you," said Liv tightly as Mary took her breakfast in her private quarters. "Before the wedding."

Of course they did. They still disapproved of her marrying Darnley, which only made Mary want to marry Darnley more.

"Bring them in now," Mary directed. "Let's get their dramatics over with."

Liv frowned (even the very sight of the uncles filled Liv with dread), but she did as she was asked.

"My dear," said Uncle Francis jovially as the two men swept into the room in a flurry of fine silks and velvets. "You look radiant. Congratulations on your happy, happy day. We are so pleased for you."

Uh-oh, thought Mary. The uncles did, indeed, seem pleased. They were smiling, in fact. As if everything was going according to their plans.

"Thank you," Mary said slowly. "I know this isn't the match you wished for me, but I believe . . ."

"Oh, we like Darnley now," said Uncle Charles. "He'll do, in a pinch."

"But . . ."

"Like you said, he is of royal blood," added Uncle Francis.

"Together you'll have a much stronger claim of the thrones of both Scotland and England. And your son will be the undisputed ruler of the entire realm. Darnley is a wise choice. You're developing quite a sharp and discerning political mind, aren't you? Good for you. Smart girl."

Alarm bells were sounding in Mary's head. Her plan had been to defy her uncles and send them packing back to France. She didn't know what to do with them if they were going to claim to be on her side.

"I . . . uh, why, thank you," she said.

"We will, of course, have to move up our plans for dealing with Elizabeth," said Uncle Francis.

"How so?" Mary had her own plans. All week she'd been composing a long letter to Queen Elizabeth putting forth a new idea: that the two of them be allies. Mary had decided that she had no true desire to rule England, no matter what her uncles said. Scotland was enough for her. So it made sense to align herself with Elizabeth, who was, after all, another woman simply trying to keep a tenuous hold on her crown. They could be sister queens, is how Mary had phrased it in the letter. Perhaps even, in time, friends.

"We've had word that a contingent of English soldiers crossed the border in Scotland yesterday, heading fast for Edinburgh," said Uncle Francis.

Mary stared at him. "English soldiers? But why?"

He shrugged. "To stop the wedding, of course. Elizabeth will see your marrying Darnley as an act of war, a move to take the throne of England. Which of course it is. She'd do anything to keep that from happening."

"But I'm not trying to . . . I don't intend . . ."

"Don't worry your pretty little head about it, my dear," said Uncle Francis, patting her hand. "Elizabeth's men are too far away. They won't reach here in time to stop the wedding. And even if they do, we've rallied an army of our own to defend you. Plus we have triple the usual men guarding the castle, and the captain of the guard has the only key to the castle gate, and we're told he has the heart of a lion. You will marry Darnley in peace, I swear it."

Droppings, thought Mary. But her uncles being for her marrying Darnley (and Elizabeth apparently being against it) didn't mean that Mary still shouldn't marry him. Did it?

She needed to think. Unfortunately there wasn't much time for that.

"Thank you," she said. "Now if you'll excuse me, I must prepare myself."

"Of course," said the uncles in unison, and bowed, and saw themselves out.

"Well, they were entirely too pleased with themselves," said Liv, her brow furrowed.

"I know," murmured Mary. "I know."

Flem came bustling in then, bearing a huge bouquet of red roses. "From Darnley," she said, beaming, but then sobered. "For you, I guess."

Mary took the bouquet. She'd never cared for roses. Red roses were meant to represent love. She'd told Darnley not to expect love. So what was he doing?

"There's also a note," said Flem, and handed a piece of parchment to Mary.

For my red queen, it read. *To symbolize my utter devotion to you, if not my love.*

All right, then, Mary thought. Darnley would do in a pinch, as her uncle had put it. She must take things one step at a time.

Speaking of steps, a bent-over old woman had inexplicably appeared in Mary's chamber now—how had she gotten in?—and for some reason was thrusting a pair of shoes at Mary.

"Blue shoes for your blue gown," the woman croaked.

"Thank you, but who are you, madam?" Mary asked.

"I was a maidservant to your mother," the old lady answered. "I know she would want you to have these today."

"These were my mother's shoes?" Mary shouldn't have been surprised. Most of what she'd been wearing since she'd arrived in Edinburgh had once belonged to her mother. But this felt different. As if, through this old woman, her mother was reaching across the chasm to give her a gift.

Blue suede shoes.

Which could count as something old and something blue.

"Yes. She was most grieved that she could not be there on the day of your first wedding," rasped the old woman.

"I felt her absence keenly that day," replied Mary, although looking back on it now, it seemed to her that it really had been the happiest day of her life. Things had been going markedly downhill for Mary since then.

The old woman grasped Mary's hand, her grip surprisingly smooth and strong. "Your mother is with you, my dear. Whether or not you can see her, she's always with you."

Mary nodded. "Yes, yes, in my heart. I know."

The woman gave a brittle laugh. "And she is proud of you."

Would she really be proud, though? Mary didn't know the answer to that question. Certainly Mary de Guise knew what it was like to marry a second time for an entirely political reason. *Like mother, like daughter*, Mary thought.

"Excuse me, but your other guest—the one you had me send for—has just arrived," Flem interrupted. She paused and cocked her head at the sight of the old woman, her nostrils flaring. Then she shook her head as if to clear it. "He kept calling me *you, girl*. He's a disagreeable fellow, isn't he?"

"Yes," Mary said, taking the blue suede shoes from the old woman and giving her a gold coin for her trouble. She straightened her shoulders. "Please send him in."

"Why have you called me here?" John Knox said loudly, glancing around as if he was expecting to be attacked.

Mary, who had been standing at the window gazing down into the garden, turned to look at him. "I have a favor to ask of you."

He scoffed. "A favor? Why would I do you a favor? Why just days ago—"

"You were trying to burn down my castle and run me out of the country, I know, I know," she interrupted. "I was hoping we could get past that. I'm getting married today, you see."

He scratched underneath his beard, which was still the most terrible beard in existence. "I know. It's outrageous, if you ask me. Why, your last husband is hardly cold in the ground and here you are throwing yourself into the arms of another man."

Mary's hands clenched into fists, but she forced herself to relax. "My marriage is entirely political, as I'm sure you can appreciate."

"I'm sure I can't," he said. "So what is the favor you would ask of me?"

She really disliked John Knox, but he wasn't one to beat around the bush, which she found refreshing.

"I'd like you to marry me," she said.

His mouth dropped open. A fly fluttered out of his horrible beard and almost into his throat, but then he closed his mouth again just in time. "You want to marry *me*?" he sputtered. "I am already married, and you . . . you are . . ." All at once he took in her attire. She was still wearing her dressing gown, without jewels or finery, her hair loose about her shoulders. "Is there no end to your depravity?"

With great effort, she produced a smile. "You misunderstand me, sir. I don't want to marry you. I wish you to marry me. As a man of God. Today. To Lord Darnley."

"Oh." Knox scowled. "Of course I would never do that. I am

an Eðian, as you know, and you are a treacherous Verity of the worst sort. If I were to marry you it would seem as though I supported you and your reign. Which of course I do not."

"Oh, come now," Mary said. "We are not so different, you and I."

"We are completely different," he argued.

Behind him, Liv closed the door and locked it.

Knox startled in alarm. "What is the meaning of this? You think to take me prisoner? The people of Scotland will not stand for that, you know. Why, right now they—"

"Are you sure?" Liv asked Mary softly.

Mary nodded.

"Release me at once!" screamed Knox.

"Oh, do shut up," said Mary. "Just watch."

She looked him in the eye and changed. Light flashed, and she was a mouse. She moved easily from the folds of her dressing gown to stand, tiny but proud, before the gaping Eðian minister.

Liv bent and scooped her up. She held out her hand to Knox, with Mary sitting calmly in her palm.

"Her Majesty wishes you to know her true nature," Liv said. "So that you will realize what the two of you have in common."

His eyes were fixed on her. Mary suppressed a shiver. Then she glanced at Liv.

"Please turn around now," Liv ordered Knox. "So that the queen may return to her human form with her modesty intact."

Knox's face turned red, and he spun around to face the wall.

Mary changed and quickly put on the dressing gown again.

"If you tell anyone what you've seen here, I'll deny it," she said to Knox's back. "But I wanted you to know that I am no Verity tyrant, bent on the destruction or suppression of Eðians. I mean to have peace in my kingdom, and tolerance among my people, whatever their beliefs."

He slowly turned around again.

"You're still a woman," he said stiffly. "And women still shouldn't rule countries."

"We'll just have to agree to disagree about my qualifications for my position," Mary said. "I am to be married today. And one day I might have a son, who will be king of Scotland after me, and I wanted you to know that, as well as being the rightful king, appointed by God, as I have been, he will be an Eðian supporter, as I am. That I can swear to you. I don't think you could find anyone with royal blood enough to claim the throne of Scotland who could offer you the same."

Knox thought for a long moment. Then he sighed. "All right, fine."

She smiled. "Wonderful. And if you could perhaps cease with distributing that awful pamphlet about me, that would be nice."

"Very well. It needs to be revised, anyway. I'll marry you today. But I can't promise that I won't try to overthrow you tomorrow," he warned.

She nodded. "Let's take this one day at a time, shall we?"

* * *

Her uncles were confused when she arrived at the Holyrood chapel for her wedding that afternoon with John Knox and a large company of Knox's men. The uncles were even more confused when they were told that the ceremony was to be performed by Knox, not Uncle Charles, the cardinal.

But they didn't protest. The uncles didn't want to make a scene, not today.

It was an odd assembly of onlookers, then, when Mary came down the aisle, not on any man's arm this time. There were Eðians and Verities; her brother, James, and his men; her uncles and their men; the Scottish courtiers and their men; and even a large group of the common people, who Mary had invited at the last minute.

It didn't have the grandeur of her wedding to Francis. But it would do.

"You look . . . ," Darnley started as she came to stand beside him in her resplendent gown of blue velvet and golden trim.

The dress reminded her of Francis's blue doublet. Her favorite on him. But she was not going to think about that.

"You too," she said to Darnley, and took the hand he offered her.

Together they turned to face John Knox.

She did try very hard not to think of Francis.

Francis and the silly high-heeled shoes.

Francis saying the vows, his blue eyes fixed on hers, the rest of the world fading into the background as he'd murmured, "I take you to be my wife . . . forsaking all others . . . keeping faith and truth in all matters between us . . . until death us do part."

"If anyone knows of a reason that these two should not be joined in holy matrimony," Knox was saying. "Speak now or forever hold your peace."

Mary's bottom lip began to tremble. But she didn't speak.

The chapel was utterly silent. It seemed that everyone approved of her marrying Darnley. Only her heart screamed a protest. But she was determined that she would overcome her heart this time. She would do what was best for Scotland. Which meant marrying. And producing an heir.

Still, the image of Francis kept floating up in her mind. *With this ring, I thee wed.* She remembered the smile in his voice as he'd said that to her.

With this ring.

Her breath caught. She was still wearing Francis's ring.

Which was bound to get awkward when Darnley wanted to put his own ring there.

"Wait," she said softly.

Everyone in the chapel froze. Was she going to back out now?

Mary pulled her hand from her future husband's and turned to her ladies. She gave her bouquet to a grumpy-looking Flem. Then she slipped Francis's ring from her finger and handed it to Liv, who nodded and closed her palm around it solemnly. Mary took the bouquet back from Flem—red roses, not white cowslips. Then she faced Darnley and took his hand again.

He smiled wanly. He'd looked worried for a second there.

"Very well," Knox said, clearing his throat. "Let us continue with the business at hand. Marriage," he said, and there was something funny about the way he rolled his r's with his thick Scottish brogue. "Marriage is what brings us together today."

FORTY-FOUR

Ari

"Are you ready, Sire?" Ari asked Francis. He was staring pensively in the direction of Holyrood, as if he could sense that the wedding was beginning and he could stop it using his will alone.

Francis startled and then nodded. "I'm ready," he said steadily.

Ari turned to the six English soldiers who had accompanied them from London. She tried not to dwell on how small a number they were, when going against so many. This would not be a battle of strength but a battle of wits. She unstoppered a large vial from her chest of potions and handed it to the first soldier. "Once you take this, we'll have about ten to twelve minutes. So we have to move fast."

The soldier looked less than thrilled at the idea of drinking some mystery concoction. Ari had explained how it worked while they'd gone over the details of the plan—her plan!—but of course nobody but Francis had believed her.

"I still think this is a ridiculous plan," said the soldier.

"Yes," agreed a second soldier. "We liked the one with the fireproof cloak and the wheelbarrow better."

"But only mildly better," said a third.

The fourth pulled out the voluminous black cloak. They had picked it up at a street market. It hadn't been advertised as a fireproof cloak, until Francis had mentioned to the vendor that they needed one. Then it was suddenly a fireproof cloak. And they'd bought it. But when Ari had tested it out by lighting a corner on fire, she'd singed all the hairs off her arm. So that put an end to the idea that they'd scare the guards off using a tall guy on fire yelling, "I am the Dread Pirate Roberts!" as she had seen in her previous vision.

The day wasn't going to be won with her visions, she'd decided right there and then. It was going to be won using her true skills. Namely, potions.

"Just drink it," she ordered the first soldier.

He held the vial up to his nose. "It smells bad."

"It's not meant to be perfume," she pointed out.

"Drink it," said Francis from beside her, using his I-am-the-king voice, even though he was not the king of this particular man.

"Just one swig should do it," suggested Ari.

The soldier took a swig. His face immediately squished up in an expression of disgust. "It tastes terrible!"

"I didn't have time to flavor—" Ari started to say, but then stopped.

Because the soldier's face had vanished. Along with the rest of him.

There was an exclamation of surprise among the remaining soldiers. Ari grabbed the potion (which now seemed to be floating in midair) and thrust it at the second soldier. "Hurry! We have to go!"

The soldiers each quickly swigged and disappeared.

"Look at that!" she heard one cry. "I'm invisible!"

She grabbed and tossed the vial to Francis, who took a sip. "It really doesn't taste so bad," he said as he literally faded into the background. "A bit lemony."

He was trying to be nice. She kind of wanted to hug him for that. But how did one hug an invisible king?

"Let's be off," she said.

The invisible men (and Ari) moved quickly along the outside of the wall that surrounded Holyrood Palace (and the abbey, where the wedding was taking place even as they ran), to the north side, where the gatehouse was located. This was the only way in if they didn't want to descend some impressive-looking cliffs, which had felt like insanity to even consider. Ari rather wished that she could have taken her invisibility potion as well, but she had another potion to ingest in a few minutes, and she wasn't fully certain of what would happen if a person took two of the potions at once.

She tried to walk casually, like she was just a serf out on serf business, as they got in position in front of the gatehouse. There were twenty men standing outside of it, but how many were inside?

She removed another potion from her belt and drank it. Then she looked at the gatehouse again.

"Ten," she whispered. "There are ten men in there. Wait. Eleven. But past the gatehouse there is no one. It's a straight shot to the side door of the church."

"What's going on in there?" came a voice she knew as Francis's. "Has it started yet?"

Ari shook her head. "I can't see that far. I have to get closer." She blinked a few times, suddenly dizzy. Seeing through walls was so disorienting.

"You there! Boy!" one of the guards on the outside of the gatehouse called out, having spotted her. "What are you doing?"

Ari fumbled with her pack. Her fingers closed around a sloshy packet, which she'd heated over a fire a few minutes ago. It was like grabbing a hot potato, burning her already singed fingers, but she gritted her teeth and lobbed the packet at the line of guards. It burst, sending a plume of green steam into the air around them.

For a moment nothing happened. The guards just looked at Ari in anger and confusion. And then their faces started to turn green, and all hell broke loose.

"Now!" Francis shouted.

The six invisible soldiers rushed the unsuspecting guards. Some of them were already panicking and bolting away, because it's simply not natural for one's face to turn grass-colored. And the others were dispatched quickly enough, because it's difficult to fight an enemy one can't see.

"This is a most wondrous plan!" she heard one of the soldiers exclaim. "I wish we could be invisible for all our battles!"

They were down to sixteen guards now, outside the gatehouse.

Ten.

Six.

But they still had to deal with the men inside. And they no longer had the element of surprise.

"Francis?" Ari called.

"I'm here," said a voice next to her.

She held out a bow. It was indeed strange to watch it wobble in the air as he lifted it.

"I don't know why you picked me for this particular task," he complained. "I'm only a decent shot. Mary is much better. You should have picked her."

"Mary's in there," Ari reminded him, pointing at the church beyond the wall.

"Right. I'll do it."

Ari handed him the arrow with the weird bulbous tip she'd fashioned on it. "Remember, aim for the exact center of that tiny window."

"I remember." Francis nocked the arrow. It was noisy. The soldiers were shouting. The remaining green-faced guards were shouting. The guards inside the gatehouse were shouting. Francis blew out a breath.

"This is going to work," Ari said, more to herself than to him. "As long as you hit the target exactly."

"So, no pressure," Francis said. "It's only my entire life, my future, and the future of France at stake."

"And England and Scotland," Ari provided helpfully.

"Gah!" Francis said in exasperation.

"But I believe in you," said Ari.

Francis loosed the arrow. Ari held her breath as she watched it sail in a clean arc toward the gatehouse.

And then into the wall.

"*Merde!* I told you I wasn't very good!" Francis cried.

Ari handed him the second, just-in-case arrow that she'd also prepared. "Try again. You can do this."

She really hoped he could, because this was their last chance to get into the gatehouse. And if they couldn't get into the gate-house, they couldn't get into the church. And she had a feeling that the wedding was already well underway.

"What if we're too late?" Francis asked, as though he were reading her mind.

"We only have to get there before they say man and wife," Ari replied.

Francis abruptly appeared next to her as the potion wore off. His face was red. "She's *my* wife!" he roared, and then drew back the bow and shot the arrow perfectly through the tiny window of the gatehouse. Within seconds something like smoke began to curl out of the window, and the shouting from inside turned to frantic screaming. Still able to peer through walls, Ari watched the remaining guards begin to panic.

"Come on!" yelled Francis, and sprinted toward the gatehouse.

Ari hoped the six English soldiers were still alive and behind him.

As he reached the door, it burst open and a guard ran out, clutching at his face. "I'm blind!" the man screamed. "I can't seeeeeeeee!"

Francis pushed the guard to the side and entered the gatehouse. Ari ran in behind him, a bit unsteady with her double layers of vision. Inside it was chaos. Most of the guards had been blinded by the *Not There* potion and were either cowering or stabbing out wildly at nothing. The rest were being handled by the invisible soldiers.

This was actually going the way Ari had hoped it would.

But then she ran to the inner door. And it was locked.

"Francis!" she panted. "It's locked! What are we going to do?"

Francis, clearly caught up in the moment, screamed out a battle cry and charged at the door, bashing it with his shoulder. It didn't budge. He fell back, panting.

"Ow," he said. "Surely one of these guards must have the key."

They both looked around and at the same moment spotted a single man whose uniform was slightly different from the others, trying to slink inconspicuously away from the fighting. Francis grabbed him by the collar and flung him against the wall.

Mary would have been impressed with him, Ari thought.

"You're the captain of the guard, aren't you?" she asked the man. "Where is the key?"

"I have hidden it where you will never find it! I will never give it up!" the man yelled. His eyes narrowed on her. "You're a woman!"

"So?"

"You're a witch!" he concluded. "WITCH! WIIIIIIIIIITCH!"

"Now that's not very nice," said Francis, looking embarrassed on Ari's behalf. "She's merely good with potions. She's not—"

"I am a witch," said Ari, drawing herself up as best as she could.

Francis's mouth fell open. "You are?" (In this time, dear reader, being a witch was even worse than being an Eðian.)

"I am a witch, and if you don't give us the key, I shall turn you into a toad."

The man scoffed. "I don't believe you."

Ari gave Francis a meaningful stare. "I absolutely will turn you into a toad. Or at the very least, a *frog*."

"No," Francis groaned.

"Yes. I shall."

Francis closed his eyes for a moment, mortified at her suggestion. Then he sighed. "Even I don't believe you have the power to do that."

She fake scowled at him. "You don't believe it? Now I am displeased with you, as well. I'll show you." She lifted her hands toward Francis in as witchy a way as she could manage. "Alaka-zam!"

Light flashed, and when her eyes adjusted, she saw a small green frog sitting where Francis had been standing.

"Dear God!" exclaimed the captain of the guard.

At that moment, the rest of the six soldiers began to material-ize in the room, one after another. Ari was relieved to see that they were all still alive.

The captain of the guard began to tremble. Ari turned to him with an icy expression and lifted her hands again. "Ala—"

"Wait!" The captain of the guard drew the key out of his dou-blet from a long chain around his neck. "Here! Take it!" He yanked the key free and threw it at her, then bolted away.

Ari caught the key and hurriedly unlocked the door. There was a flash as Francis transformed again. She moved quickly into the courtyard to give him a moment to get into his clothes.

"You owe me," he muttered as he appeared next her, fully dressed. "But I already owe you so much that it doesn't matter."

There was no time for thanks or pretty words. Ari was star-ing with her enhanced vision through the walls of the abbey. It was crammed with people. Mary and the man Ari assumed was Darnley were standing at the far side under a giant stained glass window. And a few steps from Mary stood Liv, beautiful even through a wall.

Ari's heart leapt. "Liv," she murmured.

"Ari, focus," said Francis.

Ari blinked and remembered why they were there. "The wedding has started!" she reported, and grabbed Francis's hand and ran across the grass toward the church.

"I should burst in at the part where they ask if anyone has an objection," Francis said as they reached the side door. "That would be the best time."

"We're well past that!" Ari watched in horror as Liv stepped forward to give Mary a ring. A ring that she was about to place on Darnley's finger. "Go, Your Highness! Go now!"

Francis threw open the door and stepped into the chapel.

FORTY-FIVE
Francis

Finally, after what felt like a thousand years, Francis saw her.

Mary.

She was standing right there in a blue dress, looking up at the man before her. *Lord Darnley*, Francis thought bitterly. He was taller than Mary, and undeniably handsome.

Francis straightened his shoulders. Now was not the time for despair. In fact, now was the time to stop this, because as he stood there, staring jealously while his wife married another man, the man performing the ceremony was just getting to the part where both parties were to say "I do."

Darnley had already said it, in fact. And behind Mary, her ladies were lined up, looking somber.

"Do you, Mary Stuart—"

"Stop!" Francis lurched forward as all the gazes in the chapel swung toward him. "I object!"

"It's too late," someone said. "We already did that part."

"Who is that?" someone else asked.

"What does he think he's doing?" another asked.

The old Francis—the Francis from a few months ago—would have withered under their curious and judging stares, but now, he just raised his voice. "I am Francis Valois, king of France. Mary Stuart, Queen of Scots, is *my* wife."

The words echoed for a moment as Francis focused completely on Mary. Their gazes locked, and Francis's heart nearly stopped under the force of her attention. But the grief in her eyes turned to recognition, then shock, then wide-eyed understanding that he was alive, and he'd come for her.

"Francis." Her voice was soft, barely a whisper, but he felt it deep in his chest. The beginnings of a smile touched the corners of her mouth.

For Francis, the whole world could have stopped spinning right there. Nothing else mattered, nothing except crossing the chapel to take Mary into his arms. His Mary. His wife. His queen.

He didn't notice the commotion of the crowd, all the people asking, "What is going on?" and "That's the king of France? I thought he'd be taller." He didn't notice the shuffling of various groups, the hiss of swords sliding out of sheaths, or the whispered instructions from various nobles to their men.

Tension hummed throughout the chapel, but Francis had eyes only for Mary.

She took one halting step toward him. "Francis. You're—"

"Alive!" Duke Francis peeled away from the congregation. "My boy, you're alive."

"I'm aware," Francis said, still staring at Mary. He didn't know what to do now. His entire plan had been focused on getting to the wedding before Mary said "I do." And now he'd done that.

"This is indeed the best news we've had all day." Cardinal Charles pushed forward, along with his brother. "We're overjoyed! We thought you were dead."

Francis tilted his head. "You're overjoyed?"

That was a bad sign.

"Yes!" Duke Francis was practically beaming.

Surely— But oh, if Mary was still married to him, and he was king of France, then Mary was still queen consort of France, and that gave them power. Of *course* they were happy. Removing Francis from the throne had been Catherine's play—one that had forced the uncles out of French court.

"No!" cried Darnley. "You said *I* could marry her."

"That was before we knew Francis was alive," Cardinal Charles said. "It's nothing personal, my boy. It's just that he's a king and you're, well, not."

"I knew it!" shouted Mary. "I knew you two were behind this. Well, I suspected it since this morning, anyway."

Duke Francis shrugged. "You'd be disappointed in us if we didn't try."

"I'm disappointed in you because you're terrible, murdering schemers." Mary's lip curled. "And you tried to trick me into marrying someone who could benefit you."

"I could be king of England," Darnley said to the uncles, as though Mary hadn't spoken at all. "One day."

"Ah," said Duke Francis. "That *one day* is the difference. Francis is king of France *now*, and frankly, France is more important to us."

"Technically," said the man with the awful beard who'd been performing the wedding ceremony, "Charles the Ninth is the king of France. That Verity scum."

"Illegally!" Francis countered. "I was kidnapped so that my own mother could put another son on the throne."

"I said I was sorry," Ari said behind him. "Geez."

"And I forgive you," Francis said quietly. "This is mostly for dramatic effect."

"Oh, that's fine, then," Ari said. "Carry on."

Meanwhile, Darnley—who'd never moved past the fact that he wouldn't be marrying Mary today—seemed to come to a decision. "If I can't have her," Darnley said darkly, "no man shall." A knife appeared in his hand (who goes to his own wedding with a knife?!), and before Francis could shout a warning, the blade was at Mary's throat. The steel gleamed against her pale skin.

Everything unraveled from there.

"Men, to arms!" called Duke Francis, and all of his men raised their weapons. At the same time, the English soldiers who'd accompanied Francis and Ari rushed into the chapel, their swords drawn.

"Defend the queen!" came another voice, one the reader might know as James's, but Francis hadn't yet met Mary's brother. Swords and bows lifted.

"Eðians, attack!" That was John Knox. (Although Francis didn't know his name, just that he was the minister and the call to violence didn't seem very man-of-God-like to Francis, if you asked him. No one had, though.)

Suddenly, James's men were shouting. And Knox's Eðians were shouting. And the uncles' soldiers were shouting. And the English were scowling in a most put-out sort of way. All at once, swords clashed and the battle was on, although who was fighting whom, Francis could hardly understand. Everyone was moving this way and that, and with half of the combatants dressed in wedding finery, it was difficult to tell who was on what side.

"Get to Mary," Ari said. "I'll be right behind you."

Francis scanned the room for Mary, but she was still under the stained glass window with Darnley's blade at her throat.

"Help Mary!" he called to the English soldiers, but the noise of violence swallowed his voice. Then he lost sight of her.

Blades flashed, moving lightning fast as Francis ducked around to the outside of the room. If he could just get to Mary, everything would be well again. He had to believe that.

"The British are coming!" cried one of James's men.

"They will never take our freedom!" another man shouted, just an instant before he was engulfed in a flash of white light and emerged as an angry boar.

"Remember the Alamo!" yelled someone else, even though the Alamo hadn't been invented yet.

Francis slipped around the side of the room, weaving in and out of the battle. Everyone was fighting everyone, or so it seemed.

It was honestly one of the most confusing moments in history, but here's what our research provides:

James's men were fighting the uncles', who were fighting Knox's, who were fighting the English, who were fighting Darnley's. And then there were some men who just wanted to watch the world burn. They were lighting more candles.

"Mary!" Francis called. "Mary, hang on!"

As he made his way around the chapel, he caught the movement of her blue dress, flashes of light as two of her ladies changed form, and the panicked cry of one ex-almost-husband. By the time Francis pushed through the battle, Mary had taken Darnley's knife, and now she had the tip of the blade pointed directly at his Adam's apple. In her other hand, she held the bouquet of red roses, which was smashed from her using it as a club.

"Don't even breathe," Mary said.

"Grrr," said Flem, who was in her dog form, her jaw clamped around the man's right hand.

"Squawk," said Bea, who was perched on Darnley's head, her talons inches from his eyes.

"Well done, Mary!" said Duke Francis. "We always knew you had it in you."

"You!" Francis (our Francis) drew his own sword and lunged toward the uncles. "You killed my father. Prepare to—"

"Don't be ridiculous," said Cardinal Charles. "We don't kill anyone. We have people to do that for us." Both of Mary's uncles laughed.

"I know all about Montgomery." Francis's sword arm trembled a little. He'd never been good at violence. The idea of harming another person was abhorrent. But these men had caused so much damage.

"What are you going to do?" Duke Francis asked. "Tell us to prepare to die? You wouldn't. You've always been weak."

Red flared around the edges of Francis's vision, but he didn't move. He didn't have to. Ari had stuck by his side this whole time, as she'd promised, and now she was creeping up behind Duke Francis and Cardinal Charles, unstoppering a glass vial.

"Now!" Francis said, and Ari didn't hesitate. She splashed the liquid onto Duke Francis, and he vanished into a burst of white light.

"What did you do?" Cardinal Charles screamed. "What did you do to him?"

"Oh, nothing," Ari said. "I've just helped him embrace his inner Eðian." With that, she whipped away the pile of clothes to reveal a large, hairy spider. In one smooth motion, she turned the vial over and trapped Francis-the-spider inside. "He'll go back to normal in three, maybe four days."

"Now," said Francis, "call off your men."

"But we're on your side," Cardinal Charles said, unable to take his eyes off his brother, whose legs were sliding off the glass as Ari turned it over and stoppered it once more. "We want you to stay married to Mary."

"You're a murderer," said Francis. "Whether or not you held the lance, you were the hand that directed it."

"Not to mention, you tried to assassinate Queen Elizabeth." Ari held up the spider. "I believe the king of France gave you an order."

"Very well," said Cardinal Charles. "I relent." He signaled to his men to stand down.

"Now you." Mary's voice was low and deadly as she looked from Darnley to John Knox. "And you. Both of you, call off your men, and you'll live out the rest of your days in my dungeon."

"Don't you mean *or*?" Darnley asked. "Call off our men *or* we'll live out our days in your dungeon?"

Mary arched an eyebrow.

"Oh." Darnley gulped. "All right. I'll call them off."

"And you?" Mary asked Knox.

"Why should I do what you say?" he asked. "You're not my queen."

"Are you Scottish?" she asked.

"Yes."

"Then I am your queen. Tell your men to lay down their swords. As I told you earlier, I will be fair to Eðians and Verities alike. All have a place in my kingdom. But if you insist on demeaning me for no reason other than that I am a woman, *you* will not."

Francis couldn't help but smile as John Knox backed down, and within moments, the English and Scottish forces (James's men) had Cardinal Charles, Francis-the-spider, Lord Darnley, and John Knox all under arrest—for murder, attempted murder, more attempted murder, and general unlikability. Knox would probably be released because being an unlikable jerk wasn't a crime, but for the moment, it was satisfying to see him frog-marched out of the chapel. (Although not like Francis would march as a frog. Obviously.)

But now that all the official stop-the-wedding business was over, Mary's attention was on Francis again. His heart jumped to his throat. He'd crossed two countries to reach her, battled (sort of) everyone imaginable to stand here, but now that he was before her, he hardly knew what to say.

She moved toward him, her gaze never leaving his. The knife and the tattered bouquet of red roses she'd used to beat her fiancé about the head dropped from her hands. "Francis," she said softly.

He even loved the way she said his name. Like he was *her* Francis.

"Hello, Mary," he whispered.

FORTY-SIX

Mary couldn't breathe. Francis (her Francis!) was alive and apparently well, and he was standing a mere ten paces away from her. Staring at her.

Everyone was staring at her. As usual. Every courtier who hadn't yet fled the room, and even some who had returned out of curiosity as soon as the fighting had ceased. Every soldier. Every commoner. Every castle servant and lady-in-waiting. They were all staring, waiting to see what Mary would do.

She swallowed, her heart galloping.

What would her mother tell her to do now? Mary knew exactly what she'd say:

Be calm and composed.

Be a queen.

This was going to be a tall order, indeed, as her dress was torn after her struggle with Darnley, one sleeve completely missing. Entire sections of her hair had come undone and were sticking out at odd angles. Her crown was askew. She looked (as they would have said back then) a fright. But it didn't matter.

Francis was alive. He was looking at her with eyes that said that he'd missed her. That he had come all this way for her, to be with her. That he forgave her, for leaving him before, and for believing that he was dead, and for agreeing to marry someone else so quickly. That he was still her husband.

"I love you," she said loudly. She didn't care that so many people were listening, and that it might not be the most appropriate time for this revelation. She'd run out of time, before, to tell him that she loved him. She was not going to make the same mistake again.

His eyes widened. "I love you, too."

"No, I mean, I *love* love you," she said. "As the poets write about. As the bards sing in their romantic ballads. That is how I love you, Francis Valois. And I always will."

His eyes were shining. He smiled. "I *love* love you, too. I always have."

She ran to him, tears streaming down her face, and flung herself into his arms. They hugged each other for what should have been an awkwardly long time, but somehow wasn't awkward at all. For Mary it was wonderful, the solidness of Francis's body as it pressed against hers, so warm and good and right. He even seemed a bit taller. His chin fit perfectly into the curve of her shoulder, his breath against her neck. He was saying something, but it was muffled by her hair and she didn't understand—something about a frog? Why was he talking about frogs at a time like this?

Why was he talking at all?

She pulled back a few inches so that she could kiss him.

Now, we as your narrators could describe this kiss—the way their lips parted as they tried to get even closer to one another, the exact angle of their faces, Mary's fingers on the back of Francis's neck, his hands on her waist, pulling her to him, how the kiss contained everything that they were both feeling at the moment, which was a lot. It was passionate, to say the least. But we can't really do it justice with words. You're just going to have to believe when we say that it was an epic kiss. If you take into account that the two of them were fairly inexperienced when it came to kissing, having done it just the one time before (in the last decade), it was pretty freaking amazing. By the end Mary wasn't wearing her crown anymore, and Francis's hands were buried in her tangled auburn hair, freeing it from the rest of its pins and trappings, and Mary's hands were—well—they were under Francis's shirt.

Which was when someone approached the couple and began to clear her throat loudly. "Excuse me. If I may have a moment."

At last Francis pulled back. He smiled and tucked a strand of hair behind Mary's ear. Mary blinked at him dazedly. Then she started to lean in, because she'd forgotten why they'd stopped kissing. She wanted to keep kissing Francis. Possibly forever.

But the throat cleared again.

It was an insistent throat.

Reluctantly Mary turned her head to see who would dare to do such a thing. It was the old woman who had come to her room earlier, who'd given Mary the blue suede shoes. Only the woman wasn't actually old, Mary realized with a start. She was . . .

"Mother?" Mary gasped.

"What?" said Francis. "This is . . . ?"

"My mother," murmured Mary. "That's my mother."

"My clever girl," her mother said.

"But you're . . . dead," Mary said breathlessly. "James told me you were dead. My uncles killed you. Or you died of 'the Affliction.' Or something."

"James told you what I wanted him to tell you, and nothing more. James has been a trooper, hasn't he, helping me fake my own death and all, helping you become the ruler of Scotland in more than just name. Thank you, James," Mary de Guise called over her shoulder.

"You're welcome," he called back.

Mary de Guise turned back to Mary, Queen of Scots. "Now, you see? I didn't actually die." She waved at the crowd around them. "I'm still alive, everyone. Surprise!"

"That's been happening a lot lately," piped up Ari wryly.

"Ari!" Mary exclaimed, turning toward the seer's voice. "You're here, too!"

"Yes. I couldn't seem to help it." Ari was standing beside Liv, holding Liv's hand. Mary's heart squeezed for them.

Mary de Guise cleared her throat again. "So, yes, I'm not as dead as it first seemed."

"But why fake your own death?" asked Mary.

"I was feeling trapped. My messengers were being intercepted. My enemies were growing bolder every day, and I could sense that your uncles were up to no good. Catherine de Medici was not to be trusted with you, either. No offense, Your Grace," Mary's mother said to Francis.

"None taken," he said with a shrug.

"I thought if I were to 'die,' then you would return to Scotland and be out from under the influence of those who would try to control you." She smiled triumphantly. "I was so right, wasn't I?"

"But why didn't you reveal yourself sooner?" Mary sputtered. "Like—I don't know—yesterday?"

"I wanted to see how you'd handle the responsibility," her mother said lightly, as though this made perfect sense. "It was time for me to let you spread your wings and see if you would fly. And you did, my darling. You did beautifully. You kept your wits about you even when you were physically in danger. You learned to compromise and negotiate. You made sacrifices for the good of your country. You ruled, my dear. I am so proud of you."

"But I would have married Darnley today," Mary said. "I nearly did!"

Her mother nodded thoughtfully. "Yes, and that would have been a grave mistake that would undoubtedly have cost you your crown, and maybe even your life. Darnley would have tried to be king himself. And he probably would have made even more enemies for you, and perhaps done something dumb like getting himself murdered, and then you might have been framed for it, which would have turned out to be the ultimate downfall of your reign. Who knows? But perhaps you would also have borne him an heir who ended up ruling England and Scotland someday. It is difficult to know these things in advance. You did your best, my dear."

"Oh." Mary thought for a moment. "So what happens now?"

Her mother tapped her chin with her finger. "I don't know. You seem to have won over the Eðian faction here, for now, or at the very least they don't despise you as they did, so it might be possible for you to split your time between France and Scotland. James and I can manage things, in the meantime, while you're away."

Mary turned back to Francis. "What do you think we should do?"

His eyebrows lifted. He seemed bemused but pleased that she was consulting him. "I think we'll figure it out, together."

She reached for his hand. Their fingers interlaced. She smiled.

"Yes," she said. "We'll figure it out together, from now on."

FORTY-SEVEN

Ari

A week later, Ari was staring out at the waves of the English Channel, reminiscing on how different this journey was compared to their first. Back then, they'd been posing as peasants. Now, they were going back to France as a royal party. Queen Elizabeth was coming with them—to lend legitimacy to Francis's claim—which meant her ladies and her guards and her advisers and her favorite cook were coming as well. Plus the entourage that would be traveling with Mary and Francis, which included Ari now, but no longer as a lady, or a squire.

She had a new title. It was the king's Official Advisor, Grand Potion Master, and Prognosticator of Prognosticators (although that last one was mostly for entertainment).

The only thing that hadn't changed was that she still dressed in boy clothes. Not only were boy clothes more comfortable than the corseted girl clothes, but they were also logical when it came to running a laboratory. Less flowy fabric meant less chance of something catching fire.

Ari looked farther down the ship, where Francis and Mary were enjoying the view as well. At least, they were enjoying the view of each other, without much of a care for anyone or anything around them. Ari was happy to see it. Something had changed in both of them. Even though not much time had passed since their wedding, they had grown, Ari thought. There was nothing like separation and rumors of death to make a person appreciate another person.

"A livre for your thoughts?" Ari hadn't realized that Liv had joined her.

She smiled because Liv's face always made her smile.

"I was just thinking about what life in France is going to look like now. Francis and Mary are together again. Queen Elizabeth is here as an ally. And a month ago I was living in a hovel with a frog."

Liv laughed and then took Ari's hand in hers. "And Mary has decided not to marry me off to some nobleman. Ever."

"Oh dear," said Ari. "She's not exactly fulfilling her queenly duty then, is she?"

"No. But I forgive her. And what about your own future?"

"Well, as the king's trusted adviser," Ari said, summoning up her most grandiose voice, "I can definitively state . . . I don't know."

"What about a vision?" Liv asked.

Ari snorted. "I think I'm going to take things as they come."

They both were silent for a moment as they looked out over the water. The ocean breeze was salty and fresh. Sailors bustled about, readying the planks and adjusting the sails. The first signs of land could now be seen just off the bow.

Liv cleared her throat. "Will you take the official adviser's quarters? Or will you stay near the laboratory?"

"Well, I've been thinking about it. As much as I complain about our time in the hovel, there was something very freeing being there. Finding my own herbs. Building my laboratory from the ground up."

"But that hovel was in Calais," Liv said, her voice worried.

"I know. I'm not talking about that particular hovel. I'm talking about a cottage that is within the palace grounds. I'd be easily available, and yet still on my own."

"Oh," Liv said. "Oh, good." She squeezed Ari's hand.

"You know, the cottage is rather large. I mean, it's definitely bigger than any of my previous residences."

"Well, you'll need room for your father, of course. Once we rescue him. And we will rescue him."

Ari felt a stab of worry. She nodded determinedly. "We will rescue him. But then he'll probably want go somewhere solitary to work on his book in peace. So I'll have the cottage to myself, which seems excessive, since it's so big. I should probably get a roommate."

The corner of Liv's mouth quirked up. "I think I might be able to find you one."

Ari's heart did a backflip. She hoped Liv wasn't talking about Greer.

"I'm not talking about Greer."

This was going better than Ari had hoped. She pulled Liv closer until their foreheads touched. "I missed your face."

Then the two of them turned their attention back to the water and the approaching land with a little more clarity as to what their new lives would look like. From where Ari was standing, it looked like happily ever after.

FORTY-EIGHT
Francis

But there was one last thing to do before happily ever after could officially begin for Mary and Francis.

They finished crossing the English Channel and made their way from Calais to Paris. Francis had not sent word of his arrival—as far as he knew, no one in France was aware he was alive (aside from Catherine, who believed he was in Calais living as a frog)—but Mary and Elizabeth, as queens, had standards and expectations. The escort sent to, ah, escort the royal party to the capital was as grand and lavish as any vision of King Henry's. At the palace, the group was welcomed with trumpets and wine and a literal red carpet.

Charles IX—or more likely Catherine—knew the value of a good show.

Finally, the doors to the throne room were opened wide to greet the foreign royalty, and the queens stepped through to meet the audience of admiring courtiers.

No one noticed Francis as he, Ari, and Liv followed behind Mary and Elizabeth, not at first. He was dressed well, but people were used to overlooking him. For now.

On the throne, Charles IX sat with an annoyed look on his face, like he understood that being a boy king with a regent left him with little power. Catherine sat next to him, on a lesser throne, but no one would doubt that she guided the kingdom.

"Welcome," Catherine said, rising to look at the sister queens straight on. "Please, come forward. I'm sure there's much for us to discuss."

"Much," Mary said. "I cannot wait to tell you everything that has happened since I left for Scotland. But first—"

Mary and Elizabeth stepped aside.

"You've got this," Ari whispered encouragingly.

Francis moved forward. He took a deep, fortifying breath. He was here, back in his palace, in his throne room. Whether he liked it or not, he'd been born to be king. This was his moment.

"Hello, Mother," Francis said. Murmurs rippled through the crowded throne room as people finally noted who he was. He didn't look much different than he had a few months ago, but he did hold himself more like royalty than he ever had before. It was amazing the things that posture could convey.

"My son," Catherine began, but Francis didn't let her finish.

"Rumors of my demise have been greatly exaggerated." Francis strode toward the thrones. "I've come for my crown."

"You can't!" shouted Charles IX. "I'm king now."

"No." Francis didn't raise his voice, but still, it projected across the throne room so that everyone heard. "I was poisoned. Spirited away in the night. Kept against my will. But now, I return to France with my wife, Mary, Queen of Scots, and my dear friend, Queen Elizabeth Tudor of England, both of whom support my claim to the French throne. I *will* have my crown back. Know that if you plan to make me fight for it, I am prepared for that battle. But I hope it will not come to that. We are, after all, family."

"But—" Charles IX started, but then Mary and Elizabeth stepped forward, one on either side of Francis, and their soldiers stepped forward behind them. Ari, too, came forward, and Francis heard the slosh of a potion, but he didn't turn around to see what she held.

"All right," Charles IX said. "You can be king now."

"I'm so glad you've returned to us," Catherine said, gliding forward, her arms outstretched. "I thought you dead. Your ear looked really bad."

When she reached Francis and hugged him, he did not return her embrace. "I am glad to see you, Mother," he said softly, "but I haven't forgiven you for what you did to me. While I won't have you arrested, you won't be my regent. You will not rule France through me. I don't care how many mousetraps you threaten us with."

"Who knows," said Ari softly, coming forward with her potion in hand. "You might find your inner Eðian, too."

Catherine stepped back, uncertainty on her face for just an instant before it was smoothed away beneath the mask of haughty competence she always wore. "What I did, I did *for* France, my son.

Because you were not prepared to be king."

"I'm prepared now," Francis said. "You may go to the Château de Chenonceau. I know that you seized it after expelling Diane from court."

Catherine lifted a hand to cover her mouth. "You would send me away? My son?"

"You are not good for France, nor are you good for me. So yes. I would send you away, rather than any of the other possibilities. And I hope you will repent of your wickedness."

We, as your narrators, think this is highly unlikely.

"Fine," she said. "I will go. And you take your crown. But if you ever need me—"

"Goodbye, Mother." He said it as kindly as possible.

She swept away, flanked by guards. Ari darted off to find her father and returned shortly, smiling in relief.

"Nostradamus is safe. I told him you had returned, and he said, 'I told you so.'" She grinned. "He predicts that you will have a long and prosperous reign."

Francis recovered his crown from his younger brother. He didn't wait for anyone to put it on him. Francis crowned himself, took his throne, and held court for the rest of the day. He was king, wasn't he? And he had a job to do.

Later, after court was finished and a feast (which one might describe as grand, but certainly not *lavish* or *extravagant*) had been held, Francis and Mary walked toward their rooms. Alone.

"Now is it time?" Mary asked.

Francis raised an eyebrow. "To jump on the bed?"

"For our happily ever after." Mary laughed, but then tapped her forefinger to her chin and looked thoughtful. "Although I suppose that could involve jumping on the bed as well."

Francis took her hand and kissed it. "Anything you want, my love."

And now, dear readers, it's probably time to give those two some privacy. For reasons, you know. (We know.)

Acknowledgments

We had so much fun coming back to the Eðian world to write this book. And, as usual, we have a lot of people to thank for getting us this far:

First off, our wonderful team at HarperTeen, starting with Erica Sussman and Stephanie Stein, our incredible editors, who always find every single one of our jokes hilarious (or at least they act like they do—thank you for that). Our amazing cover designers, Jenna Stempel-Lobell and Alice Wang. And all of the behind-the-scenes people: Alexandra Rakaczki, Louisa Currigan, Sabrina Abballe, Ebony LaDelle, Cindy Hamilton, Jennifer Corcoran, and Anna Bernard.

Secondly: Lauren MacLeod, Katherine Fausset, and Jennifer Laughran, our agents, who continue to play well together. You all get cookies. We'd also like to give a shout-out to Holly Frederick, our film agent, and to Gemma Burgess, for becoming such a great cheerleader of the Janies while working your own Janie magic for the small screen. And Maggie Cahill at Parkes+MacDonald, for believing in our story of ferrets, horses, and assorted shenanigans.

To our families: Jeff, Sarah, and Jill; Dan, Will, Madeleine, Carol, and Jack; and Carter, Beckham, Sam, Joan, and Michael.

And as with *My Lady Jane*, we'd also like to thank our Eðian inspirations, our pets: Hush and Hildy; Poesy, Frank, Stella, and Max; and Pidge and Jewels.

And finally: thank you to the army of librarians and booksellers who get our books out into the world, and to our readers, who are, quite simply, the best.

More can't-miss books from the Lady Janies
Also by Cynthia Hand
The Afterlife of Holly Chase
The Last Time We Say Goodbye
The How & the Why
With You All the Way

Unearthly
Hallowed
Boundless
Radiant: An Unearthly Novella (available as an ebook only)

Also by Brodi Ashton
Diplomatic Immunity

Everneath
Everbound
Evertrue
Neverfall: An Everneath Novella (available as an ebook only)

Also by Jodi Meadows
Before She Ignites
As She Ascends
When She Reigns

The Orphan Queen
The Mirror King

The Orphan Queen Novellas (available as ebooks only)
The Hidden Prince
The Glowing Knight
The Burning Hand
The Black Knife

Incarnate
Asunder
Infinite
Phoenix Overture: An Incarnate Novella (available as an ebook only)

Only slightly **The electric, poetic, and monstrous tale of MARY SHELLEY.**

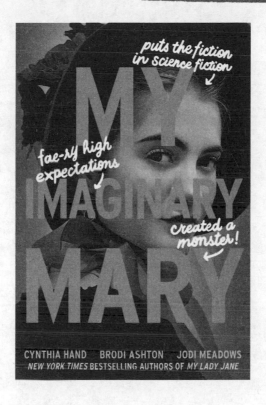

puts the fiction in science fiction

fae-ry high expectations

MY IMAGINARY MARY

created a monster!

CYNTHIA HAND   BRODI ASHTON   JODI MEADOWS

NEW YORK TIMES BESTSELLING AUTHORS OF *MY LADY JANE*

Keep reading for a sneak peek!

Mary

ONE

It was a dark and stormy night. Again.

Mary peered out the carriage window at the black clouds gathering in the sky. Most nights had been dark and stormy lately, but Mary didn't mind the rain. Storms always made her want to write . . . *something*. Something epic. Something terrible and wonderful and spine-tingling. But she didn't know what. Currently she was amusing herself by imagining the clouds as a herd of wild horses galloping through the sky, streaming lightning behind them. (As we've mentioned, Mary had quite the imagination. You'll see.)

"Hmph, what dreadful weather," remarked Mary's stepmother, leaning to look out the window, too. "Really, William, must we be going out in this? You know I hate getting wet."

Mary sighed. Her wicked stepmother obviously didn't

understand anything about finding the beauty in nature.

"It doesn't look too bad," her father responded cheerfully.

At that moment, the thunder boomed so loudly it caused the walls of their shabby carriage to shudder. Then the sky opened and poured down rain.

Mary's father was undeterred. "We can't miss this party, my dears," he said, raising his voice to be heard over the deluge. "It's such an honor to be invited."

There was no arguing with that. They all knew that to be invited to a party at the house of Mr. Charles Babbage was no small thing. Mr. Babbage, a brilliant scientist and inventor, was very selective about who attended his soirees. Over the years his guest lists had included all the best minds in England. That Mary's father was receiving invitations to Babbage's parties again was a relief. It meant that the family hadn't fallen *too* far in the world's esteem, in spite of their recent money troubles. Perhaps it even meant—as her father hoped—that they were on the rise.

"Of course I know that, my darling," Mary's stepmother said with an elaborate sniff. "But I don't care for Mr. Babbage. He's appallingly plainspoken. He says what he thinks, without a care for how it might be received."

Mary, who had never before met Mr. Babbage, thought this would be a refreshing quality for a person to have. But her stepmother obviously didn't understand anything about people and their complexities.

"I quite like Mr. Babbage," said Mary's father. "And there's always at least one reading from a famous author at these parties, and multiple scientific demonstrations. Mr. Babbage himself might reveal one of his latest inventions. This evening is sure to be exciting."

BOOM! went the sky, followed by a stab of lightning that briefly illuminated the carriage.

"I don't care for exciting, either." Mary's stepmother drew the curtains across the windows.

Mary resisted the urge to roll her eyes. Of course her stepmother didn't understand anything about adventure.

"I'm keen to see all of the newest fashions," piped up Jane, Mary's (only a tiny bit wicked) stepsister, from beside her mother. "I'll be content to simply go about looking at everyone, like they're an assortment of brightly colored birds, and I, the happy ornithologist." She fiddled with one of the glossy curls that framed her face. "I'm especially interested in specimens of the male variety."

"Hmph," said Mrs. Godwin. "I do hope there will be a few *appropriate* young men for you to associate with at this party." She eyed her three woefully unmarried charges critically. "Otherwise, what's the point?"

"Now, now, dear, this isn't that type of party," admonished Mary's father. "This is not some ball for the ton. The point is to enlighten our minds, not to trot out our girls like prized ponies."

Mary rather loved him for saying that. William Godwin was a forward-thinking man. But then, he had the luxury of being forward-thinking. Because he was a man.

CRASH! BOOM! went the sky.

The carriage lurched to a stop.

"Oh, good," said Mary's father. "We're here."

"Mr. Babbage!" Her father rushed forward to shake hands with the host the moment they arrived in the parlor where Mr. Babbage was greeting his guests. "So good to see you again."

"Ah, Mr. Godwin," replied Mr. Babbage. "So good of you to come."

Mary's father stepped aside to reveal his slightly damp family. "You already know Mrs. Godwin, but may I present my daughters, Fanny, Mary, and Jane."

Fanny, the oldest sister, performed a small curtsy but said nothing. Fanny almost never said anything. (In fact, if we hadn't mentioned her, you would never have known she was there.)

"Good evening," said Mary, also curtsying.

"You have a splendid house!" exclaimed Jane.

"Thank you," Mr. Babbage replied. He was older than Mary would have guessed, a bit stooped but still stately, with lively green eyes under bushy gray brows. His gaze wandered between Jane, Mary, and Fanny. "You say *all three* of these are your daughters, Godwin?"

Color rose in the face of Mary's father. "In spirit, sir, if not in blood. Jane is my wife's daughter from a previous marriage. Fanny is the daughter of the novelist Gilbert Imlay and my late wife. And Mary is my own daughter, with my late wife."

Mary felt that jolt of yearning inside her that happened whenever someone mentioned her mother. Mary Wollstonecraft had died of a fever when our Mary was just eleven days old, but Mary somehow still managed to miss her.

"Charming woman, that last wife of yours," Mr. Babbage said gruffly, "and an undeniable genius." His eyes skimmed over the current Mrs. Godwin and landed on Fanny. "Are you a writer as well?"

Fanny shook her head. Her passion was needlepoint. (It was a quiet passion.)

"And you?" Mr. Babbage's focus shifted to Mary, which was unfortunate, because she didn't have the faintest idea how to answer his question. Everyone expected her to become a writer, as both her parents were famous writers. There were times she quite enjoyed building her "castles in the air," as she called them, writing about far-off people and places and things. But there were other times that she doubted she had any talent at all. Certainly nothing she had written up to now was good enough to be (gulp) published.

"I would like to be a writer," she said after an awkward pause. "Someday." But deep down, she wasn't sure that this was ever going to happen.

"She's constantly scribbling," reported Mary's father. "I am quite certain that she will be as brilliant a writer as her mother ever was."

"Is that so?" said Mr. Babbage appraisingly. "What do you write?"

5

That was the question, wasn't it? Her stories were just imaginary incidents for people who lived only in her mind. They weren't fit to be seen by anyone but herself.

"I'm only seventeen, sir," said Mary. "I've had little opportunity to experience anything extraordinary in life. But once I do, I'm sure I will write . . . something . . ."

Something, well, extraordinary. Something marvelous.

She hoped.

"I've never been very good at writing, myself. It was always my poorest subject in school," said Mr. Babbage. "I'm a numbers man at heart, but I can appreciate the talents of others. I look forward to seeing all that you have to offer the world, Miss Godwin." He glanced off toward the ballroom. "And now, if you'll excuse me, I have some more important matters to attend to."

Then he walked briskly away.

"Well, that was brief," said Mrs. Godwin.

"I thought he was nice," said Jane. "Not at all as unpleasant as you made him out to be, Mother. Oh, look, there's cake! I adore cake!"

Having now performed the necessary introductions with the host, the family set out to enjoy the party. It was even more lavish than Mary had expected. Mr. Babbage's house was blazing with noise and color and light, so much so that the outside storm was drowned out, as if the weather itself was too impressed by the gleaming parquet floors and plentiful velvet drapes to make a scene. As Mary's father had promised, there were numerous groups of seasoned intellectuals standing about, earnestly discussing issues of philosophy and politics and so forth, with the aforementioned readings of poetry being held in the smaller side rooms, along with a number of scientific displays.

But there was also music. And dancing. And (as Jane had so enthusiastically pointed out) cake.

"Oh my goodness," exclaimed Mary's father. "Is that the Duke of Wellington?"

They all turned to look.

"He's a fine figure, isn't he?" said Jane. "Not young but definitely handsome."

"Although something about him says 'nefarious villain' to me," mused Mary.

"Villain?" Mr. Godwin huffed. "He's our country's finest war hero!"

Mary shook her head. She was fairly certain, for some reason she couldn't quite put her finger on, that the Duke of Wellington was a villain. (But that's literally a different story.)

"It doesn't matter. He's married." Mrs. Godwin sighed. The majority of the guests were older, distinguished men—scientists and artists—and their wives.

There were only a few *young* men.

"Dibs on that one," Jane said around a mouthful of cake, nodding her head to indicate one of the more finely dressed boys who seemed to be approximately their age. She pinched her cheeks to pinken them and brushed crumbs from her dress. "Watch me go, then."

Mary observed in a kind of awe as her stepsister swept off

toward the unsuspecting young man. She was familiar with all of Jane's moves—the casual, seemingly accidental bump, which Jane referred to as the "meet-cute." The charming introduction, followed by the demure-but-flirtatious smile. The gaze from under Jane's thick lashes. The way she moved her body slightly in time to the lively jig that was being played in the next room, to suggest that she herself might wish to—ah yes, the young man had asked her to dance. And off they went.

"Good on Jane," said Mary's stepmother. "I believe that one is in line to be an earl someday. Lord King something-or-other. He'd be an excellent catch, wouldn't he, dear?" She looked to Mr. Godwin for a confirmation, but Mary's father had gone to introduce himself to the Duke of Wellington.

Mrs. Godwin sighed again.

"He's not exactly handsome, is he?" remarked Mary, meaning the boy and not the Duke of Wellington. This future earl was neither handsome nor homely; indeed, there was nothing striking at all about his appearance. Lord. King. Earl. That guy was a confusing combination of titles.

"But he's rich," said Mrs. Godwin. "That's all that matters, in the end."

"You don't think that's somewhat vulgar?" Mary suggested lightly. "Treating it like some sport, I mean? The hunting and trapping of rich young men?"

"That's life in the real world," snapped Mrs. Godwin. "At least *my* daughter is showing some initiative. Unlike you two lumps."

Mary wanted to fire back a sharp retort in defense of herself and Fanny, fellow lumps, but by the time she thought of something clever and cutting enough, Jane had returned from the ballroom.

"Lord, he was a bore, that one. I take it back, about the dibs." Jane's dark eyes trolled around the room. "If only there was someone else who—" She gasped. "Look, there's Shelley!"

They all swiveled around again.

The young man in question was standing near the door, having just come in from the rain. Mary's breath hitched at the sight of him. He was undeniably handsome, neither too tall nor too short, slender of build, topped by a mass of fluffy brown hair that he could not seem to help but constantly run his fingers through. He had bright blue, inquisitive eyes that seemed to drink in his surroundings, and an impish, yet not quite rakish, smile.

BOOM went the thunder. Or was it Mary's heart? (Reader, it was thunder. But he did have one of those heart-boom-inducing smiles, so we can hardly blame her for the confusion.)

"Shelley!" called Jane so loudly it caused Mrs. Godwin to flinch. "Shelley, over here!"

The bright blue eyes swung in their direction.

Mary resisted the urge to pinch her own cheeks as he strode across the room.

"Hello, Godwins! I did not expect to find you here!" he exclaimed. "What a delightful surprise." Then he seemed to remember the formality of the situation. "Mrs. Godwin," he said with a slight bow.

"Mr. Shelley," Mary's stepmother returned stiffly, but even she was inclined to smile at him.

"Miss Imlay," he said to Fanny. She said nothing, as usual, but as her gaze fell to his intricately embroidered waistcoat, she began to fan herself as if she was suddenly too warm.

He turned to Jane. "Miss Clairmont."

"You're a sight for sore eyes, Shelley," Jane declared.

"Your sore eyes beheld me only this afternoon," he reminded her playfully.

Mr. Shelley was a writer—having recently published his first book of poetry to modest success. Almost a month ago he had turned up at the Godwins' bookshop at 92 High Street and requested an apprenticeship, of sorts, with Mr. Godwin. He claimed that Mr. Godwin was his favorite author (even though Mary's father hadn't been able to sell any of his own novels in years) and had declared that Mr. Godwin's ideas—especially the bits about how society must overthrow its outdated and oppressive institutions, like marriage for instance—had been transformative in Shelley's life. And that was that. Shelley was in. But instead of being paid by Mr. Godwin for his work, Shelley had agreed to pay Mr. Godwin for the honor of being mentored by such an esteemed and influential author. So it worked out well for everyone.

"Dance with me, Shelley," cried Jane.

"Oh," Shelley said awkwardly. This was forward of Jane. Inappropriate, even. He glanced at the floor, then up briefly, covertly, at Mary.

She gave a slight, almost imperceptible nod.

"I'd be delighted," said Shelley, extending his arm to Jane. And off they went.

"See?" crowed Mrs. Godwin. "Initiative."

It was true. Jane had game.

"They make a fine pair, don't they?" said Mrs. Godwin as they moved to the doorway of the ballroom to watch Shelley and Jane dancing. "He's undoubtedly handsome."

Undoubtedly.

"And intelligent. He gets on so well with your father that he feels like family already," remarked Mrs. Godwin.

Indeed.

"And his father is a baronet. So he's rich."

"But not as rich as an earl," Mary pointed out.

Mrs. Godwin waved her off. "Rich is rich. Mr. Shelley is perfect for Jane."

Mary smiled a secret smile and then quickly suppressed it. Shelley *was* perfect. He was clever and sensitive and forward-thinking. If one believed in marriage, he'd be the ideal husband.

But not for Jane.

"You're Mary" is what he'd said when they'd met that first day in the bookshop.

She'd blinked up at him, startled and embarrassed because she'd been so focused on the book she was reading that she hadn't noticed him approach. "Yes," she'd said, blushing at the intimate way he'd addressed her. "And you're—"

"Percy. But everyone calls me Shelley. What is it you're reading that has captured you so?"

She'd glanced down at the slim volume of poetry in her hands.
"Tennyson. He's—"

"Beautiful," Shelley'd murmured, and then from memory he'd
recited: *"For ere she reach'd upon the tide / The first house by the water-side
/ Singing in her song she died / The Lady of Shalott.* I love how he wrote
it—*singing in her song.* The way it sounds. The way it makes me feel."

And, with those words, Mary had known a simple truth. She
and Percy Shelley were the same. They understood each other.

Mary had also known very well that her stepmother would
never approve of Mary becoming romantically involved with Shelley (rich boys only belonged with her own daughter), so Mary had
made an arrangement with Jane, who'd been all too happy to cover
for them in the name of love. And now Jane was the one who got to
dance with Shelley, to be held in his arms, to smile up at him. But
that was just how it had to be.

The song finished, but instead of lining up for the next dance,
the couples began to exit the ballroom in a flood.

"Back so soon?" Mrs. Godwin said as Jane and Shelley
rejoined them.

"They're setting up some sort of presentation now," Jane
reported.

As if on cue, Mr. Babbage appeared again. "May I have your
attention?" he asked, not so much a question as a demand. "Please
join me in the ballroom for a demonstration of the most thrilling

nature, given to us by one of the world's most cutting-edge scientists in the field of electricity."

"Electricity? How shocking!" Jane cried, and then giggled at her own joke.

They shuffled toward the ballroom. It had been set up in rows of chairs facing a long metal table, upon which there were two mysterious objects shrouded by white linen.

In front of the table stood an even more mysterious man.

The scientist. Mary felt an inexplicable chill shoot up her spine at the sight of him.

"Who is he?" Mrs. Godwin asked, squinting. "Is he wearing a wedding ring?"

Ew. This man was at least fifty. His hair was a dull yellow in color, brushed purposefully forward to lie across his brow. He had impressive sideburns and a long, sharp nose—indeed, his entire face was pointed, except for his chin, which seemed to be trying to burrow inside his cravat to hide.

"That's Mr. Aldini," said Shelley. "The famous galvanist."

At the same moment Mary's father appeared beside them, eyes alight with excitement. "Ah, hello, Shelley," he said, clapping Shelley on the shoulder. "I wondered if I would see you here tonight." He gestured toward the front of the ballroom. "How fortunate we are, to be able to see Signore Aldini in person. Hurry; let's get a seat near the front."

They were able to procure seats in the third row, Mary silently negotiating with her sisters for a place between Fanny and Shelley.

After the guests were seated, the lights in the room were extinguished save for a tall candelabra flickering beside the table. The room quieted, and Mary could once again hear the steady patter of the rain and howls of the wind. Her heart, she found, was pounding. Her skin felt tingly. It was as though some part of Mary could sense that something in her life—something big and powerful and as unstoppable as the storm that raged outside—was about to change. And so it was.

But Mary could never have imagined what.

Mr. Aldini held up his hand. "What is life?" he asked.